CROSSING THE PRECIPICE

ELUDRIANS

BOOK 2

L N HEINTZ

Crossing the Precipice, Eludrians II, by LN Heintz

Edited by Steven Moore
Cover by MIBLART

www.LNHeintz.com

Download printable maps: www.LNHeintz.com/maps

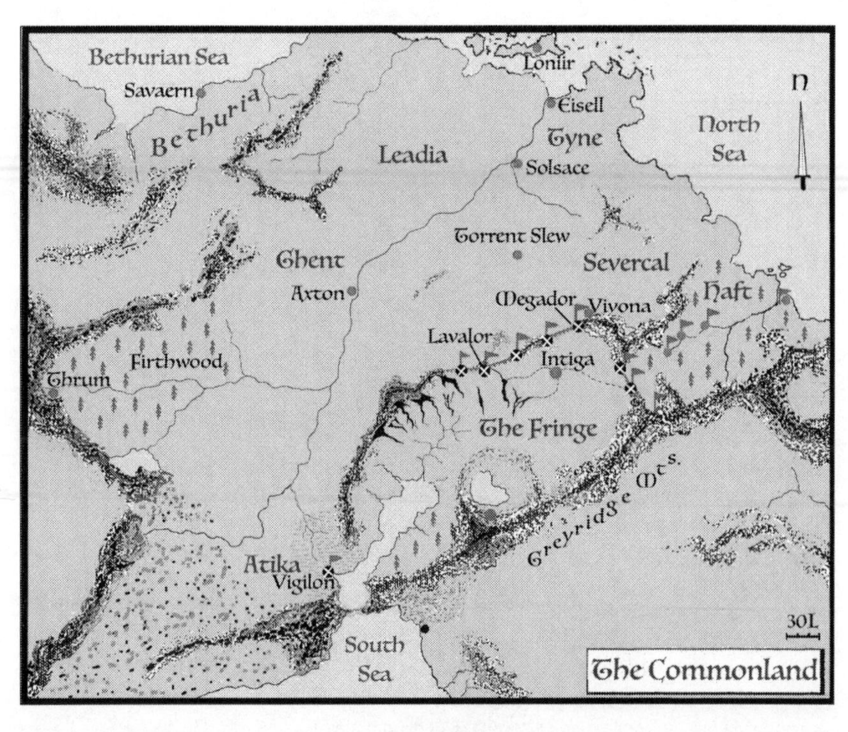
Bethurian Sea
Savaern
Bethuria
Leadia
Lonúr
Eisell
Tyne
Solsace
North Sea
N
Torrent Slew
Ghent
Axton
Severcal
Haft
Megador
Vivona
Lavalor
Intiga
Firthwood
Thrum
The Fringe
Greyridge Mts.
Atika
Vigilon
South Sea
30L
The Commonland

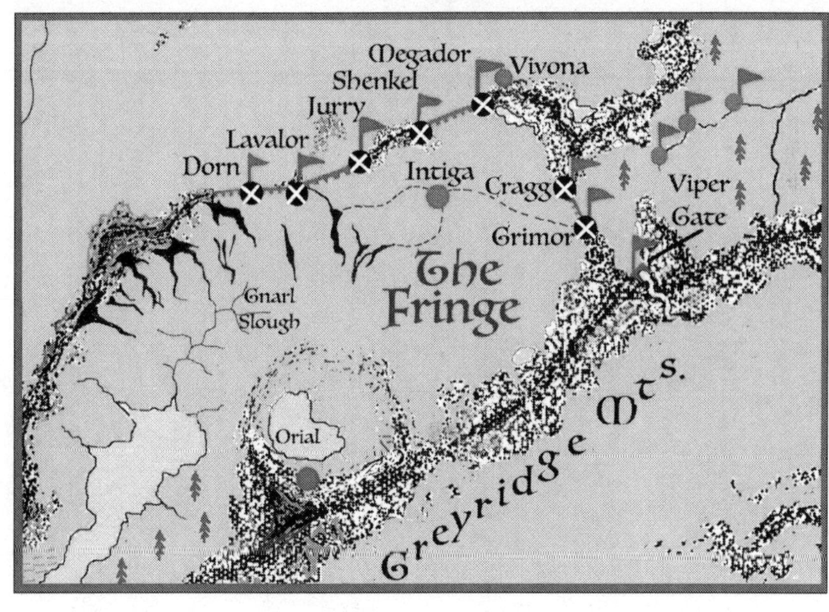
Megador
Vivona
Shenkel
Jurry
Lavalor
Dorn
Intiga
Cragg
Viper Gate
Grimor
The Fringe
Gnarl Slough
Orial
Greyridge Mts.

1

There wasn't much time left, judging by the approaching roar.

The falls were just yards away. He heard Runt yelping in fear, its cries half-choked with water. The mutt was nearby, but the swift current of the castle moat was making it difficult to get eyes on the tiny creature he had somehow let into his heart. If he didn't find him before they went over the cliff, this ill-advised attempt at rescue would be for naught—or worse.

Again, a yelp. Closer.

Katonkin Weir jerked his head toward the sound and saw the poor creature bobbing on the surface. The sad thing barely had his snout above the choppy water. It was a miracle Runt wasn't already drowned. His arms windmilled as he surged toward the panicked animal. The distance between them halved within seconds, but now they were at the cusp of the falls.

His body dropped as the entire river plummeted into the cracked earth below. He barely had time for one more gulp of air before becoming fully submerged in the white and green avalanche of water. Weir thrust out an arm in the direction he had last seen Runt. When he pulled it back, he was astounded the thrashing animal was firmly in his grasp. Jhalaveral had smiled on them both, so perhaps they had a chance after all.

Too late to put his feet forward, he pulled Runt into his chest, cradled him tightly within both arms, and rolled himself into a tight ball as the falls dragged them down to the plunge pool. They struck hard, but the vertical column of cascading water had also saved them from fatally slamming into the river below. The falls punched through the surface, bringing Weir and Runt deep into cold dark water that frothed with bubbles and confused swirls of agitated currents. The seconds turned into minutes, or so he imagined. He felt Runt kicking frantically next to his chest, no doubt struggling for air the same way he was. The watery prison refused to let them go. They were cast about furiously in all directions, tumbling over and over amidst the fury of these headwaters. More than once he was thrust into underwater boulders, threatening to bash in his skull if they should meet.

The bottoms of his bare feet came in contact with something solid. Another boulder. He reacted, and thrust away from it with every bit of energy his Atikan muscles could manage. He sped in a direction he hoped was upward, a spear in the dark, angry water. He saw light, and began pulling himself toward it with one hand. By this time, Runt had ceased his frantic movements, the light had begun to fade into darkness, and Weir's vision was failing.

Must . . . keep . . . fighting . . . .

A mixture of air and water surged into his lungs. He gasped and coughed desperately, expelling unwanted water, accepting air whenever he could, until finally he breathed normally. The roar of cascading water again accosted his ears. The mist fell all around him as he rolled over onto his back and lifted Runt onto his neck.

Drowned!

Weir pointed his eyes upward, into the mist. He couldn't see anything at first, but the current quickly drew him downriver and he saw the twin waterfalls—two identical ribbons of white spume—plummeting from around the southeast corner of Castle Lavalor far above. It occurred to him it was unlikely any person had ever seen the

Lavalor Falls from this perspective. Or if they had, they had likely never lived to tell about it. He was determined to be the first. And perhaps Agmar, the man who had thrown Runt into the moat, would later have his chance.

Runt wasn't breathing, but Weir refused to let him go. Instead, he began kicking downriver, letting the current take his body, and using his free arm and his kicks to help guide him to the southern side of the gorge, the closer side, where he hoped there'd be a spot he could exit the water. The river was fast, so he closed quickly with the cliff off his left shoulder. The current soon buffeted him against the rocks, and he had to constantly use his feet to push himself away from the boulders. Several times he noted short gravel-laden strands where he might find safety. But the waters didn't cooperate, and he was swept cruelly past them, only to crash brutally into more boulders or even the sheer face of the southern cliff of the gorge.

Finally, he saw his chance, a tiny gap between two boulders, and he kicked and pulled himself closer to it. He was just beginning to think he'd gain the shore when the current started moving him away from his goal. But at the last second an eddy caught him and whipped him back toward the opening.

"Jehlude Jhalaveral!" he gasped as he clambered onto a mound of gravelly mud.

Weir dropped to his side in exhaustion. But a life depended on him. He rolled onto his knees and lifted Runt in both hands. Poor thing wasn't breathing. He lifted the tiny mutt by his hind legs, his curling tail above his head. He shook the creature a few times, and massaged his abdomen.

"Wake up!" he implored. "I went over this damn cliff for you. Wake up!"

Nothing happened, just water seeping like slime from out of Runt's blunt snout. Weir shook him some more. He glanced back at the river a few feet behind him, then quickly peered up the side of the cliff.

How do we get out of here?

More shaking. More squeezing. But still, no sign of life.

Weir turned Runt over, his drenched snout facing him, his eyes closed.

"Never tell anyone I did this," he whispered to his beloved dog, and then he took a deep breath, stuck Runt's snout into his mouth, and blew. He did it six more times before the pitiful creature in his hands began gasping for air and then opened its eyes. For the first time in history, laughter echoed loudly between the sheer walls of Lavalor Gorge.

2

Castle Lavalor had fallen. That much was clear. Vilemaster magic had broken through the Cadia Gate and Bipaquan redfaces riding gigantic lizards had overwhelmed pretty much everything else. Oh yeah, and the ogres. How could he forget? Boson Rheev watched Katonkin Weir disappear into the rapid waters of the moat, heading fast toward the falls and on to Little Dog Gorge. The vaunted warrior, his leader, had severely hurt the Vilazian commander, Lazlo Urich, and possibly his demon, Haem, and now he was dead set on finding them and ending this battle once and for all. Boson wasn't sure he'd choose the Lavalor River as his means to get behind enemy lines, as Weir had done, but he'd never dare question that man's motivations or reasons for doing anything. If Panthertooth was willing to risk going over the falls, then he had a good reason for doing it.

Boson stood on the lowered drawbridge of Lavalor Gate. A fierce battle between men and monsters raged just feet away inside the portcullis tunnel. The humans—mostly vangards wielding Atikan battle axes or swords—were desperately trying to keep the giant lizards at bay. They hoped to confine them to the interior of the castle as long as possible. Hundreds more of their fellow countrymen were now attempting to withdraw to nearby Lavalor Village, where the defeated Commonlanders planned to gather in order to reconstitute their forces. The more time they had, the more of them would be saved.

The way he saw it, he and his fellow vangards had two big problems. Who would protect their imminent withdrawal? And how would they keep these lizards from following them to Lavalor Village and continuing the battle there? His people needed time to regroup, if they were to have a chance at survival this night. Desmund Poole's spurs had already left the scene to escort most of the others away from the castle. But some of them would return shortly to assist in the vangard retreat. Upon further reflection, he decided to focus on the lizards instead.

One problem at a time.

He looked at the black iron spikes up above—the portcullis—barely protruding from the ceiling of the tunnel. This one was the outer grating, nearest the drawbridge. But there was another one, too, at the far end of the tunnel. If he could just lower either barricade, it would keep the lizards inside the castle long enough for the Lavalorans to get back onto their feet. He hoped.

With no other ideas springing to mind, Boson plunged into the fight. He yelled for his warmates to make way for him as he muscled his way further into the tunnel. Few of them heard his calls over the sounds of fighting—the battle cries, the screams, the hissing of the lizards and their wails of misery as Blue and Gold resolve bit deep into their angular heads.

Nearer the front now, he saw one of the snake-like lizards vault over the leading line of vangards blocking all entry into the passageway from the interior of the fortress. It aimed for the side wall, to Bosun's right. Several vangards struck out at the creature with their weapons, extending their bodies as far as possible, trying to stop it. But their blades whistled by, inches short of their common target. The four legs of the lizard immediately gained purchase on the coarse stone blocks of the tunnel wall and pulled the thing higher, away from Lavalor's defenders. It then jumped into the middle of the human throng, right at Bosun.

He instinctively lashed out with his sword, a mercenary, whose blade already had the gore and viscera of over a hundred lizards, and quite a number of Bipaquans, covering it. It struck home, piercing the pale throat of the creature beneath its head. Several more nearby vangards, two to be precise, also stabbed at the thing, then all three of them pushed or punched the ten-foot creature to the ground and resumed attacking it until it lay motionless.

Boson renewed his efforts to get inside the castle.

"Let me through," he yelled at the next vangard in his path. The man somehow heard him, and let him by. So did the next one. Boson aimed right and squeezed past the final vangard and the front corner of the tunnel, also at his right. A black shape with two rows of white teeth lunged toward him. Boson dove to the ground and rolled forward, under the snapping jaws. He regained his feet, turned right, and ran along the interior wall of the castle. Almost immediately he was confronted with a wooden structure in which he knew was housed a forge and a greeting stable. He angled left toward the large, square doorway of the building, jumped over the swishing tail of one of the lizards, and ran inside. Another of the riderless lizards was there. It attacked immediately. Boson plunged his mercenary deep into one of its eyes then used the black leather grip of his sword to help him swing around the screaming beast. Now he only had his two longknives, one at his right hip, the other slung behind his left shoulder.

Boson had been born in Lavalor, so he knew his way around here, though the interior was dark at this hour. He'd also spent time working in this forge when he was young. He aimed for the back wall, around the cold forge and its bellows. He saw what he was looking for. Another door. It was closed. He grabbed the left edge and pulled. It opened easily, sliding to the right. He checked for lizards. None. He entered the stable area, turned left, and quickly found himself in open air once again, in moonlight. He stepped onto the edges of a water trough just outside the building. How many times had he done this before in his youth? A hundred? He hooked his hand around a large, square wooden post and heaved himself onto a cross beam behind the trough. With his other hand he grabbed the edge of the roof and pulled himself upward, and onto it.

He stood up now, on the stable roof. He saw the full moon in a mustard sky, spying at him from above Lord's Keep. He whirled around and there was the main interior wall of the castle twenty or thirty feet away. But there was also a buttress that angled up from the left. He ran toward it, his boots pounding the haleburl boards of the stable roof. A few seconds later he jumped over onto the lower part of the rising buttress and began running up its steep, ascending slope back toward Lavalor Gate. Once there, he reached up, and hauled himself up onto the northern allures of the castle.

A lizard lunged at him from the right. He unsheathed his hip blade and quickly blinded the creature with a series of lancing stabs. He sheathed his blade as he ran past the wailing creature and on into the gatehouse. He turned left, into an archway, ran ten feet or so, then another quick right. There! The windlass! And at his right shoulder, the fully retracted grate of the interior portcullis.

3

Lorgan heard the clackety clack of the spinning windlass above, and the screech of iron against stone. The portcullis was coming down. *It's behind me!* He finished prying the spike of his war axe out of a lizard's skull and simultaneously barked a frantic warning to his warmates.

"Fall back," he screamed. "Fall back!"

A quick glance to the rear revealed movement. And those at his side were frantically trying to disengage from their individual battles so they, too, could get clear of the iron grate.

"Move it," he bellowed, just to be sure everyone had heard his warning.

But the grate was fast. Half the men abreast of him danced backward, ducking under the spikes of the descending barricade. He was one of them. But the other half didn't make it, five vangards, though not a single skink did either.

The portcullis completed its journey at break neck speed. It thunked into the skulls and necks of several thrashing lizards, killing them instantly, though their long black tails continued to swish violently.

Lorgan glanced back at the second portcullis, still retracted. He had a bad feeling about it.

"Keep going" he continued roaring to the men at his back. "Out of the tunnel! Now!"

The weary men obeyed him and quickly made their way out into the open air and onto the drawbridge. Meanwhile, the five trapped men were still fighting. Their backs were to the grate and the skinks were at their throats.

"Under the barricade," Lorgan shouted to the five, after noting the portcullis had a two-foot gap at the bottom because of the dead lizards caught within its spikes.

The five fell to the ground in random order, several of them at one time, onto elbows and knees, then rolled to safety through the gap. Within seconds, all of them had successfully made it back into the tunnel—except one man who had a foot caught in the hungry jaws of a lizard.

Lorgan rushed over to help. He got down, grabbed onto an outstretched hand below the partially closed grate and pulled, trying to free his warmate. But two more beasts joined the first, and the man's screams began to echo into the tunnel.

Lorgan held onto the man until his hand went limp and his shrieks fell silent.

He quickly stood up, and backed away from the lowered portcullis. After ensuring no one else was left behind, he turned and ran as the second portcullis began descending. He had to dive to clear the grate, but he did so, with inches to spare.

Several pairs of hands reached down and lifted him to his feet.

"Let's go," said one of the men, a good friend named Brawk, also a vangard. "To the village!"

Lorgan peered toward the smaller walls of the distant village, about a quarter-league atop a wide hill. Usually at this time of the evening he'd expect to see the ramparts there lit up with torches or lamps. Not tonight. Lavalor village had been evacuated several days ago and now it was but a dark husk standing below a set of monolithic cliffs from which the Lavalor River originated. His eyes flicked back down to the road, which ended here at the drawbridge. Then he traced it back toward the village. He could see hundreds of small shapes moving on it in the darkness—warriors on foot, and hundreds of horse riders—withdrawing up a gentle rise toward the village. Because of the full moon, no one had need of a torch.

Some of the shapes got closer, getting larger as they neared. Horses and riders. He spotted Pennon Desmund Poole approaching on the lead animal. He had brought a company of his spurs to help the remaining vangard force to safety.

"Everyone make it out?" shouted Poole, his features too hard to see in the gloom.

"Aye!" returned Brawk, who then slapped Lorgan's shoulder and turned to leave.

But Lorgan stood his ground. He spun around and gazed to the top of Lavalor Gate.

"Someone's still up there," he shouted. "In the gatehouse. He's the bastard who lowered the barricades on us—for us."

A dozen vangards reversed course and joined ranks with Lorgan, each of them peering toward the top of the main gate of Castle Lavalor. The remainder, three-score or so, continued up the hill to the village, spurs beside them, oblivious to what was happening here at the gate.

"Who is it?" demanded Lorgan loudly. No one answered. He scanned all their faces.

"No one saw who it is?" he asked. No response.

One of the vangards waved tentatively. "Boson," he said, not entirely convinced himself.

"I think," the man added.

"You saw him up there?" asked Lorgan.

The man shook his head. "He pushed his way through the tunnel as we were holding those skinks back. He was trying to get to the front. I saw him cutting one of them, then when I looked back, he was nowhere to be seen. I'm sure he got inside. I think that's where he was headed."

"Who else could it be?" said Brawk.

Lorgan nodded to himself. It all made sense now. Boson Rheev was last seen trying to get inside the castle. A few minutes later the barricades were released.

They heard commotion from the direction of the village. Poole, Lorgan, and his mates jerked their gazes in that direction. *What now?* Even in the darkness of the early gray evening he saw it, a dark line in the sky that corkscrewed upon itself, wider on top, narrower at the bottom.

"The demon gyre!" said Poole from atop his horse.

The gyre was already near ground level, just above the road. Then it touched down. It began to move away from them, slowly following the road up the gentle slope toward the village, causing panic and angry warnings as it went. Strangely, there were no sounds of swords, or any other weapons. Lorgan knew why. Steel couldn't hurt demon dust.

Lorgan tried to think of something he could do. Nothing. He was too far away, and the demon was gaining distance with every second. He suddenly cursed for allowing himself to be distracted.

Boson!

"Off the drawbridge," Lorgan yelled, whipping his attention back to matters he could control. He gestured wildly to either side of him. "Spread out along the edge of the moat. Keep eyes on the ramparts. If Bosun's still alive, we need to find out where he is. He's gonna have to jump, if he wants out of there alive."

The men reacted. Some moved to the left of the drawbridge, some to the right. Lorgan was one of those moving left after stepping off the winolkan heartwood of the drawbridge.

"We need to be ready for him," he continued. "Don't forget he's Bethurian, so he might be hard to see in this darkness."

"There!" shouted Brawk almost instantly. He was pointing at the top of the wall about thirty yards to the right side of Lavalor gate. Sure enough, it was Boson Rheev.

Without delay, the Bethurian jumped, his black arms whirling at his side, before spearing into the moat directly below. The heads of several angry lizards popped out over the allures just behind him, though they didn't follow him over the wall.

"Get him!" ordered Lorgan, though he wasn't sure how they'd do that.

Boson surfaced. He started swimming in a desperate attempt to cross the moat. The current carried him quickly toward the drawbridge, and Lorgan wasn't sure his friend would get close enough to their side of the channel for them to pull him from the drink. With every second, the Bethurian managed to get closer, but in that same span of time he travelled four times the distance along its length because of the strong current.

He won't make it!

Lorgan wished he had some rope. But he didn't. All he had was his axe.

Knowing that Boson had exactly one chance remaining to avoid going over the falls and into Little Dog Gorge, Lorgan hustled back over the drawbridge and centered himself over it at the point where he judged Boson would be carried underneath it.

Boson must have seen him. He briefly raised an arm before slipping back under.

Lorgan raised his axe in both hands, showing it to the Bethurian after he again resurfaced.

He was much closer now.

Did he see it?

Lorgan ran to the far side of the drawbridge and threw himself flat on the boards with chest and head overhanging its edge. He lowered his axe toward the rushing water, gripping it firmly with both hands—then waited.

Maybe four seconds passed. *I missed him.* But a sudden weight took hold of the axe from below. He saw a pair of muscular black arms sticking out of the water and desperate hands encasing the axe head.

Got him!

The axe suddenly grew heavier. Really heavy. It started pulling

Lorgan over the side of the drawbridge. His first impulse was to let go, but he resisted. He called forth all his will, and squeezed down even tighter on the wooden handle.

Someone jumped on him from behind, trying to anchor him where he lay. About that same time someone else grabbed his ankles and pulled.

~

Harder this time.

Maybe it was because he was older. Or perhaps it was the exhaustion of battle. Or maybe it had been pure luck that he and Runt had emerged at all from these dangerous waters all those years ago.

Weir lay on his back on the river bank deep in Little Dog Gorge. He was shivering badly while gazing back towards Lavalor Falls. Havless Tower could just be seen within the swirling mist, an apparition hovering over the brink, its upper extents glinting in the growing moonlight. It seemed a world away.

How could I have failed Lavalor? Twoheart?

Has Jhalaveral abandoned me? All of us?

He heard himself grunt out of defiance. He had survived these hazardous falls once again and he had severely hurt Lazlo Urich and his demon. Clearly, Jhalaveral still favored him. There could be no other explanation.

Despite his shivers, these later thoughts comforted him and eased his heavy heart. He also reminded himself that Twoheart yet breathed and was being looked after by friends. The boy and girl as well. With renewed purpose, he sat erect, crossed his legs, and began to meditate. The first thing he needed to do was restore body warmth. His arms and legs were largely nonfunctional at the moment, and he doubted he could fight right now, much less climb this treacherous cliff. With hands on knees, he closed his eyes and began to take deep breathes as he attempted to tame his panting and calm his mind.

Silence. Tranquility. Awareness.

Five minutes.

Ten.

Fifteen.

The shivers succumbed to Panthertooth's crushing will.

4

Everything seemed red to her. And blurry. What little she could see. She felt depleted beyond comprehension. Exhausted. Burned. Vague shapes moved around her. Horses. Warriors. Lots of noise and urgent words. She was being carried through a gate, and had then been set down onto the hard ground under a warm, cloudy sky. Yellow moonlight.

Where am I?

Who am I?

A man's face appeared before her and filled her vision, blocking the night. Clearer now.

"Ada," he whispered closely. "Can you hear me? Wake up."

That helped.

I'm Ada Halentine. I'm an eludrian. There was a battle.

"Wake up," came the male voice once more.

"I'm alive," Ada managed to whisper, barely.

"Yes, you are alive," confirmed the man. "How do you feel?"

Ada forced her eyes open wider. She peered more closely at him. It took a moment for her to focus. She didn't recognize him. But she started remembering things.

"How's Galager?' she asked, her voice cracking and raspy. "Where is he?"

The man fed her some water from a bladder. Just a few sips, but it was life-saving.

"Galager?" she again asked, grateful for the water. "Tell me."

The man lifted his gaze. He aimed it over to the other side of her body.

Ada turned her head, looking in the opposite direction. A body next to her. A man. It took her a moment to realize it was Galager. His face was angled toward her, his tongue lolled in her direction. Unconscious. Eyes closed, but breathing.

There were others nearby. People laying on the ground. Dozens of them, maybe more. Some of them were moaning. Some of them looked dead.

She heard yelling. Warnings were shouted. She tried to lift her head to see what was happening, but she was too weak, and it fell back to the ground. Her temples pulsed with pain.

"Demon," someone shouted. And again. Someone began shouting orders, but she couldn't fully concentrate.

Something appeared above her. The gyre! Black and elongated, twisting like a whirlwind. It was right above her and Galager. She tried to roll over to get to her feet, but it was hopeless. Still too weak, she breathed in some particles. Dust, lots of dust. Her awareness grew dim. She felt light, as if she were floating. Then she blacked out.

~

Castellan Malick Havless growled as he stood atop the southern wall walk of Lavalor village. A dozen soldiers stood alongside him, including a soaking wet Boson Rheev, each languishing in despair and defeat. They watched smoke rising from the distant castle, once thought unbreakable. None of these men were flags. Both Pagan Tellor and Lucious Morl—Havless's chief military advisors—had been slaughtered by Haem on Lord's Watch while the fortress crumbled around him. A lot of faces were absent.

"How did it happen?' asked Havless, his back to Boson.

Boson had arrived just minutes before. Lorgan and a few of his other vangard warmates had miraculously pulled him from the moat, and Poole's spurs had then brought them all to the village. Boson soon heard rumors. The two eludrians had been taken by the demon. No one else, just Ada and Galager. And now those rumors had been confirmed, a heartbreaking development.

"We couldn't stop him," said Pennon Adam Stoddard, young, wiry thin, boyish features but unafraid to pick a fight with anyone. "Our weapons mean nothing to the gyre. It came down from out of the night sky, and the next thing we knew, they were gone."

In a gesture of immense frustration, Havless cradled his head in his arms. "And Katonkin?" he asked. "Where is he?"

"Panthertooth has gone to kill Lazlo," uttered Boson.

Havless dropped his arms and turned to him, his eyes weary. Other questions were issued. Boson answered them all. When the others learned that Weir had gone over the falls, everyone fell silent. Their capacity to be shocked was nearing its limit.

"He'll get them," stated Boson, trying to sound calm and reassuring.

"Who?" asked Havless. "Our two young eludrians? Katonkin doesn't even know they've been taken."

"He'll figure it out," replied Boson. "Lazlo needs medical assistance. He must have already returned to his camp to be healed."

Boson examined his boots for a moment, thinking it through.

"Lazlo didn't kill them," he continued. "He took them. There must be a reason he's keeping them alive. The Vilazians will be celebrating their victory tonight. News of their capture will spread quickly through the enemy camp and reach Panthertooth's ears too."

Havless shook his head. "No, no, no. Bad decision. Even if they're still alive, that's a fool's mission. Not even Weir can hope to kill Lazlo and then rescue Ada and Galager. The obstacles are too many. The odds too unfavorable." He pointed over the parapet in the general direction of the castle.

"You see those bloody lizards crawling all over everything?"

Boson reflexively cast another glance at the fortress.

"That's just the start of his problems."

"Lord," replied Boson, "it's Panthertooth we're talking about."

Desmund Poole stepped closer to Havless. Both men had yellowish hair, but Poole's was a bit longer, a little browner, had a little less blood in it, and it fell to his shoulders rather than just his ears. It was also parted in the middle. He tended to squint, even in darkness, and it made it seem as if he was always calculating things—or people. "Aye, Lord," he said. "Don't start doubting Panthertooth. Not him. Not now."

"Our concerns," said Bosun, "shouldn't be for Katonkin—or the eludrians. We have more important things to worry about tonight."

Pennon Quinton Collier nodded. "We've lost some good men," he said, the tip of his white beard bouncing as he talked. "What we decide in the next few minutes may decide how many more will perish in the coming days. Or even the next few hours."

"We need a plan," agreed Havless. He scanned the grim faces near to him. "But as Pagan would say, any plan needs to be based on facts, opportunities, and potential pitfalls." Nods and murmurs followed that comment. "Let's be quick about this. If we fail to stop the Vilazians here at Lavalor, the entire kingdom may be imperiled. We can't allow this breach to stand."

"Lord," said Pennon Arvil Sovron, a stocky man with no neck whose eyes barely came up to Bosun's collarbone. He was maybe five years older than Bosun and had a clever wit. His bulky head was rather flat on top, and his closest friends affectionately called him Arvil the Anvil because of it. "I watched almost two hundred of my men fall on the western curtain tonight, Bryson Corg among them." Groans escaped the throats of several of their number. Not everyone had heard the grim news about Corg.

"I estimate we lost twice that number in totality," responded Collier. "We need an accurate head count. Sooner the better."

"I never thought I'd see Lavalor fall," said Havless. "But all of you listen to me. We're going to take back our home. Maybe not tonight, maybe not tomorrow, but soon. Mark my words, we will find a way to defeat the Vilazian Multitude and send it back into the Fringe."

"Aye," came a chorus of deep voices.

"You all fought bravely," said Havless. He surveyed the alleyway behind the village wall and pointed at hundreds of other soldiers and warriors down on the grounds below them. There were others on the walls. All of them exhausted. All of them waiting for orders. All of them ready to sacrifice everything for the cause—the defense of the Commonland.

"Everyone fought well," he said. "I couldn't be more proud of you. We—we just weren't prepared for those damn lizards."

"Too many of them," said Poole. "I had three companies of my spurs, firing at will, almost point blank. But they just kept coming."

"Your men were magnificent," replied Havless. "And they'll soon have another chance to avenge our fallen brothers."

"What do you have in mind?" asked Sovron. If any of the men here tonight looked as if he wanted to kill more of the Vilazian Multitude, it was him.

"We stay here," said Havless. "We man these walls. Our enemy's numbers are diminished now. We should have a better result next time they dare challenge us."

Madness, thought Boson.

"Unless," added Havless, "anyone here has a better plan." He scanned the darkness, checking faces. But no one spoke.

Will no one oppose his absurd plan?

Finally, Havless inspected his visage and the young vangard took it as an invitation to loosen his tongue.

"Lord," Bosun began. "Master Vreman is dead. His head is laying atop Cadia Gate, if one of those lizards didn't swallow it yet. Ada and Galager are captured. We have no magic to aid us. Even Sanguir is gone."

"Speak on," said Havless. "Where are you going with all this?"

Boson cleared his throat, surprised he was given a chance to complete his thoughts.

"The castle's walls are stronger and higher than these ones under our feet. And there's no moat encircling these parapets. But worse, these walls are at least five times the total length of the castle's, making them harder to defend because we just don't have enough men."

Havless stabbed a dubious look at him. "What do you propose?"

Boson knew they wouldn't like his idea, but he told them anyway.

Several of the men immediately objected, in particular Pennon Sovron, who reacted rather angrily at first. Defeat affected everyone in their own way, but Sovron was eager to avenge the deaths of his men on the western wall. Boson's plan would delay that.

"I agree with Boson," stated Collier unexpectedly, tilting the argument irrevocably in the Bethurian's favor. Until now, Collier had remained silent on the matter as he considered everyone's observations.

"We can't defend the village," he further opined. "That was never a contingency we planned for. Lavalor was supposed to be unbreakable. We don't have the manpower to properly defend these walls against Lazlo's army and his confounding lizards. And there's no moral imperative to defend the village because it's already been evacuated."

"I also concur with Boson," responded Banner Ledon Jule, commander of the Lavalor Gate, the man who had rung the bell that sounded out the retreat from the castle.

Havless seemed to be on board. "What do we need to make this plan work? We better get started on it."

All eyes turned to Boson. "Rope," he instantly answered. "Lots of it. And torches. Some oil lamps will be good too. As many as we can carry without slowing us down."

"And stretchers," suggested Sovron, finally giving in to logic. "Lots of my boys can't walk now."

"Where would we get those?" asked Stoddard.

"We'll make them," answered Collier. "Won't be a problem."

"We all agree, then?" remarked Havless suddenly.

"Aye," said every man within earshot.

"So be it," said Havless confidently. He looked at Boson. "And until Weir's return, you are my acting Pennon Vangard."

That troubled Boson. It felt like a betrayal of Katonkin Weir. Winkite Berda'weir, too. "Are you sure, Lord?"

Havless grimaced. "Don't make me regret this," he said.

5

Lazlo Urich growled as the healer slid the broken arrow shaft out of his back.

The healer flinched, and cast anxious eyes at him. The man had no need to fear him though. Eludrians with gifts of healing magic were always in critical need, and they were highly valued.

The healer's assistant, a fetching young lass with honey hair and alluring full lips quickly jammed a substantial piece of folded cloth against the entry wound over his right breast, an inch below his collarbone. The healer hurriedly grabbed up a similar piece of cloth and held it against the exit wound under Lazlo's right shoulder blade.

Lazlo stared at the woman's lips as he reflected on the moment that Atikan had shot him atop the castle gatehouse. Oh, how he'd love to get a chance to burn that man! Perhaps he still would, in the coming days.

A red-jacketed soldier entered the tent.

"Is it done?" asked Lazlo.

"Yes, Lord," replied the officer, Captain Tsalon. "It'll be several hours before they can awaken from the tincture."

Lazlo grimaced as the man and woman attending to him wiped more blood from his skin. Although the pain was palpable, it reminded him of his victory in Lavalor this evening. Two victories, actually. His first one was in breaking the legendary fortress, Castle Lavalor, although it had cost him an arrow in the shoulder. And his second victory came later, when he managed to steal the boy and girl, both eludrians, right from under his enemy's noses.

The stories I'll later tell about that!

"Shall we start?" whispered the healer, standing behind him.

"Please do," replied Lazlo.

"This shouldn't hurt too badly," said the younger man. "But it will sting a bit as it heals and cauterizes your wounds." The man had something else he wanted to ask. "It seems your wound did not deplete you as much as I would have expected. Did you do something to alleviate its worst effects? Before arriving here, I mean. It is a serious injury."

Lazlo replayed some of the final moments of the battle in his mind. A small gurgle of laughter escaped his lips despite the burgeoning pain he now experienced. The two Commonlanders, themselves eludrians, had been hurt because of an explosion, no doubt some kind of magical outpouring triggered by the boy, or maybe the girl. He also remembered the boy's impossible gold aura and his deadly use of magic as he ascended a ramp to the top of the massive gatehouse. *Remarkable!* Although Lazlo had at first been forced to flee the scene because of a life-threatening injury suffered at the hands of an Atikan vangard, he soon discovered it was but a nuisance once he became the demon's passenger.

"It was the demon," answered Lazlo. "When in an incorporeal state, as I was, blood loss apparently is halted. A total surprise on my part, I assure you. And quite fascinating."

"That might have saved your life," the healer said. "You were lucky."

Lazlo grimaced again. "We are still learning about these demons. They are new to us, as you know. And the pain, it actually became bearable as I became one with Haem, as if my sensory nerve endings were largely muted. Not completely, mind you, but enough so I could take my time and see to important business. Each time we fly, it's as if

I've been drugged. I'm aware of everything, but the experiences are more . . . dreamlike. And time seems to be more of an abstraction, if that makes sense. An hour can elapse though it only feels like minutes to me. It's the only reason I was able to return to the village and claim the two Commonlanders despite being hurt." He sighed. "Begin," he ordered. "There's still much I need to do."

A red sheen suddenly illuminated the dark interior of the large tent. The healer had invoked his aura. A second passed before Lazlo felt the magic in his back where the arrow had torn his flesh. The sensation quickly penetrated him, following the arrow's destructive path. The magic became hot as it worked to repair what a vangard's missile had rent.

"Lord," said Captain Tsalon, once the aura had subsided. "Why the need to medicate the Commonlanders? They were already unconscious."

"They're eludrians. They're dangerous."

"But they have no eludria."

"They may have . . . gifts. That's why they are here. It's why I risked my life to return to the village to get them. We shall need to use extreme caution with those two. We can't let them regain consciousness, not until we better understand them."

"Why not kill them?"

Lazlo lifted his face to the officer. He was an apt aide, but not much of use for anything other than that. "There may be others like them. I'll need to bring the boy and girl to Intiga. Leave them with Vashti. Perhaps she can discern the nature of their gifts. I'm too busy with this war to take the time to fathom their nature myself. Until we understand their magic, they are a threat to Azinor."

"How long will this take?" said Lazlo, directing his words now to the healer working at his back. As if on cue, the healer walked around to his front and faced him after the honey haired woman stepped aside to give him space.

"Not long, Lord," he said. Your back wound is already closed." He pointed at Lazlo's chest. "Now for this." Once again, the red magic sprung forth from his clenched fist and he extended it forward.

"Captain," uttered Lazlo, his voice affected by the magic and the pain, "bring the Commonlanders to me. We shall be departing for Intiga shortly."

"How long will you be gone?" Tsalon asked.

The healer continued to lave him with red magic. "I'll likely return here near sunrise, or thereabouts."

The officer bowed his head, then quickly departed the tent.

Lazlo quashed another groan as the healing fire increased in intensity briefly to cauterize him. He lifted his head back and focused on the sloping tent ceiling as the healer and his attractive assistant worked to make him whole again. He lowered his eyes and studied the woman closely as she assisted the healer, admiring every feature of her lovely face and longing to run his hands through her flaxen hair. Perhaps after his return from Intiga, he would enquire as to whether this woman might like to join him in the privacy of his tent for a different kind of healing. Of course, that depended on how matters were progressing here at Lavalor on the morrow, and whether he needed to organize another attack, perhaps against the village. No doubt that's where the enemy would reassemble after this evening's rout of the castle.

Five minutes passed, and the healer's magic subsided, although he continued his administrations. Shortly thereafter a half-dozen men entered the tent along with Tsalon. The two unmoving Commonlanders were carried upon a pair of stretchers. They set them down on the rugs near the exit and quickly departed after Lazlo ordered them all to leave.

The girl's hair was cut like the vangards, and she was dressed like them too, though she was an eludrian, not a warrior. She had performed admirably, despite being a pupate—a common Vilazian military term reserved for novices. She had shown great bravery and stamina though her efforts had been doomed to fail from the start. The boy had red hair, and lots of freckles. Lazlo had to admit he was frightened of him. It wasn't like him to feel that way about anyone. He'd seen what this redhead had done to those ogres with his gold magic, and even Haem seemed afraid of him for some reason.

Lazlo pushed away the healer, withdrew eludria from his belt with his left hand, and invoked a malediction to summon the demon. "Anon doss Haem, tagk'liotz!"

A half minute passed before a crack in the air flowed in through the entryway and into the darkest shadows at the back of the tent, where it wrapped itself into a ball of seething dust and effectively became invisible—unless you were looking for it. Lazlo had learned days ago that Haem often needed to remain in this incorporeal state whenever it was near any of his men. Otherwise, some of them would panic upon seeing the demon namril standing in their midst. In truth, Haem's man-like form was an insidious sight to gaze upon—even for him.

Lazlo waved for the healer to continue his work.

"Remove this bloody rag," the young eludrian quietly instructed. His assistant did as commanded. Lazlo tucked in his chin and peered down. The wound was closed. The healer used another bit of clean, wet cloth to wipe away the remaining smears of blood.

Lazlo secured his eludria, then tested his injured arm, smiling because of the absence of pain or restriction.

"Well done," he said. He made to slide off the table, but the healer placed a hand on his bare shoulder.

"Be careful," he admonished. "I will need another thirty minutes with you to ensure you are completely healed."

Lazlo shooed him away, dropped his feet to the floor, and donned his black robe. The woman took several steps backward. But realizing she had approached Haem's dusts, she reacted quickly and moved to the side, away from the lurking demon.

"Looks healed to me," replied Lazlo. "Feels that way, too."

"Appearances are deceiving," replied the healer. "Would fifteen more minutes instead suit my Lord?"

Lazlo shook his head. He approached the sleeping boy and girl and studied them as he further tested his arm. "No need," he slowly replied. "You've done well."

"Thank you, Lord, but I beseech you not to test your arm needlessly any time soon. You need to be care—"

Lazlo jerked his gaze back to the healer.

The man suddenly looked terrified.

Lazlo caught himself. He was not one to shy away from harshly disciplining his inferiors, but this man was especially competent. And Lavalor was finally in ruin, so he was feeling . . . generous this evening. He opened a calming palm toward the man.

"You've served me well. I therefore ask you to enjoy the comfort of my shelter while I am at Intiga. Command my cooks as you will. Have them prepare a feast of your choice." Lazlo smiled at the shocked man. "Within reason, of course."

The man bowed deeply. "You are indeed gracious, Lord. I thank you for the opportunity to serve you."

Lazlo considered the woman, who, like Haem, was trying to remain invisible and unnoticed. She really was quite pretty. And shy. She kept her gaze lowered to the elegant rugs covering the ground. But then she gave it away when she stole a glance at him. She had the faintest glimmer of a smile on those beautiful lips.

Perhaps in the morning, my dear.

Lazlo faced the demon. "Haem, it's time."

The dusts separated from the perimeter shadows and approached Lazlo and the two unconscious teens. The healer stepped back, deeper into the dark spaces behind him. Lazlo studied the black crack at the center of the small cloud through which the creature's soot billowed. Remarkable, as always! He breathed deeply of the particulates once they had surrounded him and immediately felt his body begin to transfigure, becoming lighter. He sensed that familiar heat and sound—which he surmised was the distant lake of fire and the dreary drone of millions of voices, both barely perceptible. He checked the Commonlanders. They, too, were breathing the dusts and were becoming shapeless as their bodies were transfigured into dust and conjoined with Haem.

"Intiga," ordered Lazlo, already a bodiless voice.

6

The five-hour climb had been arduous, not unlike the first time he had negotiated this soaring cliff-wall that towered three-hundred feet, at least. Back then he had a barking dog to contend with, tucked safely away in a rear waist sack he had made with his tunic. Today he had only his two longknives. And they were hungry.

Weir forced old memories from his mind as he concentrated on matters at hand. Thirty more feet and he'd be safe in the forest that delimited the southern extent of Lavalor's impalement field. He'd almost fallen to his death twice, both occurrences caused by rock crumbling away underfoot. Despite the dangers, he figured this was the best way to gain entry into the enemy encampment. All other routes would be fiercely guarded. The gorge was an unlikely threat to the Vilazians and it therefore afforded him the sole opportunity he needed for a stealthy intrusion. There'd likely be sentries up above somewhere, but probably not many.

He chanced a glance down at the Lavalor River and saw only darkness because of the late hour, though he could hear it faintly hissing like a snake in the grass. The upper half of the far side of the steep canyon was bathed in moonlight. Some of it reflected his way, allowing him to see details over on this side. He estimated the next twenty feet would be the hardest.

The wall at this spot was daunting. It was as flat and flawless as a mirror. *But I've crossed it once already.* He spied a perturbation in the stone several feet above his head. Hardly seemed big enough for a bird to alight onto. Yet it was all he had. He pushed up on his toes, extended his right arm as high as he could, and carefully wrapped his fingertips over the narrow edge.

He took a deep breath, exhaled half of it, then pulled his body up until his head was near his straining fingers. He dangled for a moment, then observed another rock bump, several feet to the left, but a little higher. He'd have to pendulum himself closer to that next handhold to continue upward. One more breath, and he was ready. He swung his body over and grabbed a six-inch wide protrusion with the fingertips of his free hand. Almost instantly, his right hand snapped over to join its sibling.

He had no choice now but to go straight up—or straight down to that watery grave. Without delay, he pulled on the tiny ledge of stone with all the explosive energy stored within his arms and shot upward about two vertical feet. He momentarily lost sight of the bit of rock he had intended to grab onto. He panicked, and slapped the stone face with his right hand, hoping to find a handhold. Luckily, his fingers found purchase, and now he was dangling.

He started to tire, but he dared not pause.

He noted some seams and edges further to the left, and swung toward them.

Twice more he repeated similar movements in that same direction. His breathing started to sound louder. He found a small ledge, a place on which he could rest a big toe.

He glanced up and saw the top of the cliff not more than a dozen feet away.

Almost there!

As tired as he felt, it took energy even to remain unmoving, hanging as he was by the edges of his fingertips and by a single toe.

One mistake here and he'd be a pulp of flesh and bone on the river rocks far below.

This time he found a crack. It angled upward steeply, to the right. It made for easier climbing as he could jam his fingers into the crack for proper, safer grips. He made short work of the next ten feet and found tree roots protruding from under the lip of the canyon rim. One such root had almost killed him and Runt on that earlier day when it tore away from the rock face. A desperate hand and another root was all that had saved him then, so only with extreme caution did he now dare to try it again. Finally, he completed his perilous ascent of the cliff and carefully, slowly, he crawled his way onto grass —beautiful, flat grass.

He remained flat on the ground for some time and took deep, silent breathes as he scanned his surroundings. Tall pines mostly, but some firs and yellow jakroots stood in abundance here. The full moon hung brilliantly over toward the west at this early morning hour, but the density of trees blocked most of the light from reaching the ground. It cast an array of confused shadows everywhere.

He remained flat for a while longer, staying absolutely silent, and letting his heart slow. Luckily so, for he eventually saw a sentry hunkered down against the foot of a wide fir tree about twenty feet away, directly in front of him. Weir spent another minute, searching for more Bipaquans, but so far, only this one.

He couldn't tell if this redface was sleeping or not. His face was in shadow. Weir had a choice: either charge the man and quickly kill him, or choose a more cautious and time-consuming option. He chose caution. There could be others nearby.

He began to inch forward slowly, his torso barely off the layer of dried pine needles that dominated here. He moved like those lizards that had lain siege on the castle, arms and legs alternately moving forward.

His hand crushed some dried jakroot leaves. His body went rigid.

Did he hear that?

Another minute passed, but no movement from the redface. Weir proceeded forward. He got to within two strides of the Bipaquan when the man finally realized he wasn't alone. Weir observed his legs tense first, then his upper body began to lean forward. The element of surprise gone, Weir burst into motion and pulled *Vengeance* from its hip sheath. Redface was halfway to his feet when Weir kicked him solidly in the chest with his bare foot. The warrior crashed back into the trunk of the tree, grunting loudly from the impact. So far it was the only sound either of them had made. Weir's blade pierced the man's neck, pinning his head to the course bark behind him. He expired shortly thereafter with Weir's other hand clamped over his mouth.

But sounds! More sentries!

They had heard their warmate's death-grunt and were already charging through the trees toward him. Four Bipaquans, Weir counted, based on the sounds of bare feet tearing through pine needles and dried leaves. An instant passed and he saw their shadows flitting toward him, two on either side, substantial gaps between each of them. Weir crouched, to make it harder to be seen, and moved away from the dead man. He would need more space for the coming skirmish. He was surprised these sentries hadn't yet called out any warning. He attributed this to confusion. They didn't yet know exactly what had happened to their warmate, or whether a warning was even required. Weir would have to act fast with these remaining four, and hope there weren't others.

The second man to die dropped silently when he came within range of Weir's bloodied longknife. *Vengeance* streaked unseen in the darkness and sunk to its hilt in the Bipaquan's neck. Weir spun around and withdrew his second blade, *Mercy,* this one from over his shoulder, and killed a third man—a Bipaquan wearing a wolf head-dress—with yet another expert throw, again to the neck. Weir pivoted once more and dashed toward the dead man who was wearing *Vengeance* as a piece of neck jewelry. He snatched the blade from the still figure just as another redface loomed in front of him. The warrior finally realized the danger and his mouth began to form a scream. He swung a sword toward Weir's shoulders. Weir sidestepped the attack, and cut him down after just a partial word had escaped into the darkness, his longknife yet again causing bloody carnage within a Bipaquan throat.

One last sentry—rushing directly toward him.

This final Bipaquan also began to scream a warning. Weir threw *Vengeance,* but because of the added distance and poor light, it missed, and bounced off a nearby tree somewhere close behind the man. He went abruptly silent. He must have caught a glint of steel in the fragmented moonlight, and he jerked aside in reaction, an abrupt maneuver that caused him to cease his verbal utterings in mid-phrase. It gave Weir the time he needed to come charging in behind his flying weapon. The two men met where the wolf man had died, *Mercy* still lodged deep in that man's throat. Weaponless, Weir leapt in the darkness and swept his feet in a horizontal arc. His first kick missed, but the second connected solidly with the man's ear and sent him sprawling to the ground as his sword fell. Weir bent even lower as he spun, deftly snatched the man's sword in mid-air, and continued his circular attack. He brought the weapon around, gripping it in both hands, and sunk it deep into the Bipaquan's chest.

Weir dropped to a knee beside the expiring redface, who gasped several times before heading toward the eternal abyss. Weir remained unmoving. He trained his eyes and ears to the nearby forest, looking for movement, listening for threats. Maybe a minute passed. But beyond some leaves rustling above him in the trees, nothing. No sounds. He had been lucky there weren't other sentries around.

He stood, took several steps, and peered down at the wolf man.

He had an idea.

He knelt, removed the headdress from the deceased man, then draped it over his own head. He thought this thing would be useful, as it might disguise his own identity. Perhaps it would allow him to appear as a Bipaquan. Atikans and Bipaquans were very similar in appearance, after all. The headdress was basically the partial pelt and head of a wolf without its skull. Weir found he could pull it down over his forehead, and when he dropped his head low, the snout and ears would partially mask his upper face. The headdress also had long, wide strips of fur hanging over his shoulders and back, including the animal's appendages, and they further served to mask the fact that he was Atikan. After adjusting the headdress one more time, he retrieved *Mercy* from the man's neck, and cleaned his blade and hands on the Bipaquan's clothing. Weir found that one strip of fur on the headdress had ample amounts of the man's fresh blood on it. He cut it off and used it to smear blood on his face.

Weir went searching for *Vengeance*. He found it sticking upright in the pine needles a few yards away. It had taken several precious minutes to find it in this darkness, but the time spent was well worth the recovery of a valued weapon.

That made him think about Galager's ruby—Roln's ruby. *I still have it!* He reached down and felt for it in his trousers, confirming it was still there. At least he hadn't lost it going over the falls. He cursed himself for not handing it over to Bosun earlier. Lot of good it would do him now.

He meant to depart the scene when he realized he had to do something about the bodies. If they were discovered, it would initiate a pursuit he couldn't afford. There was also some risk in taking the time to dispose of these bodies, for it might generate more noise and attract unwanted attention. He ultimately decided it was a risk worth taking. Checking again for threats, and finding none, he grabbed the wrists of the wolf man and dragged him over to the edge of the gorge, laid him sideways to it, and then pushed him over the edge with a heel. He heard the body thumping against rocks several times over the next five or six seconds before hearing a faint splash. A few minutes later the other four bodies, and their weapons, had been similarly dumped over the cliff. Finally, he proceeded west through the forest, in the direction of Lazlo Urich's encampment. It was time to end this battle—on his terms.

7

The sun blinded her that summer morning and filled her sight with orange rays of eternal bliss. The double doors of her bedchamber leading to the eastern terrace of their mansion were wide open, letting in not only the light, but the Jasmine breeze flowing in from the nearby village. Jana stood in the doorway, verbally compelling her older sister to get out of bed.

"Come on Adriana," she coaxed. "The Jasmine festival starts this morning. You promised to go with me, remember?"

Ada threw a pillow at her. It missed and almost knocked over a crystal vase with fresh cut yellow roses sticking out of its mouth. Ada peered at her younger sibling through eyes fuzzy with sleep. Jana looked like an angel in the orange and white brilliance, her white shift billowing up like wings, and dusty rays silhouetting her slim figure. It made her smile even though Jana would never stop referring to her with anything but that horrendous name she so hated. Not even the fierce Edward Halentine, her heroic father and the Mayor of Vivona, dared use Ada's proper name.

Jana skipped forward, deeper into the room. She jumped onto the bed at Ada's side and poked her beautiful, exuberant smile into her face.

Ada laughed as she yawned, then grabbed Jana and hugged her close. "Do I have time for one more hour of sleep?"

"We need to go!" Jana said. Her breath warmed Ada's neck. "Master Worill said if we get to his shop before the mid-morning bell, he'd let us pick out a bottle of Jasmine perfume from his collection, one for each of us."

"I don't like perfume."

"But you're a girl, Adriana. Of course, you like perfume."

Ada laughed again. "Okay, I'll pick one out. And give it to you."

Jana returned her laugh and hugged her big sister once more.

"But don't you tell Master Worill I gave it to you," said Ada. "He may want it back."

"Don't worry," Jana squealed in delight, her amber eyes glinting like fire and emitting rays of goodness and innocence, "I won't tell him."

"I love you, Adriana."

"I love you too, little girl."

~

Ada's eyes popped open. In an instant the happiness in her heart vanished, replaced with fear and depression. Right away she saw the woman, and it startled her. Why wouldn't it? Last time she was truly, fully conscious she was with Master Vreman and Galager atop Cadia Gate. She remembered the battle and that moment when Galager came to save them. *The explosion!* It had temporarily blinded her—a kaleidoscope of red and blue—before it sent her into oblivion. Some amount of time later she had been carried somewhere. Lavalor Village, she was sure. She remembered Galager lying next to her in the dirt. That's when Haem took her.

Galager too?

The woman stood in the doorway of the bedchamber. The door frame was constructed of white stone blocks, many of them misaligned as if they had been shaken loose by an earthquake. The entire room spoke of its former affluence. Various architectural elements decorated the chamber, including plaster cornices and columned door and window casements with entablatures. Many of the plaster pieces were broken, although any fallen debris had been removed and the dust swept away long ago. Tall candle stands, at least a dozen, were scattered throughout the room. They cast low golden glows on the white walls. An open window draped with scarlet curtains framed a black sky beyond. A red pennon with black heraldry markings hung on the wall near the door. More broken plaster. Night air—cool and moist. Signs of dawn approaching.

Where am I? Somewhere high. She aimed worried eyes back toward the woman. Her arms crossed. An amused expression pinned on Ada. Middle-aged. Creases around her eyes. Black hair with hints of gray, wavy and long, falling to her waist over an elegant ankle-length gown, sleeveless, and rose-brown in hue. It wasn't Jana, though this woman was as beautiful as her.

Her eyes flicked back to the red pennon then the woman. *Vilazian!* Her heart sunk with despair. This could only mean one thing. *Lavalor is lost!*

Ada was shocked to discover she was in a bed even more enormous than Arthor Hadron's white monster. Keeping her eyes on the woman, she tried to lift an arm but found her wrists shackled to chains. The chains were secured around rear posts of the bed, both substantial. She tested them anyway, yanking the chain on her right arm as hard as she could. The square post didn't so much as vibrate. But the shackle bit harshly into her skin. Parts of its iron edges were sharpened, no doubt to mitigate intransigence.

Ada scowled at the Vilazian. Saw her steal a glance to Ada's right. Ada followed her glance. *Nothing there!* A few pieces of furniture—a chair and a large wardrobe, red curtains filling each of the room's corners. Ada tested the other shackle, but again, the only result was a slightly bloodied, and stinging, wrist..

"Careful, girl," said the Vilazian woman in the common-tongue. Her accent was strange to Ada's ears, but her speech was perfect.

Ada furrowed her brows as a small amount of blood dripped slowly from her shackles and onto the dirty linens beneath her.

The woman chuckled. She dropped her arms to her side. A silver chain of a necklace slipped out from between the fingers of a hand, revealing a glimpse of scarlet light therein.

Awareness stung Ada. *Eludria! Vilemaster!*

"But you're . . . a woman!"

The Vilazian smiled wider. Perfect white teeth.

"She talks," said the woman. "So astute of you to notice." But then she chuckled. "Ah! You're a clever one. You discern I'm gifted, although I'm female."

The woman again furtively glanced to Ada's right, then took a small step into the room.

"Vilazians don't allow matters of gender to interfere with one's innate nature. All of us—man or woman—are free to express ourselves and explore our gifts. Perhaps you are gifted too?"

"How are you able to speak common-tongue?"

The lady waved her empty hand dismissively.

"Prisoners, of course. We learn much from them. Every Vilazian eludrian learns your language. I am fluent in three languages, proficient in two others. The Vilazian Winds extend into many lands." She leered at Ada. "Do any of your eludrians speak my language? I suspect not many do."

Seemingly as an afterthought, the woman uttered a short phrase, in Vilazian, for some reason. "Yours are a disgusting and uneducated people."

Ada's bile rose, and she almost responded. But a wiser voice inside her warned her not to react. She ignored the comment.

"Am I your prisoner?" Ada asked without emotion.

Another chuckle. "Not so clever after all."

Trying to anger me. Don't let her. "I mean—why am I your prisoner?"

The woman took another step forward. She seemed afraid to come too close.

"What is your name?"

No harm in answering. "Ada."

"Your full name, child?"

"Ada Halentine. Who are you?"

"Vashti Dal'falkoz. And it's my honor to host you during your short stay here. You remind me of someone."

"Who? Someone who cast an ugly spell on you?"

Okay, that was lame.

Vashti laughed. "I'd be disappointed if you didn't exhibit such spirit."

"What happened to my friends? Where are they?"

Vashti secreted another glance to Ada's right again. *Why?*

"Do you mean the boy?"

Ada sat up higher. "Yes, Galager. Where is he?"

Vashti lifted fingers, caressing her lips in thought before dropping her hand to her waist.

"What do you remember of him?"

"Tell me! Is he alive?"

"My dear, I don't wish you to despair like this. You remind me of my poor Carleea. Not your ugly shaven hair and filthy clothes, of course. But your blue eyes and complexion. Same as hers. And your spirit. Yes, he's safe. He's here."

Ada sighed with relief.

"There, you see. You feel better already. I can tell. The poor boy is still unconscious. My servants informed me you were on the verge of awakening, so here I am. But it appears this Galager of yours, well, he hasn't even blinked since arriving here a few hours ago."

"How did we get here? Where are we?"

"Lazlo brought you here."

"You mean that demon, don't you? Haem?"

Vashti smiled in acknowledgement.

Ada again scanned the room. Old. Broken. Elegant. Tall ceilings and doors. White marble everywhere, with plaster accents. *Old? Broken?*

"Intiga!" she uttered in sudden astonishment. "I'm in Intiga!"

"My Carleea was also gifted with such intelligence. I think I like you."

But Vashti's cheeks turned downward and she frowned. "And for that reason, I am dismayed I have to do this."

The Vilazian took one more step. She now stood at the footboard. She raised a clenched hand and pointed it at Ada. A silver necklace chain dangled from it as a growing aura enveloped her entire fist.

Ada flinched in terror and scooted back against the headboard. She instinctively tried to search within her garments for her own eludria, but her shackles bit deep.

Red magic began pouring from the vilemaster's fist. Her emissions quickly formed a cone of scarlet energy that she interposed between herself and the Vivonian.

"What are you doing?" Ada asked. "Stop it!" she yelled.

The Vilazian's magic bulged toward her and became more elongated.

Ada heard a sound at her right, a rustling of fabric, but Vashti's attack was commanding all of her attention.

"I am so sorry," said Vashti, "but I have no choice in the matter."

The silent magic was just inches from Ada's face now. Powerless to defend herself, she closed her eyes, thought of her sister, Jana, and waited for finality.

8

Panthertooth carefully stalked through the section of forest separating him from the Vilazian Multitude, and hopefully, that bastard, Lazlo Urich. The enemy encampment wasn't hard to find. Numerous campfires had served as a beacon and led him straight to it. He saw the fires through the trees almost the instant he departed the area of Little Dog Gorge.

He constantly searched for sentries. The closer he got to the encampment, the more there were. For the most part he had been able to steer clear of them, but several times he had come within a few yards of roving Bipaquans—one with a wolf headdress like Weir's. But not once was he challenged. The headdress he had taken for himself had been a boon. So far, no one had given him a second look.

Weir paused beside an old jakroot. He estimated the dead and rotting thing would soon be lying on the forest floor. Perhaps one more good storm might do the trick. Dead limbs were already strewn around its wide trunk. The earliest rays of dawn were striking the topmost branches of the ancient tree. Soon it would be daylight. It had taken him the entire night to get here.

He peered intently into the enemy encampment once he neared

it. Tents everywhere, stretching off to the west. Too many to count and pretty much identical. They were constructed of brown oilskin tarps strung up between trees, and probably a third of them were adorned with two-pointed red pennons with an imperial black griffin coat of arms. Most of the soldiers and warriors were still asleep. No signs of ogres—or those lizards. The monsters were kept somewhere else, he figured, somewhere comfortably away from humans.

Another visual sweep confirmed no sign yet of Lazlo's shelter. It would be bigger than all the others. Unfortunately, he'd have to venture deeper into the encampment to find the murdering ass. He stepped around a tangle of dry jakroot branches and proceeded forward at a normal pace and bearing. Sneaking around now would only make him stick out.

He passed through the first row of tents, his eyes always searching for threats. A sleepy Vilazian soldier strolled past him, heading in the opposite direction, probably off to take his morning plink. Weir lowered his chin as the man came near, but the redcoat didn't seem to notice him. With every step he took, the band of yellow sunlight at the tops of the trees sunk lower to the ground. He would have to work fast to find Lazlo.

A Bipaquan warrior suddenly appeared from the flap of a tent. Weir almost ran into him. He deftly sidestepped around the man and moved forward, keeping his chin down, his eyes covered by the headdress.

The warrior directed a phrase of gruff words at him. Weir placed a palm on the grip of *Vengeance* and wondered where he might hide the body, if it came to that. In a tent perhaps. He turned his shoulder halfway back toward the Bipaquan and waved an indifferent arm and grunted something unintelligible. He resumed a casual walk toward the center of the enemy encampment, although the next few seconds felt as if there was a target on his back.

Weir fought the urge to look over his shoulder to check on the Bipaquan, for to do so might appear suspicious. He took several more paces and turned right, between two other tents. Only now did he pause. He heard no signs of exigency. No shouts. No hurried footfalls on the forest floor. Satisfied that no alarm had been raised, he resumed his incursion into the center of the Vilazian encampment. He suddenly spotted a smudge of red above and behind one of the tents ahead. Not a pennon, but a flag.

He continued on, his steps a bit brisker now. After maybe another dozen or so rows, he finally saw Lazlo's command tent. There could be no doubt. It was round, unlike any of the other tents he'd seen. It had a diameter of maybe twenty feet and had a tall center pole sporting a red Vilazian flag with that same black coat of arms. A pair of long spears served as support poles for a rectangular entryway, each with a red pennon at its head.

Weir inwardly cursed his bad luck. There were no guards at the entryway. And that likely meant Lazlo wasn't here. At least not right now. He instinctively checked his surroundings again. So far, so good. But the encampment was fully illuminated by the early sun at this time. Before too long everyone would be awake.

He hesitated, considering his options. Withdrawing was one of them. Maybe he could find a place to hide, and come back later, perhaps after sunset. Under cover of the long, dark night he could then exact his style of revenge on the leader of this army. Option two was more to his liking.

He again scanned for threats. Seeing none, he walked briskly through one more row of tents and then darted into the square entryway of the eludrian's abode, a modest vestibule designed to keep the elements from the main lodge just ahead. Once inside the short space, he paused, and listened.

He heard snoring. *Might Lazlo actually be here? Could I be so lucky after all?*

Panthertooth carefully separated a pair of leather panels and peered into the main chamber. The lodge was rather sparsely appointed. Animal rugs—lion, bear, panther, buffalo, and others—were heaped upon the ground. They were enough for Lazlo's advisors to comfortably recline together as they plotted and planned their murderous schemes. A single man in an ochre-colored robe currently lay amongst their center. He didn't think it was Lazlo. The day before,

Lazlo had worn a black robe. Next to the snoring figure were several pewter trays that contained the half-eaten remnants of various meats and fruit. The Vilazian slept face down, his head in a crook of his right arm, with his left extended behind him at his side. A bit of red light, an aura, glimmered from the man's left fist.

Vilemaster!

Four small tables stood equidistant around the perimeter of the tent. Each was amply covered with numerous candles of various lengths and diameters. Maybe a quarter of the candles were lit. A larger table stood off to the right of the entryway. A short smear of blood was visible on its surface as well as a pile of bloodied bandages or rags. Despite the candles, the space was still rather dark.

Panthertooth removed the wolf headdress and set it silently on the ground. He stepped carefully as he moved toward the sleeping eludrian. Subduing a vilemaster wasn't without risk—even a sleeping one—especially when one had to simultaneously disarm him and keep him from making any sounds. One mistake now, and it would be over. And killing this Vilazian wasn't an option either. Not yet. If this wasn't Lazlo, Weir needed information from him.

He decided to disarm him first then deal with the man's mouth afterward. These wizards could conjure fire in a heartbeat. Weir could be dead before he hit the ground.

At the man's side now, he observed the eludria glowing like a chunk of hot coal through loosely clenched fingers. He bent low and snatched the vilemaster's left fist into one hand, as if he had just grabbed the head of a viper. He simultaneously kneeled on the man's upper arm, to keep him immobile, and grabbed his fingers with his other hand and squeezed. He heard bones snapping as the ruby fell harmlessly to the brown fur inches below. Weir flicked at the talisman, sending it flying safely toward the shadows.

The vilemaster awoke instantly and began to squirm and buck. The nascent utterings of a scream escaped his terror-stricken lips, but Panthertooth pivoted, straddled his back, and encircled the man's neck with his constricting arm. He had the man's head nestled deep in the bend of his elbow while he squeezed mightily, shutting down his air supply as well as the blood flowing through his neck arteries. Weir lifted his head, bent him backward, and encircled his face with his other arm, further muffling his terrified utterings and applying even more pressure. Seconds later the Vilazian slumped and Weir let him drop.

With blood flowing within his arteries again, the Vilazian began to self-revive. Weir quickly turned him over and sat on his chest, straddling his arms. He slid *Vengeance* out, rested its tip lightly on the man's larynx, and planted his other palm firmly on his mouth.

Weir grinned insidiously as the Vilazian's eyes registered, first, awareness, and then shock. He wisely didn't struggle though. He wasn't a stupid man. Weir shushed him. He did it again and the Vilazian realized what Weir wanted and nodded slightly.

Weir tentatively withdrew his hand from around the man's mouth, ready to plunge it back down again if needed. But so far, not a chirp. This Vilazian didn't want to die.

"Do you understand my words?" Weir whispered, speaking in the common-tongue.

"I do," muttered the man. "Please don't kill me."

Weir smiled. "No need for that. If you cooperate with me. What is your name?"

"Harll. I have a wife, and two children."

"As do many of my men who died last night."

"I'll do anything you ask. But I beg you, please, don't kill me. I've never harmed any Commonlanders—or Atikans. I'm just a healer."

"Silence."

Harll's eyes widened even further as his lips snapped shut.

"Where is Lazlo?"

"He's not here."

Weir let the tip of his blade penetrate lightly into the man's skin, drawing a bead of blood.

"Gone. He's gone."

"Go on."

"He took them to Intiga. To the mausoleum."

Them? Weir was confused. If this man was speaking accurately, Lazlo had gone to Intiga, but he had taken several people with him.

"Who went with him?"

"The eludrians."

Something wasn't right. This man clearly wasn't referring to Vilazian eludrians.

Oh no!

"Tell me about these eludrian," Weir urgently demanded. The point of his blade dug a bit deeper into the man's neck. "Are they Vilazian?"

"No, no! Commonlanders. Two of them. A boy and a girl."

Weir tensed. His eyes became narrow slits. His blood ran hot. He wanted to lash out at something, someone.

The healer sensed the anger rising in Weir.

"Don't kill me!" he pleaded again, fearing for his life. "Please, don't kill me."

Silence. Tranquility. Awareness.

"I won't," Weir finally replied, his body less rigid now. "But only if you truthfully answer my questions."

"Of course," the man said. "Of course. Anything."

"When did they leave for Intiga?"

"Last night. After I healed Lazlo. After the battle. Lazlo is evil—even more than those horrible creatures—the slake. I don't have a choice being here. Our people are forced to help the Lord Masters. Please don't kill me. I beg—"

"The boy and girl, are they hurt?"

"No! I checked them myself."

"The demon, Haem. It brought them here? It carried them away?"

"Yes. But Lazlo is supposed to return here in the morning. Soon. Very soon. He intends to leave them with Vashti, at Intiga, so she can examine the prisoners—and understand their gifts."

"Can these demons be killed?"

Harll didn't answer. Instead, he was busy thinking. His eyes began to fill with resignation. He was probably starting to believe he had no escape from this encounter, so why answer any more questions.

"You are doing fine. I shall show you mercy if you provide but a few more answers. I will bind and gag you—to give me time to escape this camp. You will be able to return home to your family. Now listen carefully. This is important."

Harll nodded.

"Can Haem be killed?"

No hesitation. "Kill Lazlo. Kill the demon."

"Is that the only way?"

"I—I don't know. But, oh! The malediction. It can send the demon back to the abyss, if you are gifted, and know the correct words."

"Malediction?"

"It's a phrase bound to magic. When used with a demon's name, these words bind the creature to the will of the one summoning it from the pit. We think these words were crafted by Ethelliphus himself so he would be the master of anyone or anything entering his fiery domain. Like I said, the malediction can also be used to compel Haem to return back to the abyss or to issue any order to the creature. Surely this knowledge is worth my life?"

"Tell me these words."

"Anon doss Haem, tagk'liotz."

"Again."

The healer complied.

Weir had other questions. But time was of the essence. It was morning. Lazlo could return at any moment. "You have been helpful. Thank you."

Weir felt his face tighten with grim determination.

Harll saw it. "Please. I won't tell anyone you were—" But then he went silent. He knew his pleas were futile. When he closed his eyes, Weir struck him brutally on the temple with the pommel of his longknife. Harll went out instantly. Weir sheathed his weapon, quickly rolled him over and again wrapped his substantial arms around Harll's neck and mouth. Afterward, he silently squeezed the life out of him.

Weir remained unmoving after the body went still. This death hurt him. He believed everything Harll had told him. The Vilazian people themselves were victims of their own Lord Masters.

But what choice did I have?

He strangled the guilt from his mind, rose to his feet, and crossed the dim interior to retrieve Harll's talisman. After pocketing it where he wouldn't confuse it with Galager's ruby, he returned to the dead Vilazian and rolled him back over.

Did he lie about having a family?

He saw the food tray nearby and hungrily consumed most of the remaining scraps of meat and fruit. He saved one hefty chunk of ham and jammed it into Harll's gaping mouth, deep into his throat.

Rolling him over one more time, Weir picked him up, arms grappling his chest, and carried him around one of the tables with candles on it. Finally, he violently threw the vilemaster's body against the table and knocked it over, causing the lit candles to fall onto the animal rugs. They ignited instantly, their flames rising high and spreading to the other rugs layered over the hard ground. Weir ran around the flames to the exit and donned the wolf headdress. He suddenly realized a mistake, and withdrew Harll's ruby from his pocket. He tossed it over toward the burning figure. Then, once he was sure the flames had touched the ceiling of the tent, he headed out into the despondent morning with a new mission. Lazlo would have to wait. Right now, he had to go to Intiga to find the teens, and return Galager's ruby to him.

9

Boson Rheev climbed over the village wall an hour or so after midnight. He was the last man to do so. He slithered down one of the six ropes he and his friends had used to lower everyone to the ground. It had taken the better part of three hours to get their army over the wall, including the injured. Deception required they avoid the easier path through the gates.

A fist of other vangards, including Lorgan and Brawk, imposing shadows in the darkness, were waiting for him below. The six men quickly pulled down the ropes and hefted the heavy coils over their shoulders. Without a word they slipped away into the night, making haste to catch the withdrawing army somewhere up ahead. With luck, the Vilazians would never figure out where they had gone.

Boson didn't feel lucky.

Quinton Collier's report was part of the reason. Collier had ordered a head count during the few priceless hours the battered army had been allowed to sleep. Once it was completed, he reckoned almost eleven hundred soldiers and warriors—not counting the spurs—had made it out of Castle Lavalor after the battle. All five hundred of Poole's Spurs were accounted for, and so were several dozen donkey-cart boys and their animals. But two hundred and forty-seven soldiers—swords, arrows, and spears—had perished on the western curtain wall alone. That was about half the men assigned there on the final night of battle. Lavalor's Vangard Corps hadn't fared so well either, for twenty-three of their number failed to answer roll-call, almost a quarter of their total. The remaining losses—one hundred and thirty souls, according to their best efforts at producing an accurate accounting—had occurred in random locations throughout the embattled fortress. The majority of these were on or near Cadia Gate.

In addition to the fatalities, well over two-hundred other men had suffered significant casualties of one form or another, many of them life-threatening. Despite their heavy losses, Boson considered themselves lucky more hadn't died. Considering their circumstances, their only major weakness at this point, besides having been ejected from their home, was the absence of eludrians within their numbers, and, of course, that was a huge problem.

Boson's plan was simple.

First, Poole's spurs would quietly, but not secretly, depart the village through Jurry Gate. Their goal was to proceed with all speed eastward along the Severcal Road to later meet up with reinforcements from Jurry. Many of the injured would be taken out on horseback, forcing at least as many spurs to share their mounts.

In the meantime, everyone else—all those who could walk, a good number who couldn't, and all led by Havless—would secret themselves over the eastern wall where it met the northern cliffs. The vangards would accompany them. This ground force had one simple goal: escape, and then fight another day, hopefully after its standing had improved. As long as darkness permitted, Bosun and the others would make their way around the eastern extent of the Lavalor cliffs and follow an old, treacherous hunting trail, a trail he knew like the back of his hand.

In justifying this plan, Boson had reasoned that if the spurs and foot-soldiers instead remained together as they withdrew from Lavalor, they would be too slow, too exposed, and the enemy would easily track them, catch them, and lay waste to them. Lazlo and his demon would be the ones doing most of the wasting. Survival, Boson suggested, depended on the horse units taking advantage of their speed to draw the enemy away from the slower land force, which would take an entirely different route to an agreed-upon meeting place. With luck they'd all meet up with the boys from Jurry before anyone found them. Hopefully, the units from Jurry would include an eludrian or two.

The donkeys, however, were a different matter altogether. They had been left behind in the village. They were just too slow to keep up with the horses, and too loud. It was heartbreaking to leave these faithful servants behind, no doubt to be slaughtered by the lizards if they attacked. But there was nothing else they could do. One other benefit to be gained by leaving them behind was that their sporadic braying might induce the enemy into believing the village hadn't yet been evacuated, lending precious time for withdrawal.

The major risk of this plan was what would happen if the Vilazians were able to deduce Lavalor's defenders had split up. For if that occurred, Boson knew the slow-moving ground force could very likely be obliterated, especially if Lazlo and Haem were part of that reckoning. It was with great concern, therefore, that Boson kept wary eyes toward the rear as he trudged northward with his warmates.

Sixty minutes into their difficult trek, he became disconcerted with their slow progress. The injured and wounded were slowing them down, not to mention having to find their way along the edges of dangerous crags and ravines in almost utter darkness. Many of their number also hefted bundles of torches, a necessity, if they reached their destination later this day—yet another reason they were sluggish. The moon was up, but did little good hidden behind the mountains that formed Lavalor Cliffs.

His patience wearing thin, Bosun selected a brace of his Atikan vangards and a similar number of arrows, and together they dropped to the rear of the long procession. A first attack, if it came, would come from behind, and he wanted to be ready if it did.

The ground force veered north-east after clearing the worst of the rocks, and disappeared into the heavy pine forests that seemed to stretch forever northward to Torrent Slew and other distant locations. Its members needed to get some distance between themselves and the Vilazians as fast as they could. If their ruse was discovered, it would only be a matter of time before the enemy would come for them. The land at their front was hilly and rugged, but easily crossed, so long as they stuck to the winding draws and vales. Later in the day they would turn due eastward, into a chaotic system of crisscrossed canyons and another expanse of higher rock lands that some reckoned were caused by the Sword of Jhalaveral all those centuries ago.

One way or another, they'd have to find a way to stay ahead of the enemy and survive the remainder of this day, and then the unwelcome night. Bosun had an idea how to accomplish that, but it all depended on reaching the rock lands before they had been located by the enemy. If the Vilazians managed to spot them before then, their chances at escape would plummet, as they'd be forced to stand and fight before rejoining with Poole and his spurs the next day. Even if they miraculously made it through the night, the real challenge might be the run they'd have to make to their final destination—a place known as Grassy Creek—the following morning. If everything went as planned, that's where'd they'd rejoin with Poole and his spurs, not to mention the units from Jurry. As for now, though, all they could do was to keep carrying their most severely wounded, keep moving, and keep checking their rear.

10

Vashti leered contemptuously at her after extinguishing her magic. It had never touched Ada, and never burned her.

"Remove her shackles," the Vilazian stated in her native tongue.

Ada flinched as she heard sounds over to the right of her.

A Vilazian soldier in a dirty red tunic and tan trousers stepped from behind the curtains in the corner of the room. He had been hiding there all along. He approached her bedside, withdrew a key, and unlocked her shackles. Once she was free, Ada leapt from the bed to make a run for the door. But the man blocked her escape and wrestled her back down onto the mattress. He was just too big for her, and she was still feeling a bit pathetic from her recent exertions and experiences.

"Stay!" he said. As if she were a dog.

He was a big man with a nasty frown immersed within a long black beard. His dark eyes were encased in a mess of angry wrinkles. He was barrel-chested with thick arms and legs and he tended to stand with a hunched over posture.

Still near the footboard, Vashti draped her necklace over her head and around her neck, then crossed her arms, and glanced at the soldier.

"Thank you, Ficx."

"You sure you're safe?" he asked.

They're afraid of me. Why? I have no eludria.

Both were conversing in Vilazian, utterly unaware of her proficiency in their language.

Vashti smiled disdainfully toward Ada. "This one's harmless."

"Anything else, my Lady?"

"Stay close for the time being."

Not so safe after all, are you?

Ficx bowed in deference. He went to stand watch at the open window where traces of morning sunlight had started to beam in.

Ada's thoughts returned to Vashti's aborted magic attack. *Testing me? Trying to provoke a response from me? And why was this man hiding behind me? Was it in case I became a problem for her?*

"Why am I still alive?" asked Ada, content for now to sit on the side of the mattress. "Isn't it like you people to murder your prisoners? Or turn them into ogres? Instead, here I am in this fanciful bed."

"In time, dear," the vilemaster said, allowing a bit of coldness to affect her expression. "In time. Until then, I'll keep those shackles off you as long as you cooperate."

"If the tables were reversed, I'd have lain you to earth the moment I saw you."

Vashti chuckled. "You people are animals."

Ada ignored her.

"Why have you eschewed your femininity, your greatest resource? You look and act as a man does."

"My purpose is to defend Severcal. The Commonland. I'm a warrior, not a lady." Ada suddenly realized she had never slain a single enemy soldier or eludrian. So how could she dare consider herself a warrior? After all, here she was, a prisoner of a sworn enemy. Her life had been a complete failure. She and Master Vreman had even failed to protect Lavalor. Her dreams of becoming a storied eludrian were already in ruin, and if she wasn't depressed before, it rent her in two now. *Is Vreman alive or dead?*

Vashti sensed the change within her. Her taunting smile vanished.

In its place her colored lips became compressed as wrinkles of concern formed around her eyes.

"Now dear, sweet child, I'm not going to hurt you."

"Yeah, right."

"There! See? Just like my Carleea. You pout just like her. I so miss her."

Vashti seemed sincere. Ada watched her as she gazed longingly through the steadily brightening window and off into the distance.

"She's in Azinor?" asked Ada.

Vashti shook her head. "Gone," she whispered.

"What happened to her?"

Vashti stared blankly, perhaps considering whether to share intimate details. "She was your age. Same auburn hair and blue eyes. Skin like porcelain. You are beautiful, Ada Halentine, and really should learn to be a woman, instead of—" The vilemaster allowed a bit of revulsion to affect her features as she pointed at Ada's beartail and then her clothes. "—whatever it is you think you are."

"You must miss her."

Vashti's voice softened. "I couldn't save her."

"What happened?" Ada whispered after a beat.

"She got sick. Fifteen years ago. Nothing I did could save her."

She had that faraway look again.

"I'm gifted with considerable healing arts, and yet . . . powerless. I summoned the best healers from Azinor, but to no avail. She withered away, as did many within Vilazia that year."

Her voice hardened. "A curse, perhaps, from one of our many enemies who sought to destroy Azinor and enslave my people. Lord Zaviel himself lost a wife from the same curse. The same malady."

"I'm sorry. About Carleea."

Vashti peered at her warily, suspiciously.

"How many did the curse claim?"

"Too many! More than we could count."

Fifteen years ago, Ada wondered. About the same time people stopped transcending. *Could there be a connection?*

She glanced at Ficx. He was still at the window, staring luridly at her, his hairy arms wrapped across his massive chest. A shudder ran through her spine at the thought of possibly being alone with this creep. Hopefully, Vashti wouldn't let it happen, but she decided to try to get further on her good side, just in case.

"What was she like?"

Vashti began to slowly pace at the end of her footboard. "Innocent, sweet. She didn't deserve what happened to her. That pain!" The Vilazian lifted a finger to an eye. "She loved animals. Especially horses. She had a beloved Gargan Pacer, a brown and white one named Jewel. He had a diamond on his forehead." Vashti glanced at Ada.

"Horses are very smart and empathic. Did you know that? The sad creature knew when Carleea left this world. He became depressed—much as you are now. He'd spend the entire day, every day, angrily pacing the paddock fence closest to the mansion. Poor thing, it broke my heart every time I looked out the windows at him. For months he mourned her. But—"

"But what?"

"He broke my heart."

Ada squinted her eyes in confusion. "How so?"

Vashti rotated her palms upward and shrugged. "One morning, after awakening in a rather good mood, I went to him. You see, there I was, feeling hopeful for a change, and Jewel, well, he was still angry. Because of Carleea. And, of course, the damned creature was so sad."

Ada sensed she wouldn't like where this story was going. "What did you do?"

Vashti lifted her chin and looked down at her from above her nose, steeling herself. "I had to. Jewel was making me unhappy. Prolonging my own misery."

"What did you do?" Ada repeated.

"What anyone would do in my circumstance. I burned him."

Ada covered her mouth with a hand. "You burned Jewel? Her horse? You killed him?"

Vashti stared out at the sunlight. "I showed him mercy. He was in pain. And I interred him alongside Carleea, reuniting them. I think she'd have loved that."

"And you call *us* primitive?" said Ada.

Ficx burst toward her from the window, triggered by Ada's rising voice. But Vashti held up a palm. "You disapprove?"

She wondered if Galager was truly still alive. If so, she had to get control of her emotions. If not for herself, then for him. If he really was still alive, his only chance at getting out of here might be if she could somehow take advantage of Vashti's apparent fondness for her. It was a pathetic plan, but it was all she had right now.

"I'm sorry for your loss," Ada slowly uttered, restraining herself, and trying to sound sympathetic. "I can't imagine how horrible your suffering was. To lose a daughter must be—heartbreaking."

She wondered if her own parents would agree with that sentiment.

Ficx backed away to the window as the redness in Vashti's face lessened.

"I like you, Ada. But do not think I shan't hurt you if you abuse my good nature—or try to escape."

Ada checked her wrists. They were no longer bleeding.

"Would you like to see Galager?"

Ada jumped to her feet. "Please—yes!"

Vashti pivoted toward the exit, her rose-colored gown swirling in the dusty rays of sunlight piercing the room's interior. She stopped in the doorway and turned.

"Come with me! If you're lucky, he may be awake."

11

Lazlo's tent was a spectacle of heat and fire. Panthertooth slinked away as fast as he could without attracting any attention toward himself. Bipaquan and Vilazian warriors ran toward the raging pyre from all directions. Weir took a random path as he exited the camp, generally in the direction of Little Dog Gorge. He kept near the tents, keeping away from the centers of the walking spaces, often dipping his eyes or turning around as numbers of the enemy came running toward him from more-distant locations. As they approached, he would temporarily face the show of destruction he had ignited until the threats had passed then turn back and walk briskly again toward the camp perimeter.

The tents finally thinned out and fell behind him. He felt relieved to once again be surrounded by nothing more than trees. He could hear the chaos back in the encampment—men shouting at one another as they tried to manage the tiny crisis. Unsure as to the cause of the fire, they'd soon assume the worst and send out patrols, looking for those who might have dared enter their perimeter. He needed to put as much distance between them as possible, and do it as soon as he could. And that meant he had to take risks. He couldn't afford to take too much time skulking his way to safety.

He scrutinized everything as he walked, looking for sentries. They were here, he just needed to spot them before they saw him. Not long afterward, a sparrow burst from a tangle of wild muscadine thirty yards to the front and right. He froze, then slowly shifted his form to merge more fully with a nearby fir tree. He spied another movement near to where the bird had taken flight. *Redface!*

Weir slithered around the giant fir, putting it between himself and the silent Bipaquan. So far, no warning. No sound of a weapon sliding from a scabbard. No rush of careful footfalls on the detritus of dead leaves and pine needles.

He dropped low, slinking forward in a crouch, away from the sentry, partially doubling back before veering south again within a slight depression that gave him a bit of cover. If he was detected now, he doubted he'd escape the fervid pursuit that would inevitably occur. They'd chase him all the way to Intiga, if he even managed to get that far. His only chance would be to throw himself into Little Dog Gorge, but without the falls he knew he'd likely be crushed as he struck the river far below.

The Bipaquan settled back down into his hiding spot just a few seconds later. Weir hurried forward a few feet as he did so. It was enough to get him past the immediate danger and to resume a more reasonable pace, excruciatingly slow as it still was.

He heard the first patrol crashing forward from behind somewhere. It sounded as if they were headed directly toward him. He wondered if they were following his tracks, but he believed that unlikely. An entire army had occupied this area of forest for the past few days so it was nearly impossible to identify his tracks from the others. Still, he had to admit it wasn't impossible—he could have done it.

He went on for several minutes without encountering anyone. He was beginning to think he had gone past the outermost ring of sentries. He heard a shout from behind, perhaps a hundred yards away.

"Faster," he whispered to himself.

His path grew straighter, and his pace, quicker. He was familiar with these woods so he knew his way. Just ahead he'd find a small streambed angling toward Little Dog Gorge, a trench of natural erosion no larger than five feet across and about two feet deep. It ran wet only after a rain, and a storm had passed through these parts just recently. He figured there was an even chance it would still contain water. Or so he hoped.

When he finally came upon it, its bottom was a muddy tract. He wouldn't be able to use this channel to hide his tracks. Instead, he jumped over it and continued forward. He quickened his pace even more. He came upon two more streambeds, both muddy, both worthless. He began to jog now, his eyes scanning the forest ahead and to the sides. He considered heading directly to the gorge at this time, but the cliffs were still fatally high this close to Lavalor. Another league and perhaps—perhaps—he might safely jump to the river below. He certainly had no time to climb down, and it was inherently more dangerous that way, too. There was also greater risk heading south while remaining close to the cliff, due to there being fewer paths of escape, and greater chances at running into an enemy picket.

Another minute of uneventful running passed, when something almost imperceptible caused him to stop in his tracks and crouch low to the ground.

Hissing up ahead. *Lizards!*

The hisses arose on his right flank as well. He paused, taking in quiet breaths, listening for the advancing patrols and also trying to get a gauge as to how many of the skinks he was facing. Almost simultaneously, he heard a human voice from behind—still about a hundred yards away, drawing nearer. A dozen of the black reptiles became visible in the shadows of the forest ahead. More of them came into view at his right. Any path directly south or west was blocked. Weir rose to his feet and jogged slowly to the left, toward the gorge. It was the only way out now, unless he fought his way to safety.

He wasn't sure if these creatures had seen him. *Might I be able to skulk past them if I hid somewhere and let them pass? Climb a tree and wait?* He paused, crouching again in shadows, waiting to see where the lizards were heading. He could see them in the distance, between the trees, moving in his direction. That seemed to answer the question. He had to assume they knew he was here. So far, though, not a sign of any Bipaquan riders, so that was one thing in his favor.

The hissing got closer. He turned to the south east, hoping he could outflank the skinks. He darted through a stand of hemlock, but the lizards had moved laterally with him, blocking his path further south. A full left again, toward Little Dog Gorge. It shouldn't be far now. He encountered another muddy streambed, jumped over it, then adjusted his path parallel to it. Another streambed angled in and joined the first one. The mud at the bottom gave way to rocks and gravel. Weir launched himself into the channel, his feet landing solidly on a boulder set deep into the mud. He bounded forward, from one rock to another, always staying in the streambed. This channel would be faster for him—no more having to dodge around trees or bushes or having nettles scrape at his skin, and the rocks precluded any tracks being left behind.

He paused. But the hisses had encircled him—except to the east, the direction of the gorge. It was starting to appear as if he would have to climb down that treacherous cliff. But, on second thought, having seen how these monsters had climbed Lavalor's walls, he didn't think such a descent was a safe option. Jumping might be better.

He wondered, why are these things here? Did they wander aimlessly to this location from yesterday's battles? The absence of redface riders suggested that was a possibility. He remembered how they'd attack in pairs, one longer skink and a shorter one with a rider. Perhaps when a rider was killed, the lizards he controlled were no longer constrained to where they were being led. A thousand lizards or more had attacked the night before, so it seemed reasonable to believe a good number of them had gotten lost, and now he had found them.

Several more dry streambeds angled in and conjoined in a chaotic, crisscross pattern as he ran forward. Some of the naturally formed furrows dug deeper into the earth. He plunged ahead into what he figured was the main channel.

He instantly didn't like the way the channel walls were getting higher as he ran. Already they were at shoulder level. If they got too high, he could be trapped. The gravel-laden streambed rose a bit, but ten yards later it descended rapidly as the walls began to close in and serpentine through the earth, narrowing first, to almost shoulder width, then closing in altogether above his head in short sections. He had to duck low whenever the ceiling closed in and joined, and then he'd pop his head out and briefly scan his surroundings whenever the ceiling again opened up.

When he arrived at Little Dog Gorge, he had to crawl on his knees to cover the last dozen yards or so. The low ceiling here had formed a virtual tunnel that exited just below the lip of the cliff. The tunnel had a triangular cross-section, wider on the bottom, with its rock-encrusted walls narrowing in to form a two-foot-wide ceiling overhead. The final three feet of the tunnel had no ceiling, however. It had likely crumbled off and fell into the gorge.

He peered over the edge of the gorge and his heart sunk. The sheer stone cliff here stood at least two hundred feet high—much too perilous at this location to survive a leap into the raging river. He would have to patiently climb down at least a portion of this vertical sheet of stone, probably while fighting off those murderous skinks. It didn't look good. He gazed longingly across the gorge to the safety of the far cliff, only a few hundred feet away. One of the wolf appendages of his headdress swung forward into his vision. He couldn't believe he was still wearing it, so he tore it off and cast it into the gorge.

From this vantage he could perhaps see four or five hundred yards of the white-tipped river before it vanished behind the curving gray granite walls. He spotted a dozen or so monstrous forms caught within the misty rocks at the river's edge below—dead skinks from the previous day's battle. Hundreds more no doubt had been washed downstream. There were likely a few dead Bipaquans down there as well.

He considered doubling back, to look for another way out. But the hisses were just yards away. He could hear them on all sides of his location. He was trapped.

The tunnel suddenly collapsed a dozen feet from where he knelt. One of the lizards had fallen through. After the dirt settled, the black creature saw him and thrust its way deeper into the shaft. The only thing keeping the frenzied thing at bay was the narrow confines of the tunnel.

But Weir wasn't safe, because another skink immediately attacked from the opposite end, where the tunnel let out to the gorge—just about where he was kneeling. Black jaws lunged at him from directly above as the lizard straddled the tunnel. Weir reacted by quickly scooting further inside, directly under this second lizard, away from the gorge and those razor-sharp teeth.

A black foot ripped through the ceiling just inches from his beartail. The thing was the length of his forearm and it angrily raked the air with four massive claws. Another twelve inches of ceiling fell in, so the new gap overhead was two feet long now. The foot disappeared. In its place now he could see the writhing gray underbelly of the monster as it worked to dig Weir out of the ground. It was one of the longer skinks, the ones the redfaces didn't, or couldn't, ride.

He checked his rear. The skink plugging the tunnel there was closer. It was using its tremendous weight and fury to bore through the constricting shaft. Weir would have to decide soon on a course of action. Both monsters were seconds from their prey—him—and he could hear the hisses of countless others outside.

The skink overhead moved forward, closer to the gorge, its head curling in deeper toward him, getting ever closer to Weir. If the frenzied thing wasn't careful, it could very well lose its balance and fall into the gorge.

Weir looked to his rear. Teeth.

He looked to his front. Teeth.

He looked up. A scaly, gray underbelly.

An idea finally sprung to mind. It seemed irrational at first. Even fatal. But with jaws slashing just inches away, front and rear, he knew this was his last chance at surviving and later finding Galager and Ada. He also knew it would be a miracle if he survived this crazy idea.

But what choice do I have?

12

They turned right after leaving the bedchamber, Vashti leading the way in the outside corridor and Ficx following behind a barefoot Ada. They hadn't allowed her to don her boots, assuring her she wouldn't need them for the foreseeable future. They passed several doorways on either side, each a statement of luxury with their stout oaken doors polished to a high gloss. The walls and floor were white granite with white marble insets. Ada spotted a variety of imperfections—cracks, joint misalignments, missing pieces, repairs—probably due to the cataclysm caused by the Sword of Jhalaveral, an event that had ushered in the Age of Blood, an expanse of time now in its six-hundred and thirty-first year.

They proceeded forward on a continuous three-foot wide red and black rug covering the center third of the corridor. They passed through a short section of the hallway with dozens of stone boxes laying on recessed shelves on either wall. That got Ada's attention.

A *gigantic, marble tower containing bone boxes? In Intiga?*

The mausoleum!

She had heard of this ancient place—reportedly one of the few structures in Intiga remaining almost entirely intact after the apocalypse. It was hard to believe she was actually inside it. And who would have known all this artwork was here? On every section of wall, exquisite paintings of various sizes were hung in elegant frames. Sconces with thick, cream-colored candles—all lit—were frequently placed alongside or among the artwork and served perfectly to illuminate both the corridor and the art. The paintings and drawings were mostly of important looking people, Vilazian, no doubt, most probably vilemasters, generals, and other leaders. But she caught glimpses of landscapes as well, perhaps scenes of the Fringe, or even Vilazia?

Vashti continued along the elegantly adorned passageway, turned a corner, and came upon a pair of opposing portals with stairways in each, the right one heading downward, the other, rising. A pair of swordsmen dutifully stood guard here. She barely acknowledged them as she turned into the descending stairway. Down, they slowly spiraled, passing two other floors. A glance into the first of these revealed yet another opulently decorated passage, but the second was bedecked only with the dust of centuries. Vashti exited onto the third floor they came to. Brightly lit, it instantly revealed its age and state of disrepair. Like the floor immediately above, the structures here hinted of their status as it existed immediately after the apocalypse.

They turned left. Just ahead stood a group of Vilazian soldiers gathered around an open portal, talking and laughing, completely unaware of Vashti's approach. One of them finally saw her and snapped to, the others following urgently.

Vashti speared her way through their presence. "Has the boy awoken yet?"

Before anyone could answer, she veered through the doorway, Ada hurriedly following with Ficx's hand on her shoulder urging her through the group of soldiers.

"Not yet, Excellence," said one of the men from behind. "He's out cold."

They entered a larger area with no windows, but lots of grime and age, and it was cold here. The oil lamps here revealed a stunted hallway with several rooms on either side, each demarcated and separated by black, iron bars. A dungeon. Six cells, three on each side.

"Why keep him in this filthy place?" Ada reacted angrily. "If I deserved better, shouldn't Galager as well?" She instantly regretted her outburst, for as they proceeded forward, she noted other prisoners in the cells they passed. Several of the captives sat up with sudden interest upon hearing a female voice speaking the common-tongue.

Vashti ignored her and stopped at the last cell on the right. She peered through the bars to examine the occupants. Five men in linen undergarments, stripped of armor and boots. The surrounding darkness fooled her for an instant, but then she realized these men before her had black skin—Bethurian wardens! And there beside them, Galager! He was heaped upon the floor against the far wall in his normal clothing, his shuttered eyes pointed directly toward her.

Ada gripped two of the bars and thrust her face in between the narrow gap between them.

"Galager! I'm here!"

No movement, except from the Bethurians. She heard more prisoners rustling behind her, the captives in each of the six cells rising to their feet. Some of them uttered words of astonishment. One man somewhere in the darkness sobbed lightly. Her heart ached as she turned, and tried to count the human shapes obscured in shadows and partly hidden behind iron bars. She lost count at fifteen, including the five Bethurians and Galager. Each of the prisoners had shackles on their wrists with a short length of chain securing them to an iron loop in the floor. As these countrymen and allies stood erect, they had to stoop down a bit because of the short chains that limited their movements.

"Galager," she said in a firm voice. "It's me. Ada."

Still no movement.

"Galager! Wake up!"

"My Lady," uttered one of the Bethurians, the man laying closest to Galager. "What magic beguiles my eyes so, that a lovely vision such as yours visits us in this hopeless space? As to your friend, he's not moved since arriving, although he's breathing deeply and steadily. He bears no sign of injury that I can discern." The man's voice seemed to have a natural gravelly quality to it, but Ada also detected an unhealthy rasp to it. He had the look of resignation and grief on his ebony face, as did his four warmates. But they all seemed hale, except for one Bethurian who cradled a limp right arm in his other hand, as if he had broken it. If it were not for her concern over Galager, she'd have been in utter shock at seeing these Bethurian wardens as prisoners in this dungeon. These were not the kind of warriors who allowed themselves to be captured. It just didn't happen!

"Thank you, Warden." Ada gestured toward the man with the injured arm. "He's hurt." She glanced toward Vashti and then Ficx, a yard behind her, but they showed no sign that she should cease communicating with these prisoners. Ada turned back to the Bethurian. "Who are you, Warden? What is your name?"

"My mother calls me Civato Jeregoth. As do my friends."

Humor, even in such darkness.

"My warmates and I are out of Savaern, via Castle Shenkel. We were shamefully captured four days past—by a shape-shifting creature of soot and steel whose skin was impervious to the edge of our swords. My Lady, you may take this as ravings from a desperate stranger, but the demon transfigured us one-by-one into cinders and then brought us here."

"Warden Jeregoth," said Ada, "the creature you speak of is familiar to me and has a name—Haem. He's a demon. And it's clear his intention was to capture, not kill, you, otherwise you'd be dead. Galager and I were brought here by him as well. And your shame is misplaced. I fear Castle Lavalor has fallen, in large part because of my own insufficiencies." Groans escaped the throats of some of the other prisoners. She instantly regretted the mention of Lavalor's demise. These men needed hope, not despair. "I'm not entirely certain of Lavalor's final fate," she added. "I was rendered unconscious before the battle ended."

Vashti's cackle echoed through the vaulted chambers. "I'm afraid, my dear, Lavalor is no longer a thorn in the Vilazian heel."

Jeregoth let the vilemaster's subsequent laughter die before speaking. "My Lady, this is grim news."

"I'm sorry," whispered Ada. She again glanced toward Vashti, but the vilemaster seemed content to allow the conversation to continue.

"Your name?" enquired Jeregoth.

"Ada Halentine." She pointed across the cell to the unmoving bundle near Jeregoth. "His name is Galager Swift."

"Lady Halentine, should Jhalaveral look upon you with favor and see to your freedom from your own unfortunate and present dire circumstances, I beseech you to let others know of our fate here."

"Of course, Warden." Ada again noticed his raspy voice. "Have you taken food or drink since your capture?"

Jeregoth shook his head. "But that is the least of our worries."

Ada whirled toward Vashti. "You must feed them at once." Ada pointed at one of the other cells. "All of them. And we need a healer."

Vashti's lips curled upward in an amused smile. "Food is scarce. And dead men don't eat."

13

It wasn't looking good for Weir. If he left this tunnel, the swarm of lizards outside would eat him alive. If he stayed put, he'd eventually be torn out like a rat snatched from a hole by a hungry snake. If he jumped over the cliff, he'd be crushed when his body crashed into the raging waters far below. And if he climbed down the wall or tried to run, the skinks would easily overtake him.

That left only one other option.

He gulped down the last of his reservations and peered through the hole in the ceiling at the writhing lizard above. It was time to get to work. He unsheathed a blade and sunk it to the hilt in the grayish underbelly of the skink. Blood spurted and the creature howled. He stabbed again. Another shriek of pain, but less intense. On the third thrust the skink went nearly silent and unmoving. *Now or never!* He thrust *Mercy* into the creature's belly one last time, grabbed the black leather hilt with both hands, and began sawing.

Just . . . a . . . few . . . more . . . seconds . . . and . . .

The monster's innards finally relented to Weir's ferocity. Intestines and other organs gushed through the slit Weir had created in its underbelly. He withdrew his blade as the viscera poured over him, slid from his chest, and dropped onto the ground between his knees. He sheathed his blade, reached up, and pulled the slit apart with both hands, causing more of the bloody entrails to plop downward. He shook off the gore, lurched to his feet, and thrust his head and shoulders deep into the dead creature's innards. At last, he pulled up his legs, pushed off the earth near the ceiling breach with his feet, and wiggled himself further inside the disemboweled monster.

Now the hard part.

With no time to lose, he fought his way forward into the warm cavern of slippery flesh. His plan was to get far enough forward so that his added weight would cause the reptile to fall over the cliff—with him inside. It was a miracle the thing hadn't done so already, and it was the only way Weir could imagine surviving an impact with the river from this height, though by no means would that be certain.

He quickly discovered it was nearly impossible to breathe as he zealously fought for life, grabbing organs and other sinewy tissues and wreaking even further havoc on the dead reptile from within. He kept his eyes and mouth shut tight as he pulled and kicked his way forward, inch by gory inch.

It soon appeared he had miscalculated. Nearly out of breath, he knew he wouldn't last much longer entombed as he was within this monster. Rather than give up, though, he fought harder. Retreat wasn't an option. His right elbow brushed against what he could only imagine was a ribcage. It was behind thick layers of tough, slippery flesh, but he could feel the bony encirclements protruding inward. He tried to pull his arms up to push against the ribs with his hands, but the confined space didn't allow it. He next tried contracting his legs to use his feet to push off the massive ribcage, but again, the constrictions stopped him. He only just managed to check that his longknives hadn't caught on anything. They hadn't. Lastly, he fanned his elbows out and felt them come in solid contact with the flesh-covered ribs on either side, locking him in tightly. With this new found leverage, he pushed with his elbows, and fortunately, slid forward a half foot or so. His lungs on fire, he repeated the maneuver and slid forward again, this time impacting a giant blob of rubbery tissue he could only assume was the creature's hot, lifeless heart.

His way forward was blocked.

But he had come far enough.

The entire body of the serpent-like creature gave way from its muddy perch.

It slid over the cliff.

It went into free fall.

Weir ceased struggling and let his body go limp. He tried his best to curl into a ball, not really succeeding. He had fought valiantly for a favorable outcome, and now everything was in the hands of Jhalaveral.

Silence. Listen to your heart and to your surroundings.

Tranquility. Accept this moment, this life, who you are, and why you are here.

Awareness. I am spinning in mid-air like a galaxy of stars. I am protected within the enfoldments of a creature that wanted me dead but which instead will bear me to safety. Thank you Jhalaveral for my time on this earth and the sun in my eyes. Thank you for those I have helped, may their struggles continue, if mine does not.

I love you, Twoheart.

They slammed into the river like the Sword of Jhalaveral.

Weir had never been hit so hard in all his life.

Whatever air remained within his agonized lungs was instantly expelled because of the sudden force of the impact. Weir was ejected from the creature, like shit from an anus, only faster and more violently. For the second time in hours, he sucked in a mixture of air and water as he bobbed on the surface of the Lavalor River, its frigid, blessed waters cleansing and invigorating his uninjured body.

"I'm alive!" he dared pronounce once he had caught his breath, his words echoing from the walls of the narrow canyon. "Do you hear me, Ethelliphus? You had your chance—but you failed!" It was unlike him to challenge the devil so, but having survived the battle, the falls, the encampment, the skinks, and now this plunge over the cliff, he had emerged with a sense of destiny fortifying his heart and soul.

"Ada! Galager! I am coming for you!" he yelled.

He glanced to the clifftop from where he and the skink had fallen.

Lizards were crawling all around its cusp, looking for the quarry they thought they had cornered. He didn't see any sign of redfaces anywhere.

"I am coming," he repeated, not quite shouting this time, and aiming his exuberance and his joy south along the slowly curving gorge. "Galager and Ada. I am coming!"

He started shivering—already. These waters were freezing and would kill him if he didn't get out of them soon. He used his arms and hands and flippered himself around, scanning the choppy water in every direction. The skink that had saved him was behind him, upstream—about ten yards away, but it was sinking fast. He spied another of the monsters just behind the first one. It was floating belly-side up with its short legs splayed out on either side of the long body. Weir figured his big splash must have dislodged it from the bank where it had been stuck for the past day or so.

Another idea sprung to mind.

He fought the current and allowed the bloated lizard to catch up to him. He approached it behind one of its front legs and tried to climb onto the creature. But his weight caused the half-submerged corpse to partially roll in the water, causing Weir to fall back in. He lashed out, grabbing a clawed-foot. He paused, evaluating the situation, and decided on a different tact. He swam to the skink's rear, ducking under the surface of the water to pass its rear leg. He clamped his arm around the body at the point where the long tail met the torso. Thankfully, this was a female. He inched his way over the tail, the genitals, and onto the rear end of the skink. This time it didn't roll. Shivering violently, he slid his way forward slowly, being careful to keep his weight evenly centered. It was maddening progress, but it was progress.

He arrived at the center of the roundish belly a short distance in front of the rear legs. He paused, taking several deep breaths, his arms reaching sideways for stability and balance. He was still sopping wet, but at least he was out of the water. He glanced at the walls of Little Dog Gorge slipping silently and quickly behind him, and decided they weren't currently a threat. As he watched the tall cliffs recede, he wondered how long he'd be able to remain atop this monster. With a little luck, it would take him all the way to Bone Canyon—if it didn't sink first. That could save him at least a day of travel time, putting him halfway to his goal, Intiga.

Once at Bone Canyon, he'd have to disembark and get back onto solid land before going over another set of waterfalls where the Lavalor River was sucked down in its entirety into the deeper canyon. From that point on, he'd have to get to his destination on foot. In his estimation, he wouldn't arrive at Intiga until the next night sometime, perhaps toward midnight—if everything went perfectly. *But when did anything ever go perfectly?*

14

Lazlo caught sight of the smudge of dark smoke while still leagues from his encampment, south of Lavalor. The two Commonlanders had been safely delivered to the exquisite Vashti in Intiga—she'd get to the bottom of their gifts—and now he and the demon were winging their way north along the Lavalor Gorge, back toward the defeated fortress, and back to what remained of his diversionary army. They had taken a beating the day before, but had nevertheless managed to take the fort. He estimated he and Haem were four or five hundred feet above the gorge, slightly west of it. As a passenger within the demon's dusts, it was as if he was held firm in the clutches of a griffon's talons as it soared through the air, except there was no sensation of the cool wind against his skin or in his hair. Indeed, he was quite comfortable, protected within the demon's preternatural enfoldments. And such exhilaration! Lazlo could hear the rush of air, even breathe of it, and see his surroundings, but he felt nothing. The first few times he had tried this, he had become severely disoriented, but he soon became accustomed to the thrill of flight and quickly learned to love the experience.

At first, he mistakenly believed the tendril of smoke to be from blazes set during the previous day's battle. But as they neared the encampment, he realized this black snake reaching into a hazy brown sky of day-old smoke was fresh and originated from within his camp. Haem steadily descended as he neared the vanquished fortress, a speck on the horizon. Lazlo noted a group of slake clustered against the edge of the gorge as he and Haem flew past. There were perhaps fifty of the giant lizards down below, a tight bundle of frenzied activity that caused him to wonder if perhaps this commotion was connected to the smoke.

"Lower, Haem. Let's get a closer look at these slake."

Haem responded to his command. Within seconds they were a mere fifty feet above the roiling creatures. One of them had dug its way into a narrow water course that dumped out into the gorge, but as he watched, the black thing extricated itself from the partially covered defile and began lumbering over others of its kind. There was a bit of blood and gore in the trench. With no sign of any human activity here, Lazlo concluded these slake had most likely cornered a deer or other unfortunate animal. Satisfied there was nothing amiss, he ordered Haem to continue to the encampment.

They landed near the source of smoke, materializing behind hundreds of his gawking men gathered around a heap of glowing ash that the night before had been his tent.

Captain Tsalon shouldered his way out of the staring throng and aimed for him.

"Lord Urich!" he said, dipping his forehead deferentially. "Welcome back."

"What's happened here?" Lazlo growled. "Did intruders cause this? Have you found them?"

Tsalon shrugged in doubt and his empty palms rose to his trim waist, answering Lazlo's questions even before he opened his mouth.

"I've dispatched patrols into the surrounding areas," said Tsalon. "But we've had no sign of anyone penetrating our perimeter. I believe this fire an accident."

Lazlo made his way toward the smoldering ash heap, Tsalon following. The gathered soldiers made way for them as they neared.

"How can an accident happen in an empty tent?" Lazlo asked. But an instant later he remembered the healer.

"The healer, where is he?"

Tsalon gazed steadily at him. He didn't know.

They stopped walking at the perimeter of the tent fire, which had already died for the most part, though it had consumed nearly everything. The blackened remains of rugs and the tent enclosures were heaped around the charred center pole, still standing. Only one panel of the tent still stood, as did the entryway.

Lazlo carefully stepped into a darkened area of the ash heap, testing for heat in the bottoms of his boot soles. He took a few more tentative steps, scanning every detail and searching for answers. He saw someone—burned to a crisp, almost invisible because of the wisps of smoke coming off of everything, including the body.

He approached the still form, avoiding any glowing embers yet remaining, but considered retreating when his boots began to get hot. He sidestepped, circling around a pile of charred rugs, and then he was squatting near the body, which was face down in the ashes. A man, his hair burned away, his scalp a tiny landscape of bubbled flesh. Lazlo reached under the man's forehead and tilted his head up.

He recognized the face—the healer.

The man's face looked as hale as it had been the day before. Even the front of his neck was burn-free, although there was some bruising. Lazlo let the face drop back into the ashes and abruptly stood. One more quick scan informed him there weren't any other bodies.

"Get him out of here," Lazlo ordered loudly.

Two soldiers immediately responded, entered the blackened circle, and pulled the dead eludrian onto green ground. Lazlo remained where he stood, his eyes still searching. It appeared that one of the tables with candles had been knocked over. The other tables were still erect, though badly burned. His attention went to the toppled table—on its side. The candles once atop it had been scattered nearby, each a tiny glob of melted wax where they had come to rest. The candles on the other tables, though, had melted where they stood, leaving a larger pool of collective wax on each tabletop.

He spotted a food platter and a wine flagon. He nudged the flagon with his boot tips. Empty. He examined the unburned portions of the animal skins where the healer had been found lying. He bent low, grabbed one of the rugs and pulled it from its resting spot. Something small fell from the edge of the coarse-haired skin and disappeared into the blanket of ash below with a small puff of soot. Lazlo jabbed a hand there, and retrieved the object—the healer's eludria ruby.

"Lord," said Tsalon, "there's something in his mouth." Tsalon was on a knee aside the healer's body.

Lazlo left the blackened circle. He dropped to a knee near Tsalon. He reached down and peered into the healer's jaws, which Tsalon held open for him.

"Choked on his supper," said Tsalon. "Knocked those candles over whilst struggling to free himself of it. That's my guess. Probably was breathless before the fire got him."

"I think you are correct," said Lazlo. "It's the only explanation. Unless there's been any evidence of those vangards getting in here unnoticed." Lazlo unconsciously rubbed his shoulder where that Atikan had shot him with an arrow. The healer had done a fine job with the wound. So far, no real pain, just a bit of numbness hardly worth mentioning. The man would be missed.

Tsalon shook his head. "I've heard nothing like that," he said. "But as I said, some Bipaquans are out looking, just in case. If anyone can find those vangards, it's the Bipaquans."

Lazlo regained his feet. "You're quite sure there's been no enemy activity in the camp since I left for Intiga?"

"Not that I've heard," Tsalon replied, also rising.

"Any of our men missing?"

"Hard to tell. We haven't really got completely organized since yesterday's fight. We sure as hell lost lots of Bipaquans because of the battle—not a single one of our men, though, since we didn't properly enter the fray—so it might take some time before we figure out if anyone's missing because of snooping vangards."

Lazlo studied the eludria in his palm, rolling it slowly, back and forth, along his lifeline. He glanced at the healer's body. Something wasn't right. A sense of doubt tugged at him, but he couldn't place the reason for it. Those neck bruises—could they have been self-inflicted by someone desperate to get air into his lungs? If not, could a vangard have snuck undetected into the middle of his camp, killed this eludrian, and then covered up his tracks by setting a fire? He thought of the Atikan—the one who had shot him after single-handedly slaying the mighty Daquin. But would such a man risk his life to come here, alone, in the slim hope of killing him in his own camp? Or perhaps it was those two eludrians—the boy and girl—that would compel the Atikan to risk everything to save them?

"Prepare another tent for me. And then find that woman, the healer's assistant."

"It'll be done," said Tsalon. "Anything else?"

Lazlo nodded. "I want you to check everything. See if there've been any other problems."

"Problems?"

Lazlo glared at the man. "Ask around and see if there have been any reports of anything strange happening. Or maybe someone is missing. Maybe our patrols have seen or heard something. If so, let me know at once."

"As you command," said Tsalon.

15

He rose from a knee after examining the dirt. He was barefoot, like all the other Bipaquans here. Linen loin cloth with sleeveless jerkin. Lean, tight, long black hair with dark brown eyes. Brown skin, used to baking in the hot sun.

"East," the man said, one of Gainhu's best trackers. "Men and horses. Moving slowly. Trying to be quiet."

"How many?" asked Gainhu as he observed a Vilazian soldier peeking over the gate parapet at their rear. The village itself had been empty of enemy warriors and animals when they arrived here—except those ugly, noisy horses, and a few dogs.

"Counting is impossible," said the tracker. "Too many men and horses."

Gainhu could indeed pick out both human and horse tracks on the road. They were going to make a run for safety rather than stay and fight. He figured it was their best option.

"Their entire army?"

The tracker shrugged. "Perhaps."

Gainhu hesitated, his eyes sweeping over the entirety of his nearby force—fifteen parties of elite warriors, each man awaiting instructions and eager to fight once more. He was eager too. He wanted to get moving right away, follow these Commonlanders, catch them unawares somewhere, kill them all.

But he felt he was rushing things. He decided to be careful. He gestured to the village walls behind them and looked at another of his subordinates, another of his best trackers.

"Take your team to the western side of the village," he told him. "Let me know what you find."

The man dipped his forehead smartly and departed, taking fifty warriors with him.

To his best tracker, Gainhu then said, "you and your men search along the eastern wall of the village."

He wanted to look things over here a little more before he committed all his men to following the horses. He needed to be sure other units of the enemy hadn't snuck out from this walled village at some other location.

In the meantime, the corrupt and pampered red-coated Vilazians —five more parties, or companies, as his new friends would refer to them as—were inside the village with orders to raze every building after plundering them all of valuables and supplies. Already, scores of black smoke plumes pierced the early sky. He quickly chose another warrior from his remaining forces and sent him into the village to inform the Vilazians about the fleeing horsemen and in which direction they were headed. Afterward, he gave orders to the remaining Bipaquan forces to remain near this gate.

"Rest while you can," he told them, and then jogged to join up with the small tracking group moving along the right flank of the village.

It didn't take long to discover the place where a large force of Commonlanders had slipped down from the walls during the night. The small team of trackers he had accompanied was nearly at the end of the eastern wall where it joined with the cliffs rising up behind the village. That's where they found tracks leading into the higher elevations at the northeast. The Commonlanders had escaped into what looked to be a hunting trail snaking off in that same direction. Yet again, his prized tracker couldn't be sure how many of the enemy had come this way, but it was a good number. Even Gainhu could see that.

Yet, he was worried. What about the tracks they had found on the road? The ones accompanying the horses? Why did the Commonlanders send some of their ground forces along with the horse warriors to slow them down, only to send so many of their other brethren this way? Almost immediately the answer came to him. There could be only one explanation. The human tracks on the road were the horse riders themselves. They had temporarily dismounted to make it appear their entire army had gone that way. *Clever!*

Gainhu needed another messenger. He barked orders to an older warrior who was staring at him with arms crossed over his proud chest. The Commonlanders had departed hours ago. Their head start was significant, and that meant he and his men had a lot of running to do this day if they were to catch them. He was glad most of his men were younger and well-conditioned.

"Get the others," he said to the veteran, who seemed annoyed he was being left behind. His compressed lips and burning gaze gave it away. "Order everyone to follow us as fast as they can. Then inform our friends in the village where we are going. I'm going to catch up with our enemy and keep an eye on them until we're ready to engage them again."

"I prefer to remain with you," said the warrior.

"You're too slow—old man," replied Gainhu. Some of the others laughed.

The veteran spat on the dirt. "I can still outrun you."

Gainhu spat as well. "Perhaps, my friend, but not today."

16

Civato Jeregoth didn't know exactly how many hours had passed since the girl, Ada Halentine, had visited them. Perhaps four or five, he thought. Such a miracle she had been—a light in the inimitable darkness that had descended over him and his men after being captured by that insuperable beast. Her mere presence, as brief as it had been, had given flame to hope, though the flicker had turned to ember and allowed the reemergence of a throbbing heartache that immediately reminded him once again of his dilemma and the likelihood he would never again set eyes on Bethuria.

Lady Halentine had revealed to them that the Sunder Line had most likely been breached at Castle Lavalor. This horrible news had made it all the more urgent for him and his team to get out of here alive. For if the enemy had indeed breached the Sunder Line, it would only be a matter of time before the war finally reached Bethuria. With all his heart, he felt he needed to be there to protect the homeland. He rubbed grief from his eyes as he again wracked his brain for a way out of this hell they had been dropped into. But if there was a path to freedom, he couldn't see it. He had failed his men, failed the Commonland, failed Bethuria, and even failed Jhalaveral.

He again checked on the boy lying next to him—Galager Swift—

just another unmoving form on the cold stone of this dungeon floor. If the boy had an injury, Civato couldn't see it, but he dared not make firm conclusions. With vilemasters and demons in the mix, injuries needn't always be of a visible nature.

The girl had begged her captor to show pity on Galager—and the other prisoners—but that monster would have nothing of it. Instead, she had terminated the brief visit and took Ada away from them before he could learn anything more about her. Two Commonland teens from Lavalor—that's all he knew about them. Probably eludrians, otherwise why would the Vilazians have taken the effort to bring a boy and girl here to Intiga? On the other hand, it was well known the Vilazians executed enemy eludrians without pause or fanfare, so maybe he was wrong about them. If so, who were they? Why were they here? What mystery was playing out here?

In the gray light, he saw his friend, Uri, shifting his form, trying to find relief from the shattered forearm he had suffered during the brief fight with that demon. His other three friends were again sleeping, as were most of the other strangers in the nearby cells. Sleep was a kind escape for these prisoners, a way to forget the stinging wounds of the iron shackles around their wrists, the dull ache of empty stomachs, and the icy angst and anguish torturing their skins and minds. They all were locked securely in cells protected by iron bars and also had these irons around their wrists, so why in hell was there a need for these restraints to have edges on them? Edges that had the capacity to cut deeply into their skin? He had to admit, though, that those sharp edges limited their movements and sliced away at a man's desire to explore any means of escape. Still, the barbarity of these Vilazians never ceased to disgust him.

"Civato," came a whisper from the darkness.

"I'm awake, my friend."

"Four days," muttered Uri. "I fear my hour is nearly upon me."

"No," said Civato firmly, though still whispering. "You mustn't give up. The suffering is—"

"It's not the pain, brother. It's my heart. It beats a song of finality. For me, if not also for you or the others."

"Need I remind you? You're not an oracle."

Uri laughed.

"The pain and this hunger," said Civato. "It deceives you, and clouds your thoughts with despair. But you must fight it."

"Civato. I grow weak, that is true. But Jhalaveral has spoken to me in my dreams."

"Then you are deluded."

Uri laughed again, a little louder this time.

"Has he also told you how you will leave this world?"

"Eludria."

Civato hadn't expected such an answer. He wanted to rebut him. But everyone knew what inevitably happened to Vilazian prisoners—transfiguration. The likelihood they all would soon become an ogre and let loose into the Fringe was something he had been dreading.

"I shall release you to the creator before I allow that to happen. I will snap your neck myself. All of you!"

"And who will snap yours?"

"Someone will."

Civato lifted his shivering shoulders off the floor and sat upright on his ass. He then glanced at the boy beside him, Galager Swift. "These Commonlanders, the boy and girl. There's a reason they're here."

"To rescue us?" uttered Uri, dubiously. "Them? A boy and girl? You seriously think they will save five wardens, and all these other prisoners as well? I propose you are the one who is deluded."

"Perhaps."

Uri, too, sat upright. Even in the grayness, Civato could see his friend's ever-present smile. Rare were the times he hid it. Even here.

"They're eludrians," whispered Civato, hoping it wasn't a lie.

"How can you be sure? And even if they are, what use are they without eludria?"

The more Civato thought about it, the more he was convinced Ada and Galager were eludrians. Ada had as much implied that when she said her insufficiencies had in part contributed to the breach at Castle Lavalor. She certainly must have been referring to magic.

Nevertheless, without eludria, magic was an impossibility. And if there was an escape from this infernal prison, it had so far eluded him.

"Have faith," said Civato. "Jhalaveral has put these two here for a reason."

"But you heard the girl. She said Lavalor's been broken."

"Then we shall unbreak it!" He uttered that a little more loudly than he'd intended. Some of the other men rustled at the sound.

"Civato, that's why you are loved so, and why you are our leader. You never give up on us—or the homeland."

"And all I ask from you in return, old friend, is not to give up on yourself. I need you."

"But I speak truth, my brother. Jhalaveral has revealed to me my fate. I shall be with you for a short time after I perish from this life, but it won't be me."

"That makes no sense."

"Of course, it does. I'm to be transfigured. Those words were whispered to me as I slept. The Commonlanders—I only wish it were true, and that the boy and girl were eludrians and could—"

Chains clinked behind Civato as Uri ceased talking and stared in silent surprise over his shoulder. Civato turned around and saw the Commonlander pushing himself off the floor and rising to his knees. For a few moments all three men just stared at one another before the Commonlander spoke.

"Yes, I'm an eludrian. But where the hell am I?

17

Gainhu brought his fifty-odd warriors to a halt at the side of a wide stream. They had been following the Commonland ground forces since shortly after dawn. It was almost noon. He and his small group had set a fiery pace. It wasn't difficult tracking an army. Only two or three other Bipaquan warriors had managed to come from behind, running ahead of the main army, and join his party. He had laughed when the veteran he earlier sent back as a messenger came running up alongside him, a look of victory etched on his aging, but determined face.

Heavy stands of pines lined both banks as far as he could see. The slow-moving stream was clear and shallow, perhaps ankle-deep, and its bed was a blanket of small green river rock. Beyond the stream the forested land rose steeply.

He was just thinking this would be a good place to be ambushed when a line of Atikans burst from the dark shadows opposite the bank and ran toward them, whooping and hollering, splashing madly across the gently rippling waters and throwing battle axes. His first instinct was that these enemy brothers—people of similar skin—had made a mistake, for they were outnumbered five to two. But the axes brought down five of his men before anyone could react, and then he suddenly heard the staccato release of bow strings snapping taught behind the Atikans. More of his men went down because of the lethal volley of arrows that came streaking from the higher trees up ahead. His brain screamed to withdraw, but pride wouldn't let him. Besides, his men would just be exposed to another round of missiles if they ran now. Instead, he yelled an order to advance.

Their axes expended, the Atikans withdrew those two little swords they each carried. But as both forces collided in the center of the stream, those little swords whirled almost invisibly and began cutting down more of his men. One of the enemy had black skin, and the man was coming straight for him, teeth bared like white grave markers and his hair like a nest of baby vipers. Their blades sang and weapons clashed. The black man spun—one moment he was standing directly in front of Gainhu, and the next he was at his left side aiming one of those tiny swords directly at his neck while sinking his second blade into the stomach of that veteran, who had come to Gainhu's aid despite his earlier treatment.

Gainhu quashed a sense of loss for the old warrior, ducked the black man's blade, lunged forward, and wheeled in the direction of his opponent. Their weapons clanged together—that little sword somehow getting the best of things. Gainhu was forced to take a step backward because of the strength of the black man's attack. He heard screams in all directions, and hastily scanned the array of warriors on either side of him. His men were dropping like boulders in a landslide. Fifty men—being slaughtered by a mere twenty as easily as if they were sheep.

Gainhu screamed an order to retreat. His remaining men reacted instantly, disengaging from the Atikans and running back the way they had come. Thankfully, no more arrows came at them as they entered the shelter of the pines, probably because the vangards were in their line of fire. Ordinarily, he would have cursed his men for retreating like this, but he was right behind them. He vowed the next time he wouldn't be so careless. And he'd have more men.

18

Vashti sighed. "I told you. Their fate is written."

Ada resisted the urge to cross the room and gouge out her eyes. Anger would only make things worse. She instinctively knew it wasn't the right tool to win concessions from this deranged woman. *Make her like me. I remind her of her daughter. That's her weakness.*

They had gone to Vashti's bed chambers after their brief foray into the dungeons. Her own room—the one she had awoken in—was a short distance down the gallery hall. Once again they were surrounded by the trappings of luxury, only this time in a much larger space. Vashti was comfortably ensconced within an immense chair upholstered with leather and furs. Unable to shake images of her mistreated countrymen secured away in the dank prison below, Ada remained standing nearby. Her guilt would not allow her to repose herself in a similar chair across from her captor.

"But why can't you show them mercy? Lavalor has fallen, things are going your way, and unless I'm mistaken, my Lady, *you* are clearly in charge here. Surely, we are both civilized. Hasn't there been enough death and misery already?"

Vashti pointed a slipper of yellow leather toward her as she considered her request. She swept an icy gaze of disdain her way.

"Not at all, child. The war has only just begun." A thin smile of malevolence flared up when she saw Ada shrink in despair.

"Then Galager. Can't you at least—?" Ada fell silent with self-disgust. As much as she wanted him to be safe, she wouldn't ignore the fate of the other prisoners. It horrified her that she had almost done that.

"Oh my," said Vashti. "I didn't expect that from you."

Ada glowered at her. "Why are you doing this?"

Vashti glanced at the closed door of the entryway. She had guards out there, waiting, in case of trouble.

"Sit down, Ada. You're annoying me." An order, not a request.

She decided it was better to comply, so she reluctantly slid into the luxurious chair as a thousand swords of shame pierced her body.

"You're learning," said Vashti as a look of satisfaction etched her aged features.

"We're all going to die anyway."

"Not everyone." Vashti chuckled. "Not necessarily."

"You mean—everyone but me?"

A tiny shrug.

"Is there anything I can do to change your mind?"

"I can't change my plans for you, dear."

"What plans?"

"You'll soon find out." A look of exultation affected the vilemaster's face. It caused a shiver to run down Ada's spine. This bitch was going to do something terribly evil to those men—to Galager. She again considered attacking her, here and now, putting an end to this vile woman's filthy life. But reality took hold. She wouldn't get a step before Vashti's eludria erupted in fire. And then there were those men outside in the hall.

Ada knew she had to get control of herself if Galager and the others were to have a chance at survival. An image of Katonkin Weir sitting cross-legged under that oak tree near Havless Tower came to her. She instinctively told herself to calm down as she remembered his instructions. *Silence. Tranquility.* Awareness. *Breathe deeply and slowly. Listen to your heart beat.*

"What are you thinking?" asked Vashti. "Your mother, perhaps? You grow less tense with every second. That is wise."

"It's just something someone taught me. I'm alright now."

"Need I remind you, I'll hurt you, if you force me to?"

Ada nodded dejectedly. "That won't be necessary."

"I'm happy to hear that. I rather like you, although you are a barbaric Commonlander."

Me? Barbaric?

Vashti withdrew something from the folds of her gown and displayed it in an open palm.

Galager's sandbag!

Ada tried not to react. "And isn't that precisely why I must eventually die?" she said. "I'm a Commonlander?"

"Ordinarily, that would be true. But—"

"But what?"

"Very well," said Vashti, leaning forward and offering the sandbag to Ada, who snatched it up almost too hastily. "I think it's time to get to the heart of the matter."

Ada examined the toy, turning it in her hands, then pocketed it. She needed to stay focused. No distractions.

"You're an eludrian, dear Ada. Or are you going to deny it?"

"Oh," replied Ada, surprised at the question. "I thought that was understood. Why else would I be here?"

"And, of course, we know your boyfriend is also gifted."

"Yes, he is."

She wondered, *does she know Galager can invoke magic without eludria?* Is that why she feared me at first? Why she tested me? Lazlo must have seen us that night on Cadia Gate and told her everything. She felt herself shudder at the thought of what that creature Fasar had become. The terror emanating from that demon was unlike anything she had ever experienced. She remembered Galager stepping forward. The resulting blast as their magic touched. The fire. The light. She suddenly realized there was something about that light. The moment their magic comingled a massive outpouring of blue light had surrounded her.

Am I imagining that, or did it really happen?

Vashti reclined back into her chair again. "Tell me about him."

"What do you want to know?"

"What kind of family does he come from?"

"His parents are poor. He hasn't seen them for quite some time. It's his stepfather—they had some difficulties."

"And his blood father?"

"Galager never really knew him. A soldier, perhaps. I haven't known him very long."

Vashti searched the air for questions and insights. "What kind of training has he had?"

"He attended a sword academy back in—"

"Magical training, Ada. What kind of magical training has he had? Who taught him?"

"I trained him."

Vashti pulled her head back in surprise. "You?"

"Lazlo and Haem killed our teacher, Arthor Hadron. You must know that. It happened before our studies with him could commence. Both of us recently transcended. Unlike Galager's father—stepfather—my father is in government, and he knows people. Eludrians among them, so I knew things."

Vashti still appeared shocked. "So . . . you . . . "

"That's right, before the battle I showed him everything I'd been taught. Other than that, he's received no training from anyone. Only me."

"And what did you teach him?"

Ada shrugged. "Just the normal stuff. How to invoke an aura. How to create ball auras. How to meditate. We performed a blood meld too. But we never got the chance to raise a nimbus before your people started murdering everyone."

Vashti ignored her provocation. "And that's it?"

Ada nodded. "What is it you think he can do?"

Does she know?

Vashti seemed mystified. "Apparently, not much at all, if I'm to believe everything you are telling me."

19

Boson squinted briefly at the early afternoon sun. "How is she? Is she improving?"

Twoheart lay still and silent on her stretcher in her linen wrappings and blanket. Only her face, neck, and long black hair were exposed to the cooler air at these increasing altitudes. The skin on her face, redder than normal, had begun to blister, but she was breathing steadily and deeply. A medicinal balm, originally conceived and concocted by the Listener, had been applied to all of Twoheart's scorched skin the evening prior. Hopefully, this miraculous salve would help this woman come back from the brink, as it had done for so many others over the years. Such a boon Sanguir had been to Lavalor, for so many reasons. But now she was gone.

"She'll live," said the stretcher-bearer laboring at Twoheart's feet. He was a civilian, a tailor from the village who, like so many others, became a warrior on those days when needed—days like the last few. Boson didn't actually know the man, but he had seen him around during the course of his life. Being the only Bethurian born in Lavalor, every man and woman in the village knew him—or knew of him. It had been like that as long as he could remember. He would encounter a villager in some random happenstance, a person whose name he did not know, a person who then acted as if he knew him, often referring to Boson by name, asking questions about his father or mother, or even about things going on in his life as if they were close friends. Boson would always be embarrassed he didn't know their name, though indeed he would often know their occupation, having briefly met them before in a shop or other place. In these uncomfortable moments he'd just pretend everything was normal, exchange pleasantries, politely answer their questions or discuss some unexpected topic for a few minutes, and then move on after bidding the man or woman a good day.

There were a good number of villagers he did know by name, however. He had a good number of friends too. Being the son of a Bethurian warden married to a Lavaloran woman, and now a vangard himself, everyone in Lavalor seemed to love him—well, respect him, maybe, in any case. But he did love them all. And he loved Lavalor and his station as a member of the Claw and as a vangard warrior. He would die for these good people, if needed. Despite the color of his own skin, despite the fact he was half Commonlander and half Bethurian, he was one of them, and that's the way they treated him as well.

"Her eyes," the stretcher-bearer said, "have flitted open several times today. She's even ranted out a few words—Atikan, I'm afraid, so I don't know what she said. But I reckon she's still a bit delirious those moments she's awake."

"Twoheart's stronger than most," replied Boson. "She'll make it."

The tailor nodded as he and the man at the other end of the stretcher continued plodding forward. Boson smiled at the tailor, hefted his war axe over a shoulder, thanked him for everything he had done for Lavalor's wounded, and picked up his pace. The previous evening, when the call went out for folks to build stretchers and bindings for those unable to walk and then later, to help carry them, this man had contributed his entire supply of linen, wool, and muscle toward the effort.

Boson glanced forward, up the winding game trail rising ever higher into the rock lands. As far as he could see, their stretcher-bearers struggled up the precarious incline with their loads of injured Lavalorans. Their pace was maddeningly slow, even halting at times. More vangards and archers—led by Lorgan and Brawk—had been sent rearward to give the army time to escape up this escarpment. Boson wanted dearly to rejoin them—there would be more rear-guard skirmishes with the Bipaquans—but he had to make sure Havless, at the head of this long procession, knew where to aim his army. The procession was nearing a critical juncture and he had no choice but to be there to ensure everything went as planned. His anxiety as high as these boulder-strewn hills, he started running forward, passing the stretchers, then the walking wounded, and finally several companies of exhausted but rough and ready swords, spears, and archers, many of them carrying bundles of torches. It took him a good half hour before he finally caught up with Havless and his guard, and then another fifteen minutes when they, together, reached a place known as Flattop.

"This is it?" asked a panting Havless, bent over with his hands on his knees. "Flattop?"

"Aye, Lord," replied Boson. "This is where our futures may be determined."

Havless gestured aimlessly across a seemingly endless table of undulating granite. "How far does this go on?" he asked.

"In some directions," began Boson, "a league or two."

"Which direction are those caverns you told us about?"

Boson pointed to the southeast. "That way. About a league, though it will get a bit rougher before we arrive there."

"Brilliant," said Havless as he straightened up. He examined Boson's face. "What are you waiting for? My permission? Get on with it!"

"Aye, Lord," said Boson. He set off at once, Havless near his side, and the Castellan's retinue of two fists of swords following in single-file order. Behind them came Havless's army, one Lavaloran at a time.

"Stay behind the man in front of you," said Bosun to everyone within earshot.

He lowered his voice so only Havless would hear him. "I've left instructions with the vangards to remain here at the entrance of Flattop. They'll ensure every man and woman understands what they must do. And once the last of them passes this way, the vangards will fall in behind them and ensure we've left no stragglers or sign of our passing."

"You're sure the Bipaquans won't detect which way we go?" asked Havless.

"Not across this desert of granite," said Boson. "We'll be on solid rock from this point forward—until we enter the caverns. Once they arrive here, the enemy will have to disperse in every direction in the hope of picking up our path again. The cavern entrance is hidden well. It's possible they'll never find it. And if they do, they won't have torches."

"What about our rear guard?"

"Once they've concluded their business with the lead elements of the Bipaquans, they'll head a bit further north, bypass the caverns, hopefully draw the enemy away from our path, and then rejoin us in the morning after we exit the caverns below this mountain, closer to Grassy Creek."

"Do they know the way?"

"Lorgan's been to the caverns before, though it's been a while. He assured me he can find the exit and catch up with us again."

"I'm concerned for their safety. What if they can't elude those redfaces?"

"Our vangards surpass the Bipaquans."

Havless nodded. "Of course they do. What about the arrows with them?"

"They'll be protected. As long as Lazlo doesn't find them."

Havless glared at him.

"We've done well to reach Flattop," added Boson. "We've now avoided the worst-case scenario—being caught before reaching the caverns."

"What's the next thing to worry about?"

"The morning. We'll have to make a run for Grassy Creek in

daylight. The enemy could still catch us in the open. Lazlo Urich will decimate us if he finds us then."

"Why not make that run under the cover of darkness?"

"Pennon Poole won't arrive at Grassy Creek until sunrise—if he comes at all. He doesn't know precisely where the cavern exit is. It might take time for him to find us. And Lazlo, with his magic, can find us even in darkness. Our best chance is to hope Poole finds us before Lazlo does."

"Brilliant!"

Havless fell silent. Boson took that as a cue to pick up his pace, though he was careful not to get too far ahead of the others. The undulations of the smooth granite soon began to increase in frequency and amplitude. Boson did his best to find the easiest routes between these ripples of rock—the injured and the stretcher-bearers were already taxed to their limits and it would only get worse in the caverns. In many locations, rain water had accumulated in the deeper grooves lacking drainage pathways, but he had no difficulty finding ways around these long, narrow pools. He often checked his rear to ensure the single-file army was making good progress. Thankfully, it was.

A short time later he came to stand near a long, deep crack in the rock running across their path. Havless and others gathered around him while peering down collectively into the long fissure. Easily several hundred feet deep here, its width was fairly consistent, between twenty or thirty feet across.

"Where's the entrance?" asked Havless.

"This way," said Boson. He wheeled to the right and jogged alongside the fissure while examining its depths. Two minutes later he found what he was looking for as the fissure started widening. At this same point, the interior walls of the crack started deviating from being sheer and straight, to having ledges and protrusions, some of them rising to the rim and looking like narrow ramp ways. He pointed at one of those ramps.

"That's it?" asked Havless. "This is where we go down into this crack?"

Boson shrugged. "Either that, or go back the way we came."

Havless gazed into the black depths beyond the ledge. "Looks dangerous."

"We'll manage," replied Boson. "The entrance is hidden further below—well, not so much hidden as hard to spot because it is so tiny and masked within shadows."

Havless shook his head doubtfully and spoke wistfully. "I've always wanted to visit these caverns. But I've never known anyone who knew where to find them. I thought them to be childhood tales." He backed away from the precipice and looked at Boson. "How did you find them?"

"My father," answered Boson. "He, in turn, was shown the entrance by a friend from the village one day while hunting. My father was retired by that time. He and I spent a lot of time in the wilderness around here, hunting, learning the ways of the forest and mountain. He taught me how to take care of myself."

Havless smiled. "He taught you well. I knew him—your father. Amarin Rheev. A good man. Your mother, too. Elouheth, wasn't it?"

Boson nodded, returning the smile. He studied the Lavalorans who were gathering around their position, more arriving every second. They were tired and hungry, but at the same time strong and resolute.

"We better get moving," he said.

He stepped over the rim of the fissure and onto the narrow ledge leading down into the shadows. "Stay close!" he yelled to his rear.

20

The shorelines of the gorge were black because of the sheer numbers of skink corpses caught up in its rocks. The Vilazian —the healer he had murdered—had called them slake. Skink! Slake! Who gave a panther's tail what you called them? The castle defenders had slain a great number of the monsters during the Battle of Lavalor, and those that had simply been maimed or had the good misfortune to fall into the moats had perished in the cold waters hours ago.

The current was fast as Weir watched the cliffs slip steadily by. The number of dead slake diminished the further south he travelled, as did the height of the rock walls on either side of him. An hour later he had seen the last of the dead slake, and the walls were perhaps about one hundred feet high on average, less than half the height where he had risked his life to escape those monsters. With nothing else to do but hold on, he closed his eyes and meditated.

But he couldn't clear his thoughts. He felt troubled. That healer, he wasn't a soldier, and Weir believed him when he had said he never hurt anyone. Weir reminded himself the man was only a Vilazian. He had killed so many of them over the years, after all. But his conscience wouldn't let it go. Killing was different than murdering, at least in this case. *Maybe I acted too quickly?* Maybe there were other options he hadn't considered? He wondered if he should have instead tied that man up even though pursuit would have inevitably followed. Or maybe he should have beaten him half to death, rendering him unconscious for a good many hours, or days, giving himself plenty of time to get away from the enemy encampment—and giving that man a chance at life.

But like blood seeping through a bandage, images of Galager and Ada being carried away by Haem and Lazlo filtered up through his memories. They reminded him that bastard Lazlo Urich had his demon to chase him down regardless of any head start he might have fashioned for himself. There'd be no lead favorable enough to guarantee his escape from a flying dust and its master. Besides, that healer was killing Commonlanders and Atikans every time he made whole other Vilazian combatants. The man wasn't so innocent after all.

He re-opened his eyes in frustration and scanned the gorge for dangers, high and low. None. He did note, however, this monstrous corpse he was sprawled onto was deeper in the water than it was when he first started this absurd journey. At this rate he wouldn't be carried all the way to Bone Canyon as he had hoped, and that meant it would take longer to arrive at Intiga. Depression was also beginning to take a toll on him again. *I've failed them! Failed everyone!* He shook his head, trying to slay all bad thoughts. He thought back to happier times. He remembered his father, a Kuneteje Master, and their times hunting for deer, spearing fish, spending countless hours training with him or meditating and learning the techniques of mindful existence. *I miss him.*

He missed his mother too. It was a blessing they both were still alive, still in Bridgefoot—his birth place—still making their annual springtime journey beyond the Stallion Mountains to their secret place in the shadows of the unattainable Amaranthine Springs. Many years prior they had happened upon that spot by pure chance. They were young and full of spirit, two adventurers deeply in love, much like himself and Twoheart. On one of those journeys they dared try for Amaranthine Springs, high in the Stallions, though no one had ever successfully scaled those soaring mountains in that area, with more than a few perishing. The attempt nearly killed them too, but they came into a small hidden forest high up in the encompassing rocks. They found a tiny spring emitting from a crack in a cliff. His father immediately named it the Trickle, and laughed at how the force and arc of its discharge reminded him of a stream of piss. Other waters there dribbled, oozed, and sheeted from the surrounding rocks and cliffs, but none of them emitted forth in the same manner as the Trickle. There, in their high secret vale, they leisured and rested from their effortful ascent, and there and then—so goes his father's story—is where and when Katonkin Weir was conceived.

He grew up hearing stories of that sacred place, the enveloping mists, the Trickle and its unique and bitter-tart taste, the huge cone pines that were easily four times the height of any others anyone had ever seen, the distant echoes of constant thunder at the pinnacles far above—where existed, it was reckoned by most, Amaranthine Springs, accessible only through Firthwood, on the far side of the mountains. His parents would later return to the Trickle, after realizing their son had somehow been born with exceptional gifts of physical prowess. No other boy near his age could match his speed, or strength, or reactions. Even his sight and hearing were superior.

They eventually remembered those giant cone pines—bigger than they should have been—and they recalled how reinvigorated and robust they themselves had temporarily become during their short stay in that tiny vale. Falle Vaydal, his people would later call it, adopting Firthan words to name this place. *Valley of Life!* His mother always claimed the water in Falle Vaydal—the Trickle—had magic in it. And eventually, his father—continually astonished by his son's evolving abilities—believed she might be right. They finally returned there a few summers later, intending to carry home some of that vitalizing water, but they found the Trickle dry. Frustrated, but not deterred, they returned there numerous times over the coming months, and eventually figured out the Trickle flowed only for a few days in late spring after the peak of rainy season.

With several casks of water carried by leather straps in their straining fingers and slung across their straight backs—and their energies and muscles refortified from consuming the Trickle's blessings—his parents returned home and began visiting those among their people who were sick and ill. It was astonishing when, within days, they all showed improvement, with many being completely healed. The water wouldn't repair the scourges of the permanently crippled or bring back the dead, nor would it immediately turn anyone into the physical rival of Katonkin Weir, but its potency to cure was considered miraculous by all Atikans.

From that day forward, the Atikans caravanned to Falle Vaydal every rainy season and collected precisely half of the special water, leaving the other half for the giant trees that still depended on it. The collected water—about seventy barrels each year—would then be brought back to Atika and distributed amongst the far-flung villages and mixed with ordinary drinking water supplies so that every Atikan could benefit from the Trickle's gifts. Within half a decade, all newborn children showed signs of superior physical abilities and the health of all Atikans improved to the point where illness and disease became a thing of the past. The Atikans had become a super race among races.

~

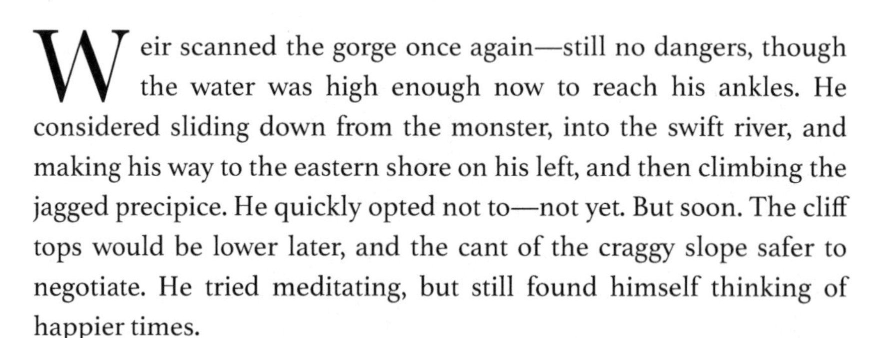

Weir scanned the gorge once again—still no dangers, though the water was high enough now to reach his ankles. He considered sliding down from the monster, into the swift river, and making his way to the eastern shore on his left, and then climbing the jagged precipice. He quickly opted not to—not yet. But soon. The cliff tops would be lower later, and the cant of the craggy slope safer to negotiate. He tried meditating, but still found himself thinking of happier times.

He was fifteen when he was sent alone into the wilderness—to Sojourner Falls—with only leather leggings and a knife to prove he was a man. By now, he was more than a physical match for any other Atikan, regardless of age. Still, he had need to become a man himself, and the only way to do that was to survive alone in the back country for one entire moon, as per the Atikan custom. He cherished those solitary days, being alone during the clear nights with a blanket of stars providing his spiritual warmth, exploring the canyons, gorges, and river ways of the Shattered Hills. On his first day of his adventure, he cut a sapling of jakroot then made a spear—with his knife as its tip—to catch the speckled whitefish that inhabited almost all of the waters where his people lived. He ate their flesh raw, until on the third day of observing the wildlife and its ways he found some flint and thereafter made fire every night. On the fourth day he fashioned a proper spear head from a second piece of flint he had reserved for this purpose, using damp strands of fiber torn from the inner sides of jakroot bark to secure the head to the shaft. Once those strands dried and shrunk, it was nearly impossible for the spear point to fall off.

Those were the days he was becoming a man, but what truly changed his life was what happened on the very last day of his sacred journey. He had come across the tracks of a large pack of rock wolves. He estimated their numbers to be at least a dozen, but probably more —perhaps as many as two dozen, as many of the members were likely shadowing the main pack. This was disturbing, as rock wolves preyed on Atikans and any animal they happened on, including the brown bear and the rarer panther. Sometimes the wolves would come down out of the nether regions of the foothills, where they usually preferred to live, out of the way of human kind. And now was one of those times. Hoping to avoid the wolves, Weir was about to continue on his way toward Bridgefoot when he spotted another set of tracks. A woman! Whoever this person was, she was barefoot, probably Atikan, and she was running—and the wolves were on her scent. Their big paw tracks had left numerous imprints over hers. She was being hunted.

Weir remembered wondering that day if he should run to Bridgefoot, gather up some warriors, and then return to save the woman. But he was still many leagues from the village and he doubted this woman would remain alive long enough to be rescued, if he didn't try to help her right away.

It then occurred to him it was the last day of his sacred journey into manhood. This was a test! What else could it be? Either he had to save this woman, and himself, from these ferocious rock wolves, or he would return home a failure, if he returned at all. A heartbeat later he began running in the direction of the wolves.

Cold water splashed on his thighs, interrupting Weir's reverie. Atop the skink, he was entering some rapids, and the bloated monster wasn't faring too well in these rough waters. The rougher it got, the deeper it sank. Weir peered forward and saw white boulders sticking out of the rapids like hungry teeth. He could hear a roar of turbulent water not far ahead. He had known about these rapids, had seen them many times from the safety of the canyon rims, but he had hoped he and this skink would somehow be able to negotiate this section of the river. It would turn smoother, not too far ahead, but until then he was entering dangerous territory.

He checked up ahead again and saw tangled logs and a few skinks caught in many of the boulders. The recent storm had dislodged the logs from their former resting areas on the banks or from the canyon rims, and now they were presenting themselves as a trap for unwary skink floaters such as himself. He suddenly realized he was in grave danger, if he attempted to pass those trees and boulders. He slid off the skink and urgently began swimming toward the left cliff face. He needed to get there before he reached the rapids that continued to rush closer and closer every second.

21

Over twenty men dead. Including that obstinate old man.

Gainhu figured it was his fault.

He should have seen the signs. The clues. They were there all along, in that forest trail, in the last section just before the stream and the ambush. Barefoot tracks, increasing in number, trampling over boot prints of their fellow Commonlanders. They had sent more of their Atikan vangards rearward, but they had erred, left telltale signs of their tactics, and he nevertheless had failed to take advantage of it and instead ran—not walked—into their trap. He cursed himself, wanting to blame his lead scout, but knowing in his heart it had been his own fault for hurrying them along.

No more mistakes!

The only saving grace was that his army had finally caught up with him because of his subsequent retreat. He no longer had to fear being outnumbered. Next time they encountered those Atikans, things would be different. And next time he'd be more careful not to let them dictate the circumstances of the fight.

The pine forest soon thinned, and they exited it as they were presented with a meadow leading toward some rising hills. Off to either side higher peaks rose, though nothing as rough as those jagged mountains behind Lavalor village. Free of the trees, he decided to again pick up his pace, and gestured toward lead elements behind him to stay close. He had to make up lost time, and this seemed the best chance. It was easier to track the enemy here in this tall grass that rose no higher than his knees. No ambush possible here.

They proceeded forward, quickly following the trampled vegetation. An army had passed here today, no doubt. The meadow narrowed as it rose, and the hills on either side began to close in and grow higher. Within thirty minutes the lush grasses gave way to a dry stream of rocks and boulders. He started doubting himself. Where was this narrowing vale leading? He could easily imagine he was entering a long canyon, one in which the only way out would be to reverse direction and go back the way they came. *Another trap?* He peeked to his rear, seeing all those men trying to keep up with him. To reverse course now would mean turning his army around, and that would be seen as a weakness in his skills and leadership. Swallowing once, he decided to keep going forward.

As he had feared, they soon found themselves in a canyon with walls rising higher and higher on either side. They could climb them, but they would be vulnerable while doing so, especially the further they progressed. He considered turning around. They were certainly entering ambush territory again. But, still, he didn't want to be seen as weak and cowardly by his countrymen.

Forward!

A half hour later their circumstances hadn't improved. In fact, they had worsened. They had just gone around a curve in the narrow canyon when he saw them, about a bow-shot ahead, standing defiantly amid some large boulders plugging the narrow canyon. The vangards—about thirty of them, mostly Atikan—were brazenly waiting for them out in the open, their little swords sheathed, but their axes nowhere to be seen. Gainhu figured the rocks upon which the vangards stood made it more difficult to wield the heavier axes. Either way, the only way forward would be to get past these enemy warriors.

He checked the ridges above him. No one up there, especially those archers.

At this point he had two choices, turn around and send his army running like cowards, or do battle with the vangards.

He decided to charge.

The war cries of his men echoed from the narrow confines of the canyon as they closed with the waiting enemy. He immediately realized that, while his force outnumbered theirs, the narrow confines of this canyon made it impossible to leverage that strength. Blades crashed together as the two sides met, those little swords of the vangards whirling almost impossibly.

He briefly wondered about that black warrior he had faced earlier, and felt shame as he realized he was glad he wasn't here. He fought off his humiliation and fear with anger as he finally crossed blades with one of the enemy. Some of the war cries on either side of him turned to shrieks of pain, and more than a few were death screams. He almost panicked when someone crashed into him from behind.

Pushed forward against his will, he ducked a near-fatal thrust of a little sword aimed for the spot between his eyes and then stepped to the right to avoid being pushed further toward the enemy. Another little sword came slicing downward toward his neck, but he desperately parried and instinctively jumped onto a series of boulders increasing in height. His movement afforded him a moment of respite from other attackers, so he quickly glanced at his rear and saw that his army had bunched up behind the leading fighters.

His units further back, eager to join the battle, were still advancing though, and causing everyone at the front line to become jammed together, thereby impeding their movements. Many of those engaged with the vangards were trying desperately to keep from being pushed further into the maw of the vangard trap. The logjam was fatal to at least four men in the few seconds Gainhu observed the fighting.

"Back! Back!" he shouted over the heads of his valiant warriors while waving his arms to get their attention. He was careful to avoid issuing the traditional order to retreat. He wished the fight to continue. For now. Nonetheless, his men didn't notice the difference and they all suddenly began to reverse course.

"No! No!" he shouted, trying to stop the ill-intended withdrawal. No use, he quickly realized.

We'll have to regroup!

Gainhu returned to the field of battle, intervening in several fights in sequence, adding just enough force to allow several of his men, in turn, to escape the skirmish with their lives. The two sides separated, his men moving rapidly back the way they had come, and the grim-eyed vangards standing their ground, a wall of steel and muscle preventing passage through this defile of red rock. Before he turned his back to the vangards, he counted eight men lying still on the ground. None of them vangards.

Despite repeatedly screaming out orders as he ran, Gainhu didn't regain control of his army until the walls had curved enough to block visibility between the two opposing forces. Some of his men looked embarrassed, most angry. A change in tactics would be required to breach that vangard wall. No longer would he attack with everyone at once. Reminding himself that his strength lay in sheer numbers, he pointed at the leader of one of his best war parties and ordered him to get his men ready for another advance. If needed, he would take the day via attrition—attack again and again with smaller-sized, yet more capable units.

He invested a few precious minutes telling his chosen men what he planned. He stressed that panic and speed were not their friends. Once he was sure everyone understood, he gave the order to slowly advance. The party of one-hundred Bipaquan veterans—his best fighters—circled around the curving walls slowly and deliberately. Their weapons were held before them as they checked the canyon rims for enemy archers and scrutinized the rocks and boulders gathered at the foot of those vertical walls for other traps. He wished he had ordered his men to carry their lances with them—used with great effect the night before. He had thought they'd be a nuisance while on the run, but now he saw his error. He had also considered employing his archers here, but the vangards had too many boulders to hide behind. It would be a waste of his precious arrows.

The Atikans were still waiting for them. In the interim, they had stacked Gainhu's fallen warmates like a pile of logs in the middle of the canyon directly in front of the vangard position.

But one of his men atop that pile of flesh and bone was still alive. He could see movement in his limbs. Two vangards—Commonlanders—stood over the fallen warrior, both straddling him, each with a foot planted on the small of his spine, and another foot on a wrist. The vangard at the front had the warrior's black hair clenched in a fist and was pulling the poor fellow's head up cruelly, thereby exposing his neck and chest toward Gainhu and his advancing war party. Judging by the blood smeared across his neck and shoulders, the man was grievously injured—a head wound by the look of it. He felt a measure of pride, however, to observe the victim's steely eyes and determination. Yes, suffering and fear could be seen on that face, but they were tempered by immense courage. If the purpose of this tragic display was to humiliate Gainhu's man and demoralize his companions, the vangards had failed.

He led his party forward. They had formed themselves into a ten wide, ten deep formation. He would remain a member of the rear-most rank for now, looking for dangers, shouting instructions, maintaining control of everything.

Should have done it this way the first time.

Rather than charge the enemy position, he would this time send one rank in at a time—ten Bipaquan warriors arrayed against an equal number of vangards standing in their way. He would give them the space they needed to show their mettle. And if one of his men in that line met a grisly fate, the one behind him would immediately take his place. The vangards up ahead were organized similarly, only their formation was ten wide, three deep, as it had been in their previous skirmish here. The narrow canyon in this location wouldn't allow for a broader front. If needed, he'd return with another war party, and keep repeating the entire process until the vangards were routed. He had the numbers, and if the vangards were smart, they'd have to eventually retreat—or die standing their ground.

But, where are their archers? He checked the canyon rims again, satisfied not to see any movement anywhere up there. Their absence would make it easier for him and his men.

The two forces were about twenty yards apart when the nearest vangard standing over his man suddenly plunged his tiny sword into his captive's neck, deep inside his collarbone, killing him instantly. Afterward, he withdrew his bloody weapon and the two Atikans, laughing and hollering, leapt from the stack of Bipaquan bodies and returned to the safety of their warmates standing closely behind them.

A wave of disgust and anger exploded within Gainhu. His men, too, as the ten-by-ten formation suddenly lunged forward, threatening to lose its integrity as the individual men within surrendered to angry impulses to run forward to avenge their friend.

"Hold!" screamed Gainhu. "Hold!" Thankfully, they all heard him and did as ordered.

"Advance!" he then yelled. "Maintain ranks. Time to kill these Atikan dogs!"

The fighting, this time, was more competitive at the start. Two Bipaquans went down in the first thirty seconds, but then a vangard body slumped to the ground with a sword stuck deeply within his stomach. As planned, the two empty spaces in the Bipaquan front line were immediately filled by fresh fighters. Gainhu, and those of his men not yet fighting, cheered as the enemy warrior fell upon the ground and then went still.

"They're not invincible!" he screamed, seizing the opportunity to embolden his men. "Maintain ranks!" he again reminded with a mighty bellow. "Kill the dogs!"

His eyes flitted upward. The rims. What was that? And then he saw them—the archers.

Commonland heads popped up over the jagged rock formations atop the walls, directly above them, a dozen on each side. Bows were drawn, their cords thrumming, arrows speeding towards him and the others. A dozen Bipaquans in the middle ranks screamed, a similar number of men fell. Ahead, at the lead rank, another Bipaquan warrior met his fate at the hands of an Atikan berserker, a man screaming with bloodlust as his two little swords whirled and buzzed.

Another volley of arrows.

Gainhu scanned the ground nearby and counted three dead vangards and at least ten of his elite warriors still on the red dirt, several more writhing in agony. Two more quickly joined them because of the confusion rippling through his formation and enemy knowhow.

Gainhu cursed silently.

What should I do?

22

Lazlo Urich disentangled himself from the woman and rolled off the pile of furs. A soft hand reached out for him in the dim tent interior and beckoned for him to return. He took it and gently kissed it.

"How long have I slept?" he said.

He twisted around further and stared into her lovely eyes for a few breathtaking moments. He fought a longing to accede to her silent wishes, but he remembered the urgency of his duties, and so he stood.

She turned onto her back and gathered her yellow hair over her far shoulder.

"A few hours," she whispered. "Must you really leave me?"

"We both have work to do," he said, donning his black robe over his shoulders and arms and letting the garment fall to full length. "The wounded need you, and I have an army to find and destroy."

The woman, that dead healer's assistant, sat up and pulled a thick panther fur up with her to cover herself. He didn't even know her name. In truth, he hadn't even noticed her until after the battle the day before, when that vangard arrow was sticking out of his shoulder.

He would never admit this to anyone, but in the days leading to this confrontation, he had been riddled with stress and anxiety. His entire focus had been on preparing for this engagement and getting his army formed up and positioned without having the ogres and the slake tear into each other. What a nightmare that had been, especially the slake. But the Bipaquans were a remarkable breed of man and a boon to Vilazian efforts, not just here in the Sundered Lands, but in many other locations as well, where the Vilazian Wind was saving the world from itself.

And now Lavalor had fallen—quite unexpectedly at that.

The slake had been of far greater value than anyone could have guessed. Such a shame it had taken the Bipaquans so many years to learn to control these black lizards. Otherwise, the plan known as The Grand Unraveling may have been set into motion years earlier.

Then last night, watching this beauty while her master worked on his injury, and feeling his worries dissipate, his burdens grow lighter, and the euphoria of victory overwhelming him, he had remembered he had other needs to be looked after. The woman was merely in the right place at the right time. And seeing the way she smiled at him now as he donned his robe, she was feeling the same way.

He considered asking her name. Changed his mind. He had a wife back in Raiil, and it somehow felt better if he just kept things simple.

"I won't have need of you when I return," he said. "Not anymore."

Her eyes dropped.

"Don't presume otherwise, or ever behave in front of me as if these last few hours happened."

She returned her gaze to him. A strong woman, already she projected an indifference to this development.

Strong. Smart. Beautiful. I like her.

Perhaps later I'll change my mind.

"Did I displease you?"

"Of course not," he said, snatching his sword and belt from a peg on the center tent pole.

She looked confused. "I embarrassed you?"

"Nothing like that."

"Then what?"

He finished buckling on his belt, and adjusted his weapon.

"You were but a momentary pleasure," he said. "Better you understand that now, rather than think something more has happened here. I don't have time for later distractions. Including any unwanted attention from you."

"I see," she said, appearing unhurt.

"Get dressed and go," he ordered unemotionally.

He then ducked through the entry flaps and into the bright sunlight. He reached into a fold of leather under his robe and withdrew a ruby. He acknowledged the two guards seeing to his safety, squinted into the warm light, and let the astonishing warmth caress his cheeks as he willed forth an aura.

"Anon doss Haem, tagk'liotz!" he uttered loudly.

The woman exited the tent in her own robe, glanced his way, then pivoted and walked away toward the infirmary tents on the opposite side of the encampment.

He returned his attention to the skies, scanning them, waiting. Several of his men saluted and drifted past as he stood there. Finally, he spotted the ribbon of dust. It came swooping in between tall pine trees and then hovered over him.

"Up," said Lazlo.

A tendril of dust swirled down toward his face. He breathed deeply of it. He immediately felt a tingling sensation throughout his body as he changed form—into dust—and then was assimilated by the demon. He listened for the anguished voices, but today there were none. He didn't care why.

"North," commanded Lazlo. "Over the fortress."

They rose at once and veered in the indicated direction. How he loved doing this—flying while disembodied.

He estimated he and Haem were about a hundred feet over the trees when they left the perimeter of the forest and flew directly over the pole where he had transfigured that vangard into a vrecht. Beyond the impalement field, just ahead, loomed the castle. Smoke still rose from the massive gatehouse where he had snagged an arrow. He studied the impalement field as they crossed over it. The bodies of dead slake, Bipaquan warriors, and ogres met his gaze wherever he aimed his eyes. They were propped up on those sharpened stakes, or laying in pools of bloodstained earth with arrows and iron-tipped bolts protruding from their bodies. Even from this height a maleficent odor of rotting flesh reached his invisible nostrils. It was an astonishing sight, and he was glad it wasn't his fellow Vilazian soldiers that had suffered down there. Not that he much cared for them either, but to lose men always had an impact on his army's morale and fighting effectiveness.

He and Haem crossed the moat, kept free of corpses because of the swift currents that surrounded this proud, hulking fortress.

Lower.

They dropped closer to the moat near the end of the long causeway.

Here! Hold!

Haem obeyed.

Lazlo smiled widely as he examined the broken gate. His eludrians had done their jobs to perfection. There was virtually nothing left of the Winolkan heartwood, just a few bits and pieces attached to the chains at the top. All the rest had most likely blown off and got ejected into the moat once the magic had gotten to the huge wooden gate and done its work.

Forward. Through the gate. Slowly.

Haem again obeyed.

The first portcullis was a melted line of black iron on the stonework lining the bottom of the dark tunnel. As they slowly drifted forward, Lazlo felt heat radiating from the slag below them. The walls here were blackened, with more heat radiating from those as well. The second portcullis was a twin to the first.

They emerged into the open area on the interior side of the gate.

Hundreds of slake were curled up on the ground in front of him, their viper heads laying over their long tails. Most of them were alive, basking in the sunlight. Dozens more were slowly ambling around on their short legs, exploring the area or finding somewhere satisfactory to set themselves down. Dead Commonlanders were everywhere, their bodies savaged beyond recognition.

Higher! They rose slowly.

Turn around! The rooftop of the gate circled into view.

The ash heap atop the stairway turret still smoldered, but only a few visible embers remained now. Again, dead men everywhere he looked. Ogres and slake too. He spotted the vrecht—still, unmoving, lifeless. These Commonlanders had put up a valiant fight, he had to admit.

Higher!

They rose above the massive barracks structures on the left after turning north again. They were now about the same height as the central watch tower where he had watched Haem brutally assault Lavalor's leadership the evening before. Poor fools had no idea what they were in for.

He glanced to the right, toward that massive tower where Haem had slashed the throat of that eludrian all those days ago, when he first set things into motion here, the opening movement of The Grand Unraveling.

Higher!

Now he could see the entire castle. The western wall, where the slake first breached this castle, was a cemetery of vanquished Commonlanders. He moved his gaze eastward. A gazebo in the gardens of the inner keep garnered his attention briefly. *What is that? No matter!* Slake were there too, in the keep, sleeping or crawling. And more were in the other two wards of the castle as well. Indeed, it appeared as if most of the slake the Bipaquans had brought here were reposed somewhere below, contentedly basking in the sunlight. The entire castle was full of them.

As good a place as any to keep these things out of the way.

Not a single living human, though.

He got bored. And he had other matters to attend to. Lavalor village, ahead, was an inferno of fire and smoke. Lacking the protective haleburl used extensively in the fortress itself, the village was far more vulnerable to the ravages of fire. And by the looks of things, his men had already looted the village and razed it.

Time to find their army!

23

Gainhu hoped the fourth assault would finally turn the tables. The third attempt had gone pretty much the way the previous one had, with a score of Bipaquans meeting their untimely end, though not a single vangard had fallen that time. The enemy archers had again been the difference. They had made it impossible to advance on the Atikans without suffering unacceptable casualties. In the end, he had to give the order to turn around before he had gotten within thirty yards of the enemy line.

But this time he decided to fight fire with fire. Scores of his warriors—unseen by the enemy—had scaled the walls, half of them on each side of the canyon. Armed with swords and bows, they were waiting for him up there now, ready to move forward when he gave the order. Their goal would be to sweep clean the tops of these ridges, kill as many of those archers as they could get to, or send the rest scurrying away like rats exposed to the light. Under their protective cover, his main force, down here in the canyon could then attack the vangards without fear of arrows decimating their ranks. It would now be the enemy who would have to deal with a deadly rain of steel-tipped missiles.

Satisfied all was ready, Gainhu gave the signal to move forward.

He would lead from the front this time. The peering faces up on the rims, and their other men, hidden within cracks or behind boulders, immediately disappeared. In a matter of moments they would encounter the enemy archers. In the meantime, he took the first steps down the canyon, a hundred elite warriors following close behind.

Once again the walls curved around them as they marched forward. Gainhu listened for the first sounds of battle up above, but heard nothing. That surprised him. He could now see all the way to the vangard blockade, but again he was surprised. No one there, except his own dead.

The vangards had fled!

What now?

He instinctively began trotting. He heard his men behind keeping up with him. He scanned every inch of rock and dirt, looking for traps. But there were none. He arrived at the pile of Bipaquan bodies near to the line of boulders. He leapt onto the first rock in his path, then another, as higher and higher he climbed. He stopped at the highest boulder, about ten feet above the ground upon which his men waited below. The canyon floor ahead rose steadily in elevation.

Still, not an Atikan or Commonlander in sight.

He heard his name echoing between the walls. "Gainhu," came his name again—from the top of the ridge on his left. His men were up there, silhouetted against the bright blue sky.

"What do you see?" he shouted.

Their leader shrugged. "They're gone."

"Over here as well," came another voice from the opposite ridge.

He felt relieved. This was not a fight he had liked.

"They're running!" he shouted so all could hear. This stand of theirs had been nothing more than a delaying tactic.

He again studied the pile of bodies below. A measure of anger returned to him. He noted that the vangard bodies, those few that had been here, were gone. They took their dead.

He swung his gaze upward again.

"Proceed forward—carefully. The canyon is rising. We'll rejoin somewhere ahead." He heard acknowledgments then watched as the men on the ridges pulled away from sight.

He shouted more orders to the warriors waiting below and behind.

"Get the others. Tell them to come forward."

He burst into motion, in the direction the vangards had gone. As he had thought, the canyon continued rising and eventually melted away as it converged with higher ground. His two teams of ridge attackers were waiting for him up ahead.

His forces rejoined, they proceeded forward again, climbing ever higher as the land rose, the game trail underfoot twisting in the rock formations like a river. The view to the left was amazing. Gainhu could see forever in that direction. Another pine forest stretched off into the distance below them as they followed the switchbacks higher and higher.

They crested the elevations maybe an hour later and encountered three vangard corpses laying aside each other on a sheet of endless granite. Three smiling Bipaquan warriors hunched down over their unmoving forms and took scalps. A few of his other men then swooped in and urinated on the bodies.

Gainhu scanned all directions. Behind him were the switchbacks and the infinite pine forest abutting the lower slopes they had just ascended. Otherwise, all he saw was a flat expanse of granite wherever he looked—north, east, or south. It undulated gently and was broken in places, but still, it was only rock. He cursed as he studied the stone underfoot. He didn't see anything that would betray the path of the army he had been chasing. Only those three dead vangards—left behind, no doubt, because their wounds would drip blood and point the way the withdrawing army had gone.

"Go!" he ordered to his lead tracker, milling nearby. "Take your men. Search for them. Look for signs of their passing. Report back to me when you find their path." Without delay, the tracker and his party dispersed in different directions.

More of his men began arriving, including more of his trackers. He sent the first of them off searching too. Not long afterward his entire army had arrived, many of their numbers kicking the dead Atikans or pissing on them. But lacking an enemy to fight or a path to follow, he had to order them to again wait for further developments.

More time passed, and his frustrations were getting the better of him. The afternoon was late. It was as if the enemy had disappeared from the face of the earth. Not a single sign of their passing had been found after this point. He started wondering if he had missed something on their way through the upper extents of that deadly canyon and the ascending switchbacks. Surrendering to those concerns, he sent several trackers back the way they had come to find out if the enemy had secretly escaped into that pine forest they had skirted.

At one point, the men nearest him alerted him to something in the sky. His heart skipped a beat as he instinctively feared it might be the wizard, Lazlo Urich, and that loathsome creature.

It was.

The dust creature settled down a few dozen yards away. In moments, Lazlo Urich and Haem were standing side by side as the Bipaquans nearest them withdrew to a safe distance.

Gainhu wondered whether his failures this day would now cause his life to be forfeit.

Swallowing his fear, he stepped toward the wizard and hailed him.

Lazlo smiled when he heard his name. "Gainhu," returned Lazlo. "My friend, good to see you."

Gainhu saluted as the two met. He had learned long ago that this man's smile and good disposition meant nothing.

The Vilazian spoke once more, but Gainhu had a hard time understanding him. He had been learning their language in recent years, but still had difficulty with much of it.

"You have come a long way," said Lazlo. The vilemaster noted the enemy dead.

"Yes," said Gainhu in Lazlo's tongue, relieved that Lazlo had simplified and slowed down his speech for his benefit.

"Long way."

The eludrian's smile fell from his face. "Where are the Commonlanders?"

Right to the point. "We follow them here. They fight. Try stop us. We still come."

Lazlo nodded in satisfaction, or perhaps in feigned satisfaction. He turned around, slowly examining his surroundings.

"I don't see them." He casually pointed at the bodies nearby. "Except for them, of course."

Gainhu gestured toward the rock below their feet. "We look now." He pointed behind Lazlo in several directions. "Harder find them now . . . rock. I send many tracker to look. They come back soon."

"I see," said Lazlo, lips tightening, eyes narrowing. He glanced randomly at other Bipaquans. "Tell me about these fights."

Gainhu sensed a darkening shift in Lazlo. Indeed, the wizard produced a magic stone from his spacious robes. Gainhu could see the faint red glow even in the daylight.

"You fought them?" demanded Lazlo.

Gainhu nodded vigorously. "Yes, we fight."

A smile again. "Good. Tell me everything."

Fifteen minutes later Lazlo finally seemed to have understood the entirety of Gainhu's actions since leaving the encampment that morning.

Lazlo considered him for a full minute while clenching his magic stone. But in a surprise, he then secluded it back into his black robe. "You did well," he said.

"Did well?" asked Gainhu, relief starting to filter through his body, his sense of dread carefully passing.

Lazlo placed a comforting hand on Gainhu's shoulder and leaned in close to whisper in his ear.

"I am impressed with you. You instinctively knew time was of the essence. You kept my men informed with your messengers. You opted for action over caution, forced the enemy's hand every chance you had, despite the risk of losing a few of your own. And you are still on their tail, despite their deceptions."

Gainhu wasn't sure of everything Lazlo had just said, but he sensed he was out of trouble.

Lazlo separated from him and walked back to his creature. A tendril of smoke reached for the wizard's face. As he turned to dust he said, "You know what to do—we both do."

24

Lorgan glanced over his shoulder. "Stay alert!" he warned, just loud enough for everyone to hear. "They could be anywhere."

As planned, they had veered due north after arriving at Flattop—a brace and a half of vangards and another brace of arrows, about fifty in total. They had lost three good men in the unfriendly confines of that canyon. He was glad it wasn't more. Had Lazlo Urich been there, things would have been worse—far, far worse! Lorgan's eyes flicked upward and quickly scanned the blue sky. *Where is he anyway?*

They were running as fast as they could, trying to find cover at the northern limits of Flattop before being discovered. Lorgan bemoaned losing three men, then having to leave them behind because of their bloody wounds. No way to carry them across this expanse of rock without leaving a trail of blood.

Despite their losses, things were going precisely as hoped. Their delaying actions had allowed Havless and his main ground force to reach Flattop without being observed. And that in all likelihood meant all his friends had by now found their way into those life-saving caverns. He hated the idea of running like this, but without Arthor Hadron—or those two young ones—to protect them from Vilazian magic, they really had no other choice. The hope was they'd all be able to meet up with the units from Jurry sometime in the morning. No doubt they'd have an eludrian within their ranks to counter that homicidal vilemaster and his demon.

If they didn't—

Lorgan again scanned the sky, looking for signs of the dust.

Clear!

"Keep your sorry eyes open, boys," he warned again. "If Lazlo finds us now, we won't see sunset."

The long expanse of granite finally came to an end. Down below, beneath the lip of granite that had now ended like the rim of a gigantic plate, they could see over a descending, treeless slope that then met pine forest further down—yet another woodland that seemed to stretch forever.

"Let's get moving, boys," he ordered, checking the skies one more time as he leapt from the granite plate and onto dirt, four feet below. He led them east, along the granite lip, staying near to it in the hope the rocky terrain they traversed underfoot might make it harder to track them. They didn't have time to erase their tracks, but thankfully the ground here was still pretty rocky and rough. It appeared the granite plate had at one time extended well past this descending area where they now ran, but had broken into various-sized pieces ranging from pebbles to boulders as big as buildings. They did their best to leap from rock to rock, and stay off the grassy loam, but sometimes they had no choice.

Brawk yelled a warning. "Dust!"

Lorgan whipped his head around back west. Sure enough, there it was, high up, a tiny smudge in the clear sky, just coming over the plate lip. It stopped moving and began to hover.

"Under the ledge!" ordered Lorgan. "Quick! Before he spots us."

Lorgan lunged into the dark shadows cast by the projecting rim of the granite plate and then slammed himself against the short, vertical wall beneath it, about eight feet high at this point. The others did the same, all of them crouching low.

Had they done it fast enough to prevent themselves from being seen?

Vangards ought not be hiding like this.

Hidden as they were, there was little else they could do. It would be impossible to continue moving east while crouching like this. So they waited.

A minute passed. Lorgan wondered what their best course of action might be if Lazlo and Haem found them. Could Lazlo burn them while in dust form? He had no idea. Could they in turn hurt the Vilazian when he was in that state? If they could, he didn't know how.

Another minute passed. Nothing.

Where is he?

Another minute.

He should've been here by now, if he's gonna find us at all.

Lorgan decided to check. "Stay here," he ordered the others.

"What are ya planning?" came Brawk's voice, a few men to the left.

"Just gonna poke my head out and see's if he's still there."

No one objected.

"If he sees me," added Lorgan. "I'll make a run down this slope and hope he doesn't see the rest of you. Once he's taken after me and is out of sight, you all keep heading east as fast as ya can."

"Nah," said another man disdainfully. "We'll fight 'em together."

Lorgan grunted. "No, you will not!" he snorted. "Make a run for it. He's probably gonna spit me out like snot once he's done with me, and then come after you anyway. You can fight then."

No response for a few moments, then Brawk broke the silence. "Well, get on with it, ya bastard. Always jabbering away like a woman, you are."

Cautious, low laughter rose up all along their line.

"Awright, awright," he said, laughing too. "Jus' remember what I told ya."

"Yeah, yeah," said Brawk.

Lorgan's fingers separated from the cool walls and he stepped out of the shadows.

Studying the skies in all directions, he saw nothing. "He's gone," he reported back seconds later. "Didn't see us."

"Jehlude Jhalaveral," stated Brawk as he and the others immediately clambered out into the sunlight.

Lorgan proudly and slowly examined each man—vangards and arrows. They had done well. They had given Havless and Boson a fighting chance to escape without being tracked. He also knew they were lucky not to have been spotted. Indeed, they were lucky they were still alive.

But we won't be for long, if I stay here acting like a fool.

"Let's get moving," he barked. "And keep your eyes peeled!"

~

Hold here.

Haem ceased moving.

Lazlo wondered how far up they were. A thousand? Two? It was difficult judging.

Can they see us from this height?

Lazlo ordered Haem to retreat a short distance, using the stone ledge to help obscure them from the vangards.

He had spotted the fleeing men the moment he had crossed the edge of the granite, and watched as they reacted, leaping into the shadows and then under the short projection of stone, trying to stay concealed from his searching eyes.

He instinctively wanted to go after them, but then a better idea occurred to him.

No doubt they were heading back to their army to rejoin it.

So instead of obliterating these few now, he would follow them.

And obliterate everyone afterward.

Everyone.

25

The young man pushed himself off the cold floor and tried to stand. “We’re prisoners?”

“Watch it!” Civato tried to warn him—too late.

“Ouch!” blurted the Commonlander, Galager Swift, as he fell back down, hard onto his ass. He sat up. He adjusted his shackles, trying to keep the concealed edges inside the cuffs from biting deeper.

“Ouch!” he hissed again. “Who the hell tortures people like this?’

“You need to ask?” whispered Uri, a slight laugh affecting his weakened words.

The boy peered through the darkness around him, slowly swiveling his head, taking note of his surroundings and the other prisoners—and then the bars. Civato could faintly see the boy’s eyes widening as the reality of his circumstances finally took root in his mind.

“Where are we?” the boy asked. He scrutinized Civato, again with shock registering on the eludrian’s face as he realized the men sharing his cell were Bethurians.

“And who are you?”

Civato gestured toward the boy's wrists. "Be careful with those. Don't make it worse than it has to be."

The boy blinked. He seemed confused.

"What do you remember?" asked Civato.

"Remember?"

"Yes, from Lavalor."

Confusion continued to affect the boy's face. "How do you know I'm from there?"

Good, a smart one.

"Your lady friend told us."

"Ada Halentine," whispered Uri.

Galager reacted at the mention of Ada's name and suddenly tried to stand again.

"Huzzah!" he yelled when the sharpened shackles brought him back down.

"Be careful with those," warned Civato again. "Don't try to stand."

Mindful of the chains and shackles, the boy again gathered himself into a sitting position and peered closely at Civato.

"Is Ada alright? Is she hurt? Where is she now? When did you see—"

"She's fine. No injuries."

The boy closed his eyes and sighed in relief.

"She visited us earlier this morning. She was very happy to see you."

The boy started to blurt out more questions, but Civato interrupted. "We're captives—in Intiga. All of us, including you and Lady Halentine, were captured and brought here by a demon. Do you remember anything now?"

The boy dropped his gaze to his lap, searching for memories. "I remember the chapel. Master Vreman—he burnt me with magic. But everything after that . . . I don't know—just dreams, I think. I think I fought Haem somehow, the demon, then some other kind of . . . monster that was trying to hurt Ada. And an explosion."

The boy lifted his troubled eyes toward him.

"Just fragments of dreams. That's all."

"Perhaps not dreams at all," whispered Uri.

The boy seemed to remember something.

"What about Lavalor?" he spurted. "Was there a battle?"

It was Civato's turn to drop his eyes. "Your friend said Castle Lavalor was most likely overrun. Both of you were captured by the vilemaster, Lazlo Urich."

The boy no longer seemed capable of speech. He lowered his face into his hands and remained unmoving for a good minute before he again faced Civato.

"The Grand Unraveling," he groaned. "It's happening."

Civato started to ask him to clarify, but several dozen Vilazian soldiers burst through the dungeon entrance and made their way along the vaulted hallway to their cell. A man with a black beard withdrew a ring of keys and swung open the heavy door. It squealed like a pig. The soldiers entered the cell, fanning out and surrounding the boy. Civato thought they were going to take him away, but instead they accosted him, taking turns kicking and punching the young eludrian, who attempted to escape the sudden assault by curling into a fetal position. Civato made to stand, to try and help the Commonlander, but several of the soldiers intervened and knocked him back onto the floor while one of them grabbed his chains and pulled viciously, sending waves of pain into his wrists and blood dripping down his forearms.

"Leave him be," growled Civato.

As fast as they had started, the beatings ended. But because these soldiers didn't understand a single word Civato had uttered, he doubted it was because of anything he had said.

The soldiers backed away from the boy. Realizing the attack was over, the boy dared lift his head from the security of his armpit to check on his assailants. He glanced at Civato with questioning eyes, wondering what the hell was happening. Except for a trace of nosebleed, they hadn't hurt him too badly. It didn't make sense. Why come in here and rough him up like this, but not seriously hurt him?

One of the soldiers feigned another attack and Galager flinched and briefly tucked his face back into his protective arms before pulling it back out again after realizing the attack wasn't coming. At this point, the soldiers turned away, left the cell, and disappeared the way they had come after slamming home and relocking the iron door.

"What was that about?" asked Uri.

"Good question," replied Civato. The boy uncurled, and pushed himself up into a sitting position once again. "Are you hurt?" asked Civato.

The boy shook his head. "Why'd they beat me?"

"If they had beat you," answered Civato, "you wouldn't be speaking right now."

Uri coughed. "It's like they were trying to get the boy to react."

"Doesn't make sense," said Civato. He looked at the boy. "You have no idea why they did that?"

"None at all."

"Is there anything you're not telling us? Something we need to know?"

"What's to tell? Those assholes just came in here and started hitting and kicking me. It sure felt like a beating to me, by the way."

The boy suddenly noticed Uri's condition, his limp arm, and the other Bethurians—men sapped and demoralized by days of deprivations and abuse.

"I'm sorry," he said. "You've all been through hell."

Civato grunted. He was starting to like this kid.

"Where you from?" Galager asked. "Which castle?"

"Shenkel," replied Civato. "We left for the Fringe the same morning we heard some kind of warning about Arthor Hadron and a demon. Something happened at Lavalor that morning, but without confirmation or details I thought it a bad idea to delay my patrol. It's a mistake that cost us dearly."

"Word? Pigeons?"

"No, over the Thrum. From Arthor Hadron, Lavalor's eludrian."

"He's gone," stammered Galager. "Lazlo and Haem infiltrated the castle and killed him. I was trying to help him when he died."

Civato encouraged the boy to provide more information, and

for the next ten minutes Galager divulged details concerning a litany of events that had transpired from the time he had transcended in the Solstice Military Academy to the time Master Valter Vreman had lathed him and rendered him unconscious. But there were a lot of things the boy seemed fuzzy on, or was reluctant to discuss.

The sounds of Vilazian boots again echoed outside the dungeon entrance. The soldiers were returning. The female vilemaster, Vashti, was with them this time. Civato watched helplessly as they again marched down the hall and opened their cell door. Galager tried to squirm closer to the wall behind him, but the short chain securing him to the floor kept him where he was.

Vashti swept into the cell after the iron door swung open. Her men followed closely as her gown swished over the dirty stones of the floor. She stopped in front of the boy and crossed her arms. Her left hand was clenched into a fist with a neck chain dangling from between those same fingers. She obviously had a ruby clamped inside those straining digits, traces of an aura easily visible in this dark space.

"You are Galager Swift?" she stated as she peered down at the sad figure on the floor.

"That's right," the boy responded. "Who the hell are you?"

Civato cast a short smile toward Uri.

Vashti revealed her necklace for Galager to see—a glob of eludria affixed to its end. "It doesn't matter who I am, except that the moment I feel you aren't useful to me anymore, I may decide to kill you." She dropped her arms to her sides.

"Well," said Galager with a hearty grin plastered across his face, "if you let me out of these chains, I'll teach you a lesson about how to properly treat your guests." One of the prisoners in an adjacent cell guffawed lightly at the comment.

Vashti laughed. "You? I rather doubt it." Her entire form suddenly turned red with aura and a bolt of crimson light swallowed Galager for a brief instant. The boy jerked and yelped in pain, but the magic was already gone.

"No need for that," said Civato. He turned to the boy. "Don't you mouth off anymore. She *will* hurt you. Do you understand?"

Galager nodded, but his expression was still one of defiance.

Vashti smiled. "Let's start over, shall we?"

"What do you want?" asked Civato.

"Information." Vashti pointed at Galager. "From him."

"He will answer truthfully," said Civato. "There's nothing he knows that can help you anyway. He's just a boy."

Vashti angled her cold gaze toward Civato. "Then you are ignorant of who he is and of his value to me." She immediately returned her gaze to Galager. "Tell me about your golden aura."

The boy looked perplexed. "Golden aura?" he asked.

Another bolt of red magic briefly swallowed him, and again he yelped.

"I don't know what you're talking about. Really, I don't."

Vashti lifted her arm for another jolt, but Civato intervened. "Give him a chance! He doesn't understand what's happening here." Her arm dropped.

"Very well," she calmly said, her eyes still locked on the boy. "Here's what will happen, young man. I will ask you questions, and you will carefully gather your thoughts each time and answer truthfully. If I don't like your answers, well—"

"Okay, okay, lady," replied Galager. "No need for your magic."

"Your gold aura. Why did Lazlo see you with one?"

"I don't remember any gold aura. I don't even remember the battle."

"You don't remember the battle?"

"No," Galager responded urgently. "Master Vreman—he's the eludrian who replaced Arthor Hadron—lathed me a day or two before the battle began. I've been out ever since. I never even saw the battle and didn't learn of its outcome until I awoke a short time ago."

Vashti seemed confused. "*Lathed* you?"

"I know of the magic he speaks," said Civato. "I don't know your word for it, my Lady. It's a kind of magic that resembles a nimbus in appearance, but is designed to punish another with magic fire without leaving any physical marks, much like you just did to the boy."

"Ah, thank you, Warden."

Again to Galager. "Why would this . . . Master Vreman . . . do that to you when a battle is imminent?"

"Punishment," the boy immediately answered.

"Punishment? What did you do?"

He hesitated.

"What did you do?"

Again, Galager hesitated. Without warning, another bolt of red fire briefly consumed him.

Galager screamed, then mumbled some unintelligible words.

"I didn't understand that. What did you do?" demanded Vashti. "Quickly!" she yelled.

"I killed Roln," hissed Galager. "My friend. I killed him. It was an accident. I didn't mean to. I left my eludria where he could find it, and he infused it. They had to kill him after he transfigured. It was my fault."

Vashti looked frustrated. She placed fists on her waste. "This isn't helping." She paused a few moments. "Lazlo told me someone hurt Haem with magic. He thinks it was you."

"That actually happened?" he asked. "I thought it was a dream." The boy's eyes scanned his thighs, searching for answers. But he still came up short.

"And the gatehouse?" said Vashti. "You don't remember walking up to its roof? Those ogres you killed? The vrecht? The explosion?"

"Maybe . . . bits and pieces. Fragments, images, from a dream, or so I thought. I think I saw some kind of monster attacking Ada and Master Vreman, but that's the last thing I remember."

Vashti extended her arm out. Civato thought she was going to incinerate the poor kid. But she dropped her arm back down to her side. She suddenly turned and moved toward the exit.

"Because you refuse me," she said, "I'm going to kill that girl."

"No!" cried Galager, fighting against his chains. "I swear what I told you is the truth."

Vashti acted as if she hadn't heard him, and she and her goons departed the cell.

"Touch her and I'll kill you," screamed Galager as the heavy door slammed shut. "I'll kill every last Vilazian in the world."

Vashti abruptly stopped in the hallway outside and peered between the iron bars toward the boy. "I believe you think you could," she whispered, and then left.

Galager turned to Civato. "I've got to get out of here," he shrieked. "Ada's in danger."

"Calm down," stated Civato as Galager grabbed the chains in his fists and resumed heaving against the iron floor loop. "Calm down."

"What do you mean, calm down! She's gonna kill Ada."

"No, she isn't," replied Civato. "At least not now. I think she believes you."

Galager caught his breath and ceased pulling on his chains. "Are you sure?"

"Yes, my friend. I am sure."

It was evident even to Civato that the boy couldn't answer her questions in any detail. Whatever had happened after he had been lathed, he clearly couldn't remember it. But if Vashti had left frustrated and without any information valuable to her, Civato now knew that some kind of mystery was indeed playing out here. Vashti had accused Galager of being able to conjure gold magic. And what the hell was that? As far as he knew, gold magic didn't exist. And if it did, and this boy could wield it, then perhaps he and his men had reason to hope after all.

26

The tracker pointed over the lip of the long crack. "This way," he said.

Gainhu peered into the darkened spaces below. His eyes followed a narrow ledge leading downward. Form up here he couldn't see where it led. The crack was deep, perhaps hundreds of feet, or more. No telling what was down there unless they went in.

The tracker's finger aimed closer. "They descended this ledge."

"How can you tell?" asked Gainhu.

"I followed it down. This narrow ledge leads half way into the crack and then goes east. Parts of the fissure collapsed long ago. The largest pieces of fallen and shattered rock have plugged the fissure after that point. There is lots of gravel caught on the surfaces of the fragmented rock. Some of it has been disturbed where their army passed over it. This ledge is the only way down."

"What else?"

"I returned to inform you of their path. I didn't yet follow it very far."

"Could this be a trap? Could their army have gone somewhere else?"

The tracker shrugged. "They came this way. I am sure. Traps? Perhaps."

Gainhu shuddered at the thought of Lazlo returning and having to report to him that no progress had been made in locating the enemy. The Vilazian wouldn't be happy this time just knowing where they had been. Without hesitation he stepped over the ledge and dropped a few feet to stand on the descending path of stone.

"Wait here!" he loudly ordered his men gathered along the long fissure. As to the tracker, he demanded he follow.

He moved carefully along the stone ledge, the tracker immediately behind him. It was only three feet wide at first. He wondered, could an army safely go this way? A fall from here would be fatal. He followed the ledge for several minutes as it slowly descended, the walls of the fissure rising above him. As his man had said, the ledge eventually leveled off and then widened considerably as it disappeared under a titanic pile of rubble that had broken loose from the side walls and gotten jammed between the walls of the fissure. The only way forward now was over boulders and rocks of all sizes and shapes that formed a tenuous path leading over the fissure. As he stepped off the ledge and onto the first boulder, he knew if these rocks plugging the gap shifted and fell further into the long crack, so too would anyone standing on them.

Gainhu leapt onto another of the nearby boulders. It held. He stepped onto another. Again, it held—not even the tiniest of movements. At that point he gave up all caution and jumped from one rock to another, heading east through the fissure that towered over him now. He went on this way for many minutes while scanning the rock formations for some sign of where the enemy had gone to.

He heard his name being called from behind. It sounded urgent. He retraced his steps and found the tracker standing near a pile of horse-sized boulders heaped upon one another and laying against the south side of the fissure wall.

"Have you found something?" But the moment he completed his question, Gainhu caught the scent of something familiar—faint, almost non-existent.

The tracker smiled.

"Torches!" Gainhu gasped in astonishment, sniffing the air for more traces of burning wood and pine resin. "But from where?"

The tracker beckoned him around the pile of boulders and pointed down at a triangular slit of blackness hidden behind the largest of the rocks, a two-foot-wide opening about the height of a man.

"A cavern!" whispered Gainhu, returning the tracker's broad smile. If one weren't standing directly in front of the entrance, it would be virtually impossible to see. Gainhu poked his head into the slit and sniffed. No doubt about it, he could detect the faint scent of burning torches emanating from the opening.

"They forgot about the smell of their torches," said the tracker. "Without it, I'd have never found this cavern."

Gainhu's mind began whirring. *Where are they* going? *Just hiding?* If so, they had miscalculated, and they would die inside this mountain. *Or is there another way out from this place? Yes, of course!* They intended to escape through his cavern and exit somewhere else. That had to be it.

Gainhu frowned inwardly. He wondered if his wisest course now was to circumvent these caverns and these mountains and try to pick up enemy tracks elsewhere at the place where they exited this cavern. *No! Impossible!* Not with an impatient wizard putting constant pressure on him for fast results measured in blood. There was only one way he could satisfy his Vilazian master and himself survive this expedition. He had to go after the enemy—into the caverns. But that meant he had another problem to deal with.

We need torches!

"Stay here," ordered Gainhu. "I'll send some men here to block their way out—in case they foolishly reverse course."

"What are you planning?"

"We're going in after them."

"But the darkness."

"I have a solution, though it may delay us a few hours as we get things ready."

Gainhu returned the way he came. Upon reaching the flat shelf of granite above, he immediately sent a party of warriors into the fissure, telling its members to look for the tracker and to kill anything coming out of the cavern. He posted another two parties at the rim of the fissure to ensure his men below wouldn't be accosted from enemy units hidden elsewhere, though he doubted that would occur. Finally, he ordered half his remaining men to follow him back down toward that canyon where they had last fought the vangards. They had to return to the pine forest they had passed on the way up here.

Thirty minutes later he and his men had descended the switch-backs and were again surrounded by pine trees. He quickly explained what he wanted done, and his warriors—no strangers to this kind of task—quickly got to work. They dispersed at once, looking for the materials they needed to construct an adequate supply of torches.

First, they'd collect several hundred amply-sized conks—growths of durable fungi that clung to the bottom sections of pine trees. They'd have to use their knives to cut or pry them from the bark, choosing only the largest of the conks, half-spherical in shape about three inches thick, and eight to ten inches in diameter. Conks were living things, full of moisture, and held a flame for several hours. They could be reused several times before having to be discarded. But they were often hard to find, and indeed, it took over an hour before they had a good supply of them.

The next step—making handles—was easier. They had no difficulty finding short branches that were suitable to this purpose. Gainhu's men either cut them from trees or found them on the ground. Each handle, after being trimmed of unwanted outgrowths and cut to length, was about two feet long and had a forked end with short branches that they then sharpened and stuck into the sides of the conks, which they had hollowed out. The final step entailed cutting thin strips of pine resin from the trees and enfolding and packing them firmly into the hollowed-out conk bowls. Once lit, a single torch could burn for almost an hour and would be held horizontally at waist level. A knife blade stuck into the handle halfway down its length served as a grip to prevent the heavy conks at the far end from rotating the handles upside down and dumping flaming pine resin onto the ground.

It was nearly sunset when he and his men returned to the cavern entrance with several hundred conk torches and a good supply of pine-resin protectively encapsulated between wide shavings of pine bark to serve as torch refills.

Gainhu was the first man into the cavern despite the risk of being shot by an enemy archer as he stepped into the darkness. He was never afraid of doing the things he ordered his men to do. He held the sputtering and smoking torch before him at waist level as he carefully squeezed between the two rock faces forming the triangular opening. He popped into a larger space, its extents barely visible in the dim torchlight. Further ahead he saw only blackness; the way forward. He was thankful the enemy hadn't ambushed him.

He leaned toward the light raying in from the opening.

"Let's go!" he yelled to his men waiting outside.

They had some time to make up.

27

Ada judged it to be midnight when Ficx and two other soldiers came for her, dragged her out of bed, and brought her to the rooftop observatory of the mausoleum. She quickly estimated the square, open-air rooftop to be about fifty or sixty feet across on each side. At three of the roof's corners, a substantial rectangular turret rose above her, each capped by a four-sided gold-leaf pyramid thrusting toward the heavens like tall spires on a chapel. The architects had rotated the square turrets by an eighth of a turn from the main footprint of the building so that anyone exiting the stairway portal would be aimed straight toward the center of the roof.

She exited from the middle of the three remaining turrets.

Where the fourth turret should have been, opposite from her, was nothing at all. Instead, it had been torn away along with a sizeable part of the rooftop. No doubt, this damage had been done during the apocalypse. There were other visible sources of damage up here too —parts of parapets missing, sections of the turret coverings carried away by winds or fallen inward, and cracks in the marble that webbed out from the place where the missing turret once had stood.

A gigantic block of white marble sat at the center of the observatory, just ahead. Its long side faced her. It was an altar, rectangular in shape, perfectly flat on its upper surface, but exquisite because of the marble itself and the chiseled adornments covering every square inch of its sides. It sat diagonally in the center of the roof.

The rooftop was brightly lit by torches ensconced upon the turret walls and the ramparts, and by several flaming braziers a short distance behind the altar. No doubt the mausoleum's illuminated crown was visible across many leagues on this clear night.

The moon was high at this hour, nearly full and round. Another sinking feeling in her gut told Ada this celestial body was part of the reason they were here. In her brief career as an eludrian, only weeks in the making, she had already learned coincidence was rarely involved when the full moon was out.

The two soldiers who had brusquely led her here dragged her to the right, across one side of the observatory and forced her onto her knees at the center of the nearest rampart. They then posted themselves at her sides. Ficx stood behind her.

She soon heard sounds emitting from the stairway turret, the same one she had used. She noted a red and black Vilazian standard hanging limply from a long black pole affixed to the peak of that same turret. It riled her gut to see a foreign flag on Commonland soil, especially in this sacred city and on this fabled building.

The noises grew louder and then three men spouted forth from the portal—one Bethurian warden enfeebled by days without sustenance or warmth, and a Vilazian soldier at either side of the struggling man. A few steps behind came three more men, again a warden and two armed escorts. And then more men, and by the time the tail of the procession had made its way onto the rooftop, a dozen Bethurian and Commonland prisoners had been chained to iron loops, each one set into the stone floor so that they formed a circle about fifteen feet in diameter, with the altar anchoring the circle.

Nine more men welled out from the same stairway portal. Two Bethurians—Uri Hauer and Civato Jeregoth—and Galager! And their escorts.

Free of the portal, Civato suddenly grabbed the arms of his escorts, roared like a bear, and pulled mightily on their limbs as he took a long step backward, surprising all. The two men he held in his grip crashed together, one falling to the marble floor and the other struggling to remain on his feet. But by now there were dozens of Vilazian soldiers nearby, and a fist of them quickly attacked the rebellious Jeregoth and began punching and kicking him until he was bloodied and subdued. Afterward, they roughly pushed him to the end of the altar closest to Ada and secured him there to a hefty iron loop embedded within that side of the marble block. Uri, meanwhile, wounded and weak, and barely able to walk, had been dragged toward the front of the altar, while Galager was chained up at the far end of the large marble block, opposite Civato.

"Galager!" cried Ada, once the chaos had diminished. He was awake and looked hale. He had been staring at her since emerging from the stairway. For just a moment she felt all the pain bleed away as he aimed his amber eyes and a loving smile at her.

"Are you alright?" she asked desperately across the space. "Have they hurt you?"

"I'm okay," he said. He studied her closely as a wrist iron snapped shut.

He glanced toward the subdued Jeregoth. "Civato told me you visited us in the dungeon. He told me Lavalor has fallen. Is it true?"

Ada felt a tear stream across her cheek—she wasn't sure if it was from happiness at seeing Galager alive, or from sorrow at having to tell him their home of the last week or so had been overrun by the enemy.

She answered with a nod.

Why doesn't he use his magic? He doesn't need eludria.

"Panthertooth?" he asked. 'Twoheart?"

"I don't know. The explosion, it—"

"The explosion was real?"

He doesn't remember.

Ficx leaned over her shoulder and grabbed her hair, pulling her head back.

"Shut up," he said, whispering insidiously into her ear.

The Vilazians had chained Uri to the stone rooftop about a body length in the front of the altar, facing it. They'd used two chains, both attached to an iron loop set into the rooftop between Uri's feet. The other ends were secured to his wrists, one at each shackle. The poor man, obviously suffering from his injuries, could stand, and perhaps take a short step in any direction, but that was about it. Ada recalled the horrible day, just a few days earlier when Lazlo Urich transfigured the vangard, Fasar, into a monster. A shiver ran down her spine and she instantly suspected Uri—perhaps all of them—would soon meet a similar fate.

Laughter rose up from among the enemy soldiers. They were enjoying this.

Vashti's angry voice pierced the night. "Free her!" she yelled as the eludrian stepped onto the rooftop from the same turret portal from which everyone else had emerged.

The two soldiers at Ada's sides quickly obeyed, and unlocked her shackles. Afterward, they backed away from her.

Ada rose to her feet and rushed across the rooftop. She circled around the back of the altar, over to Galager. She rounded the big block of white marble and clumsily wrapped her arms around her friend's shoulders, who was unable to return the gesture because of his shackles. His chains were just long enough to enable him to stand straight.

"She's an eludrian," Ada whispered into his ear.

"I know," he said. "Why did she have you unlocked?"

"I remind her of her daughter—or something."

Galager smiled. "Well, there is a lot to like in you."

She ignored his witticism. "Listen to me. She won't let us live. She's playing with us." He didn't know how to respond.

She started to ask him why he wasn't using his magic. *You don't need eludria!* But Vashti had come too near to them and she might overhear her.

"Enough of this sad display," Vashti ordered.

She ordered Ada away from Galager, back toward Ficx and the two men abreast of him.

Only reluctantly did Ada let go of Galager and return there.

Vashti, meanwhile, had taken a position between the altar and Uri, facing him. The warden had already fallen to his knees because of exhaustion, though Ada hadn't noticed exactly when that had happened.

Vashti returned her gaze to Ada. "My dear child, if you do anything I don't agree with, I'll have Ficx return you to those chains. And that may not be the limits of my generosity. Do you understand?"

Ada didn't say anything.

"You are indeed a smart one. I hope you remember that in the coming moments."

"Don't hurt them," Ada pleaded. "Why are you doing this? You've won! You've destroyed Lavalor. Don't kill them. There's no need to kill anyone."

Vashti laughed. "My child, the invasion has only just begun. Lavalor was but a—" She waved a hand diffidently in the air. "—distraction. We didn't expect it to fall, much less so easily. There's much more work to do before your people succumb to the Vilazian Winds. And tonight will be just one more step toward that inevitable end."

Ada's heart sunk further, if that was possible.

Vashti scoffed. "Oh, don't worry. Your dear Galager will survive the night." She stared luridly toward Civato. "And this fine specimen of a Bethurian will also see the morning sunlight. I have special plans for him." She returned her attention to Galager. "You as well."

Vashti considered the magnificent moon. "It's time," she said.

On cue, twelve of the soldiers took up positions in front of the prisoners in the circle, one for each chained Bethurian or Commonlander. They withdrew eludria rubies from their pockets and gleaming knives from their belts. None of them were eludrians—no auras. Vashti dismissed the remaining soldiers—no longer of any use—and they filed back into the stairway and out of sight. Ficx said something to the two men still behind her, and they walked to the stairway and took up positions as guards on either side of the portal.

"Stand near the exit with the others," Vashti said to Ficx. "You'll be safe there."

"What of the girl?" he said from behind Ada.

"She's of no concern."

Ficx did as Vashti asked.

One of the Commonland prisoners began to weep. It was obvious what was about to happen to him and to the other prisoners. He looked pleadingly toward Ada and spoke to her.

"You're an eludrian, my Lady. Please stop her."

"She has no eludria," mumbled one of the other dejected Commonlanders. "She's as harmless as we are."

Ada wracked her mind for a way out of the coming tragedy. *Should I tell Galager to use his magic? If she hears me, she may kill him. Or kill me for lying about him earlier.*

"I'm sorry," replied Ada impotently as the man broke down.

"Get ahold of yourself," scolded another prisoner. "You ain't no coward."

The sobbing man reacted at once, lifted his head, and stood rigid and proud. "I ain't no coward," he confirmed. "Hell with you, Lady," he defiantly added as he spat toward Vashti, coming up short by a good distance.

Without warning, Vashti withdrew a knife and a ruby—in separate hands—pivoted on her heels, and slammed the short blade deep into Uri's right shoulder, causing both Uri and Civato to scream. She instantly pulled it back out.

She pressed the eludria into the open wound and pulled her hand back after the talisman had been assimilated into the Bethurian's bloodstream. Even from where she stood, Ada heard the low sizzle and saw the puff of smoke as eludria disappeared into Uri's wound.

Uri began to twitch. He ignored the blood spewing from his shoulder and fixed his gaze on his friend, Civato. Pain etched the wounded Bethurian's face, yet a smile dominated his features.

"My brother, it's as I dreamt." Uri's words were difficult, but clear.

"But I have also seen other things. Good things. Have faith, my friend."

Vashti struck his jaw with the blunt end of her knife to silence him and turned back to her men.

"Now!" she commanded.

Twelve blades arced down onto human shoulders. Just as many screams pierced the night. The blades were quickly withdrawn and a ruby pressed into each man's wound.

Horror and grief pulsed through Ada's head and heart. She took steps across the rooftop to rip Vashti's heart out. But her enemy sent a sheet of red magic toward her from her other ruby—the one she wore on her necklace. The magic instantly surrounded Ada from head to toe like a net, but it didn't inflict any pain or damage. It was merely a nimbus, intended to hold her where she stood. As hard as she tried, Ada could barely lift a finger.

Civato yelled as he struggled against his chains. "I shall avenge you, my brothers. All of you!"

By now, the twelve had eludria pulsing in their veins. They were doomed. Uri, too, as he began to convulse. His fists were knots of flesh and bone, his limbs were thrashing wildly, his eyes wide with pain, saliva streaming from his mouth and dripping from his chin, and urine dripping to the stone. The twelve began to react in a similar fashion. Vashti ordered all of her soldiers, except Ficx, to exit the roof. Satisfied they were gone, she called forth more magic. It rose above her, then mushroomed out before forming separate tentacles that throbbed with crimson hues. A separate tentacle of red energy reached out to Uri and each of the twelve and enveloped them. Vashti began chanting strange words that Ada couldn't understand. Held rigid by the magic—as Ada was by hers—the twelve went silent and ceased their movements, including Uri.

Vashti continued her outpourings, the extent of her wickedness evident even in the bestial sounds of her mysterious words. Something else began to occur. The forms of the twelve began to transfigure simultaneously. They turned dark and began to lose shape. The same was happening to Uri. Images of Haem returning to his dusty form back in Fane Tower stabbed Ada's memory. Here it was, happening again, to these countrymen and allies. The thirteen men —the twelve in the circle and Uri at their center—continued transfiguring. Within moments, their chains noisily rattled to the stone floor, and they became floating balls of black dust whence they stood. The dusts of the twelve then flowed upward along the lengths of the magic tentacles, following them toward Uri's location, where the dusts then combined into one black ball of swirling particulate.

Vashti released her magic. In a blink of an eye it vanished, leaving only Uri's ball of dust floating above the spot where he had been chained. A heartbeat passed, and nothing happened. Uri's dusts swiftly congealed and increased in density. A figure of some kind was taking shape. When it was done, Ada gasped. The form of a demon namril was on its knees where Uri Hauer once existed. Uri was gone, and so too any trace of the twelve.

Vashti turned to Ada. Almost as an afterthought the Vilazian then waved a hand toward her and dismissed her nimbus.

"What have you done?" Ada whispered, in complete shock at the horror she had just witnessed.

28

Katonkin Weir made fast work of the precipice. In no way could it compare to the deadly cliffs further north in Little Dog Gorge where each new finger and toe hold was but one mistake shy of certain death. He took some time to rest after cresting the cliff, laying on his back while thinking of Twoheart. She had been gravely injured during the Battle of Lavalor, but not before slaying Fasar, one of his vangards. The man had been transfigured by Lazlo Urich into some kind of monster that could kill with nothing but fear as a weapon.

But Twoheart was no match for a vilemaster, no one but another eludrian was. He guessed she must have also attacked Lazlo. She was protecting Galager and Ada. But that magic—she never had a chance. He wondered how she was faring now. Had she regained consciousness? Is she in pain?

Is she alive?

His heart ached with the desire to go to her. But without him, the teens would never see the Commonland again, assuming they were still alive. Sanguir had told him they were important somehow. He believed her. They had both transcended within days of one another, seventeen years since anyone else had done so. Curiously, that was also their age. He had grown fond of them, that was for damn sure. He'd never show it, of course, for that would weaken them.

Thinking of them caused energy to flow back into his limbs. He rolled over onto his side, rose to his feet, and began a moderate sprint southward along the eastern side of the rift. The thick forest to his left threatened with its darkness, but it dared not encroach too closely to the gorge. The rocks here weren't proper perches for their tentative, searching roots.

Weir bounded from boulder to boulder, veering closer to the forest whenever he encountered a smaller defile or ravine shooting into the main gorge. After an hour, he began sweating, but he wasn't breathing very hard yet.

The smaller ravines increased in frequency after another thirty minutes, and it was then he made his way into the black and green tree line and put some distance between himself and the dangerous and unpredictable confines of the Lavalor River. He listened for threats as he ran. Ogres were his main concern. They normally infested the woods of these areas, so he constantly wondered where they were. He was starting to think they had been called elsewhere, perhaps to be used as pawns in Zaviel's and Lazlo's greater invasion plans. No doubt there'd be other attacks along the Sunder Line soon, and it concerned him he wouldn't be there to help. Nonetheless, he had come to believe Galager and Ada were too important not to be rescued.

Two hours later his chest began to rise and fall in rapid synchronization with his surging arms and legs. His lungs sucked in copious amounts of air with each step and screamed at him to stop running. Desperate not to even slow, he closed his eyes as he ran, and tried clearing his thoughts.

Silence! Tranquility! Awareness! Breathe!

He continued forward urgently. Eyes still closed. Dodging trees, veering toward less dense foliage when he sensed it. Listening for birds and other sounds. Hearing faint echoes, always seeking those vectors devoid of audible reflections. He could sense the blade of a sword as it threatened, so anything else was child's play. Deprived of sight, his concentrations allowed him to better channel his energies into his legs. His arms then began to slow their piston-like churnings, and even his breathing slowed as he maintained his torturous pace, but with longer, smoother strides.

He had no idea how long he had been running blind when something struck him across the forehead. It slapped him down onto his back like an ogre's fist. The air in his lungs exploded out of his throat as his back slammed into the forest floor beneath a low, meandering limb he hadn't sensed. His eyes finally open again, Weir gripped his head in both hands and fought back an impulse to scream in agony. If ogres were near, they'd hear that.

Awareness again flooded into him through all his senses, and among the horrible and painful things they were telling him was that fire was pulsing in his limbs and chest, especially his lungs. He could barely contain himself now, as he repeatedly gulped down huge amounts of air into his hungry mouth. His body needed air—lots of it!

For what seemed like an eternity he lay there, drawing in air from out of the damp forest surroundings, resting his limbs, waiting for his heart to slow and the pain to dissipate. He wanted to get back up and run. But he couldn't just yet. If an ogre attacked him now, he'd be helpless to defend himself. *Hell, if a rabbit attacked me now, I'd be finished!*

He laughed. It made him think of Twoheart again—about that day he was instead running to save her from those rock wolves. If he could turn back time, that's where he would go.

~

He remembered, first, the distant howls, then the throng of bestial growling as he got nearer. He finally came upon the scene of a battle between several dozen wolves and the woman. Trying to escape her pursuers, she had run into a draw. *What's she doing out here?* She had obviously hoped to climb her way to safety and at the same time use the narrow confines of the draw to keep herself from being surrounded by the bloodthirsty beasts.

But luck was not with her, as the draw had come to a dead end against a series of daunting rock shelves stacked atop each other, impossible to climb while beasts yet tried to rip her legs from her body. The woman—an Atikan who looked to be about the same age as himself—was trapped against these barriers of jagged rock, but she had managed to get to a bit of high ground, if three feet was considered high.

As Weir approached, she repeatedly swung her sword at every snout and set of teeth that dared to try to tear at her. Having no other plan, he picked up speed, hoisted his spear, and threw it as he neared the yapping pack. One wolf went down, the long wooden shaft protruding through its shoulder and then sticking straight up like a flag pole in the writhing creature. Weir howled as he breached the perimeter of growling animals and ran straight through them toward the woman, who seemed as stunned by his sudden appearance as these wild animals were.

One wolf reacted more quickly than the others and leapt at him as he passed through the middle of the shocked group, but Weir sidestepped it and caught the huge animal by one of its ears and its neck and threw the beast behind him as he continued forward. His new path took him near to the spear he had thrown. He grabbed it and pulled it free from its quivering victim as he ran past it without losing a step. Then one huge leap, and he was standing aside the woman, and the pack was again readying for another attack, only now there were two meals in its sights.

Weir and the woman didn't say anything or even acknowledge each other. They didn't have time, for the rock wolves had decided enough was enough, and they attacked as a pack. With fangs flashing just inches away from his legs and his belly, Weir continually thrust his spear into the seething sea of gray fur and heard yelps of pain each time the spear found its mark. The woman was doing the same thing with her sword.

One of the huge beasts battered its way onto the same rock shelf they were standing on and then clamped down on the woman's sword arm. She screamed as she tried to fight loose from the creature. Weir turned to help her, but two more wolves leapt up at his back. Weir dropped his spear and fell because of the combined impacts of both wolves slamming into him from behind. He was going to die just a day before becoming a man.

But another roar filled the draw. Deeper, more resonant—a ripping sound full of death. Weir twisted around, trying to fight off the two wolves that continued aiming for his throat. He caught a glimpse of black fur and long white claws streaking toward them from above the rock shelves behind them.

Panther!

One of the wolves shrieked in pain and terror as the panther lifted it in two rows of dagger-like teeth and nearly rent it in two in a single bite, causing wolf blood to splash over Weir. The other two wolves attacking Weir and the woman, seeing a new enemy in their midst, abruptly turned tail and ran back to the safety of the pack.

The big cat hopped from the ledge and landed on all fours just feet away, interposing itself in front of the retreating wolf pack. It roared once more, and leapt again, directly into the teeming pack, easily crossing the fifteen-foot gap in one bound. Two more wolves died as the cat slashed the belly from one and then crushed the neck of another with its rapacious teeth.

Mystified by the welcome intervention of the panther, Weir returned his focus to the woman. She was trying to stem the bleeding from her right arm while keeping a wary eye on the animals.

The battle below them raged. The panther was twice the size of the biggest rock wolf, and it was also faster than any of them. Within seconds another wolf perished as the cat's furious claws and teeth became a whirlwind of white death.

But the remaining wolves now allowed their hunting instincts to guide them. They began to attack the big cat from different angles at the same time. When the panther turned to defend itself from one flank, the wolves behind it would then lunge in and nip at its flanks with their own deadly fangs, leaving bloody gashes in the black fur. It didn't require a lot of smarts to know where this was headed. The wolves were going to use patience and their superior numbers to kill this beautiful creature—and then him and the woman.

Weir snatched up the woman's sword and dove into the fray. He drove through the startled animals yet again, heading straight for the rear end of the panther. A wolf immediately succumbed to his savage blade as it split its spine in two. The cat turned on Weir, but seemed to realize he was there to help and resumed attacking the rock wolves.

Another wolf lunged in to try for Weir's sword arm. Knowing these bites were poisonous, Weir desperately pulled his arm away from the snapping jaws before they could connect. He punched out with his other arm, landing his fist squarely on the wolf's ear, causing it to stumble and ending the immediate threat of a poisonous bite. But seeing their chance, two more wolves jumped in, and Weir wasn't ready for them.

A spear wielded by the woman suddenly impaled one of the two wolves about to chomp down onto his exposed stomach, killing it instantly. At that same moment, the neck of the other wolf disappeared into the maw of the panther. It fell to the ground mortally wounded. Weir had but a moment to think things were finally going their way when at least six wolves leapt onto the exposed back of the panther, driving it to the earth. Weir's heart sank as he heard the proud beast screaming in pain. The fight had become a frenzy of wolf teeth, and he knew there'd be no escape for the panther now.

With but a moment to breathe, Weir and the woman regrouped, and quickly returned to their narrow shelf of rock as they watched the panther die in the dirt with at least a dozen of the huge growling animals with their fangs latched deeply into black fur. The sight of that beautiful animal perishing affected Weir. He decided to go back in and fight its killers. He took a step toward the seething battle, although now it was more an execution than a fight. The woman hooked a hand over his shoulder, stopping him. She shook her head solemnly.

"We climb," she whispered between pants, their first words.

The wolves must have heard her. The gray creatures collectively lifted their bloody snouts and pointed them toward the two Atikans. Weir crouched as the pack slowly drew nearer, the woman following his example.

Another roar from behind them caused Weir to flinch. A second panther jumped over them and landed in the gap in front of the remaining wolves. If the first panther was huge, this one was a giant, easily outweighing the first by half as much. Weir surmised it had heard this battle from some distance and had been running to get here. Now he understood why the first panther had attacked the wolves. It was protecting its family, no doubt concealed above somewhere in these rocks. The wolves had intruded on their territory and the panthers had instinctively defended it.

This time the wolves chose to flee. Wisely so, Weir believed. This second panther, a male whose back was as high as Weir's shoulders, was an indomitable creature that even a full pack would have difficulty with.

The panther glanced toward Weir and the woman, then sauntered over slowly and put its snout against the unmoving head of its female mate. It emitted a high-pitched wailing sound as the male nudged its deceased partner. It remained there for several minutes, wailing and nudging, waiting for a response that would never come. Finally, the male turned around and stared menacingly at the two humans.

"Slowly," said Weir, nodding toward the right. "Over there."

The woman took a tentative step in the indicated direction, then carefully dropped from the rock shelf and onto the dirt below. Weir followed her carefully and deliberately, trying not to appear as a threat to the giant panther. Once they were safely to the side of the narrow draw, the panther grabbed one of the dead wolves in its wide jaws and bounded up the rock shelves behind the spot where it had come from, disappearing in just a few seconds, probably to some nearby cave to see to its young.

~

Weir rubbed his eyes and wondered, *how many years ago, was that?* He peered through the moonlit sky as he clambered up a moderate slope of lush grass and intermittent rock near the canyon rim of Bone Canyon—so named because of its shape—on his right.

What hour is it? Midnight?

The canyon seemed like an endless void of blackness as it ran to the west and south. He had been running all day and night as he fixed his mind on old memories, using them to distract himself from the pain in his legs and the fire in his lungs. He had stopped from time to time—about once every hour—falling onto his back, heart thumping in his heaving chest, regaining energies, letting the agony drain from his limbs and body, before resuming his quest to find and rescue Galager and Ada. At times he'd run blind, for in that mindful state he could cover more distance more quickly—and less painfully—that way. Because of his earlier mishap with that confounded tree limb, however, he was more selective and careful when he did it. Last thing he needed was to run over the lip of Bone Canyon or into one of the many smaller ravines joining with it.

Hours earlier, around sunset, he had largely emerged from the thick forest that lined both sides of the Lavalor River and its imprisoning gorge. Now he was faced with a seemingly endless series of undulating hills, golden from the hot summer days, but shades of grey under this cool silver moon. Defined by that high hanging body, a crest of a long, ascending slope drew nearer with every laborious step he took. *Almost there!* And then finally he was at its summit.

His heart leaped with victory when he saw remnants of the old structure rising over him a short distance ahead. Lion Wall! Or at least a part of what was once the western end of Lion Wall. The apocalypse had ushered in the Age of Blood over six hundred years ago, and had brought down many parts of this wall, formed Bone Canyon and even Little Dog Gorge. The comet had changed the face of the land, brought eludria to this world—to the Fringe—which then attracted the Vilazians here. He didn't deign to understand why the gods did what they did, he was no philosopher, but he knew his part in it all—to kill as many of the Vilazian Multitude as Jhalaveral would allow.

He approached the jagged terminus of the Lion Wall. It appeared almost as a stairway because of the way this final section had fallen and crumbled when the world shook that day, all those centuries ago. The toppled bits had long since eroded into the earth or into nearby Bone Canyon, with centuries of natural processes covering most of them with dirt and vegetation. He climbed the weathered blocks, leaping from one to the other and using his hands to help propel him upward. In seconds he was atop the ten-foot-wide wall, thirty feet above the ground. He ceased moving and stood erect as he peered in a southerly direction toward Intiga, his first good view in that direction.

He had expected a landscape of shadow darkness, but instead—a light!

As if pulled by the mysterious emission, he went forward along the wall a short distance before his feet again lurched to a halt. His gaze fixed on the brilliant point. His heart pounded as he watched the spectacle with rapt attention. He wondered if he were imagining things. Was his mind playing tricks? What fool would create such an exhibition in these lands? It would no doubt draw too much unwanted attention—dangerous attention. As he rested and watched, and tried to understand what he was witnessing, the light changed from white to red.

Vilemaster!

Intiga!

The presence of light most likely meant Galager and Ada were there. Or so he hoped. He thought back to Galager's laving at the hands of Valter Vreman. Might this light be something similar? Perhaps he had just seen evidence of their demise—or torture. He also thought of other possibilities—Fasar, the vrecht.

Weir's body may have been exhausted, but his capacious heart was nowhere near to its limit of hope and confidence. He commanded his reluctant feet to resume moving forward along the top of Lion Wall. He was running again beneath the stars and that damned moon that seemed to know nothing else but to cause anguish and misery. He kept his eyes on that tiny red dot as it wavered in the distance, and a minute later it turned white again. A few minutes more, even the whiteness had disappeared. He came to another gap in the wall and quickly descended its ragged edge and dropped back to the earth on the southern side of the stonework. He figured he was halfway to Intiga now, with the hardest part of his two-day journey behind him. The Lion Wall—what was left of it—would now protect his left flank as it led him straight to the Commonland's ancient capital, in ruins now because of the Sword of Jhalaveral.

29

Daybreak didn't come soon enough for Lorgan. The night had helped them escape the Vilazian and his demon, but everyone was tired, hungry, and cold as the sun rose to start a brand new day. The moon hadn't helped the first half of the night, blocked as it was by the mountain Havless and his army were presumably hidden within. Their progress was slow on the treacherous slopes beneath Flattop. They made up some of the distance after the full moon finally reached its zenith, however, and they had long since emerged onto more gently rolling hills a few leagues north of the area where they would rejoin with Havless. Before them now were diminishing hills of golden grasses interspersed with pine and an occasional patch of birch and alder. On their right, the land rose sharply upward, back up to Flattop. Lorgan wondered what he'd do if he couldn't find Havless. He didn't like being away from the main force. Every man was needed in circumstances like this, and though he and his vangards and arrows had fought valiantly yesterday and had done their job to help the army escape, today was a different matter altogether. He felt as if he weren't carrying his own weight. For that reason, he kept his men running at the fastest possible pace the terrain underfoot allowed.

The land had just begun to level out before them when Lorgan caught sight of the gyre. Several of his warmates spotted it almost at the same instant and let out loud warnings. The creature came in from high up, and swooped down quickly to make contact with the earth about twenty yards ahead of the group.

"Ready arrows!" Lorgan shouted as his vangards made room for the twenty archers among them to form a line.

"This isn't good," said Brawk, at his left shoulder.

"Yeah, no kidding!" answered Lorgan as the dust transfigured into the forms of Lazlo Urich and Haem.

"Shoot those bastards!" hollered Lorgan the moment he figured there was something to shoot at.

A red nimbus flared up around both the vilemaster and his creature, causing all the arrows to fall harmlessly to the ground after colliding with the impenetrable wall of shimmering magic.

Lorgan could see Lazlo laughing at them from behind his red dome.

"Left n' right!" yelled Lorgan, not ready to give up just yet. "Arrows—fire when that nimbus falls or even flickers."

The vangards instinctively divided into two groups, about three or four fists in each, and charged around both sides of the kneeling archers.

"Jehlude Jhalaveral!" they all cried as they threw themselves toward the two enemy figures, avoiding the middle ground so as to keep the line of sight clear so those powerful Axton Longbows could do their work.

Halfway there, Lorgan let loose with his war axe, aiming it straight at Lazlo's chest. He hoped the vilemaster would make a mistake, perhaps strengthen his nimbus closer to the path of the axe—weakening it elsewhere—thereby opening up other avenues of attack for his warmates.

A dozen more war axes followed his in. But Lorgan's heart lurched when they all bounced to the ground, just as the arrows had. He wanted to retreat at this moment, send all his men running in different directions, away from these monsters. But already his unyielding vangards were surrounding the nimbus and trying to penetrate it with their longknives.

Lorgan saw an axe down in the grass and picked it up. He glanced back at the four fists of arrows under his command. Their bows useless, each man wore a look of horror on his face. They knew what was going to happen to every single one of them.

"Run!" screamed Lorgan in their direction, spittle flying halfway to their positions. "Get out of here!"

He paused just long enough to ensure they had indeed turned tail, and then he put everything he had into one last swing of the axe, aimed directly at the leering face of the man who had broken Lavalor. Once again, however, the axe failed to dent the Vilazian shield. It was like trying to knock down the Bear Wall with a carpenter's hammer.

Lazlo's nimbus expanded, steadily pushing the vangards away from both Haem and himself. The vangards fought against the red curtain, trying to stop or penetrate it, but Lorgan knew it futile. Without warning, it suddenly snapped smaller, releasing Haem from its protection but continuing to enshroud Lazlo.

Free of the magic, Haem lifted his immense sword and proceeded to attack the nearest of several vangards. Before Lorgan could react, a tendril of red magic looped out of an opening at the top of the nimbus and danced toward more of his men attacking from the right.

"Run!" yelled Lorgan. "Everyone run!"

But the magic had already wrapped itself around four of his friends, who were all dropping like dead flies.

Its first victims already on the grass, the magic then lashed out toward him like a gigantic bullwhip. Fire filled his insides the instant it touched his skin and he lost control of his arms and legs as he fell. He had never known such pain, such agony, as it ripped away his life and several more of others struggling nearby. Despite the suffering, what hurt him the most as he left this world was that he had led Lazlo straight to Havless and his army.

30

Vashti Dal'falkoz crossed her legs—mostly hidden under folds of her long silk gown—and aimed a smile toward Ada after sipping tea from a delicate white porcelain cup, its rim lined with gold bead. She placed the cup down onto a silver platter on the small table next to her chair, and then sighed happily after glancing at a simple wooden box behind the tray. Vashti and Ada sat together on opposite sides of the tea table in a tiny room with red and black tapestries covering the walls. For the second time since sitting, Vashti tugged slightly at a silver neck chain that disappeared into her bosom. It was a warning to Ada that her captor was in constant contact with eludria as it hung hidden beneath her garments. Any unwelcome moves by Ada, and she would instantly be hurt with vile-master magic. Vashti took another careful sip of hot tea. As far as this monster was concerned, everything was wonderful and the world was a blissful paradise just waiting to be enjoyed by anyone brave enough to seize it.

There was a day not so long ago when Ada might have sympathized with such a notion. How many days ago was that, she wondered. Two days? After discovering the depths of her fondness for Galager? Ten days? Before learning of Arthor Hadron's assassination and then watching Haem murder all those soldiers atop Fane Tower? A month ago? Before she betrayed her caring father by challenging his authority over her in front of the Lord Consulcior? Or perhaps the last day of her innocence was long ago, on that morning with her younger sibling, Jana, when they lay in each other's arms, basking in the glow of sisterly love like she had never felt before or since.

Why did I leave her? I could be with her now.

But she knew the answer almost immediately.

Eludria!

It had called to her all of her life. It was never a matter of *if* she'd transcend, but instead, *when.* All she had ever needed was the courage to do so—and the right time. Of course, she had often questioned this impulse within her, and even tried ignoring it. But swords were forged to thrust and cut, arrows made to shoot, and deep down inside she knew because of her earliest memories and thoughts that she'd one day become an eludrian.

She recalled the day when she first had the idea to attend the Megador Military Academy. Well, maybe *volunteer* was a better choice of words. After all, girls weren't allowed to train in those dusty blood buckets or head off to the Sunder Line to engage the enemy. Instead, their wombs were the secret weapon the Commonland used against the enduring Vilazian menace, and every fertile woman over the age of fifteen in each of the Five Realms was expected to push out as many babies as their bodies could bear. Only because of the privileges afforded her as the daughter of a nobleman had she been excused from that cursed requirement. Nonetheless, her idea seemed so brilliant at the time. Surely, by dedicating her energies and efforts to volunteering at the academy she'd fulfill that inner need to contribute to the war effort in a way other woman wouldn't be allowed to, and she'd obliterate the guilt she felt at benefitting from privileges most woman were denied.

In the end, it didn't work out that way. And in reality, being at the academy just made things worse. Every day she'd curse the cooking pots and brooms and mops she was armed with while watching all those young men beating the bloody hell out of each other, making themselves tough and dangerous. Her heart literally ached because all she wanted to do was to grab a wooden sword and jump in there with everyone else. And that ache grew every day—every month—until finally she could no longer fight it, or deny her purpose, or her destiny. One second she was helping the headmaster by writing letters of transfer for some upcoming graduates—men heading to the Sunder Line—and wishing like hell one of those documents could have her name on it, and the next second something inside her snapped, and a resoluteness flooded her mind and body and caused her to throw the quill across the room. She then marched into the headmaster's study, where he blissfully napped the afternoon away and she yelled at him to wake up. Oh, his surprise as she announced her intention to infuse eludria. He nearly fell out of his chair.

"But—but—" he stammered. "You're a girl!"

"I'm more than a girl," she yelled. "I'm an eludrian! I know I am. This is what I'm supposed to do, I know it! And I won't waste another day pretending I'm something different." She wasn't sure why she was yelling at the time, but attributed it to the need to ensure this—man!—would take her seriously.

The headmaster looked as if his heart was going to stop. "But—your father!" he then said. "He'll personally slay everyone here if I let you get anywhere near eludria!"

Another hour of arguing didn't change the headmaster's mind, so the next morning she returned to Vivona and took up the matter with a local Consulord who was a friend of her father's. Bad idea, as even he had no intention of arousing the wrath of the great Edward Halentine. What he did do, though, was warn her father of her desire to transcend. Then for the next week everyone she knew tried to talk some sense into her, most of all her father. Soon after, she managed to have a note secretly delivered to Calob Jaenks, Hamic of the Covern and Lord Consulcior, and finally, her wishes were granted after a private meeting with him and her parents. She left that meeting beaming, her father and mother, not so much.

Ada wondered why she was so different than other woman. Why

did she possess this inner drive to fight the enemy and help repulse them from her kingdom? Why couldn't she have just accepted her place as a woman? This was a man's world. A man's war. Nonetheless, she had to admit it made sense that women should, as a rule, bear children and that men should march off to do battle against the hated Vilazian Multitude. How else was it possible the Commonland could have resisted extinction these last few centuries had they not always done things this way?

There I go, thinking like a man again!

And now here she was, the prisoner of a vilemaster.

"I can find you some nice clothes," said Vashti after taking another sip of tea. The dark haired eludrian wrinkled her nose in disgust. "I'll have those sad garments you're currently wearing burned."

"I'm fine like this," replied Ada. "It's who I am. How can you sit there sipping tea after everything you did last night? Doesn't all that killing bother you?"

Vashti's eyes narrowed. "Circumstances sometimes require us to make hard choices. We do what we must, and go on living. If your people would simply learn their place and bow to their fate and the Vilazian Winds, this invasion wouldn't be necessary."

"And those demons?"

"They wouldn't be necessary either. But your people—they are so stubborn!"

"Why shouldn't we be? You're occupying our land and killing our people."

"Your land?" said Vashti. "Everything under the sun belongs to my people, including this pathetic corner of the world you call the Commonland."

Ada scoffed. "By what perverse reasoning have you come to that conclusion?"

"Because to the strongest go the spoils." Vashti sipped more tea. "Had we not deserved to be your Lord Masters, Ethelliphus would not have made us stronger than everyone else, or gifted us the—" Vashti abruptly ceased talking.

"The what?" asked Ada instantly, sensing a miscue by the Vilazian.

Vashti's eyebrows drew together, her lips compressed. She was obviously annoyed with herself for almost revealing something she hadn't intended to divulge. *But what?*

"What are you hiding?" teased Ada. "Does it matter now? Of what use could that information be to me now? How could I possibly benefit from it?" Ada chuckled, hoping it would help pry open the door to Vashti's guarded secrets.

She took the bait. "I believe your people called Cazlich's talisman a Bloodstone?"

"That's right," confirmed Ada.

"Some number of years ago we found another one, deep in the mines.

Ada felt her jaw must have hit her lap. No wonder there were demons in the world once again after all these years. It was the only possible explanation. Without any doubt at all, Ada knew Vashti was telling the truth.

"But . . . you didn't use such a talisman last night when transfiguring Uri into that demon."

Vashti chuckled. "The eludria I used was—how would you say it? —specially prepared long before last evening's events. It was previously saturated with the power of a Bloodstone."

"Where is it?" pondered Ada. "This so-called Bloodstone"

"So-called?"

"Sure," said Ada. Without thinking, she slid her ring from a finger on one hand to the same digit on the other hand. "Maybe you're lying to me about finding it. Trying to scare me."

Vashti waved dismissively at her and turned her gaze to the small box on the table and then turned it to the room's solitary window.

"As you yourself pointed out, why should I care if you believe me? It wasn't even my intention to let you know about this discovery. It's not often my tongue slips like this. Ada, my dear, you are indeed very clever, just like my Carleea. You both had—you have a way of disarming me." Vashti cocked her head in thought. "Very well," she started. "Lord Master Zaviel possesses the talisman."

"And where is he?" It was a question the defenders of Castle Lavalor often asked in the final days before the fateful battle.

"He is preparing for the main assault."

"Main assault?"

"Don't look so confused, dear. As I told you earlier, Lavalor was a diversion—to draw your forces away from Megador."

Ada wasn't sure she believed her. Megador was the most fortified place on the Sunder Line. Why would they bet everything on attacking the Commonland's most well-defended location?

Vashti must have known what she was thinking. "Defeat Megador, defeat the Commonland," she said. "And with the Bloodstone, we now have the means to achieve our goals. What you encountered at Lavalor is but a taste of what we have in store for your people."

Vashti sipped some more tea. "Actually," she said, "your people have already had a previous taste of our new power."

Ada shook her head in confusion. "How so?"

"Several years ago," Vashti said. "At Lavalor. Zaviel knocked down one of your gates. He was still learning about the talisman, which he had inherited from his predecessor. The magic was more powerful than he could control. Had he not hurt himself during that attack, Lavalor would have fallen then."

"I don't know if I believe you," said Ada. Though she did. She remembered the day not so long ago when Weir had taken her and Galager to Cadia Gate. He had told them about an earlier attack there that had destroyed part of it. "Why did you wait so long before trying again?"

Vashti shrugged. "As I said, Zaviel was hurt. It took time for him to recover and to learn the proper use of the talisman."

"Why do your people need to control the world? Why can't you just leave everyone alone?"

"The gods demand it. The prophecies state one nation shall rise, and free all others from oppression and the squalor of their primitive ways, thereby saving all people of the world from the constant struggle of life. One nation, its people, good and righteous, shall be gifted with the strength to accomplish this task and will therefore save and protect all others." Vashti sipped delicately of her tea before resuming. "That nation is Vilazia."

"Did Carleea believe that?"

"She was young."

Ada cocked her head. "So, she doubted your prophecies?"

"She would've come around, in time. You young people have . . . distractions."

"What about your husband? Why isn't he here with you? In fact, why are you here at all, and not back in Azinor? Surely, this separation must be challenging for you?"

Vashti set her cup down. "Lord Master Zaviel is the reason I'm here. His plans to destroy the Commonland once and for all have met with approval by the Imperator. Zaviel demanded I come here, to summon a demon, which he deemed necessary to win this war. It is an exhausting task, to summon a demon. No person can do so twice in any short length of time. He needed help. He deemed I alone was capable—besides himself and Lazlo, and the Imperator, of course—of summoning such creatures. Ergo, I was sent here—against my wishes, I might add."

"And your husband?"

"Home, where he belongs. He is a senator, and he is needed in Azinor. The imperator avails himself of my husband's wisdom every day."

"But if that's the case, didn't he argue for you *not* to come here?" Ada could tell she was touching a sore spot. Vashti squirmed in her chair.

"Very astute—like my daughter." Vashti straightened her spine before continuing and flipped her long, dark hair behind the back of the chair. "My husband and Zaviel are . . . political rivals. My presence here is a kind of revenge for Zaviel being here himself. Zaviel didn't want to originally be assigned to these lands. He instead had designs on the throne, designs my husband discerned . . . and punished."

Ada took a guess. "You mean, your husband revealed Zaviel's

ambitions to the Imperator? And that, in turn, caused Zaviel to be exiled here? To end his dreams of leading Azinor?"

Vashti clapped her hands lightly. "You are brilliant. Well done."

"Not so much," Ada replied. "Still, I don't get it. Why would the Imperator send you here if Zaviel and your husband are enemies? Aren't you in danger from Zaviel because of what your husband did to him?"

"It's a long story," Vashti said. "One I shan't completely divulge to you. But as I said, I have the skills needed to summon a demon. No other eludrian outside of the Sundered Land does. When Zaviel was first exiled here, there was no way of knowing he'd end up with Lord Master Azaul Jembe's Bloodstone. It was a . . . a miscalculation on the Imperator's part. And now I've paid the price."

"I see," said Ada. "The Imperator fears Zaviel now. As does your husband. Zaviel demanded you be sent here as a kind of revenge. You have been—sacrificed. It's like godevil, only with three players, and they are in mid-game, each of them seeking a suitable ending."

Vashti scrunched her face in confusion. "Godevil?"

"A board game," answered Ada. "Not important."

Vashti nodded. "You mention the rifts between the players. It reminds me of my husband's final words before I left his side to come here, before I crossed the wide ocean." She glanced wistfully toward her lap. "My love for you shall cross the precipice," she whispered.

Vashti fell silent for a few seconds, apparently reflecting on regrets and lost love.

Ada leaned forward. "Will you return home? Will they let you?"

Vashti lifted her face from her lap. It had turned resolute again. "No more questions about Zaviel or his Bloodstone. Do you understand?"

Ada sat back into her chair and drummed fingers on a knee. "Alright, then—what about the demon? Why do you need a second demon namril? Isn't Haem enough to defeat the Commonland—if you are as strong as you say you are?"

Vashti picked up her cup and sipped. "Haem is the second demon namril we have summoned from the great pit, not the first"

Another depressing surprise. "Second?"

Vashti smiled from around the gold bead.

"The one you summoned last night is a third demon namril?"

"This summoning is not yet complete."

Ada struggled to get her mouth working again. With every revelation it seemed the future of the Commonland was growing dimmer and dimmer. "Does this third creature have a name?"

"I don't have that knowledge yet. After tonight I will."

Ada remembered Vashti's cryptic comments about having a special purpose for Civato and Galager. Could it be she was going to sacrifice them tonight as a means to complete the summoning? Just thinking of that possibility made her shudder.

Vashti leaned forward slightly. "Are you alright, dear? Your face just turned even more pale."

"I'm fine." *Be strong!*

Vashti glanced at the wooden box on the table. "Would you like to see what's inside this box?"

"You told me the Bloodstone was with Zaviel."

"No, child. This box contains something else."

"What?"

"Eludria."

Ada shrugged with indifference.

The vilemaster set her cup down again, twisted around, grabbed the closed box, and hefted it onto her lap. "This eludria has been specially prepared by Zaviel."

"With his Bloodstone?"

"Correct," said Vashti. "The Bethurian I transfigured last night is still there, trapped inside the shell of a namril. There's but a tenuous connection to the demon at this point. But after tonight, the demon will be fully snatched from the pit of fire and then the summoning will be complete."

"And Uri?"

"The Bethurian? Gone forever, after serving his purpose."

Ada had to struggle to control her anger. She wanted nothing more than to destroy this smug, evil bitch, but right now she had to take advantage of her willingness to share vital information. If she could just find a way to escape, it could be critical in repelling the invasion.

Vashti opened the lid of the box, untwisted a mass of red fabric exposed within and tilted the container toward Ada so she could see inside.

Daggers! Two of them, made of eludria.

Galager! Civato!

Ada again wanted to launch herself at Vashti and strangle her. But to do so would be suicide.

Silence, tranquility, awareness.

Quite suddenly an idea popped into her mind. A crazy one, but an idea, nonetheless.

Finally, a plan!

Vashti delicately caressed one of the knives with slender fingers. "Care to touch one?"

'I decline your offer."

"So be it," said Vashti as she stuffed the red cloth back into the box, snapped the lid shut, and put it back onto the table. "Now, young lady, I have an important matter to discuss with you."

Ada stuck a tongue into a cheek. *What now?*

Vashti returned her attention to Ada. "It concerns the boy."

"What about him?"

"He is special."

"I like to think so."

"That's not what I'm referring to."

"Then what?"

"Lazlo observed the boy with a golden aura. This is unheard of, but I'm sure you know that."

Ada was genuinely surprised. "Golden aura?"

Vashti smiled.

"When did he see that?"

"You don't know?"

"No."

"On the castle gatehouse, before the explosion. I'm told it was quite amazing, and unusual."

Ada scoffed. "Galager's auras are the same as any other eludrian's —red. We both only recently transcended. The explosion was caused by Master Vreman. He used the combined power from me, Galager, and himself, to create it. He is very gifted. It was the only way to defeat the monster that Lazlo created." Ada felt her heart race as she lied about who caused the explosion. Lies had a way of illuminating the truth, if they failed to hold up.

Vashti's face turned hard. "You deny the boy had a golden aura?"

Ada once more remembered the mysterious blue magic that had protected her from the explosion on Cadia Gate. *Was that an aura? Blue? Could it be true that Galager had a golden aura? Might that explain why he called forth magic without eludria? Can I? Does this explain our anomaly?*

"I—I was inside Master Vreman's nimbus," mumbled Ada, reasoning through her own internal questions rather than Vashti's. "I was helping to feed it. Everything looked red from in there. If Galager had a golden aura, I wouldn't have seen it."

Vashti was annoyed now. "What about prior to that time? Did he ever manifest a golden aura before then?"

"Not that I know of. And if he had, he would've told me."

Ada was just starting to think she'd come out ahead on this when Vashti upped the ante.

"My dear. You're lying. Quite understandably so, of course. But Lazlo saw the golden aura. I have no reason to doubt him, but I do have abundant cause to question your responses. The only reason you both are here—and still alive—is so I can try to understand how it's possible the boy raised such an aura." Vashti paused. "Heed my warning," she added. "You will tell me what I want to know, and I will not hurt the boy."

"Even if I had your answers," Ada said, "you'd kill us both the moment I revealed them to you."

Vashti shook her head. "Not at all," she said. "You tell me the truth and I'll see to it you and Galager will live a happy life together. I won't lie to you, though. Neither of you will ever again see the Commonland or touch eludria."

Ada suddenly remembered that this bitch still didn't know or suspect Galager could invoke magic without eludria. And she was determined to keep it that way. There was no other way out of this, except to stall, not to admit to anything, and hope for the best. And hope Galager could once again wield his magic despite his lack of eludria. *Why hasn't he done so already? Why haven't I?* Any mistake now might be fatal. These Vilazians clearly feared that she and Galager might be different, and she was certain that fear would get them killed once their enemy understood everything about them that there was to figure out. The only way to save each other, she knew, was to hide the truth about their magic and make it appear as if they were cooperating.

And hope Vashti makes a mistake.

"I'm not lying," Ada said. "He's—he's new to this. So am I." She remembered what Vreman did to him. "He was lathed!" she suddenly added, hoping that revelation might end these questions. "Maybe it affected him somehow. You don't need to hurt him. He's harmless to you. So am I."

They sat in silence for a moment before Vashti called loudly for Ficx. The entry door instantly snapped open and the big man walked into the room and stood behind Ada.

"Return her to her room. I have some things I have to see to." Vashti folded her arms. "I will see you tonight—when the time comes."

Ficx clamped a meaty hand on Ada's shoulder, compelling her to rise to her feet.

"You must believe me," Ada said. "He's harmless. You know that we have no eludria."

Vashti laughed. "Like I said, smart girl, you're not fooling me with this pretense of being stupid." Afterward, Vashti waved her hand, and Ficx dragged Ada from the room.

31

It had taken them all night to descend through the caverns—hours longer than Boson had anticipated. The limitless darkness and their unfamiliarity with the complex system of descending passages and irregular cavities had slowed them terribly. With each passing hour, more and more of their torches and oil lamps expired on the underground switchbacks, raising fears they'd all be expended before finding the exit at the bottom of the mountain. Several times they had taken wrong turns, finding the way forward impassable, blocked with underground cliffs, fissures, streams, other fantastical rock formations, or caverns that simply petered out before them like a flower crushed under a boot heel. Ever the constant worrier, Havless had stalked Boson the entire time, demanding reassurances there was indeed a way out of their bottomless abyss.

Daybreak began with several tiny glows high up in the caverns where cracks and portals admitted nascent sunlight into the empty black spaces that were otherwise barely illuminated by their torches and lamps. Those slivers and spots of light grew brighter with every passing minute, lifting everyone's spirits, giving hope to every man and woman that they'd actually escape this dire place. An hour before they found the exit—an oval cave opening within which thirty men could walk abreast—their last torch sputtered out. But by that time, the morning had intensified the sparse rays of light emitted into the cavern through overhead openings in the ceiling and walls. Thus, they had no problem finding a path out of Ethelliphus's demesne of darkness.

About the same time they found the exit, reports of enemy activity filtered down through the ranks from the vangards scouting the rearward approach. They could hear whisperings echoing downward, grunts as men fell, sounds of rocks falling as they were disturbed by intruders. No doubt the Bipaquans had found the cavern entrance at Flattop and had followed Havless and his men into the mountain. Making matters worse, they were close.

Boson imagined how an underground battle might be fought, but quickly decided the real threat lay in what would happen after they exited the caverns. Inside this mountain everything was too confined to allow a real battle to be conducted, and that meant there'd likely be no significant losses on either side as long as they remained underground. He tried to figure out a way to collapse the exit, thereby entrapping the Bipaquans and sealing their doom, but without an eludrian that just didn't seem possible. Instead, they'd have to depart the caves and make their run to Grassy Creek, several leagues east of their current location. And if the Bipaquans were as close to them as Bosun feared, no doubt they'd be able to outrun and catch them.

Havless didn't like the news.

"We won't make it to Grassy Creek?" he asked.

"Not until we face and defeat the Bipaquans following us. Because of our wounded, they'll outpace us and force a confrontation."

"Do you think Lazlo Urich is with them?"

"I do not," answered Boson. "Otherwise, he'd have attacked us by now. These caverns are nothing to him and his demon."

Havless glared at him then studied the massive arch of the cave exit.

"We lack magic," stated Quinton Collier, standing nearby, reading

Havless's mind. "It'll take hours of work to undermine this archway and seal this exit behind us. Hours we don't have."

Bosun could see the exhaustion in Collier's eyes. Even his white beard seemed tired.

"We could hold them off with our arrows while we worked," suggested Ledon Jule as he approached the trio.

Collier shook his head. "They'd know what we were doing. They'd charge us with everything they had and force a battle here." He pointed at the earth below his feet. "I doubt they could defeat us in these confined spaces, but with their higher ground they could force us back, out into the daylight, before we could collapse the exit."

"Solving nothing," added Boson. "We could array our men outside the exit," he countered, "thereby preventing the Bipaquans from exiting. But at some point, Lazlo would find us."

Arvil Sovron stepped out from some shadows. "How about we retreat back into the caverns. Not far. Keep them away from the exit as we worked to undermine it?"

"I don't like it," replied Collier. "How many of our men might be trapped inside this abyss with them?"

"I see your point," said Havless. "Not acceptable."

Boson agreed with that assessment. "We have to run for it," he said. "They'll catch us, but we can send a few of our vangards ahead to try to reach Grassy Creek to find Poole and guide him back. We'll need to send them without delay."

"Do it!" stated Havless.

Boson nodded sharply and turned toward the shadows behind him where hundreds of soldiers and warriors congregated, packed shoulder to shoulder, men eager to leave this miserable dungeon of despair.

"Eulin! Melrock!" shouted Boson. "Come forward!" He glanced back at Havless. "These two are quick on the heel. They can outrun any man in Lavalor."

"Panthertooth?" asked Havless.

"Well, maybe not him—or Twoheart. But all others? Yes!"

Two Atikan vangards broke through the crowd and emerged into the sunlight pouring through the archway.

"Aye," said one of them as they came to stand before Boson and the others. The second warrior merely crossed his arms.

"Do you remember my directions to Grassy Creek?" asked Boson.

Eulin glanced out the archway. "East," he said. "A few leagues, go south near those hills." He pointed in the distance.

"That's right," replied Boson. "You'll find a stand of birch hiding the way into a vale. Take it through the first row of low hills until you come across a stream running north to south. That'll be Grassy Creek. Head south. Keep running until you find Pennon Poole. He'll be waiting for you. Tell him to bring everything he has. Eludrians, too, if he has any."

The two vangards nodded.

"Go!" said Havless.

The two Atikans took off running and headed out into daylight like a pair of arrows shot through a window. "Jhalaveral be with you!" shouted Havless behind them.

The castellan turned back to Boson and the others. "Let's get this army moving."

No one needed anymore prompting.

"Aho!" hollered Collier to the remaining men waiting in the shadows. "Time to move!"

Boson exited the cavern and stepped to one side of the large opening and halted, out of the way of those soon to exit. He looked ahead as Eulin and Melrock disappeared into a thick line of pine trees. Sovron, Jule, and Havless took up positions on the opposite side of the cavern opening. Collier, meanwhile, had come to stand at Boson's side.

Men began pouring forth from the cavern in an orderly fashion. Most of those at the front were either wounded or were stretcher-bearers. They moved all too slowly as they proceeded in the direction in which Eulin and Melrock had just disappeared. Twoheart's stretcher came past. She had one arm draped over her face, a good sign. The procession was going so slowly that Boson wondered if they'd even manage to get everyone out before the Bipaquans caught up. But a few minutes later the last of the wounded had passed by and he felt a great weight lift from his shoulders. Things would go much faster now.

Next came the soldiers—spears, swords and arrows, unhurt and still fortified with courage. It was nevertheless easy to see the exhaustion in each familiar face. Everyone was hungry and thirsty as well.

As the men entered daylight, they instinctively formed up into braces and companies, then proceeded forward to begin their march to Grassy Creek. The vangards then appeared from the shadows, the last of Havless's energy-depleted army.

Boson and the others fell in behind the trailing units. He looked down at the grassy turf, trampled and torn by a thousand men marching in column, and then winced at the fact their path would be easily seen by the capable Bipaquan units soon to come. He wondered how many of the enemy had followed them here. There would be no eluding them now. A battle was coming, and coming soon, probably within an hour or so. It didn't seem likely that Poole and his spurs would return soon enough to aide in the outcome, and that meant Havless's units would have to find their own way to victory, or at the least, hold out until help arrived.

Forty-five minutes later they veered south, then soon afterward found the stand of birch he had mentioned to Eulin and Melrock. Boson—once again the last man—had just entered the line of birch when he heard whooping filtering up through the pines from behind.

They're close!

The Bipaquans knew where they were. No doubt their advance scouts had seen them. Only minutes remained now before the battle began.

Boson ran a few yards and closed with Havless and Collier. "They're here," he warned. "It's time to make a stand."

Havless's jaw dropped. "Here? Among these trees? Are you sure we can't make it into that vale you mentioned? The narrower confines would be to our advantage."

Boson shrugged. He wasn't sure of the best course of action. He hesitated.

Collier snapped his bow string, betraying his anxiety. "We can split up," he suggested, tentatively at first. "We'll deploy half our men here," he then said more confidently, "as a blocking force in the enemy path. The rest of our boys, the wounded included, will proceed into the vale. Once there—hopefully, at an advantageous location—they can form another blocking force. Our men here will do what it takes to repulse the first Bipaquan wave, then we'll withdraw to the vale and rejoin with our brothers."

Havless speared his eyes at Boson. "Will that give Eulin and Melrock enough time to find Poole and get him back here to help us?"

Boson scanned the ground beneath his feet, trying to calculate the minutes. "I—it's hard to say."

"Don't think so much," ordered Havless. "Spit it out."

"Doubtful," answered Boson. "We'll have to hold out at least for some time until they get here."

Havless rose on his tiptoes and fell back onto his heels. "How much time?"

"As much as we need," responded Collier, a hand gripping his beard.

"Brilliant," Havless said, scratching his chin. "Alright, alright. Your plan sounds feasible. I can't think of a better one."

"We need to act fast," said Boson. "We've just a few minutes."

A sharp nod from Havless was all it took to compel them into action.

Boson and Collier began issuing orders. Havless ran forward, issuing more instructions to his units further up. Like a mountain splitting in two, a thousand men broke in half. Six companies of warriors and soldiers swung around, forming a line ten deep and a hundred yards in length.

"Get low!" ordered Collier to the nearest of their warmates. His instructions rebounded in both directions through the long line, and men dropped upon a single knee, arrows and vangards in the front, swords and spears behind them. Boson took a kneeling position at the center of the line, just behind an arrow who fidgeted nervously with his quiver full of projectiles. The man already had an arrow nocked—he was ready to fire. Boson twisted around and watched as the other half of Havless's army disappeared toward the east, toward the vale that hopefully wasn't too far away.

Less than a minute later, the Bipaquans attacked. A company of enemy archers showed themselves first, fifty yards away.

"Fire at will!" cried Collier. "With accuracy!"

Both sides let loose nearly at the same time. Three braces of vangards then stepped forward, their axes on the ground nearby, Boson included, and they withdrew their longknives and lunged into the onslaught of shrieking arrows flying towards their friends at waist level.

Blades whirled, knocking away perhaps half of the incoming missiles, sending them into the air in all directions or thumping deeply into the ground near their feet. Two vangards and perhaps a dozen other warmates went down, wooden shafts protruding from their bodies. The remaining enemy arrows simply missed their targets.

Screams from both lines, men dying or severely hurt.

Boson again checked the enemy line, satisfied to see half their number writhing or unmoving on the forest floor.

More of the enemy began appearing.

Another set of screams pierced the dark forest from ahead. War cries!

"Here they come boys!" cried Collier. "How about we lay them to earth!"

"Jehlude Jhalaveral!" came the unified Commonland and Atikan response.

Boson tried to quickly estimate the numbers of men charging forward.

Too many to count!

Fifty more enemy went down from another salvo of Commonland arrows.

Then another fifty.

"Swords!" cried Collier as the surging Bipaquan front came within twenty yards.

Their task complete, the arrows among their numbers expertly pivoted around, and leapt to the rear, freeing up space for more swords as they then came rushing forward with their eager swords. A heartbeat later the two sides met, hundreds of blades crashing together and filling the forest with anguished cries of sharpened steel. Human screams began to replace the wailing shrieks of the weapons. Boson sunk the longknife in his right hand deep into the neck of one Bipaquan warrior, laying him to earth in a blink of an eye even as his second longknife slashed the throat of another wide-eyed Bipaquan, his blood gushing like the waterfalls around Havless Tower.

They fought this way for several minutes, the Bipaquans clearly getting the worst of things as Havless's men refused to yield ground or break trust with others in their ranks. For every man Havless lost, three Bipaquans fell. Boson noticed one of the Bipaquans in particular, and realized he had already encountered this man—one of their leaders and better fighters—back at that first skirmish on the stream. They locked eyes as Boson sent another of the enemy crumbling to his knees, a longknife clean through his throat.

The two met. That Bipaquan leader, and Boson. Neither hesitated as they leapt toward each other, the bottoms of their feet three feet over the ground as they collided.

Boson easily regained his balance as his feet touched down. The Bipaquan leader, though, fell face-first into the earth with one of Boson's longknives protruding from the dead man's back.

Boson bent low, turned the lifeless corpse around, and withdrew his weapon. He checked the line, saw that it was holding, and began fighting his way deeper into the Bipaquan forces. Four other vangards noticed his incursion and advanced with him, protecting his sides, each of them mowing down any Bipaquan warrior that dared approach.

The enemy had taken a severe beating up to this point. Suddenly, the enemy was in flight—every single one of them, heading back the way they had come. Boson sucked in chests full of air as men around him cheered. He and his vangards returned to their own line. He scanned the line and counted at least twenty warmates dead on the ground and another fifteen writhing where they lay, some severely wounded. At least a hundred of the enemy had met similar fates—those who were wounded on the ground were already being sent to the afterlife by grim-eyed vangards.

We have to move!

"Pull back!" yelled Boson. He checked for Collier to see if he had survived.

There he is.

"Help everyone still alive, boys. We need to move! Now!"

"What of our warmates?" asked one of the soldiers, pointing down at a lifeless friend with a Bipaquan arrow sticking from his chest.

"No time for that," answered Collier, having finally caught his breath.

"Look after the living," added Boson. "Move it!"

Boson watched as his warmates helped the wounded from the bloodied earth and then began withdrawing. In the meantime, the Bipaquans had completely disappeared, though no doubt they'd be returning fairly quickly.

With Collier, Boson, and other leaders constantly encouraging their units to make haste, the force was soon moving at a good clip through the trees. Boson kept checking behind him as they all ran. Each of the newly wounded were draped across the shoulders of two other men. Some of the more severely hurt would no doubt die as they were carried away, but they would die if they remained.

The force finally popped free of the birch and entered a narrow valley. Several hundred yards away he saw the rest of their army waiting for them.

That's where we all shall live or die.

32

Weir held out a hand. "Let me see your arm."

The girl waved a hand at him, then used it to gather her injured arm up to her chest. "It is nothing. I'll be fine." Blood welled from between her clasping fingers as she turned away from him.

The distant howl of a wolf caused them to glance at each other.

"Don't worry," she said. "They're moving away from us." Despite her injury and their near-death experience together back in that draw, her lips were curled in a manner that revealed both humor and defiance.

Only now did he indulge in how truly beautiful she was. Her long, dark hair glistened and shone and framed an oval face of perfect, taught skin the same color and approximate age as his. Brown eyes twinkled tantalizingly though they walked in the shadows of jakroot and pine. Weir sniffed the air, trying to catch her scent, but she was clean. He wondered why she didn't have a feather in her hair like all other Atikan women. Her deerskins were a different matter. They looked old and worn, as if she had been out in the wilderness for a while. She again turned away from him and walked briskly into the forest, her hips swaying gently as she moved.

"Wait—wait!" called Weir, stepping quickly to keep up with her. "Who are you?"

"I am Winkite," the girl said without facing him, still moving briskly toward some unknown destination.

"And I am Katonkin."

The girl didn't slow down. "You fought bravely, Katonkin."

"You also. Why are you out here alone?"

She grunted.

"Why don't I know you?" he asked.

She stopped, then slowly turned toward him with feet spread shoulder-length apart like a warrior's. Women were to stand with feet closer together, a sign of deference to their male counterparts. "Have you never heard of me?" she said. Her scenic face had a look of perplexity on it.

"Winkite?" he asked rhetorically, picking through his memory for that name. "Not that I can recall."

She seemed surprised. "Are you sure?"

Weir shrugged while slowly shaking his head. He again noted blood dripping from the arm she held against her chest. He quickly stepped toward her and reached for her arm. "You must let me see that. The bite of rock wolves can be fatal, if they poison your wound."

This time she didn't resist, and unfolded her limbs.

Weir took the injured appendage and turned it slightly to reveal more of the wound. "This may hurt," he said, then carefully pried apart the largest of the cuts. She didn't flinch even a bit, but his heart sank when he saw the bead of purple pus deep within the cut.

She must have noted his reaction. "I am poisoned," she stated rather dispassionately, almost as if she welcomed the news.

Weir let her take her arm back as he nodded sharply. Without hesitating he unsheathed his knife and went to work cutting strips of leather from the legs of his knee-length deerskins. Once he had several, he tied one tightly around the bicep of her injured arm and used two more to bind and protect her wounds.

"I will die," she said. A statement.

"No!" said Weir, manifesting confidence and certitude.

"Don't lie to me, warrior boy. I am Atikan and know the dangers of this Earth."

Weir put his hands on his hips. "I am a man. Not a boy. And I don't understand why you are a mystery to me. I know everyone in Atika—or have at least seen every face. Except yours."

She didn't respond.

"You must let me help you. You'll die otherwise."

Her eyes squinted. "What are you suggesting?"

"My father and mother can help you. They always keep a small amount of Falle Vaydal's waters for emergencies like this."

"Falle Vaydal?" she asked, as if she had never heard of that place.

"Valley of life" he answered. "That's where we get the healing water."

She shrugged. "Where do your parents live?"

"Bridgefoot."

Winkite wheeled around and plunged energetically through the forest once more. "Too far," she stated over a shoulder.

Weir burst into motion, came up beside her, and took hold of her good arm.

They halted, looking at each other's faces. "You'll die if you don't let me carry you home."

"Carry me?" she said. then laughed. "No man carries me." She tried to leave him again, but his grip held her fast.

She's strong! Weir was becoming impatient. "If you are so willing to die, why didn't you just throw yourself at those wolves?" She stopped struggling to escape his grip. "I don't know anything about you," he continued. "Or why you're living by yourself out here in the wild. But I do know you are a warrior."

He let go of her. She didn't run.

"You're not some young robin that fell out of its nest. You are a zephyr soaring through the blue heavens above Sojourner Falls." He smiled at her. "I know this of you, though we only just met."

"That's where I am going. The Falls."

"Why?"

"My passage," she said.

"Only men do that."

"So you say. But I am going anyway." She lifted both hands to her face, rubbing her eyes with her fingertips. "Bridgefoot—it's too far," she repeated.

"Tonight," he responded. "I can get you there tonight."

She lowered her hands, revealing softer, more vulnerable eyes. "I can run at your side. I am strong."

"If you run, the poison will kill you long before we arrive at Bridgefoot. I must carry you. That is the only way."

She looked to the clouds, thinking.

"But your passage," she said, dropping her gaze. "Do you deny that's why you are here? When are you due to return home?"

Weir exhaled deeply. "Tomorrow," he said.

She waved her hands. "Then no! I can't ask this of you. For you to return tonight would shame you. Your people—our people—would look down upon you if you prematurely end your passage into manhood. They will exile you, as I am exiled. You must complete your passage."

"Your life matters more to Jhalaveral than my passage. It is but a ritual. Your life matters more to me as well. This is my choice."

"Mine as well," Winkite responded defiantly, once again cradling her right arm closely.

Weir snorted. He paced back and forth a few feet as he considered a response. Then he had an idea, and he told her what he wanted to do—what he insisted he do. She immediately accepted with a curt smile. Without delay Weir picked her up into his arms and began running at full speed to the west—toward home. And it pleased him when she draped her arms around his head and shoulders.

33

Boson studied the Bipaquan forces as they emerged from the blood-soaked birch some three hundred yards away, near to the beginning of this squat valley Havless's army was plugging.

"There they are," said Sovron.

"How many you figure?" asked Havless after all units of the enemy army had fully stepped into the early sunlight.

"More than us," answered Quinton Collier. "By about four- or five-hundred, I'd say."

"Brilliant!" said Havless.

"I don't see that gyre," said Boson. "Anyone else spot it yet?"

Collier, next to him, peered forward. "If we're lucky, he isn't here. Otherwise, we're done."

"They stopped," observed Havless.

"Just organizing themselves," replied Collier. "They'll be coming in at any moment, Lazlo or not."

Havless jabbed a finger over a wall of his men toward the enemy. "Maybe we should attack them before they get organized?"

Even under his white beard, Collier looked dubious. "That's not what I'd recommend. Our position here is strong. They can't flank us here. Not with all these rocks on either side of us."

Boson again checked the rugged slopes at either side of their position. He had to agree with Collier. Anyone trying to outflank them here would be easy pickings for their arrows. Either the Bipaquans attacked them head-on, up this vale, or they withdrew to try to find a way around it.

But there was another reason to stand and fight. Judging by the skirmishes they'd already had with these warriors, Boson was sure his people enjoyed a tactical advantage. The Bipaquans fought more like unorganized, undisciplined tribal folk—brave and courageous, without a doubt—but often throwing themselves into action without a plan or even without coordination or formations. Unless the Bipaquans had access to magic, Boson was sure the enemy would come up short this day despite their superior numbers.

Yet, the big question was, *did they have magic?*

Boson turned around, checking the far extents of the vale they had plugged with muscle and steel. *No one. Where's Poole? And Lorgan?*

Boson's aim drifted closer. Two companies of reserve forces were arrayed at Havless's rear—one each of arrows and swords. Immediately in front of the reserves were the wounded, those incapable of fighting. Stretchers with their occupants were now laid flat on the golden grass just a handful of yards away. He returned his gaze to Havless's front and counted eight companies of gritty soldiers and warriors arrayed across the vale, one company deep, with Havless's remaining vangards—almost three braces of Atikan axe wielders—dispersed equally through the ranks. It pained Boson that Lavalor's vangard corps was now down to fewer than sixty men, about forty short of the original hundred-and-one, including Panthertooth. And, of course, the swords and arrows had taken huge losses as well.

"Gyre!" cried one of the vangards, an Atikan over on the left. He pointed over the stationary Bipaquan units. Boson peered forward and cursed when he saw the creature rising from the midst of the Bipaquan army. He turned around yet again to check for any sign of Poole. *None!* He swept his gaze back to the front and watched the gyre slowly drift to the front of the Bipaquan line.

"They're advancing again," whispered Havless, his voice affected with horror. The castellan was fully aware of how the odds had suddenly turned against them now that Lazlo was here.

Slowly and surely, they came. No charge. No war cries. No sound. Not yet!

"What do we do?" asked Havless nervously.

"We fight to the last man," answered Collier. "If need be."

"Hold your positions, boys!" yelled Boson, as much to quell the sense of doom growing in his own heart as he did to calm the nerves of others.

"I'll let you know when to fire," Collier loudly barked—instructions to their arrows, the companies on either end of the front line. "But if you get a shot at that vilemaster, don't bother to ask, just lay him to earth and we'll deal with his pet afterward."

One of the swords at the front line yelled, "Jehlude Jhalaveral!"

A chorus of a thousand courageous voices repeated his war cry.

Boson hefted his axe, adjusted his grip, and tested the balance.

In the meantime, the Bipaquans steadily crossed the distance between them with the gyre leading the way, just over their heads.

About a hundred yards separated the two armies when the enemy stopped.

Boson's heart beat furiously under his leather war vest. He closed his eyes, took a deep breath, and tried to calm his nerves. All of this running! And for what? To die in this miserable little valley? They didn't have a chance, not with Lazlo and Haem here.

"What are they waiting for?" came the voice of Arvil Sovron from the right.

Boson's eyes clicked open again. The Bipaquans hadn't yet resumed their silent march.

The gyre, too, had ceased its forward movements.

Hoof beats!

Boson whirled around, fixing his gaze at the far end of the vale.

"Poole!" he yelled, a sense of relief flooding through him all at once. "He's here!"

He searched the distant faces of Poole's spurs, desperate to spot just one eludrian. For without one, not even Poole's spurs could change the outcome of the coming battle.

"Bloody yes!" screamed Havless. "I'm going to kiss that man when this is all over."

"It ain't over yet," warned Collier.

The horses charged closer. Boson continued searching for signs of an eludrian in their numbers. *Hard to tell at this distance.*

But finally, he spotted an old man in a dark brown robe. He had no idea who this fellow was, but he had a tiny red aura around one hand that was waving madly in the air as his horse galloped toward them.

Poole shouted something, waving vigorously as he and his spurs approached. The Pennon Spur's words were indiscernible inside the thunder of the horses, but Boson instantly understood what he wanted.

"Make way," Bosun ordered everyone. "Let them through!"

"Divide up!" added Collier. "Hurry it along!"

Poole never stopped, and in seconds five hundred spurs had poured through Havless's hastily opened gap and interposed themselves between the two armies. Two hundred more units presumably from Jurry, pulled up behind Havless's reserve force to protect their rear.

There could be no denying the sense of joy and redemption that rippled through Havless's men as the gap again closed. It was like magic. Once again the tide of fate had flipped on its head in just seconds. If there was to be a fight today, it would be a fair fight after all.

"Dust!" came a warning from ahead.

Indeed, the creature was moving again, flying steadily toward them while rising. Boson checked the Bipaquans, but they remained where they were. His eyes flicked back to the dust. It was about fifty feet high now as it came forward. In seconds it was over their spurs —but oddly didn't seem aggressive and neither did it emit any magic.

Poole's voice shattered the silence. "Hold!" he ordered his men as the dust crossed overhead. “Hold!” he again stated, twisting in his saddle to watch Haem pass.

The creature stopped, almost directly over the area where Havless and Boson were standing, both ready to fight.

“Be gone, evil creature!” cried the brown-robed eludrian from a short distance away, still on his horse. The man held up a fist with a red aura flaring even more brightly than before. A warning.

"Be gone," he again shouted as a dozen axe-wielding vangards slipped closer to the old man to aid in his protection, if needed. "In the memory of Cazlich the Redeemer, I swear the first blood to be shed in this valley this day will be yours! Be gone demon!"

In response, several dozen small objects fell from out of the dust and thudded onto the ground all around them. The creature suddenly rose higher, and then veered with great speed back toward the Bipaquan army, still holding firm a hundred yards away.

Boson returned his eyes back to the objects the dust had dropped. *Heads!*

Then he recognized some of the faces. *Lorgan's men!*

He burst into motion and began shouldering his way forward through the ranks of soldiers and warriors. He wanted to attack the enemy single-handedly and kill Lazlo. But several vangards saw his intent, caught him, and refused to let him pass.

“Stand down!” shouted Havless. “Boson get back here! Control yourself!”

The words pierced his armor, and the faint reflection of Panther-tooth's voice caused him to remember his training.

Silence, tranquility, awareness.

Boson squashed the feelings of grief and sickness coursing through his abdomen. He remembered Fasar, the vrecht, and the grim fear and despair that demon had sent into him, a vivid memory, especially now, as he looked down at Brawk's severed head and his magic-reddened face—half in dirt, half looking forward in a grisly stare through empty time. All those men, vangards and arrows. Gone!

“They're leaving!” came another report from somewhere nearby.

Boson swiveled his hot gaze toward the enemy, and indeed, the backs of the Bipaquans were turned towards them now as they began to steadily withdraw.

Havless approached Boson and placed a hand on a shoulder. “You've done well for Lavalor. Weir would be proud.”

“They yet live," Boson complained. "On our land.”

“So do we,” whispered Havless. “And that’s a worthy victory, considering what has happened these past few days.”

Havless could tell Boson wasn’t satisfied. “We’ll regroup. And then we’re going back to retake our home from these vermin. They’ll be sorry they crossed the Sunder Line. Believe me, they’ll soon regret all of this.”

Boson watched the Bipaquans begin to vanish into the broad stand of birch trees blocking the valley entrance. He then glanced at the brown-robed eludrian. “Who is he?”

"Jasper Fallowthin,” said Havless. “He’s from Jurry. Long since retired. It’s been years since I’ve seen or heard of him. He had fallen ill—and old. I guess recent events compelled him to defy his own ailments and circumstances and help defend the Blue and Gold one last time.”

“Glad he did,” responded Boson.

“Aye,” whispered Havless.

They paused, considering each other.

Havless patted his shoulder once, then wheeled around. He paused again, glancing down at the bloodied heads of his vangards. Boson realized there weren’t enough heads here to account for the arrows, but he held out no hope for them.

“Get these heroes off the ground,” the castellan barked.

34

Finally. The old city. *Intiga!*

How many years has it been? Eight? Nine?

An exhausted Katonkin Weir crammed himself further into the juncture of two limbs at the top of a grand oak he had climbed. The ancient city, the old capital of the Commonland, hadn't changed much since the last time he was here. How could it? It was in ruins, and had been that way for more than half a millennium. It was probably an hour or so before midnight. The moon was full, and rising fast. It illuminated the broken structures not too far ahead and cast sharp-edged shadows everywhere. The massive city seemed to stretch forever ahead of him, and to either side. Most of the buildings here had collapsed when the comet struck the Greyridge Mountains near Orial, presumably bringing eludria to the world and laying waste to its historical trajectory forever. Piles of rubble dominated this former metropolis, heaped in long rows along ill-defined avenues overgrown by a jungle of vines and trees. Despite the magnitude of the tragedy caused by the Sword of Jhalaveral—a disaster that affected every corner of the Commonland, and possibly the world—a good number of broken towers and spires pointed skyward like stubby fingers, snapped and shorn. One tower, though, had almost fully escaped the wrath of the apocalypse—the mausoleum.

From his high perch at the edge of the forest he could see it out there, centered within the desolation of Intiga, a black silhouette near the jagged horizon. Dim, yellow points of light emanated from dozens of openings and windows within the tall structure. He searched the city for other lights—enemy campfires—but saw none. He desperately hoped he wouldn't have to fight his way into the tower. The element of surprise was to his advantage and he didn't want to lose it. If the vilemasters—who were almost certainly within the mausoleum—knew he was coming, his chances at successfully rescuing Ada and Galager would plummet rapidly. A tiny voice inside his head—one he had been working to crush—actually questioned whether it was even possible.

He thought of Twoheart, back at Lavalor. It pained him to not know what was happening to her—and to his other friends. It had been two days since Lavalor's fall, two days in which he had destroyed the boundaries of time and distance to arrive here tonight—the night of a waning moon, but nearly full. What was happening back at Lavalor? Had there been another battle? Lazlo Urich and Haem had brought the teens here the day before, so how did that affect everything back home? Did Lazlo's journey here impede or delay his ability to begin another attack on his friends? And what other vilemasters would Weir find here—if he successfully infiltrated the mausoleum? Zaviel himself?

Weir felt the anxiety building within. He knew the next hour or so would decide whether he and the teens lived or died—indeed, whether the Commonland itself survived—and it did not sit well within his craw. He closed his eyes and tried to clear his mind of troubling thoughts.

Silence, tranquility, awareness—action!

His eyes snapped open. He peered down to the forest floor, mostly hidden in the night shadows. He launched himself into the air, hooked a long vine extending to the ground, gripped it with both hands and slid downward.

His feet on solid earth, he released the vine. He advanced carefully in the direction of the city, always keeping to the darkest of the shadows and masking his approach behind the trunks of the trees. There'd be no more running from this point on—unless detected. And no doubt there'd be sentries ahead somewhere.

He entered the city perimeter. Tall mounds of jagged rubble and broken structures were everywhere, causing him to lose sight of the mausoleum. The encroaching jungle didn't help matters. He walked the avenues slowly, staying near the sides, closer to the ruins of old homes and shops and other structures. So far, he'd seen no sentries. It was his hope they weren't expecting visitors this far from the Sunder Line.

He didn't like being in this place alone. His heart yearned for his wife to be at his side. Her presence always seemed to make the impossible a bit more possible, the night a bit less dark, and the dangers a lot more survivable. That had been true even when they stood aside each other fighting those rock wolves all those years ago, though he had thought they both were going to die that day. He'd never forget the sense of belonging the first time he was near her. Death didn't matter as long as they were together. Afterward, as he carried her across the Shattered Hills towards Bridgefoot to save her life, the energy that flowed into his heart invigorated him and gave his legs a strength and speed he had never before experienced. Her need—her life—had instilled within him a capacity he didn't know he had.

He smiled, thinking of that day. Long after he had started carrying her across the Shattered Hills, she wouldn't let him enter Bridgefoot until after midnight so he would successfully complete his passage. For two hours they waited there, at the top of Hatano Canyon, looking over the sleeping city as the poison wrought havoc within her body.

"Please, Winkite!" he had pleaded. "You're growing weaker. Let me take you now. My home is near—just below."

"No!" was her stern response, a firm hand blocking any attempt by him to pick her back up. "We agreed not to enter the city until after midnight. Would you have me die thinking you were dishonorable?"

"Then let me call for our people to come here."

She shook her head. "They would still see that as a failure on your part. No! Abide by our agreement, warrior boy."

He could only growl in frustration at each futile attempt to defy her wishes.

But finally, they heard the midnight bell echoing up from Hatano Canyon and she literally fell unconscious at the sound. Her part—saving him from certain humiliation and permanent exile—was over, and so she had let go of trying to protect him.

In an instant he had her draped over his arms as he careened down the hairpins into the darkened city below. Her breathing was shallow as he ran, and he could barely feel her heart beating as he crossed his neck with hers. He burst into the first of familiar avenues, a place he loved with all his heart, a place Winkite would not let him lose. He turned a corner and barreled down a second avenue lined with low stone dwellings, each the home of an Atikan family. Then a third street flew beneath his bare heels, and finally he was just yards away from his own dwelling, a near match to all the others he had just passed.

The thick wooden door exploded inward as his flying heels impacted them.

"Mother!" he screamed. "Father!"

Katonkin quickly crossed the small room to the spot where he normally slept. The ever-burning oil lamp glowed low on a table on the opposite side of the room. Without pausing he bent his knees and lowered Winkite onto his empty cot.

She's not moving!

He heard a door opening and saw his father lurching into the common room with an Atikan war axe in his two hands.

"Father!" he called. "She needs your help."

"Katonkin!" His father looked stunned, not so unexpected considering the late hour and that someone had just destroyed his entryway.

Katonkin's mother peeked around the bedchamber doorway. "Mother! Come! Winkite needs you. She needs the magic water. She's dying. Hurry!"

Katonkin stepped away from his cot as his parents came forward through the dark room and stared disbelievingly at the girl. "What happened to her?" mother asked.

"Bitten. Rock wolves."

"When?" asked his father.

"This morning. I had to carry her here."

"The lamp," Mother said. "I'll get the water." She vanished into the bedchamber as Katonkin ran to a table on the opposite side of the room and turned up the flame on the oil lamp. He turned as his mother reentered the room, carrying a clay flagon that held a small amount of the healing waters from Falle Vaydal.

"Her head," she said as she knelt by Winkite's cot. His father laid his axe against a nearby wall and reached down and lifted Winkite's head, allowing Mother to tip the water flagon to her lips. Drop by painstaking drop she fed Winkite a small amount of the miraculous liquid.

"Remove her bindings," Mother said.

Katonkin dropped low and did as she instructed. He then lifted Winkite's injured arm and held it up for her to examine. Father, meanwhile, gently laid Winkite's head back down on the cot.

"Find me a piece of cloth, Katonkin. Large enough to wrap her arm."

He jumped to the task, but wasn't sure where to find any cloth. Instead, he spun in the center of the room, almost panicking.

"The bed sheet from my room," Mother instructed.

He lunged through the door leading into the adjoining room, grabbed the blanket from the bed, threw it on the floor, and ripped off the white sheet covering the large feather mattress. He returned to his mother's side and ripped a piece from the linen sheet, then another.

"That's sufficient," she said, taking the smallest of the pieces and wetting it slightly with some of the miracle water. She then dabbed at

Winkite's wounds, cleaning dried blood and dirt from the area. One or two of the punctures continued to well with blood, and so she pressed the cloth against them, stemming the flow.

"Wrap her arm completely with that other piece."

Katonkin did as instructed. His mother helped, tucking away the torn ends beneath the wrappings, securing the fresh bindings. She again tipped the flagon, letting drops of the Trickle's water fall onto the wrappings, wetting the entire area where Winkite's wounds were covered by the linen. Once that was done, she again fed her more water, using her own fingers to open Winkite's lips so the precious drops could more easily enter her throat.

Three days later Winkite awoke from her brush with death. She had survived the wolf's poison and soon made a full recovery, thanks most certainly to Katonkin's intervention in her life that first day and Mother's special water. Katonkin and Winkite were inseparable afterward, though that didn't mean she willingly revealed very much about herself at first. That would come a few months later as Katonkin and Winkite journeyed to visit the home of her parents near Sojourner Falls. Unfortunately, once they arrived there, they had discovered her own mother and father had long since passed into history.

35

Weir turned a corner, and suddenly before him in the moonlit sky rose the Intiga Mausoleum, an imposing tower, almost entirely intact. It was the tallest and most glorious structure in this ancient place. He had always been intrigued by the magnificence of its architecture and its intricate system of interment chambers, stairways and corridors. This was the edifice, before the comet struck, in which the Commonland once interred its most beloved, respected, and wealthiest citizens. Along with them went their most prized possessions—jewelry, gems, and even priceless artwork—things needed for a comfortable existence in the afterlife. Weir and Twoheart had once thoroughly explored this gigantic edifice when they first came to this land to help defeat their common enemy—a year or two before the Vilazians had converted this place to a headquarters—so he knew whatever riches it once held had long ago been plundered by the Vilazians.

The mausoleum's white, marble walls, four of them, rose heavenward with sweeping marble stairways leading down to the surrounding streets from entrances on each of its broad facades. The immense edifice had three main sections, each stacked atop the other, each diminishing in size the higher they were. An intricate array of window portals studded each of the four exterior walls, allowing sunlight to illuminate the building's interior complexities during daylight hours. Right now, however, a score of them near the summit were emitting soft glows of illumination. The entire structure looked gray in the moonlight.

His eyes darted down to street level. At the foot of the nearest marble staircase leading out from the mausoleum, a corral had been built from posts and rails. He quickly estimated it contained enough horses to support a full company. Behind the corral, on the stairway, near its top where it joined the mausoleum, he could see a pair of soldiers keeping watch over the animals. From his current perspective, he could also see one other stairway, on the western facade of the tower, on the right. No one there. No corral. No sentries. His enemy thought themselves safe here—deep within the Fringe—and had therefore not bothered with guarding every entrance. This would make things easier for him. Easier, but not easy.

His eyes were suddenly drawn back to the tower's crest. Light had flared into existence from atop the observatory. He recalled the evening before as he watched that faraway pinpoint of light change from white to red, then back to white again. No doubt it had originated atop the mausoleum.

He glanced at the moon. Midnight was surely drawing nearer.

Time to act!

36

That damn moon again! How Ada hated it. She could see part of it up ahead, obscured behind the far rooftop turret.

Ficx pushed her forward through the stairway portal leading onto the mausoleum's observatory. Vashti followed from behind, a few steps below on the same stairway. The man was a brute and no doubt harbored a desire to hurt her—or worse.

Galager was already here, his wrist chain secured through an iron loop at the far end of the huge marble altar at the center of the observatory. The Bethurian, Civato Jeregoth, was similarly chained at the closer end of the rectangular marble block.

Between them, on the left side of the altar was Uri Hauer—or rather, the pale beast he had been transfigured into. He hadn't changed positions since the previous night. He didn't show any signs of movement, but was just kneeling there with his head and thick shoulders sagging down towards his massive pale chest. Ada's initial instinct had told her this was Haem, but it wasn't. She remembered Vashti's assertions that two other namrils had already been summoned from the pit.

Sanguir's words suddenly screamed in her mind.

Ne moel la velum nok. The thrum shall be thrice disturbed!

Ficx pushed her forward another few feet. She stumbled past a pair of Vilazian soldiers on either side of the portal, almost fell, but caught herself. Ficx pointed toward Galager and grunted, not bothering to verbalize anything, no doubt because he hadn't yet figured out she understood a good chunk of his language.

"Ada!" cried Galager, his voice a beacon of comfort and love.

She ran across the rooftop to him, being sure to stay away from the namril. She and Galager crashed into each other, embracing desperately. She pulled back, her hands and wrists still locked around his neck.

His eyes grew troubled. "What's happening here?"

"Isn't it evident?" uttered the Bethurian. "We're to be sacrificed, like she did to our friends last night."

Galager's eyes beseeched Ada for another explanation.

She could only lower her forehead to his shoulder. But she remembered her talk with Vashti. "I have a plan," she whispered. She glanced back at Ficx, glad he wasn't within earshot. Vashti emerged onto the rooftop from the stairway at that moment and hastily approached the two teens.

Ada turned back to Galager. "At Lavalor. You saved us all. You can do it again."

Confusion spread across his features. "How?" he whispered.

Vashti called out to her as she crossed the rooftop, coming ever nearer to the namril.

"Ada, my dear," she said sternly, "you and that boy discontinue talking. Do you hear me?"

Ada leaned in closer, pretending to kiss his cheek near his ear. "You don't need eludria to invoke magic," she uttered urgently. "Trust me. Save us—like you did at Cadia Gate."

"Ada Halentine!" yelled Vashti. "Are you daft enough to defy my wishes?"

Ada planted a lingering kiss on Galager's cheek.

Their first. Their final?

"Trust yourself," she hastily added, then pulled away from him. She pivoted toward Vashti but remained close to Galager.

"Must you do this?" she asked of her captor, feeling a wave of dread rippling through her stomach and pushing away any confidence she may have had in her so-called plan. Standing here now—this demon just feet from a chained Galager, that horrible vilemaster smiling at her in victory—her plan suddenly seemed inadequate, even foolish. This human monster could call forth magic in a blink of an eye, so what chance did she have to challenge her?

"Please don't do this," Ada said. "I'll do anything. Just don't hurt them."

Another soldier appeared on the rooftop. His hands at waist level, he carried the wooden box containing the two eludria daggers—one of which she was sure would end the life of Galager Swift, a boy from the low country she had come to adore, a boy she still could not share her feelings with, even now, just moments before he—

"Put them there," said Vashti. She gestured toward the altar as she came closer. "Between the two prisoners."

The soldier crossed the illuminated rooftop, staying clear of the inanimate namril, and placed the box onto the center of the altar. He lifted the top panel of the container, unfolded the red cloth within, withdrew the two eludria daggers and set them onto the marble, well out of reach of both Galager and Civato. After carefully adjusting the two blades so they were perfectly aligned with each other, he closed the empty box, tucked it under an arm, and departed through the stairway.

Vashti studied Ada.

"Ficx," she said.

The big brute went to Ada and grabbed her arm near her shoulder. He pulled her away from the altar, away from Galager, and toward the rampart where she had been forced to watch the horrors of the previous night.

Ada suddenly punched Ficx in the nose, hoping to rid herself of his ogre-like grip. Why she had done that, she didn't know. Perhaps she feared being irrevocably chained to this roof, to never know freedom again. Or perhaps it would be her last chance at hurting one of the enemy. Jhalaveral knew she hadn't been very adept at that before now.

Ficx merely laughed, clamped down tighter on her arm, and slapped her hard across the face with his free hand.

Galager exploded against the iron loop holding his chains to the marble block. He yelped in pain as fresh blood dripped from beneath the manacles on his wrists, and he had to cease his efforts. "Don't touch her!" he yelled, his face turning redder than his hair.

"Remember what I told you!" Ada shouted. She searched his eyes, hoping for a sign he understood, or that he'd call forth magic.

Nothing! Confusion.

Vashti came a bit closer.

"My dear," the vilemaster said as Ficx reasserted his control over Ada. "What did you tell the boy?"

Ada spat at Ficx. She would've aimed it instead at Vashti, but the distance between them didn't allow it. Ficx raised a hairy forearm and wiped the spittle from his square jaw. He wound up, preparing to strike her again, but Vashti stopped him.

"No, Ficx," she commanded.

The brute obeyed, and lowered his hand, now a fist.

Vashti touched her neck chain—a warning. She was growing annoyed with her.

"One last time," Vashti stated. "What did you tell the boy?"

Ada stared at Galager. "That my love for him crosses the precipice."

Vashti melted. She hadn't expected such a heartbreaking reply. She raised a hand to her suddenly gaping mouth and Ada swore she saw her shudder. Vashti stirred from her memories a moment later.

"Step away from her," she whispered in Vilazian.

Ficx complied.

"Don't you hurt her!" gasped Galager. "If you—"

A red tendril of magic exploded from Vashti's pointing hand and enshrouded Ada's form. She heard Galager screaming—words she couldn't discern.

A troubled expression crossed Vashti's face after she let the tendril die. The nimbus around Ada remained, however. "I'm sorry," whispered her captor.

Sorry?

"I'm afraid I've misled you."

Ada furrowed her brow, trying to figure out what this bitch was talking about.

"Summoning demons from the pit incurs a significant cost in both eludria and blood." Vashti glanced at Galager and Civato. "Two —may not be enough."

Ada still didn't understand.

"I'm sorry, but—Carleea would have liked you. It pains me I have to do this. But there's too much at stake."

Ada gasped. Finally understanding. *I'm also to be sacrificed!*

A new tendril of magic reached for Ada. She felt the nimbus grow stronger. She heard Galager yelling.

Vashti twirled around—the umbilical dying, her feelings toward Ada dying, her humanity dying—and she went to the namril.

"Ada!" shouted Galager.

"I'm okay," she answered, hoping her voice could be heard beyond her imprisoning umbrella of eludria magic. "I'm okay!"

He calmed down at that point. With his hands fully covered in blood, his fury slowly transfigured back into despair. She assumed she appeared the same way to him. She certainly felt that way— hopeless and desperate—and there was nothing she could do. Her stupid plan had assumed she wouldn't be immobilized within magic like this. And now? She could think of no way to change what was about to occur.

But—she wondered why she, alone, was immobilized within a nimbus, whereas Galager and Civato were in chains. She tried to fit the puzzle pieces together. There had to be a reason beyond the overly simplistic notion that Vashti was fond of her. To have any chance at survival, Ada needed to understand everything that was about to happen here. She needed to know what steps were involved in the summoning, and their sequence, for if she could unravel that enigma she might find a way to implement her plan after all. *It's my only chance.*

Silence, tranquility, awareness.

She reopened her eyes. Clarity had swept away all turbulent thoughts like a mighty sword vanquishing a hoard of ogres. The answer was so simple. Obviously, she was to be sacrificed *before* the others, *after* being brought over to the demon at some stage of the summoning. Chains would of course inhibit or delay such an action whereas a nimbus could be extinguished in an instant. Then at some later point, after she was gone from this world, the demon would come awake and consume her friends where they were imprisoned.

But how does that knowledge help me?

Well, for one thing, she quickly decided, it meant she couldn't wait very long to act—if she was afforded the opportunity to do it at all. She'd have to take advantage of the very first chance to intervene, and do it without hesitation or fear. *No doubts!* It wasn't much to hang your life on, but she realized just this one bit of knowledge helped her regain a measure of confidence and fortitude. And perhaps Galager would remember what he did in Lavalor, what he was capable of, and then everything would fall into place.

There's still hope!

Vashti stood between the altar and namril now, facing the horrible creature. She stood there with lips parted, forehead slightly dipped, eyes full of doubt. *She's nervous.* Vashti seemed to be gathering her own courage; she glanced at the moon as it hovered high to her rear and ordered Ficx to come closer.

"Behind the altar," she instructed, after he came within a step or two of Galager. Once her henchman was situated as she desired, she turned to face him.

"I have no way of knowing how much time this will take. It might happen quickly. You must be prepared to act once I cue you."

"You can rely on me, my Lady," said Ficx. "But what should I expect?"

Both Vilazians acted as if they were confident their prisoners couldn't understand their words. Vashti seemed not to give it a second thought as she described what was about to transpire. Ada couldn't believe her good luck, what little of it that still remained.

"I shall use a blood meld to link to this host. I will draw a life-force from the pit and into him. Then as soon as I learn the name of the creature, I will bring the girl here to succor the demon with her life, instilling within him the capacity to take the other two."

Ada almost gasped, but she made sure not to visibly or audibly react.

"At the proper moment I will signal for you to use these eludria knives. First the boy, then the Bethurian. Step clear away from each after you infuse them, otherwise you will endanger yourself to the demon's hunger."

"What about their strange magic? Will it endanger us?"

"If the boy can employ strange magic, he doesn't seem to be aware of it. He may have been incapacitated by its use, and doesn't remember. I couldn't hurt him enough to force him to remember."

"And the girl?"

"Whatever threat she poses will vanish tonight."

Vashti glanced momentarily toward Ada with sad eyes. "We lack time. The power of the moon will wane after tonight. What must be done, must be done."

"Do you need my assistance with the girl, when the time comes?"

"No. Stay behind the altar. I shall draw her closer with my power when I'm ready for her."

"As you wish," Ficx said. "Anything else?"

"Once the prisoners have been fed to the demon, I shall bind the creature to my will. Then the summoning will be complete. At that time you and I will both be safe."

Bind the creature? Ada didn't understand what that meant. She wondered, *what would happen if the binding didn't occur?* Would that be good, or bad? Would the demon return to the pit? Or might it be free to ravage the world, unconstrained by the desires and wishes of an earthly master? Were there other possibilities she didn't know about or couldn't imagine right now?

"I have confidence in your abilities," said Ficx. "Zaviel wouldn't have asked for you if he thought you were beneath this task."

"Are you ready?" came her response.

Ficx bowed his head.

"Then we begin," she said, twirling to face the demon.

She knelt before it, a diminutive figure compared to the namril, and withdrew a stubby knife from the folds of her gown—an ordinary one made of steel—then made an incision on the creature's chest, near its sternum. She struggled in doing so, no doubt for the same reason Weir and Twoheart had difficulty penetrating Haem's tough exterior when they earlier fought him. A trickle of yellow blood finally ran down the namril's chest.

That first step completed, Vashti then made an incision on her right palm, a quick flick of the hefty blade, and returned her knife to her gown as she waited for blood to drip. At the first sign of it, she embraced the namril in an almost lovingly manner and thrust her upward turned palm against the demon's chest incision. Ada drew deeply of the cool air as Vashti then invoked a bright aura that instantly devoured both figures.

"What did you mean?" asked Galager as Vashti's magic began to pulse. Vashti didn't react, but Ficx took three quick steps toward him and struck him cruelly on the back of his head.

"You keep your mouth shut!" said the brute. Yet again, Galager didn't need to understand his language to know what was demanded of him.

Ada knew at that moment that if she had the power to do so, Ficx would quickly come to regret his brutality. But with her temper rising, her training with Weir unexpectedly and automatically kicked in again.

Silence, tranquility, awareness.

Ratcheting her anger down, she pondered the meaning of Galager's query as the two locked eyes. What was it he wanted to know? Did he seek to understand her earlier comments about his abilities, or clarification as to whether or not she truly loved him?

Both? She wanted to scream out for him to use his magic, but Vashti might instantly slay him if she thought him a threat.

Ficx remained standing behind Galager while glaring with hostility at her. He was daring her to answer. No doubt he would strike Galager again if she did so.

"You're lucky I cannot reach you," growled Civato at the opposite end of the big altar, flaring like a hooded viper despite his shackles and chains. Vashti didn't react. Her efforts with the demon were demanding all of her attention.

Ficx turned toward the big Bethurian, but only returned to his assigned spot at the center spot behind the altar.

Vashti's outpourings intensified. The marble turrets and parapets glowed red because of her magical output. The namril's head lifted a bit, then his back straightened—the pale beast was coming to life, albeit slowly, inch by inch. How much longer would it be before it rose to its feet? How much longer before she and her friends were gone from this earth?

Feeling powerless and frustrated, Ada fought against the nimbus holding her fast.

No luck!

She tried again, this time with her feet. Miraculously, her right foot managed to break through the untended prison of light and energy. Hope surged as she continued struggling, and then again when she successfully freed her entire leg up to her hip.

Vashti let out an audible gasp of relief as her arms dropped suddenly to her sides, revealing a fist-sized crater in the middle of the demon's chest that pulsed red and orange at its circumference. The knife slit had grown in size and shape, but still, only traces of yellow blood could be seen dripping down the front of the beast's pale torso. The cavity looked like a portal into some other dimension.

Is she finished? Is my time here nearly over?

Ada jerked her leg back into the nimbus as Vashti rose to her feet.

Did she see that? Apparently not, as the Vilazian didn't appear to react.

"My Lady, is everything going as planned?" asked Ficx.

"It is," replied Vashti. "Just a moment's rest." Her eyes went back to Ada and she let out another long tendril of red rope that looped over toward her and encircled her waist. A second or two passed and the tendril faded away, but Ada could feel the nimbus had been refortified.

Vashti leaned back against the front of the altar. This blood meld was exhausting her.

Much sooner than Ada wanted, Vashti returned to the summoning. Her magic once again flared into existence and she dropped to her knees, reached over with her slit palm, and placed her entire hand into that glowing crater in the middle of the thing's ribcage.

Ada tried to again thrust her leg out of her scarlet prison. This time she only succeeded at getting her lower leg to freedom. For now.

Twice more Vashti repeated the sequence, succoring the namril with her own life essence, then resting—each time sending more magic over toward Ada to refortify her steadily weakening nimbus. The namril itself had finally begun to show signs of becoming more energetic. Its massive, pale arms were no longer completely motionless and instead began moving in random patterns. Its fingers repeatedly opened and closed, and its head slowly swiveled in short angles. Despite the continued rigidity of the creature's body and limbs, its eyes were showing signs of awareness. Ada could see a burning hatred in those huge orbs. Ada knew her time—and that of Galager's and Civato's—was drawing to an end unless something happened soon to change what was happening here.

Vashti finally extinguished her magic and broke away from the pale figure. The demon slowly gained its feet, almost mirroring the Vilazian as she regained hers.

Vashti emitted a loud cackle. "It's done! He's here!" she stated loudly and brashly. The namril angled its fiery eyes at the Vilazian woman who had successfully drawn it from the pit.

A sound emanated from the stairway over at Ada's left. She jerked her eyes in that direction. The two Vilazian guards on either side of the portal slumped to the floor—one with blood spurting from his chest and the other with a red gash across the front of his throat.

Standing behind the two dead soldiers was Katonkin Weir, a bloody longknife in each hand!

Vashti saw him too. She moved around the demon, stepped toward the vangard, and thrust an arm in his direction.

Weir spun in a full circle. One of his longknives streaked across the observatory, straight at Vashti's chest. An explosion of scarlet brilliance erupted from around the Vilazian's outstretched hand. At first Ada didn't know what had happened—the explosion of magic had obscured the event. But Weir's blade was now sliding across the floor toward the altar. It came to a rest when it clinked against the white marble, close to Civato but out of his reach because of his shackles.

Vashti's hastily erected nimbus had saved her life. In the blink of an eye, the Vilazian's shield was then reformed into a horizontal cone of fire that surged toward Weir as she slowly walked toward him.

He dove back into the portal as the red fire fully engulfed the stairway opening.

I have to do something!

She kicked out with her right leg. It broke free!

By pure instinct, she let the full weight of her body drop straight to the marble floor beneath her and was overjoyed when she popped free of the waning nimbus, which then hung in the air empty and formless.

Ada crawled forward furiously, trying to gain traction on the slippery marble floor. She finally rose to her feet and ran to the altar. She grasped Weir's deflected blade. She checked on Vashti to see whether the master eludrian was preparing to wash her in misery and fire, but no, the Vilazian was still advancing on the stairway while continuing to direct her outpourings toward it.

Ficx raced around the far end of the altar, around Galager.

She had completely forgotten about him!

Galager thrust out a foot as the Vilazian came racing around him, causing Ficx to crash face first onto the hard stone floor. She wasted no time, darting between the altar and the demon, and closed with the fallen man. She almost pierced the man's back with Weir's blade, but she suddenly remembered her plan. So, instead, she struck the back of his head with the pommel of Weir's longknife. She did it twice more before he stopped moving.

Everything was happening so fast now.

Vashti continued to lavish fire toward the stairway portal, hoping to burn away the unexpected threat of Panthertooth. And that horrible demon was slowly lifting its gaze toward Ada. She glanced at the vortex of red energy embedded within its chest. She had forgotten she couldn't call up an aura—a hiccup in her plan—but Vashti's magic still glowed there.

Can I meld with it?

Knowing that every second mattered, she lunged toward the creature and cut a slit into her right palm at the same moment she came to a full stop in front of it. She considered throwing Weir's knife at Vashti, but her mind suddenly filled with clarity. She knew what she had to do if they were all to survive this full moon. She had to trust Weir would distract Vashti long enough for her to put her plan into motion, and she had to trust herself that she could actually pull it off. Hoping her plan wasn't sheer lunacy after all, hoping the vestiges of Vashti's vortex would meld to her, all she could do now was plunge her entire hand into the beast's chest cavity.

37

Millions of voices struck her senses at once. Anguish and agony in each. Fire and brimstone radiating at the edges of darkness. Heat, somewhere in the deep darkness.

She was prepared for the demon's thoughts, but not these other shrieking voices. As she listened in horror, they rose and fell together like breakers, waves slamming against her mind, sprays of distress, each drop a distinct soul caught in eternal fire and misery.

Yet, one voice was what she was after. Just one.

Hungry . . . free . . . hungry!

There! The demon. Ada focused on it. She needed to learn its name.

I am free . . . pain fading . . . free . . . is it true?

Another breaker of voices smashed into her, threatening to drown her.

"Your name beast?" she shouted into the din.

Hungry . . . I . . . must . . . feed!

"Your name?" she demanded, knowing her life, and those of her friends, depended on getting a quick answer.

Feed . . . me . . . I . . . will . . . tell . . . you.

"Your name?" she uttered, "or back to the pit."

You . . . will . . . enslave . . . me.

Ada sensed time slipping away. Perhaps it was already too late. She needed the beast's name now, or everything—everyone—would die. She remembered Galager invoking magic without eludria.

Didn't I do it too, on Cadia Gate?

Another wave of agony struck her, trying to crush her to her knees, drown her in the infinite wash of despair. She fought back, gritted her teeth, closed her eyes, and with the last of her courage she screamed into the void.

"Your name creature! Now! Or I will cast you back into the abyss!"

Something blinded her. A blue light!

She heard the demon's solitary voice as her outpouring began to fade.

I . . . am . . . Cabbal.

38

Galager gripped the chains with bloodied hands and pulled at the black links with every bit of his strength. Nothing! No matter how hard he tried, no matter how desperately he pulled, he just couldn't loosen the iron loop embedded deep into the side of the altar. And now, because of his incompetence, they were all going to die.

At the far end of the altar, Civato Jeregoth groaned like a bear as he planted a foot on the altar and heaved on his bindings. But not even this mighty warrior could free himself.

Pain no longer mattered to either of them. Their bloody wrists had now become eviscerated by the sharpened manacles. It was a miracle they hadn't already bled out. They both knew they either escaped their bindings, by whatever means necessary, or they perished.

Galager again checked on the chaos around him. Two soldiers dead by the stairway on his right. Ada just feet away, but still in the embrace of that demon—her bloodied fist had vanished entirely inside the thing's chest. And the eludrian—Vashti, still heaping fire into Katonkin Weir's hiding place. Was Katonkin still alive? He didn't see how it was possible.

He heard the Bethurian bellowing in rage once more, and tilted his eyes up to see him yet again yanking on his chains.

Vashti's red magic suddenly lessened. In its place he heard that lunatic of a woman shrieking. She finally noticed Ada had escaped her nimbus, and she didn't like what she was seeing.

Galager fell against the altar, defeated, vanquished, powerless.

What can I do?

Ada said he could invoke magic without eludria, but every time he tried—nothing!

Panthertooth suddenly re-appeared in the archway up ahead as the last of Vashti's magic expired.

He's alive!

Galager expected him to leap forward and attack the eludrian, but instead Weir was staring at him while holding up something in the fingertips of his left hand.

Eludria!

Somehow Vashti sensed Weir had returned. She violently whirled around to face him one more time.

Weir's remaining longknife shot forward, straight at the Vilazian as she conjured more fire to burn him from the rooftop. Panthertooth lunged in, following his blade into the gushing fire, an act of suicide that commanded all of her attention.

Galager almost missed it. The ruby.

Weir had thrown it in a combination sidearm-underarm motion at the same time he had distracted Vashti with his knife throw and charge.

The ruby just managed to bypass Vashti's petals of blossoming magic.

It was headed his way!

Ignoring the sound of Weir's second longknife already skidding across the floor, Galager focused on the approaching talisman.

Vashti saw it too. She desperately reached out with her right hand for the ruby. Her sudden movement caused her magic to veer away from Weir and lessen in intensity.

Her grasping hand came up empty.

The tiny object floated in slow motion as it rose higher, reaching its peak just before it passed the demon and Ada. Ada finally broke free of the demon as the ruby began to drop lower—her hand withdrawing from the glowing crater, her head pivoting toward the looping eludria, her eyes tracking it, but her body too far away to do anything but just watch.

Galager jerked his hands toward the anticipated path of the ruby, but the manacles bit deep and held him where he was.

Too far to the right. Won't reach it!

Vashti's magic flared back up and she swept it across the rooftop in his direction.

Behind her, Panthertooth fell heavily to the floor as a last tentacle of red energy tore away from him.

Everyone was watching Galager now. Waiting to see whether he could get his hands on the talisman flying closer and closer. The demon, Ada, Civato, and Vashti—they were all going to witness his final failure before this Vilazian killed them all. Even Weir was looking at him as his body crumpled onto the marble.

Yet, part of Galager refused to accept failure.

It was that part of himself that was still free to do what he excelled at.

That part of himself that knew only instinct!

My feet!

With Vashti's magic reaching forward, long arms of fire seeking to touch him, Galager extended his right leg toward the approaching ruby, which was going to sail past him on his right side. He'd have to stretch for it.

It's just like a sandbag, he told himself. *I've done this a million times!*

I got this!

Time suddenly snapped back to normal as he lashed out with his right foot.

He felt the eludria impact his bare toes. Ignoring the sharp sting, he tapped the object ever so gently and watched in dreaded fascination as it changed directions and arced toward his face. He had almost directed the talisman to his fingers, but realized at the last moment that wouldn't do. Because of all the blood, the ruby would be infused within his wrist cuts long before he could use it to invoke magic.

Galager opened his mouth as wide as he could. The ruby struck his lower teeth and bounced into his mouth. He snapped his jaws shut, being sure not to close his eyes, and placed a proper thought in his mind—of a sharp, red spear of magic thrusting into the heart of the female vilemaster.

His power shot forth, pierced her advancing sheet of fire, and struck her in the chest.

She went down as if Havless Tower had crumbled over her. Her insidious magic dissipating as she fell.

For a moment he was stunned.

He couldn't believe what had just happened.

Vashti was dead!

But he didn't feel like celebrating, because so was Panthertooth!

39

Vashti Dal'falkoz hit the floor not long after Panthertooth.

Ada felt huge arms surrounding her, holding her in place, preventing her from escaping. The demon was perhaps trying to take her, feed on her, but it wasn't quite strong enough yet. She hated to think what would have happened to her had she been forced by Vashti and her magic to sate this creature with her life.

"Get away from it!" yelled Galager, trying to get her attention. His words were barely recognizable because of the ruby in his mouth.

She struggled to untangle herself from the demon's arms, and then pushed forward, and backed away from Vashti's horrible creation. She would have to deal with it later. Right now there were more immediate and worrisome things to see to.

She realized she no longer had Weir's longknife. She must have dropped it during the blood meld. She raced over to help Weir, but noticed movement from Vashti.

She's still alive!

The bitch had curled herself up into a fetal position on the floor as an aura flickered around her form. *She's still dangerous!*

Ada dove on top of her former captor and drove a knee between her shoulder blades. Vashti yelped in pain as Ada grabbed at her necklace and ripped it away. Vashti's aura flickered out as the eludria swung free at the end of the chain. Ada wasted no time and pocketed the talisman—she would infuse it later. One problem solved, she then punched Vashti several times, hard, on the side of the face. She intended no retribution with this action, but instead sought to keep this master eludrian from perhaps wielding another ruby that she may yet have had hidden somewhere else on her person.

Vashti stopped moving, hopefully unconscious, Ada thought as she grabbed her arms and dragged her straight. So heavy, for someone so small. That done, she quickly searched her clothing for more eludria, but after half a minute, she concluded there wasn't any. No doubt Vashti had used every ruby she could get her hands on for use as instruments for the summoning. Ada had found her little dagger, though, the one used to slit Cabbal's chest. She threw it off to the side, far away from the Vilazian's reach.

She switched her focus to Weir, desperately wishing to see him moving.

He wasn't.

"The demon!" cried Civato Jeregoth. "It's coming alive."

Ada whirled around. Indeed, Cabbal had turned toward her and was staring at her with eyes as hot as fire. The red cavity in his chest was much larger, too. The beast could now move its arms in a normal fashion, though it still struggled with its legs. For the moment, it remained where it was, but with every second that passed the beast was becoming more animated.

An aura erupted around Galager. He was preparing to attack Cabbal.

"Stop, Galager!" she screamed! "Don't!"

He heard her, and let his aura die. He mumbled something, but she couldn't discern his words because of the ruby still in his mouth.

"Don't attack it," she stated emphatically. "No time to explain right now."

Her eyes dropped to Ficx, laying near Galager. She ran over to him and kicked him solidly in the head. This time she wasn't so sure of her reason. She dropped to his side and fished in his pockets, withdrawing a ring of keys which she then tossed to Galager, who adeptly caught them despite his blood-covered hands. He immediately worked to unlock his manacles.

Ada saw Vashti stirring yet again.

Dammit!

She went to the center of the altar and grabbed one of the eludria knives, being careful not to use her bloodied hand. She needed this knife for another purpose.

She checked on Galager. “Once you free Civato,” she said, as the last of his manacles popped free, “help Katonkin. Get him to the stairs. We may need to leave this place before Cabbal is strong enough to attack us.”

“I can kill him,” mumbled Galager as he raced around the altar to Civato’s side, his words barely recognizable.

“No!” she yelled as she then ran toward a reawakening Vashti. “Attack the creature only as a last resort. Our lives depend on it. I’ll explain soon.”

“Carleea!” whispered Vashti as Ada reappeared at her side. “Where have you been, my beautiful child?”

She’s deluded!

Ada dropped down to her, hovering over the eludrian.

“Mother,” Ada said. “I am here.”

Vashti’s eyes glazed over.

Maybe this isn’t going to work.

“Carleea. I missed you so much.”

“I missed you, too, Mother.”

A beastly roar arose from behind her. Cabbal! She had to act fast.

“Mother,” Ada whispered. “The demon is aroused. It will soon feed on us—me.”

Vashti’s eyes gazed off to some faraway place as she smiled. “Oh, do not worry yourself over that. I’ve sent for someone to protect you.”

A pang of concern shot through Ada. She remembered that aura Vashti had called forth just before she had disarmed her. “You sent for someone? Who?”

"Carleea, my dear, Carleea. Lazlo will be here soon. Don't you worry."

Oh no!

Ada heard a moan. Her eyes flicked toward Weir and saw him trying to gather his arms up so he could push himself off the floor. Galager and Civato, freed of their chains, rushed to the vangard's aid.

"Lazlo may arrive too late, Mother. I need your help. I earlier heard you say you can bind him to your will. How can I do that? I already know his name."

"You're not an eludrian, dear. Only Lazlo has enough power and knowledge to do that."

Cabbal roared again. Ada swung her gaze to the beast and watched him take several rigid steps toward her.

"Let me stop him!" yelled Galager in a clearer voice. He had wiped one of his bloody hands clean on his trousers and held his ruby in it now.

"Listen to me!" said Ada. "Not yet! Not until I tell you! I don't have time to explain right now!"

Knowing time was short, she exploded to her feet and raced over to face the demon.

"Don't get near that thing!" shouted Galager, running to her side. Civato was alone with Weir now, helping him to stand, half dragging him to the stairway portal. "Get away!" begged Galager. "I'll blast him!"

Cabbal slowly reached for Ada, his chest cavity looking like an inverted gyre of red energy, or perhaps a tunnel into hell. She pushed Galager away. "Get back!" she demanded. "I know what I'm doing!"

Cabbal took another step toward her; he was getting faster. Any moment now and he'd be as agile and as capable as Haem.

"But—"

"I got this!" Ada insisted.

She took a few more steps, encircling the creature, aiming toward Ficx, drawing the demon with her, and away from the others. Galager stepped to the side, reluctantly letting the demon advance, though he remained nearby, behind it, in case he was needed.

"This way, Cabbal," coaxed Ada as she drew closer to Ficx. "Come over here you ugly bastard!" The demon eagerly complied.

"Watch out!" cried Galager as she felt someone grabbing hold of her ankle.

Ficx!

"Stay back!" responded Ada as she pivoted, dropped, and plunged the eludria knife deep into the brute's neck in a single circular motion of her arm.

The man screamed in terror as Ada tore herself free of his tenuous grasp and then lunged away from him.

Cabbal's eyes brightened as the eludria sizzled and then disappeared into Ficx' bloodstream. No longer did the creature have his attention on Ada, but instead, it was Ficx his murderous gaze was riveted to. Cabbal lurched forward as the Vilazian tried to crawl backward. But it was no use. Cabbal fell onto him and both turned into a single cloud of dust in the blink of an eye.

Ada and Galager met, embraced quickly, then retreated together back toward the others.

Ada suddenly remembered something.

"Wait here!" she stated, then ran to the front of the altar and snatched up the remaining eludria knife as the ball of dust convulsed violently nearby.

40

Vashti was still awake.

"Mother," said Ada, once again hovering over the injured and delirious vilemaster. "How do I bind the demon to my will?"

Vashti smiled at her. But didn't answer.

"Hurry, my Lady," yelled Civato from near the stairs. "I think that dust creature is changing back. Ada took a quick look and saw the fuzzy outlines of the namril beginning to take shape again. As for Ficx, he was gone.

"Lazlo isn't here. Cabbal is coming for me. Please tell me, Mother. How do I stop him?"

Vashti's smile vanished, and her eyes began to glint maliciously as they had before.

"You!" the Vilazian whispered. "You're not Carleea!"

"I'm sorry," answered Ada.

"Are you?"

"No. Of course not. You're a murderer. Your people are evil, yet you think you are saving us all."

"He's coming back!" warned Galager suddenly from beside her.

Ada ignored him. "You can help me," she said. "Carleea would want you to help me."

Vashti modulated her coughs with laughter. "Carleea would know how impossible it is for me to do that. I have a duty to Azinor and I am loyal to Zaviel, though he has destroyed my life. If nothing else, I am a Vilazian!"

Another fragment of Sanguir's words burned through Ada's mind. *The Lady, for her rival, shall perish before her creation, her flower twice cut from its stem as the Insight watches her love slip forever from her grasp. Her duty asks too much.*

Vashti coughed again. "Zaviel will finish what Lazlo started at Lavalor. You've already lost, all of you, though you don't know it yet. The Grand Unraveling can't be stopped."

Ada felt the hairs on the back of her neck stir.

She could feel Cabbal's preternatural strength coming closer. Galager stepped forward to protect her, or perhaps drag her away from the unrepentant vilemaster, but she held up her bloodied hand to stay him at the exact same time she plunged the last remaining eludria knife into Vashti's neck with her other, clean hand.

Vashti hadn't expected that. Her eyes bulged with surprise. She screamed in pain.

Galager reached down and grabbed Ada's wrist and pulled her up, out of the way of the demon as it raced closer—faster now—with its claws raking the marble as it drew nearer. Vashti screamed one more time as her creation fell upon her.

"We can't run from this thing," said Ada, watching as Cabbal once again turned into dust, taking Vashti with him, her screams fading into the distance then vanishing altogether.

The two teens quickly withdrew to the stairway arch, joining Weir and Civato. "We may have to fight it—if I can't turn it."

"I have my magic," said Galager.

Ada reached to him, touched his cheek. *Can magic alone stop Cabbal?*

Weir whispered something, but he was so weak from his injuries that Ada couldn't be sure what it was he had said.

Weir whispered again as Civato held him erect.

Galager moved closer to Weir. "Katonkin, what did you say?"

Again, a whisper.

"Malediction?" uttered Galager.

Weir nodded.

Ada felt her heart stop. She knew of maledictions. They were magical rites.

"What are you saying? Do you know something about a malediction?"

Weir again nodded, lifted a finger, and gestured for her to come closer so he could whisper in her ear. She did so, and what he told her stunned her.

That's it!

"Galager!" she urgently yelled, whirling once more toward the advancing cloud of dust. "Raise your aura! Around both of us! Blume my blood!"

Cabbal suddenly returned to solid form again and was half way to them by the time the red magic she desperately needed from Galager erupted forth.

"Anon doss Cabbal, tagk'liotz!" she screamed, as loudly and as clearly as she could, and hoping desperately she had heard Weir correctly. One mistake and nothing would matter anymore, as they'd all be dead in a matter of seconds.

But miraculously, the beast instantly responded to the magical rite and halted just a few feet in front of her. For a few moments it lost shape again, dust swirling around its disintegrating form, pulsing red, then finally becoming solid again.

"Yield before me," Ada spat, her words empowered with vitality and confidence. "I am Adriana Halentine, eludrian, daughter of Edward Halentine, and protector of the Commonland. Behold your master!"

Remarkably, the demon shriveled before her.

Ada held up a fist and pointed her powerless little ring at the demon. "As the strength of Constance Fane flows through me, I have heard your voice, sensed your fears, know who you are, and possess your name. Defy me at your peril, or work against me but one time and I shall cast you into the abyss of fire whence you came!"

Cabbal merely stood there, his bat-like ears twitching, coldly staring at Ada from behind that pale guise. His anger, quickly dissipated as they watched—his hunger apparently slaked by the two Vilazians he had fed upon. *Two was enough!*

Ada dropped her arm and whispered for Galager to release his aura, which he did.

"My Lady," said Civato somewhat shakily. "I—I stand here in disbelief! You have subdued this demon!"

Ada wanted to grin from ear to ear, but she was afraid to show this beast anything but strength. Inside, however, she was a roiling mess of ecstasy.

The malediction worked!

She had done the impossible! Her silly plan had succeeded!

I stole Vashti's demon!

41

It took all his strength—and the support of Galager—to be set down on the rooftop so that he was leaning his back against the altar, far away from that creature.

He had been burned deeply by the female eludrian. His skin felt like fire—his insides not much different. He had never known such torture, such agony, such exhaustion.

Now I know how Twoheart felt—is feeling.

"Are you sure I shouldn't try killing it?" said Galager. He was speaking to Ada.

She had no answer as she stared quietly at the demon.

The beast was standing motionless over near the stairway arch, its back to them, exactly where they had left it after Ada turned it. She looked unsure of herself. "It's bound to my will. If it were going to kill us, we'd already be dead."

"How did you learn to master demons?" asked the Bethurian, a warden, no doubt, who had been captured. Weir didn't know the man's name.

Ada exhaled deeply, expelling her fear and anxiety into the night air. "I earlier overheard Vashti speaking of the need to bind the demon. She didn't know I understood her language. But it was

Katonkin who gave me the words I needed to accomplish the feat. I simply replaced the name, Haem, with Cabbal, and it worked."

The Vivonian approached Weir and meant to lay a tender hand on his shoulder.

"Don't touch," whispered Weir.

Ada recoiled, a worried look on her face. "Can I help in some way?" she asked.

"I am beyond that," said Weir. "It is taking everything I have to remain awake."

"No!" responded Galager stubbornly. "We'll get you out of here. Find a healer."

Weir waved a trembling hand at him. "I am proud of you, Galager."

He looked at the girl. "You also. You both surpass the land's need."

Weir aimed his green eyes to the Bethurian. "Warden," he said, his words interrupted by a cough. "These two are the Commonland's final hope. Bethuria's as well. You must bring them back to Jurry." He coughed again. "Keep them safe. Even at the cost of your own life. Any cost. Keep them safe. They are key."

The man didn't react.

"No Katonkin, you'll bring us back!" insisted Galager.

"I cannot," whispered Weir. He looked at the warden. "Promise me," he beseeched.

"It's at least a three-day run to the Sunder Line," responded the warden. "And none of us are in any condition. This is no small miracle you ask of me."

"Three days?" echoed Galager, confusion on his face. "Katonkin, how did you get here so fast? It's only been two days."

"Ran," he answered.

"You ran for two days!" said Ada incredulously. "How did you keep up your strength?"

Weir smiled. "Twoheart."

Ada checked the archway. "Where is she? Is she alright?"

"She . . . hurt," he replied slowly. "I came alone. Lavalor has fallen.

Do not return there. Go . . . Jurry." He felt a wave of nausea coursing through his system, but fought it off.

"How did you know the words to the malediction?"

The nausea passed but his internal organs continued to quiver and rearrange themselves.

"I went to kill Lazlo," he said. "I encountered a vilemaster. A healer. He told me you two had been taken here. He revealed the malediction when I demanded to know how to defeat Haem." Even now, after seeing what Vashti was going to do to the teens, he felt guilt over what he had done to that man.

Ada nodded in understanding.

"Leave me now. Go. I already . . . cleared the tower. But more of them may return soon."

"Not a chance!" replied Galager resolutely. "We're bringing you with us."

"We can't" replied the warden. "The journey will kill him—and slow us down. We need to return at once, not just to get you two to safety, but to warn Megador of what's happening."

Galager snapped his gaze back to the Bethurian. "I won't leave him here."

Ada waved her arms to get everyone's attention. "I have a plan," she said. "We're all leaving together."

Weir glared at her, trying to reign her in to his will. She didn't fold. He swung his gaze back to the warden.

"Your name?"

"Civato Jeregoth."

Weir nodded slightly. "I am honored. I have heard of you."

"And I, you," answered Civato. "And it is *my* honor, Pennon Vangard Katonkin Weir."

"Perhaps," whispered Weir, "you and I shall fight together in our next life."

Civato smiled. "A Blight Hunt," he said. "We shall wreak terror on the enemy."

Weir grunted in approval.

Ada took a small step forward, placing herself between the two warriors. She faced Civato. "I've learned from Vashti that they intend to attack Megador. I don't know exactly when it will occur, but soon. The attack on Lavalor was simply a diversion, an attack intended to divert resources away from Megador. The fact Lazlo succeeded in breaking Lavalor was an unexpected bonus to them."

Civato wiped blood from his hands with a piece of cloth cut from the tunic of one of the soldiers Weir had killed. Galager had another piece, doing the same with his hands, and both now had strips of cloth tied around their wrists, helping to protect the wounds caused by the manacles.

"Uri also understood a few words of Vilazian," said Civato. "He overheard a guard speaking of the attack. He thinks—thought—the attack was delayed. There are rumors Zaviel experienced an affliction of some kind."

"Affliction?" muttered Ada. "Ah! I think I know what that is. Zaviel summoned another namril, and the act must have depleted him for a time."

"Three demon namrils?" asked Galager.

Ada nodded.

Weir coughed. He felt like vomiting. "Go!" he whispered. "Must warn Megador."

Ada shook her head. "I have a better idea."

Weir normally would have grown annoyed, but he had come to respect these two teens standing before him. Especially after what had just transpired—what they had done. "What do you suggest?" he asked. He noticed Ada's eyes flick toward the demon standing over by the stairway. *Ah, how could I have not seen this coming!*

"The demon," he said. "You think it will carry us home?"

"Huh!" reacted Galager.

"Why not?" asked Ada. She looked at Civato. "Warden, didn't Haem carry you and your men here to Intiga? Easily so? And that's how Galager and I got here."

She turned back to Weir. "I insist we do this."

She gestured toward Galager. "That's why I couldn't let you attack Cabbal. We need him."

Weir didn't react. Not yet.

"But we're not going home," she added.

Galager looked up from his attempts to clean his hands, though they both looked permanently stained. "Where are we going?"

"Firthwood," she answered after a slight pause.

Weir blinked.

"What's the point of going there?" responded Civato.

"You're all hurt, in one way or another," she said. "Katonkin seriously so. You need healing. We must go to Amaranthine Springs. The eternal healing waters. I think it's the only way to keep Katonkin alive."

"Amaranthine Springs is a myth," said Galager. "It would—"

Weir stayed him with a hand. "That would be foolish," he said to Ada. "Megador must be warned about the coming attack. We must go there—at once!"

"I disagree," said Ada. "There are other things you don't know."

"Like what?" stammered Galager.

Ada stuck a tongue in her cheek. "Zaviel has a Bloodstone."

No one responded. Instead, utter silence, utter shock.

"That's why they are able to summon demons. The eludria they use to snatch these creatures from the abyss has been enervated somehow with the Bloodstone. We can't hope to defeat them. They are too strong now, with their Bloodstone and their demon namrils."

Weir understood what she wanted to do, the real reason to head to Firthwood. "You seek to find Cazlich's Bloodstone."

Ada nodded. "It's the only way."

"Cazlich's Bloodstone has disappeared from history."

"I know where it is," insisted Ada.

"How? You learned that from Hadron's book?" guessed Galager.

"Yes," she said. "I told you. Master Hadron believed it to be in Firthwood, in their capital, Thrum. It was his dream to one day find it, though he ever had the chance. That Immune we discussed back at Lavalor—Darrow Stahg? He once visited Firthwood and later told Hadron it was there. That's how his dream was first ignited. It's all in his journal. The Firthans are hiding it. I'm sure of it! Hadron believed it, and so do I."

"An Immune?" queried Civato.

"Yes," said Ada. "Why ask?"

The Bethurian glanced northward. "The morning of the attack on Lavalor. The morning we departed Shenkel. Master Fellard was discoursing with Hadron over the thrum. Fellard believes Hadron was attacked even as they communicated. Hadron dispatched three final words to Master Fellard that morning."

"What words?" asked Galager.

"Demon, Immune, and Bloodstone."

Ada's jaw dropped. "You see, Katonkin! Master Hadron was trying to warn us—warn the Commonland! With his message to Master Fellard, he was trying to tell us he was about to be attacked by a demon. It must have happened quickly, poor man. He saw the beast and instantly realized someone had been wielding a Bloodstone—a second one, most likely. His message was a warning to the Commonland to trace the path of Darrow Stahg and find Cazlich's talisman. We must go to Firthwood! Must! We cannot deny this quest!"

"That's crazy!" said Galager. "But I think she's right." He looked at Weir. "And going to Firthwood can save your life. I say we go there—Amaranthine Springs!"

Weir had to admit the Vivonian had made a good argument. Indeed, he was almost entirely convinced of the wisdom of her plan—except for one detail. Twoheart had never mentioned anything about the Bloodstone although she had lived in the Firthan village of Thrum for many years before they met. He wondered, *wouldn't she know if it were hidden there?* But after a heartbeat of deliberation, he concluded that if the Firthans were in fact hiding the talisman, they might not have revealed that to anyone, not even to her. As to how Stahg had found out, he had no clue.

"My blades," he whispered.

"What of them?" asked Galager.

"Get them for me. We're going to Firthwood."

Galager smiled and invoked an aura.

"Don't you dare!" warned Ada.

"I'm not gonna hurt him," he quickly replied, referring to Cabbal.

"What are you doing?" demanded Weir.

Galager turned around and pointed at the red and black flag above one of the turrets.

"First things first," he said as he directed a stream of red fire at the Vilazian standard.

42

It was time to find out if Ada's audacious plan to fly out of Intiga would work or not. Their lives depended on it. Ada had informed them that Lazlo Urich—summoned by Vashti before she died—might very well be on his way there. Weir seriously doubted the battered and exhausted team would survive another battle with yet another powerful vilemaster and his demon, Haem.

The last thing Weir remembered was Cabbal transfiguring into dust. It was just after Ada had infused herself with that sorcerer's ruby and then commanded him to bring them to Jurry, which wasn't that far removed from their path to Firthwood. They decided to first head homeward, for several reasons. First, they could provide warning of The Grand Unraveling, Zaviel's plan to visit genocide and annihilation upon Megador and the Commonland. Second, Civato Jeregoth could be returned to freedom. And finally, the team could find Twoheart and bring her with them. After all, she needed healing too. There was also the matter that she had once lived in Firthwood, so it was possible her presence would convince the Firthans to welcome them. No one had cared to explain how Cabbal was going to be allowed in. Perhaps, he wouldn't be. Perhaps, none of them would be.

The first moments of flight were of strange, distant voices and some disorientation, but they soon receded. He dreamed of dark, moonlit landscapes while unconscious. Like a bird, he flew over many of the same hills and streams and woods he had crossed the previous two days on his mad dash to rescue Ada and Galager. He caught glimpses of the Lion Wall, Bone Canyon, and other familiar land features. He began to wonder whether it was a dream, or reality, or both.

Other voices reached his ears. Ada—and then Galager.

"Katonkin! Don't leave us!"

"Come back! Come back!"

But he was intrigued by the vistas, and the pleadings of the two teens soon left his awareness. He was so high up now, that he imagined he must be able to see all the way around the world. He peered forward, saw a land of canyons and water falls and wondered, *Atika?* But he could no longer tell one place from another from way up here above the clouds.

Twoheart would know, though, if she were here with him.

How he had been amazed—and heartbroken—when she told him her story, and how she came to be exiled from Atika by her parents and taken in by the Firthans.

"You once lived in Thrum?" a gasping Katonkin had asked at the time.

Winkite's eyes twinkled in response. "More than ten years," she said.

"But—but no outsider ever goes there!" he had remarked.

"They allowed me."

His brows furrowed in confusion. "Why?"

She shrugged a single shoulder. "They took pity on me, I suppose."

"How did you come to arrive there in the first place?"

She answered, but it was as if she had heard a different question. Instead of explaining how she had arrived at Firthwood, she told him why she had departed it.

"I missed Atika. My people. It was time I returned home, returned to the fold, regardless of the consequences."

She was shy at first, and didn't want to reveal very many details of her earlier life. And he never tried to pry them from her either. It almost seemed as if she had some kind of secret she was protecting. A few months after her life had been saved by Weir and his family, they finally decided to travel back toward Sojourner Falls, near to the place they had met, where they fought those wolves. Winkite wanted to return to her earliest home.

An empty stone dwelling met them when she finally recognized the trail leading to the place she was born. The small edifice had long ago been abandoned and taken over by bracken and weeds. They sat aside each other in the shade of one of its walls when she let her guard down and revealed her story.

She was five when her parents—ashamed of her—decided to give her away, abandoned her, like they had done to this meager dwelling where she had first come into the world. They took her to the edge of the mighty Firthwood and left her there, alone and afraid.

"I don't understand," said a stunned Katonkin. "How could they do that? Why would they do that? Why were they ashamed of you?"

She sat there casting nervous eyes at him and repeatedly scratching her head for over a minute before she answered. Whatever she was about to say was very difficult for her to reveal.

"Nature isn't perfect," she began tentatively. "It makes . . . mistakes. Jhalaveral makes mistakes."

Katonkin grunted. "What kind of mistakes?"

"I was born . . . wrong."

He grimaced, still unsure of what she was getting at.

She touched her long, black hair. "I don't have a feather."

"I noticed. Do you prefer not to wear one?"

"No, I desire one. That is why our paths crossed. I was like you. I was on my way to the falls, to see the Zephyrs. Memories of them from my childhood compelled me to return there, to finish my transition into womanhood in the same way you were becoming a man.

But Jhalaveral chose not to allow it. He, too, was ashamed of me, and sent the wolves to stop me."

Katonkin shook his head vigorously. "Of course not! He would not do that. Why would you say that?" She was on the verge of tears. "Were the Firthans ashamed of you?"

She shook her head. "They saved my life that day—when I was left in the wilderness by my own parents. They were watching when my mother and father walked away from me forever and disappeared beyond the Stallion Mountains. I had hoped they returned here but . . . they didn't. The Firthans took me in, accepted me . . . healed me. They even love me, but they are not my people. They are like the stars—beautiful, always there, but distant. I kept reaching for them, only to find them as far away from me as ever. It was time to come back to my own people."

"You were sick?" asked Katonkin. "What illness did they heal?"

"I was incomplete. Wrong."

Weir reached over and took her hands. "It's alright. I will not abandon you."

Her oval eyes looked deep into his. "Promise?"

He nodded slowly. "I swear it."

He saw the change in her at that point. She had let go of her defenses.

"The Firthans do not call me Winkite."

"They have a different name for you?"

"Lupawa."

It took a few moments for that to register in Katonkin's mind. But when it did, it was like the wall at his back had fallen over him. He knew that Lupawa was a Firthan word. The closest Atikan equivalent was berdahache. They were shaman. Magical beings that were said to bring good luck. People possessing the best traits—and physical characteristics—of both man and woman. He thought them myth. Berdahache were honored by the Atikan, not reviled or shamed.

"So," he said, wondering why her parents were ashamed of her. "You mean you are . . .?"

She could tell he finally understood. "Yes," she said. "I am berdahache."

"You do magic?"

"Of course not. That is myth."

"But you were not born the same as other woman?"

She shook her head. Her face turned down toward her lap. Suddenly remembering they were holding hands, she pushed his away.

Katonkin almost let her do it, but realizing the significance of this simple action, he held tight and wouldn't allow them to separate. She lifted her face, and they both smiled. Despite his attempt to make her feel honored and worthy, he was inwardly troubled. She was not really woman. She was . . . he couldn't say it. These feelings he had her for were real, but how could they be, if she were not a woman? This changed everything. They would never be man and wife, he suddenly realized. They would never have children. They would . . . were . . . friends, and that was all. Katonkin felt the sense of loss then, as if a sword had been stuck clean through his gut.

Winkite. Lupawa. *What do I call her now?*

She sensed his inner conflicts and continued explaining herself. "I am healed. I am woman."

Now he was really confused. "But you said you are—were—berdahache. Doesn't that mean . . .?"

She nodded. "Before. But the Firthans healed me. Amaranthine Springs. The eternal water heals all wounds, removes all poisons, reverses all natural mistakes."

Awareness dawned on him as doubt and confusion were swept away like an avalanche of rock clearing a forest. No wonder she was so strong! She was a creature of duality, and a being of the same waters as he was! Maybe more so!

"You are woman?"

She again nodded. "This is why I seek the zephyr. Why I am here. Why we met."

"What do I call you?" he carefully asked.

"It doesn't matter."

"What is your family name?"

She grimaced. "I do not remember. I was too young when my parents abandoned me, or perhaps I forget."

Katonkin's heart felt a pang of sorrow for her.

"Berdahache," she suddenly uttered, emboldened by his acceptance of her. "I am Winkite Berdahache!" She laughed loudly toward the clouds drifting lazily by. Her glistening eyes returned to his. "But you can call me Twoheart, or Winkite, if you like."

"Twoheart," echoed Katonkin, laughing with her, feeling happy that he was here with her as she reclaimed her identity—and her sense of self-worth.

"With such names, others will know," he then added. "Is that what you want?"

"Yes!" she answered confidently. "I am who I am."

A few days later they were standing together on a cliff overlooking the incomparable Sojourner Falls, just a few leagues south of the fortress Vigilon. They had decided to encamp there for a while, to get to know one another even more and exalt in the beauty of the Shattered Hills and the falls. On the morning they were to head back to Bridgefoot, they finally spotted a Zephyr high up in the blue sky. Their necks grew stiff as they watched it for over an hour gliding within and among the air currents. Miraculously, it began to spiral downward, coming closer and closer as they watched. At one point it vanished to the east, over the jagged hills leading to the Spill Blood Sea, presumably back to Zephyr Wood and the Greyridge Mountains. But an instant later it came screaming over their heads, perhaps fifty feet above the treetops. It flashed by, a streak of brown and white colors, emitting a shriek that caused their spines to tingle. The gigantic bird, gone as fast as it had come, let loose a single feather—a small one, no larger than one from an eagle. It slowly drifted downward to the pair of gawkers. Katonkin caught it before it touched the earth. He turned to Twoheart, and tied the precious gift into her hair.

She was woman, after all.

Four months later, they headed out for the Sunder Line.

Husband and wife, Katonkin Weir and Winkite Berda'weir.

43

Ada didn't know how long it had been since departing Intiga, but the sun was up now. Six or seven hours, she figured, based on the sun, although to her sense of time it had been much shorter. She and the others had sailed like a cloud across a moonlit landscape of the Fringe. When the moon finally went down some time later, everything below changed to an expanse of gray shadow and she lost sight of all detail. She often wondered how the demon knew what bearing to take to carry them to Jurry, but as time passed, she came to assume Cabbal had some special knowledge or talent. If he didn't, they'd soon learn the truth and deal with the consequences at that time.

Shortly after taking flight, she and the others became disoriented and mildly nauseous. They heard distant voices, too. But it all passed for all of them, and for the remainder of their airborne journey they mostly fell into a dreamlike state in which she often slept. Whenever she found herself awake, she often wondered whether Katonkin would still be alive when they reached their destination. He had gone agonizingly silent shortly after they first alit from the high rooftop of the Intiga mausoleum.

She and Galager also found moments to discuss recent events, helping each other to remember everything that had happened since the moment Vreman had laved Galager. Much of the past few days were mysteries to both of them. They tried to ferret out who was still alive, and who wasn't. It was frustrating to them both that Weir could have answered many of their questions, had he only been conscious. The biggest mystery to them, however, involved talk of such things as gold and blue auras, conjuring magic without eludria, Galager's dream fragments, Bloodstones, Zaviel, Vashti, Lazlo, and The Grand Unraveling.

Ada saw the fortress when it was still a dot on the landscape, far ahead and far below.

"There," she said.

"I see it," replied Galager. His ethereal voice still seemed weird to her.

"What should we do?" she asked. "We may be attacked if we simply materialize within the castle."

They were close now. Gliding in on a steep angle toward the center of the massive fortress. She saw the main wall of the Sunder Line, as straight as an arrow. It ran across an extent of open, flat terrain both north and south of the wall, or presumably so, because she had no sense of true north while flying like this. An impalement field lie to the south, very similar to the one at Lavalor.

Nestled against the northern side of the main wall was the castle. A wide pond surrounded it, fed by a channel of water coming from the north. She caught a glimpse of a river farther off in that direction where the channel originated. The castle was a long, confusing mess of angled exterior walls and interior buildings and towers of all shapes and sizes and orientations. Only now did she realize how long and wide Jurry was. Unlike Lavalor, that had a separate village, the village of Jurry was located inside the castle!

A single disappointment struck Ada at this point. She spied no sign of Havless's army anywhere near Jurry, inside or out.

"Bring us just outside the main gate," suggested Civato. "Have the demon deposit me there. The rest of you remain within the dust until I secure our safety."

"We're almost there," said Galager.

Ada turned her attention to the leftmost extent of the fortress. She saw two gates, but one of them was larger than the other. "To the left, Cabbal," she ordered. "Bring us down outside the castle. Outside that larger gate on the road."

As usual, the demon did not respond with words or thoughts. Except during the blood meld, Cabbal hadn't communicated with her at all. But he did seem to understand her, and he now altered his path and aimed them directly toward the spot she was hoping for.

Cabbal slowed as they neared the road. Ada saw Commonlanders down there, traveling in either direction to and from the castle. It was such a relief to finally be back home. Hours earlier she thought they all were going to die, or worse.

I am so lucky. We all are.

The people down below saw the demon. They split apart, giving way to the descending gyre. To a soul, they were alarmed, pulling weapons, shouting warnings in case others hadn't yet noticed the demon.

"Do not land!" shouted Ada. She wasn't sure of the proper commands. Might the wrong choice of words produce undesirable outcomes from Cabbal? And how did he know her language?

"Civato, speak to Cabbal," she said. "Order him to let you down safely. I don't know how to do that."

He responded at once. "Demon, set me down on the road as the person I am," came the deep voice of Civato Jeregoth. "Do it now."

Cabbal hovered perhaps ten feet above the ground as a black tendril of dust extended downward to the hardpack of the road. Civato materialized, safely standing as the tendril withdrew. Over to the right about fifty yards was the main gate of Jurry, as large as Lavalor Gate. Its drawbridge was already down, and its tunnel was clear of any lowered barricades.

One of the travelers closer to him threw a knife at him, but thankfully Civato saw it coming and expertly sidestepped it, letting it sail past him.

"I am not your enemy," he shouted as Ada watched from above. "I am Civato Jeregoth, Bethurian Warden. Castle Shenkel is my home. Do not be afraid. My friends and I have captured this creature you see floating above my head. It will not hurt you. I swear this!"

No more blades came flying toward him.

"What do you want?" yelled one of the travelers. He stepped forward, away from dozens of other road travelers. He was a soldier. He looked middle age, well groomed. Perhaps a pennon. Ada couldn't see his belt insignia to be sure.

Civato faced him, but didn't attempt to move from his spot.

"We come with important news. And urgent needs."

"What news?" asked the soldier.

Civato pointed to the cloud of roiling dust above him. It seemed to Ada he was pointing up at her. "Three more of my friends have come with me. One of them is severely hurt. His name is Katonkin Weir, Pennon Vangard of Castle Lavalor. The other two are Commonland battle mages."

People were gathering closer around the demon. Most had weapons in hand. Many of them exchanged murmurs of recognition at the mention of Weir's name.

"The news?" said the soldier.

The sounds of hoofbeats arose, coming from the gatehouse. A heartbeat later two fists of cavalry spurs emanated from the maw of the tunnel, heading directly toward them.

Civato waited for them to circle round him. After they came to a halt, the soldier he had been talking to conversed in low tones with one of the riders, the leader of this group.

"Civato Jeregoth," said the rider in charge, one eye on him and the other on the gyre. "Welcome to Jurry. Am I to understand you have tamed this creature, and that an injured Katonkin Weir is held within its dusts?"

"Aye," said Civato. "Where is Castellan Havless and his army?"

"They are marching to reclaim their home," said the rider.

That shocked Ada. *Already?*

Civato grimaced. "Then I face a quandary," he said.

"How so, Warden?"

"I seek the Atikan named Twoheart. She was gravely hurt during the Battle of Lavalor. We have the means to save her, but we first must find her. We need her, to continue our mission."

"Then I have solved your quandary," said the rider. "Havless left all his wounded here before marching off to Lavalor with a good number of our men."

"Huzzah!" said Galager, though no one below acted as if they had heard him.

"She is alive?"

"She is," said the rider. "But she remains in and out of consciousness. Her fate is in question."

Civato beckoned to the man. "Please bring her here forthwith. We intend to take her with us to Firthwood. They alone can heal her, as well as her husband, Katonkin Weir."

The rider paused, considering the request. "Is that all you need?"

"A leather of water. A loaf of bread. Three swords."

Civato intends to remain with us? We hadn't discussed that.

The rider turned in his saddle and pointed at one of the other riders. "You heard the Warden. Fetch her. And the other items. Bring Twoheart here immediately. If anyone objects, tell them I demand it. Do not delay." He returned his eyes to Civato.

Ada didn't know who this rider was, but he clearly commanded respect here at Jurry.

Civato bowed to the rider as his other man urged his horse forward then turned it back toward the castle, galloping away in a trail of road dust.

"Thank you," said Civato. "Now I have other things to tell you. You need to remember everything I am about to say. First, I will have each of your men here remember a single name."

The rider's face scrunched in confusion. "Names?"

Civato nodded. "Fallen brothers. Too many for any one of you to remember."

Civato is but one man, thought Ada. *Not an ordinary one.*

"I see," said the rider. "Please proceed."

Civato then walked up to each of the nine remaining riders, one at a time, and told them a single name. By the time he had completed the circle and came back to their leader, he looked up at him and told him four names, not one. Uri Hauer was the last name spoken.

The twelve! And Uri!

"Can you remember those names?" he asked to all.

Nods and Ayes.

"They died in Intiga as heroes. Please relate my condolences to their families. Tell them I am sorry I wasn't strong enough to save them. I hope to return here one day soon with more details of their fate." He looked up at their leader again. "Can you remember the four names I told you? And are you sure about that?"

"Do not worry," said the rider. "They are committed to memory."

"Come with us into the castle," added the rider. "You need more than bread and water."

Civato glanced up at the gyre above him and scratched his obsidian jaw.

"Cabbal," said Ada. "Set the rest of us down near Civato."

The riders and onlookers from Jurry were astonished when three more humans materialized in front of them. Ada immediately embarrassed herself in front of all as she fell into a fit of retching and unexpectedly regurgitated Vashti's ruby.

Mine, she corrected herself.

She quickly snatched it up, wiped it dry on her trousers, and hid it within a pocket. She suddenly remembered Vashti had given her Galager's sandbag. She swiftly patted down her pockets looking for it. Nothing. She stuck urgent hands inside them, but except for her new ruby, they were empty. *I must have dropped it somewhere.* Not the greatest emergency she had ever faced.

Weir was laying in the grass next to the road. Galager was kneeling at his side. Ada ran over to them.

The vangard was moaning.

"He's still alive!" she said, her heart pounding with gratitude.

Weir aimed a half-opened eye toward her. "It is better inside the dust," he rasped in a low whisper. "But first I need to see Twoheart."

Introductions were quickly exchanged all around.

For the next few minutes, as the two teens tended to Weir, Civato and the rider talked. The Bethurian told him everything that had happened. He told them where they were going. Why they were going there. He told them what Ada Halentine and Galager Swift had done, and of what Katonkin Weir had accomplished to free them all. And he explained the threat to Megador and the Five Realms of the Commonland—The Grand Unraveling.

Several braces of soldiers led by a single horseman marched toward them from out of the gate tunnel. Ada could see a lone figure being carried in a stretcher. *Twoheart!*

They set her down next to her husband.

He moaned, lifted his head, looked at her, and extended a brown hand over to her and touched her cheek. He spoke soft words to her that Ada didn't understand, although there was no response.

The men from Jurry brought them water, bread, and even a bit of meat. Ada helped Weir consume sips of the cool liquid and small strips of bread that she tore from the loaf they gave her. Afterward, the others hungrily consumed the meat, leaving the rest of the bread as reserve for later.

How brave these two Atikans are, thought Ada, as she, Civato, and Galager strapped on swords. They were injured like this because they had given their all to defy the Vilazian Multitude. And still, they refused to die.

"Look," said Galager, pointing to a pair of longknives laying alongside Twoheart in her stretcher.

Weir looked at Ada. "Put me back into the dust. Twoheart also. The dust lessens the pain—prolongs the body." Ada didn't understand why that was the case, but she assured Weir she would get them both to Firthwood as fast as possible. Everyone bade farewells to each other then she had Cabbal do Weir's bidding.

By the time Ada commanded Cabbal up into the air again, just minutes later, the demon had five passengers: Katonkin Weir, Winkite Berda'weir, Civato Jeregoth, Galager Swift, and Ada herself.

She could only hope that the Firthans could save Katonkin and Winkite, and that this quest would provide the team with the means needed to save the Commonland.

44

Lazlo directed Haem down over the ruins of Intiga. The eastern horizon was aflame with the first rays of daylight. A curving river divided the ancient metropolis in two. Streets and alleyways were ill-defined lines of gray powder because of the breadth of devastation here. The buildings and structures were once sharply defined, but now they were white or tan amorphous lumps rising from a green jungle that had all but taken over everything.

Dead-ahead was the mausoleum, the largest and tallest structure in the city. Golden sunlight gleamed from its three remaining turrets, a beacon for him, as such.

The gyre swooped in low and hovered over the center of the mausoleum roof. Lazlo scanned the structure, looking for signs of an ambush or a trap. Two dead sentries guarded the exit of the stairway turret, thick patches of red-stained stone under their shoulders. He peered into the dark rectangle of the turret. No one there that he could see, alive or otherwise. There was other blood up here. Twelve sets of empty chains arranged in a circle within the wider ring of braziers, blood-stained stonework near each of them. A larger red stain, halfway between the altar and the turret, and two more closer to the altar. No bodies—except the two guards. No Vashti either, although she had mysteriously summoned him near the stroke of midnight.

Smoke gently wafted from the ring of braziers. The coals were white ash, softly glowing. They had been burning all night. Almost cold. He jerked his vision to the altar's top. No eludria knives.

Had they been used? On whom?

Was Vashti alive? Had she succeeded in summoning the demon namril?

"Put me down," said Lazlo.

He felt the weight of his boots coming to rest on the stonework of the roof. Haem had set him down near the altar. He withdrew his ruby, gripped it tight, and took a moment to again survey everything, keeping an especially cautionary eye on the stairway opening.

He spotted something over by the bloodstain closest to the turret. He approached carefully, slowly, always scanning, always alert.

"What do we have here?" he whispered to himself, spying a small object in the middle of the bloodstain. He bent low and picked it up in his right hand. It was a small sandbag. A toy, mostly soaked with blood. It had belonged to that boy with the golden aura. He spotted something else in a small puddle of thickening blood in the center of the stain. A silver necklace with a broken gem-stone setting.

Vashti's necklace. The ruby was gone.

He cursed upon recognizing it, and dropped the sandbag.

She's dead!

He stood straight and rechecked the altar. The two eludria knives definitely weren't there, but there were plenty of signs of sacrificial blood around the entire roof. He couldn't be sure as to exactly what had happened here the night before, but he was certain the demon had been summoned from the pit, and the Commonlanders had killed Vashti and then escaped.

He lifted his ruby to waist-height.

A scarlet aura sprung forth from around his hand then swallowed him whole.

Lazlo listened to the thrum.

45

Two Days. Dusk. An endless stretch of forest. Mountains up ahead, behind a broad valley. Hints of lightning beyond the peaks. Ada felt like horse manure, warmed over. She wondered about the two vangards. How was it possible they had survived this long journey within the dusts of a demon as they soared across what seemed like half the Earth? The answer, she figured, was the trance-state they had been under while flying.

Every part of her body was numb, even her mind. Galager and Civato both mumbled some words expressing similar notions. Twoheart had started talking the day before, mostly in Atikan, but today there had been moments of lucid conversation in the common-tongue. Weir, not so much—a few words the day before, but not since. If Ada had to bet money on only one of them seeing another sunrise, Twoheart would be the one she'd ante-up on right now.

Cabbal set them all down at the foot of a shadowy valley opening. The demon also materialized nearby, standing rigid and motionless, watching them from behind that pale mask of human horror. Ada shuddered. She still couldn't believe what she had done. Stealing a demon from a vilemaster. She wondered if perhaps she might later regret that course of action. Still, they were alive, so what was the point of second-guessing everything now?

"Everyone alright?" asked Civato Jeregoth. His voice was deep, resonant, hale, no more raspy throat. He diligently examined his surroundings, presumably looking for danger.

"I'm living," responded Galager. "I only wish I were dead." He did a double-take and looked at Ada. "Do wishes come true because of eludria? Maybe I better be more careful with the words I use."

"You're fine," she answered. "No worries. And you're not even holding a ruby, anyway."

She stretched her arms and spun slowly, looking for Katonkin and Winkite. They were both nearby, lying on the ground within some sedge grass. Weir wasn't moving, but she saw his chest rising and falling. Twoheart had her eyes open. They were aimed at her.

Ada went to her and dropped to her knees at her side. "Do you understand me?"

Twoheart nodded. She looked better, stronger—despite the rigors of the long journey.

"Water," Twoheart whispered, her voice barely audible.

Civato rushed over and unslung the leather bottle he had obtained in Jurry. He handed it to Ada. She uncorked the narrow end and lowered the mouth of the bottle to Twoheart's lips. After maybe a dozen sips, Twoheart waved it away.

"It appears safe here," Civato reported. "So far."

The trio instinctively gathered more closely. All three knelt between the two reposing vangards within the high grass, maintaining a small target, but their vision obstructed. Civato produced the partly eaten bread loaf and began tearing off pieces, handing them to Ada and Galager as they stole furtive glances into the shadows surrounding them. The bread was stale, but Ada ate her share voraciously, as did the others. Twoheart ate some of it as well. Weir, however, was in no condition to eat or drink, although Ada carefully moistened his lips and the inside of his dry mouth with drops of water. Ada wondered if Cabbal ate this kind of food. But she decided he didn't, and returned to ignoring him.

Ada already felt strength returning to her limbs. The bread gone, all three of them—the uninjured—stood up and began studying their surroundings in more detail while continually passing the water bottle to one another, each of them taking tiny, delicious sips, in turn. She felt dirt between her toes. She was barefoot! Actually, all five of them were. Only now did she notice.

The forest surrounding them was darker than the sky. Insects were already singing, their pulsing songs arriving collectively at her ears like the sound of a sword blade on a whetstone. Far above them a single screech of a raptor. Tall, broad trees encircled them, many of them seemingly as high as Lord's Watch. Each tree was a swirl of giant limbs that curled around each other, with many of them hanging directly overhead.

Seeing no immediate threats from the forest, she swung around and faced the vale opening. Two fingers of sharp vertical ground lay before them on either side, a long bowshot in either direction. A gentle stream flowed past them over to the left. That's when she saw it. It was almost unnoticeable unless one stared directly at it—a high, transparent, curving dome that stretched across the entirety of the valley opening. The barrier seemed to play tricks with her eyes.

"Magic," stated Galager.

"Indeed," said Civato. "Something this large. Remarkable!"

A black shape swooped down from above, right in front of Galager.

"Bird!" he shouted, ducking. It came at him again, straight for his face, screeching like a common raptor, but much louder.

"Hey!" he shouted after ducking again. "It tried to grab me!" He pulled out his mercenary and swiped at the thing when it came for him again. He swung twice more, ducking upon each occurrence, then a fourth time. His weapon finally made contact and the bird fell within spitting distance of his toes.

The troop quickly gathered round the winged animal.

It's huge, thought Ada, as the creature flapped around in the grass. It was something like a cross between a vulture and an eagle, bigger, dark burgundy feathers, long golden talons and a hooked yellow beak at least eight inches long. It wasn't ugly at all, but its features made it look demonic, particularly the thing's red eyes, glowing like hot rubies. They gawked at the transfigured creature for a few seconds before Civato's sword abruptly put it out of its misery.

"What the hell!" said Galager. "Look at those talons. They could have done some damage."

"Look at the eyes," said Ada. "The Vilazians created these monsters."

Two more screeches from above.

Ada jerked her eyes up to the black canopy above her. A dark object came hurtling toward her from a small patch of sky between some of the nearest limbs.

"Watch out!" she cried while ducking. The bird swooped down, extended its talons in her direction, but Galager was there, swinging away with his blade. Once more he made contact, and a giant . . . vulture was knocked to the ground, landing with a thump and a rustle of feathers just feet away from where she stood. He struck it several more times and it went still.

Another vulture attacked Civato, trying to grab onto his head or his shoulders. He too, ducked, but fell to a knee when it became apparent the raptor was a bit more committed to drawing blood than were the first two. The denied raptor screeched as it flapped its way back into the darkening sky.

"Your nimbus," came a raspy female voice. It was Twoheart. She was on her elbows, head lifted. "Nimbus," the Atikan again croaked again, one hand beckoning for the others to come nearer to her husband and herself.

Ada ran to her, as did Galager and Civato. She produced her ruby and drew up a nimbus that she extended around the entire troop, including Cabbal, who remained motionless. They heard several more of the birds outside, saw them flitting by, screeching and fluttering their wings loudly just above the nimbus, then disappearing.

"Longclaws," Twoheart whispered, still on her elbows. "Easy to kill," she said, her face illuminated by the red nimbus, "until they come in larger numbers."

She dropped back down onto her shoulders. Ada glanced at Weir to make sure he was within the nimbus. He was.

Several more screeches pierced their nimbus. Wings fluttered somewhere close by before receding.

"Every night they attack," Twoheart said. "There will be more. Many more. You must get inside the Firthan dome. Do not delay."

"How?" said Galager. "Can we walk through it?"

"Magic," Twoheart whispered. "Strike it with magic. You will not breach it. But they will come."

"The Firthans?" asked Ada.

Twoheart grunted. Like Weir would do.

"You know this place," said Ada insightfully.

Twoheart smiled. "I once lived here. When I was younger."

The female vangard angled her brown eyes upward. "Lower your magic now," she said, her hoarse voice nevertheless heavy with Atikan accent. "The Longclaws are gone, for the time being."

Ada complied. She felt the coolness of the forest drifting back in around the troop and heard the trilling of insects.

"My turn," said Galager as he started for the magic wall, about thirty feet from their location. Ada hurried to keep up with him while Civato remained behind with the two Atikans.

She didn't watch to see her friend pull his ruby. She was examining the wall.

"Can we touch it?" said Galager.

She reached out. Her fingertips came in contact with the shimmering curtain. It felt cool and spongy, but as she thrust her arm into the barrier more deeply, it began to resist. She withdrew her hand.

"Go ahead," she said.

They took a few steps backward. A red beam of magic shot forward from Galager's left hand. He had learned well. She was so proud of him. His magic reminded her that this ginger-haired boy from the low country had defeated a vilemaster in battle, though, of course, they owed everything to Weir. *I had a part in it too.*

Galager extinguished his magic. They secured their rubies and slowly backed away from the dome, which showed no sign of damage. They again huddled around the two vangards, staring at the almost invisible dome from within the tall grass, listening for Longclaws, and waiting.

Fifteen minutes passed with nothing happening. Ada was getting close to suggesting they again knock on the Firthan door when a short length of the curtain lifted up from the ground in front of them. She was sure her heart stopped beating when she saw at least two dozen brown-skinned warriors, each one astride an immense black creature. But they weren't Bipaquans or lizards.

"Panthers," uttered Civato.

No one reacted at first. Ada wondered how it was possible the magic curtain had masked the presence of these giant cats and their riders. It wasn't until one part of it was lifted up, like a window into a different reality, that she saw them.

Ada glanced sideways to her mates. They both kept swinging their eyes back and forth between her and the Firthans. They were expecting her to make introductions.

"Friends," said Ada. That first word rang out low and weak, so she flared her shoulders, cleared her throat, and tried it again.

"Friends!" she repeated, happier with herself now. "We come from Severcal. We need your help."

Nothing. No response. She suddenly realized the Firthans weren't looking at her, but instead at Cabbal, standing ominously behind the troop.

"I am Adriana Halentine," she hastily added. "I am an eludrian."

She turned halfway around and pointed at Cabbal while keeping her face toward the Firthans. "He will not hurt you. I alone control him."

Shit! Do they understand maledictions?

She realized she had possibly put herself in mortal danger. All these Firthans had to do now, to end this demonic threat, was to put a few arrows into the heart of this girl who foolishly stood before them declaring to be the thing's master.

Civato understood her mistake and took a step forward. "Brothers and sisters," he said.

Ada quickly checked, and indeed, both men and women were arrayed before her. Things had happened so fast, she hadn't noticed until now.

"I am Civato Jeregoth, Bethurian. I am your neighbor, as are these two Commonland battle mages." He pointed at Galager and said his name aloud.

"This creature has been subdued and serves only Lady Halentine. Do not fear it. She can command its death in an instant."

"Then do it now," said a female rider near the center of the Firthan party.

"Permit me to explain why we cannot do that," replied Civato.

"War is upon us all," he continued. "Castle Lavalor has fallen. The Vilazian Multitude is again on the rise. This creature, as vile as it is, has carried us here to enable us to seek your assistance in defeating the Multitude, the Vilazians. Lady Halentine will not let it hurt anyone. We need him—it— to return us to Severcal when we are done here."

"Then you are done here," said the woman. She raised an arm above her head. Her fist glowed red. *An aura*! A swath of energy rose up to the magic archway in the shield.

"She's closing it," said Galager urgently.

But another female voice rose up into the young night.

"Shaleen," Twoheart cried from the grass. "It is me, Lupawa!"

The woman abruptly extinguished her energies and lowered her arm. She urged her mount forward after a brief pause. The others in her war party did the same, flanking her, guarding her, as she and her amazing panther closed with the troop.

The woman, Shaleen, guided her cat so it circled them slowly. It was as big as a horse, but with velvety black fur that stretched taught over a muscular frame and limbs. Yellow-green eyes with black irises scrutinized them. Long swishing tail. The only sounds it made was the rustling of grass as the regal beast stalked slowly around the troop.

Shaleen dismounted after her other steely-eyed riders encircled the troop with dozens of cats. They looked like Atikans with their black hair and light brown skin. The men even dressed like them with linen trousers and vestments. The woman instead wore short deerskin skirts and sleeveless tops. They all had leather whips coiled at their hips. Ada saw knives too, no swords. Maybe half of them carried short spears and the other half, bows.

Shaleen approached Twoheart and lowered herself onto her haunches. She placed a gentle hand on Twoheart's chest. Twoheart covered it with one of her own then the two women began talking in strange words. Firthan, Ada, supposed. She heard their names intermixed within the conversation, Katonkin's also. Shaleen went to Weir and checked on him. No response. She returned to Twoheart. Another minute or two of conversation passed between them. Shaleen stood. She faced the three of them.

"The Firthan people welcome you to Thrum," she said. She looked at Cabbal. "But not the demon. He must remain outside the valley. And you will surrender your weapons until you depart the valley."

Ada nodded, accepting the terms. "Thank you," she said.

What did Twoheart tell her?

Ada turned to Cabbal and dismissed him after ordering him to remain close to this spot. Everyone watched as the pale figure immediately dissolved into gray and black particles, formed a crack in the air, and then corkscrewed away from them, high into the trees, where it disappeared into the early evening. Several of the Firthan riders uttered exclamations into the air behind the departing demon. She wondered whether Cabbal would commit atrocities while they were separated. Yet she had no way of knowing, so she put him out of her mind.

A dozen or so Firthan riders slid from their cats once Cabbal was gone.

Swords and longknives were surrendered to them.

The men split up and gently lifted both Weir and Twoheart and carried them to two other riders, still mounted, riding bareback, as were all the others. They placed each vangard behind a rider on separate animals. Twoheart brushed back her feather and wrapped her arms around the torso of her rider, a man. He locked them in under his own arms and urged his animal toward the barrier opening. The same had been done for the unconscious Weir, but the rider uncoiled his whip and gave it to two other Firthans, who wrapped it around Weir's shoulders and underarms, then around the rider's chest, securing Katonkin to the rider.

Other dismounted riders helped Ada, Galager, and Civato onto three separate panthers. They each settled in behind their respective rider and grasped their shoulders. Shaleen and the other dismounted riders leapt onto their cats. She issued an order into the cool, evening air. More Firthan words. All the cats remaining turned as one and passed through the magical archway.

46

The panthers headed straight into the valley center, gliding through the woodland with ease, elegance, and speed. Ada could feel the power of the giant cats beneath her, muscles flexing with every step. Fearing a fall, she had at first gripped her own animal tightly with her knees, but the ride so far was smoother than she'd expected. Even when the beasts leapt over ground depressions or fallen tree limbs, the maneuvers conveyed little shock to the rider. Within minutes she found herself relaxing her grip, both on the cat and the Firthan man she clung to. Quick glances to Galager and the others revealed they were getting along just fine. Even Weir and Twoheart seemed solidly anchored behind the men conveying them toward the city of Thrum.

The trees here were more substantial than those where the troop had first landed. There wasn't much brush here, so the way forward through the trees was unencumbered. Ada chanced a glance to the sky, but all she saw was a contiguous canopy in every direction she checked. *How old these trees must be!* She tried to get a glimpse of the dome shield. *How far into the valley does it go?* But the interlocking canopy and the late hour prevented any sight of it.

She saw the first glimmer of city lights ahead in the ancient forest.

They spread out on either side of the group as they raced on. They ran past the first of them. The soft glows emanated from open doorways and windows that were built into the bases of the tree trunks. There were lights overhead in the canopies as well.

They began passing Firthan people who stopped in their tracks to watch the panthers running past them and to perhaps get a glimpse of rare visitors. The density of forest dwellers increased, as did the number of tree dwellings. Vines of various thicknesses hung down everywhere, some of them extending all the way to the ground. Many of them were intertwined together and wrapped around trunks as wide as twenty feet, maybe thicker, forming spiraling stairways into the canopy. They had entered the outskirts of Thrum. The entire forest was decorated by white lights. *Beautiful!* Ada suddenly realized not a single one of them had a flame; rather, they appeared to be small, glowing crystals.

Some of the cats and riders broke off toward other destinations. Shaleen's cat continued on, a dozen others still at her flanks or behind her. The fast-moving party broke into a wide clearing that Ada estimated was large enough for the entire footprint of Castle Lavalor to fit into. Her eyes shot skyward again. The first stars were appearing, but they twinkled more than expected and seemed a little fuzzy. She assumed it was from the effects of the dome shield. Otherwise, she saw no sign of it. For all intents and purposes, it was invisible from within the valley. Several more riders broke away from the party, their duties apparently done for the night.

The remaining cats headed across the clearing, directly toward a large structure at its center. It appeared to be a lodge, perhaps a meeting hall. It had a long, rectangular footprint and a gabled roof reaching skyward. Each wall was studded with multiple double doors, many of them open, light pouring forth from the interior. Hundreds of Firthans occupied the vicinity of the lodge, each person walking in a different direction while others stood near to each other, talking. All eyes turned their way as the panthers and their riders came closer to the lodge.

They rode past the left side of the wooden building. Ada peered into the open doorways as they did so. She caught glimpses of a massive interior space, wooden posts rising from black, wooden floors, feasting tables and benches, and several stone hearths in the center areas. She smelled traces of smoke and roasted meats.

They crossed the remainder of the clearing, leaving the lodge behind them, and reentered the forest, itself ablaze with white crystal illumination. They suddenly came to a halt at one of the big trees. Barefoot riders dismounted, sliding from the backs of the yellow-eyed panthers. Hands reached up and helped Ada from her cat. Others already had Weir and Twoheart in their grasps and were carefully carrying them into the doorway at the bottom of the tree. Ada, Galager, and Civato hustled behind them and into a lit space, a small, round empty room with a stairway just ahead leading downward. The floor was wood but it was spongy, like walking on a mattress.

They trio gathered around the two Atikan vangards after the Firthans gently set them down onto the soft floor, face up. Twoheart was awake. She tried to sit up, leaning toward Katonkin, but a Firthan man coaxed her to lie flat. She finally complied.

Shaleen went to the stairway, leaned over a banister, and yelled something into the depths below. Firthan words. An urgent, insistent, tone.

A man's voice echoed back. Two Firthans appeared from the stairway, an elderly man and woman, dressed in white robes. They were barefoot and had black hair, like most everyone else around these parts, including the two injured Atikans. Shaleen briefly conversed with them before the newcomers approached Twoheart.

Upon seeing them nearing her, she lifted her head. "No! My husband," she said sternly. She coughed. "See to him first." She seemed to remember where she was and instead spoke some foreign words. Ada presumed she had repeated her demand in the Firthan tongue.

The white-robed pair immediately did as she asked and positioned themselves on either side of Weir, kneeling at his side.

Shaleen came over to the trio. "They are wrullore healers," she said.

"Can they help them?" said Ada.

"They will try," said Shaleen. "I believe Lupawa will fully recover. Her husband . . . we will know soon." *Why is she calling her Lupawa?*

One of the healers had a leather flask. He produced a bit of cloth and soaked it with what looked like water from the flask and began dabbing Weir's lips with its moisture. He then produced a flower petal, dark purple, and carefully inserted it into Weir's mouth and placed it on his tongue. The woman, meanwhile, withdrew a globule of green crystal from her robe and set it onto Weir's chest over his sternum, causing Ada to raise an eyebrow. It was about the size of an apple.

"What's that?" asked Galager.

"Lightning Crystal," said Shaleen. "It has the power to heal. The petal is from an amaranthine flower." She raised a palm, as if asking patience and silence.

The woman in the white robe began to whisper as she worked over Weir. She placed her open palms onto his chest on either side of the crystal. It reminded Ada of Sanguir, and for the thousandth time in the last few days she worried about the fate that had befallen her.

Is she alive?

The woman's incantations grew louder, drawing Ada's mind back to matters at hand. The crystal began to softly glow with a white hue. It also had a small aura that maybe tripled in size as the woman spoke, enough, perhaps, to reach deeply into Weir's chest. The man, meanwhile, continued applying water droplets to Weir's lips and also inside his mouth as he tried to rehydrate the fallen hero. Several minutes passed and both healers suddenly moved back over to Twoheart and repeated their ministrations upon her.

When they were done, Twoheart pushed herself upright on the floor, her arm extended behind her, leaning on a palm for support. Her black hair fell behind her, as did her feather. A remarkable recovery, albeit not a complete one. When the healers tried to get her to lie back down, she refused. Showing amazing resilience, she rolled over onto her knees and crawled to her husband. She caressed his face with a hand then leaned in closer, placing her forehead gently onto his, her hair and feather falling over the sides of his face.

She gathered up her hair and let it fall over a shoulder. "We must bring him to Amaranthine Springs," she said. She switched into a sitting position aside her mate, her legs pointing past his head so she was facing him.

"Now!" she said. "We cannot delay. It's his only chance."

The two healers were standing near to her. They had hidden their water flask and the so-called Lightning Crystal back inside their robes. They looked grimly at Shaleen. The woman shook her head ever so slightly.

Ada felt her heart breaking. She dropped down behind Twoheart and helped her to remain upright on the soft floor.

"We must leave at once," demanded Twoheart. She was looking up at Shaleen, tears in her eyes.

Shaleen and the two healers stepped to the other side of the room and talked in whispers so the others wouldn't hear. When they separated, Shaleen came over to Twoheart and knelt so they were face to face.

The two women embraced, their first chance to do so since the troop had arrived in Thrum. This was no casual hug, but a heartfelt entwining of hearts, shoulders, and limbs that only really good friends—or lovers—accepted from one another.

Shaleen pushed away from Twoheart, giving her back to Ada, but she continued holding her shoulders with her hands.

"Lupawa," she whispered. "Amaranthine Springs heals all wounds and removes all poisons, but it takes before it gives."

"I'm aware," said Twoheart. "But you just helped him."

"He's not responding to our assistance," said the woman healer.

Shaleen spread her arms, trying to think of the right words. "The healers do not think your husband has the strength to survive the trial of Amaranthine Springs. And neither will he survive the ascent to that healing place. They are sure any attempt to do so will kill him. But it gets worse, I'm afraid. Even if he could survive that perilous climb, even if we carry him there, we cannot lower the shield until the morning. But he will not be with us when the sun rises."

Twoheart—Lupawa—cast violent eyes toward the two healers. Ada thought she was going to leap to her feet and slay them both where they stood. But reality seemed to take hold, and her gaze softened and dropped back down to her husband.

"I am so sorry, my friend, but he has but a few hours to live, perhaps even minutes."

"Summon the demon," uttered Galager suddenly. "Cabbal can take Katonkin to the highest of mountains. It would take only minutes."

Shaleen shook her head. "As I said, the springs takes before it gives. And we cannot lower the shield at night. The Longclaws will take hundreds of our people before morning. We will need to redeploy the shield, to keep us safe as we ascend Amaranthine Mountain, no matter the manner. We can only visit the springs in daylight. He'll be gone by then."

"Safe from what?" asked Civato.

"Jhalaveral's Lighting," said Shaleen. "At this time of year the lightning is ever present. The springs are unassailable without the dome shield to protect us from it."

Galager shrank dejectedly.

Twoheart coughed. "Katonkin is certain to die?" she asked. "Tonight?"

"I did not say that," responded Shaleen.

Twoheart's eyes brightened. A flicker of hope glimmered within them. Ada felt the same brief emotion, a blast of fire that immediately burned away at the despair she had started to feel because of Weir's fatal condition.

"Can you help Katonkin, or not?" asked Galager. "That's the one thing I've always heard about you people. You can heal any sickness and any person, right? You even healed Cazlich."

"Not everyone can be healed of everything," said Shaleen. "And we did not heal Cazlich, though he was indeed ill when he first arrived here."

"Please, m'lady," said Civato. "We've come so far. Don't let us fail now. Please tell us you can help Pennon Weir. He's given his all so we can be here. I do not know him, but already I know this world would not be right without him in it."

Shaleen dropped her arms from Twoheart's shoulders and regained her feet. She glanced at the two healers. The woman healer nodded, as if giving her consent to something.

"We have the Torpor," said Shaleen. "It is his only hope. But it's not everything *you* hoped for."

Twoheart trembled as Ada continued propping her up.

"No more mysteries," said Shaleen. "Let me explain what we propose."

"Please hurry," said Twoheart. "What is the Torpor? Why have I not heard of it?"

"We don't normally reveal the Torpor to outsiders," Shaleen began. "Not even to you, Lupawa, though you have lived here among us. We can later discuss why that had to be. But first, let me explain how the Torpor will help your husband although it will at the same time destroy your happiness. I don't mean to be blunt, but time is of the essence. When I have finished explaining all of this, I will need you to immediately make a decision. We don't have much time. You did well to bring him here when you did."

"Go on," rasped Twoheart.

"The Firthan people have lived for centuries, here below Amaranthine Springs. Yet we are a dying people, though it will take many more centuries before we all succumb to the ravages of time. I am among the youngest of the Firthans. I am over two hundred years old. Our elders are far older."

Ada heard herself gasp.

"I knew Cazlich when I was younger," continued Shaleen. "He used his green magic to discern that I was capable of safely infusing myself with the eludria. He found six others within our numbers as well. And we, The Seven, transcended. The Firthan people are the guardians of Amaranthine Springs, the healing waters, but The Seven are the wielders and maintainers of the dome shield.

"The dome shield protects us from the Longclaws, the devil birds that have cursed us since the day the Vilazians brought them here to destroy us. Cazlich responded to our need. He gave us the shield, to save us from the Longclaws. But life teaches us there are prices to pay for everything, and over time we discovered the dome has sickened us. The magic of the dome eats at our minds, though our bodies are immune from its effects because of the healing waters. We are caught in this contradiction. The thing that keeps us alive in the short term is killing us in the long term."

Ada raised a hand to her mouth. *Must everything be bad news?*

"But thankfully," continued Shaleen, "long before the need for the dome arose, we found a way to protect those few among us who grew sick or aged faster than the rest of us." She gestured to the two healers. "Our wrullorers learned to use the combined powers of the Thrum and the healing waters to allow our most vulnerable to sleep indefinitely rather than die or waste away. The Torpor.

"When we later discovered the dome was hurting us, we fortunately already had an answer. Because of the Torpor, we can allow our beloved people, those who become severely ill, to sleep indefinitely in an altered state that sustains not only their lives, but their spirits. And that is what your husband needs to undergo, Lupawa. It is the only way we know for him to continue living."

Twoheart's head dipped. Ada hugged her more tightly from behind.

Shaleen pointed to the stairway. "In a few minutes I will show you the sacred resting place of our beloved sleepers, all of those who are in Torpor. If you agree, that will also be your husband's resting place, for now."

Shaleen reached down and caressed Twoheart's tear-moistened cheek.

"Lupawa," whispered Shaleen. "Take solace. Believe me when I say there is also hope and wonder in all of this. For if the time ever comes—whether it be one day, one year, or one century from now—that we no longer need the dome shield, we will reawaken our loved ones, those we know how to heal. We have the skills to do so. And with time, we may conceive of a way to strengthen your husband so he can challenge Amaranthine Springs."

Twoheart's shoulders firmed up beneath Ada's supporting hands. She gathered her legs up beneath her and stood, albeit a little shakily. Ada rose with her and kept a hand on an arm to help keep her balanced.

Twoheart looked at her, her eyes glinting dangerously, but not as enemies. There was love in them too. This was the old Twoheart. Strong and defiant. The vangard Ada had watched battling the demons, Haem and Fasar.

"Then I have no choice," Twoheart said. She wiped the last remaining tears from her brown eyes, drying them. "We need to save Katonkin. You need to save him."

Shaleen smiled. "A wise decision."

Twoheart coughed. "I have made yet another decision," she said. "I vow that as long as zephyrs fly above Sojourner Falls and there is air within my lungs, I shall not rest until the Longclaws are no longer a scourge to the Firthan people and until I also find a way to allow Katonkin to benefit from Amaranthine Springs."

47

Shaleen abruptly went to the open doorway leading out to the forest and signaled to some men waiting outside. She allowed a handful of them to enter, then sent the remainder away into the burgeoning night. One of the Firthans had the group's weapons; swords and longknives. He came in and set the bundle against a wall, flat on the floor. He picked out a pair of longknives from the heap, presumably Weir's, and handed them to Shaleen.

Two of the men went to the unconscious Weir, sat him up, draped his arms across their stooping shoulders, and lifted his limp form to his feet. The other two posted themselves on either side of Twoheart. Although she was standing, she wasn't yet up to the task of taking stairways without assistance.

Seeing they were ready, Shaleen entered the stairway. "This way," she said.

The men carrying Weir followed first, then Twoheart and her men.

Ada waited until they disappeared below then quickly fell in behind them, followed by Galager, Civato, then the two healers. They came to another room, one level lower. A slightly bigger one, with a half-dozen narrow beds, some cabinets, and a table and chairs.

Yellow glowing crystals on walls illuminated the wooden space. Shaleen grabbed a flameless lantern from off the table. It had a white, glowing crystal affixed to it that seemed as bright as any normal oil lantern.

They crossed the room to another open doorway and entered it. Another stairway, leading down. Shaleen led them into it and descended. The two healers once again formed the tail of the procession, down into the earth.

A few minutes passed as their steps echoed off the wooden walls of the spiraling stairway. They emerged into a horizontal cavern, a tunnel, that widened rapidly as they traversed it. Shaleen was in a hurry. There were more crystals here, small yellow ones, each of them ensconced on the tunnel walls. They grew brighter, peaking in intensity as they drew near to them, then fading back into darkness after the procession had passed. Ada had never seen such a thing.

They entered a new cavern. Bigger. Darker. Cooler. Mustier. The dirt was cold and moist under her bare feet. Their immediate surroundings lit up for them as they entered. *Yellow crystals! On candle stands!*

She saw darkness further up ahead, beyond the area illuminated by their lantern and the crystals closest to it. Ahead in the shadows she spotted dark figures sitting on the ground.

Shaleen led them to the first one, just ahead, and paused.

"A jade statue," said Galager. "Like The Redeemer, back at Lavalor."

Ada was speechless. She wasn't sure what to make of this. All kinds of thoughts and possibilities started bouncing around inside her head.

"Come," Shaleen said, heading further into the cavern, winding her way around numerous other jade statues. She cradled the longknives in one arm and carried the lantern in her other hand, its light spilling out in all directions, causing a cascading effect in which other crystals within the cavern lit up when they were caressed by the light from her lantern.

Shaleen finally stopped. The men carrying Weir gently laid him on the ground, face up, on a spot where she was pointing. Twoheart lowered herself and sat on the ground next to him.

Ada studied her surroundings. They were inside a dome-shaped cavern about fifty feet high and twice that in diameter. The general area where they stood, near the center, was illuminated by the lantern and maybe a dozen yellow crystals, while the outermost areas were a ring of darkness. Yellow crystals had been distributed evenly throughout the large space. The ones closest to their location burned the brightest, and all others diminished in intensity the more distant they were from Shaleen's lantern.

"How many are there?" asked Galager, presumably referring to the jade figures all around them. They were all about the same size and shape, and had objects, or gifts, near them: fresh fruit, simple pieces of jewelry, long necklaces made of flower petals, bunches of flowers laying across knees, wooden carvings, small paintings, and the like.

"Hundreds," said Shaleen. "Our most vulnerable. They are in Torpor."

"Will this be Katonkin's fate?" asked Twoheart.

"This is where he will peacefully rest," Shaleen answered. "Until the day of his awakening."

No one reacted.

"We shouldn't delay," said Shaleen. "Lupawa, perhaps you should prepare yourself. Maybe you have some words for him? He may be able to hear you."

Twoheart bowed her head and placed her hands on Weir's nearest arm. Nothing happened for a few moments, then she bent lower and kissed her husband on the lips, lingering for a heartbeat or two. She whispered some words. Ada didn't understand them. They were Atikan. When Twoheart was ready, she sat up straight.

Shaleen signaled the two men who had helped Twoheart into the cavern. They came forward and carefully lifted her back onto her feet. Ada and Galager went to her and replaced the two Firthan men at her sides.

The man in the white robe asked everyone to give them some

space. He spread his arms and ushered them back, away from Weir. Not far, only a few paces.

With the assistance of his fellow Firthans, he sat Weir up, manually crossed his legs in the Kuneteje position, and gently balanced him so he was hunched over his knees. Both healers hastily knelt, one on each side of the stricken Atikan. The woman pulled out her Lightning Crystal and balanced it on Weir's head. They both placed their hands around Weir's skull, holding him upright but also forming a cradle of flesh for the crystal to settle into.

The woman started her verbal enchantments like before, quiet at first, then louder. The crystal began to glow, then formed a green aura. It grew in intensity and slowly spread down over Weir.

His entire body soon began to glow a bright green. The healers continued chanting mysterious words over him. A minute passed, nothing changing. Ada suddenly saw Weir's form becoming more translucent within the aura, clothes and all. The healers grew tense, their words less smooth than before. The woman had a look of pain on her face and she was sweating.

Someone touched Ada's hand. She glanced to her left. It was Galager. He had reached across Twoheart to her. She extended her left arm back toward him, in front of Twoheart, and squeezed his hand. Twoheart covered their joined hands with one of hers. Civato was standing at Galager's other side, an obsidian hand on his shoulder. Ada felt tears beginning to well in her eyes. She stole a glance at Twoheart's face. Sadness dominated every feature. But this stalwart vangard had no more tears left to cry.

The healers continued their work. Weir almost turned invisible and then a white light flared up inside him, blinding all for a moment, illuminating the entire cavern. The healers quickly jumped up and backed away from him—Twoheart's mate, Ada's friend, Galager's friend, the man who had saved them from Vashti.

The woman working over Weir had her green crystal in her hands. It no longer glowed.

The ball of light on the ground suddenly vanished.

Panthertooth was no longer there, at least not as flesh and bone.

Instead, a jade statute now occupied the space he had just filled.

Shaleen came over and faced Twoheart, Weir's blades arrayed before her, lying across her upturned forearms. Winkite Berda'weir took them, coughed, and thanked her. She took several halting steps, crossing the short precipice between wakefulness and sleep and carefully laid both longknives across Weir's knees.

"I shall return for you, warrior boy."

48

The thunder boomed, loud and close. A vortex of gray and black clouds swirled above. Lightning pulsed within the heavenly whirlpool like an irregular heartbeat. The air here at the top of this mountain was thin, cool, but heavy with mist and full of energy. Every minute or so a bolt screamed out of the clouds, striking the mountain somewhere higher up. A daunting step of rock they had yet traversed prevented direct sight of the fiery events, but the explosions of sound flowed down toward them like avalanches, accosting their ears.

Ada glanced at the last panther as it bounded back down the winding trail and disappeared behind some rocks in a blur of black fur. It had taken seven cats half a day to bring her and the others up to this lofty spot. Now she understood why it would have been impossible for Katonkin to survive this ascent in his condition. Despite being carried here by those astonishing animals and their Firthan masters, she and her friends were exhausted. It was one thing riding bareback on cats as they ran across level ground, but it was a monumental undertaking trying to hold onto them as they lurched up the side of the mountain. And they weren't even at the summit yet.

Shaleen was the only one among them still standing. Ada,

Galager, Twoheart, Civato, and the two healers from the night before —the wrullorers—were all sitting on boulders or small shelves of rock, each of them trying to catch their breath. If Shaleen was winded, though, she didn't show it.

"They don't like it up here," she said of the giant cats. "The thunder scares them."

As if on cue, a crack of thunder boomed across the mountain top. Ada felt tiny hairs on the back of her neck dancing on her skin. Pebbles rained down over them because of the blast, adding to the layer of gravel and dust already at their feet and on every visible surface.

That was close!

"We'll walk back down?" she asked. "When we're finished here?"

Ada turned a foot over on the side to get a better view of the sandals she was wearing. The Firthans had brought a number of them to the troop after breakfast and fitted the most appropriate ones to their feet. They were made entirely of wood fibers, glue, and that same type of spongy material in the healer's room. They were comfortable enough and would be put to good use in all this loose gravel.

"We won't need the cats," Twoheart said, rather mysteriously.

Has she done this before?

"They'll wait for us at the foot of the mountain," said Shaleen.

"How close are we to Amaranthine Springs?" asked Galager. He was sitting abreast Ada. Their hips were smashed against each other —Ada's scabbard caught in the middle—although there was plenty of room for separation had they wanted it. They didn't.

How can there be springs at a mountain top?

"Not far," Shaleen said. She looked up into the vortex. "We must first wait for the shield. It would be fatal if we climbed this last step without it being in place. We'll know when it's done."

"We'll be able to see it?" asked Civato, adjusting the bandages on his wrists. The Vilazian shackles he had worn for some number of days had cut deeply and caused infections. Galager had similar bandages, made necessary by the same kind of shackles. During the battle with Vashti he had tried pulling his hands from them, and had paid the price with blood. Ada touched some tiny scabs on one of her wrists. She had also felt the consequence of wearing those same shackles, and had been cut by them, though nowhere near to the degree suffered by Galager and Civato.

Shaleen nodded. "In a sense," she said. "The magic itself is transparent from below, but it will affect the vortex. It will . . . flatten a little once the shield is in place."

It had been a horrible night. Weir was gone. Ada couldn't wrap her mind around it. Shaleen had talked some nonsense about him later reawakening, but in her heart she knew that would be many, long years from now, if ever.

The day was young, but already she was tired and so were the others. She didn't think anyone had gotten any sleep the night before. She certainly hadn't, or if she had, it was only brief, fitful moments, filled with nightmares and regrets. At least the breakfast the Firthans brought them was good and made her feel strong enough for this adventure to the top of Amaranthine Mountain.

There had been so many things happening to them in recent days that she could hardly keep them straight in her befuddled mind. She wanted to talk about . . . stuff with the others. But she didn't know where to start. Maybe she just needed time to sort it all out herself before trying to talk about anything.

Twoheart coughed. Ada planted eyes on her. *What an amazing woman.* The Atikan vangard sat alone on a nearby boulder, staring off into the distance. She had put on a brave face this day, but there was no hiding her overall weakened condition. Her shoulders were slumped, she was leaning heavily on hands planted on knees, and her eyes showed weariness. When she walked, her stride wasn't sure and confident. Her breathing was shallow and labored. She was much better than the day before, but nowhere near fighting order.

Twoheart was again wearing her pair of longknives—the Firthans had changed their minds about keeping their weapons from them. Ada had assumed they thought they might need them up here on these rocky slopes—Longclaws?—but Shaleen later asserted those devils came out only at night. And never had they been seen near the springs. Whatever their reasons, Ada was glad she had been reunited with her mercenary.

Like Galager and Ada, the two healers were sitting together. The trio had barely paid any attention to them the previous evening. There had been more pressing matters on their minds. His name was Keil, hers, Willow. She didn't think they were married, or even lovers. Their relationship was more professional, she thought. Keil had traces of arrogance in his demeanor. Willow was more of a shy person. It was impossible to tell their true ages, of course, them being virtually immortal and all, but he looked to be in his early thirties, and she was maybe late twenties, about the same age range as Shaleen—maybe.

Ada wondered why it wasn't raining up here along with all this thunder and lightning.

She spied the water bottle hanging on Civato's broad shoulders. He saw her looking at it, unslung it and passed it over to Galager, who then gave it to her. After several sips, she passed it back the way it had come, and everyone followed her example, in turn.

"How do you create the dome shield?" said Galager, directing his question to Shaleen. "Do you use eludria—the way you opened a portal through it last night?"

"The Seven has the power needed to raise it," she answered. "Or to redirect it—as will occur at any moment. Cazlich taught us the skills we need after he gave us eludria."

"Will you be participating?" said Ada. "I mean, today, to help redirect it?"

Shaleen shook her head. "Only three of the seven will. But not me. Not this time."

Her answers were brief. As if she was reluctant to share too much information.

"Why only three?" asked Galager, never one to worry about boundaries, social or otherwise.

Shaleen grimaced. She glanced at Twoheart, then seemed to remember she trusted her, so in extension, everyone else here. "We only have three rubies," she said. "Cazlich gave them to us. We've not had need of more, especially after we learned the shield was hurting us as much as it was protecting us." Ada detected a note of trouble in the Firthan woman's eyes. The way they had drooped, perhaps, while giving her answer. Almost as if she were embarrassed.

No! As if she were ashamed!

"You must be very proud," said Ada. "You and the other members of The Seven have saved many lives since the Vilazian Multitude first came to our lands."

Shaleen allowed a thin smile to appear on her lips. "It is a mixed blessing to be a Firthan eludrian" she said. "You are very insightful. I am indeed proud of my brothers and sisters, the other six. I have to constantly remind them of the good they do even though there are those among us who do not value us. I only wish we could do more."

Twoheart coughed. "I am proud of you," she said. "And I am grateful for what you have done for me, both in the past and yesterday. But don't forget my vow, for I shan't. I will strive forever more to rid your home of the Vilazian scourge."

"Me too," said Galager. "And we're getting Katonkin back, no matter what it takes."

Ada was surprised to then hear herself jumping on the bandwagon. "Me too," she said, suddenly understanding that was as good as a pledge, or in Twoheart's words, a vow.

Another flash of light somewhere above, the thunder attacking their ears just a second or two later. No pebbles or dust this time.

Civato cleared his throat and walked over to the two healers, offering them the water bottle, which they gladly accepted. He turned back to the others.

"I would gladly help in any way I can," he began. *Nice words, though not a vow.* "That's why I'm here now. But first we need to remember there is a war in the making. It occurs to me that in our haste to obtain your healing miracles for the two vangards, that we have neglected to mention the other reason we are here."

"I already told her," said Twoheart, coming right to the point.

Civato sat back down. "That settles that," he said, laughing.

"Told her what?" asked Ada. "Much has happened since Lavalor fell—since the time you got hurt and went into a coma."

"I heard everything while we were flying here," Twoheart responded. She coughed several more times before continuing. "Each of you talked more than you realize as we pretended to be clouds racing across the land. I know what happened to Warden Jeregoth and his friends. I know what you and Galager did on Cadia Gate with your blue and gold magic. I know I was carried to Jurry, and that Havless and his men are at this very moment endeavoring to retake Lavalor. I know Katonkin ran to Intiga to help you. I know what you both did on that horrible tower—you defeated a powerful eludrian and submitted a demon namril to your will. I know that you brought Katonkin here so he might yet live. And I know Zaviel Vogli has a bloodstone and that we are here to find the one Cazlich possessed, for without it, the Commonland, Firthwood, Atika, and even Bethuria, might face a very dark future."

Twoheart looked at Ada. "Did I miss anything?"

Ada shook her head as another bolt of lightning impacted the mountain up above.

49

"The Firthan people do not have the Bloodstone," said Shaleen. "I would not say your journey here has been wasted, but you will be disappointed if you think Cazlich's talisman is secreted somewhere within our city."

"Then where is it?" asked Galager. He jerked a thumb at Ada. "She's been reading a book. It mentioned some guy who came here. Darrow Stahg. He said it was here."

"He was mistaken," said Shaleen.

"But you knew him?" asked Ada. Something about how the Firthan had answered Galager's query hinted as such. She had denied the assertion of the stone being here, but not that Stahg had been.

"Strange man," Shaleen said. "We would not have let him into the city, but—"

"But what?" said Galager.

"He walked through our dome shield. As if it wasn't there." Shaleen sighed. "It's never happened before, or since, and I'm at a loss to explain it."

"He's an Immune," said Ada. "Maybe that has something to do with it?"

Shaleen's eyes turned to narrow slits, filled with questions.

"I don't even know if he's still alive," added Ada.

"Immune?"

Ada nodded. "Yes, um, a person who is unaffected by eludria. An Immune will neither transcend nor transfigure, if he or she is infused with a ruby. Not many of those types running around, I suppose."

"They are immune to magic also?"

"I don't think so. But maybe sometimes they are. I'm not sure."

Civato turned up a palm. "But where is the Bloodstone, if not in Thrum?" His palm turned into a finger, pointing at no one in particular. "Would you tell us where it is, even if you knew its location?"

Good question.

"She has already told me where it is," answered Twoheart. "She understands the threat and our need."

"Shit!" uttered Galager. "Then where is it?"

"The Redeemer has it," Shaleen said.

Ada knew what she meant by that. *The jade statue in Castle Lavalor!*

"He's in Lavalor," said Galager. "I already met him."

Everyone must have been looking at him funny because he decided to elaborate on his previous comment.

He glanced sideways at Ada. "It was after Hadron laved me," he said. "I was in a coma or something. A reverie. Lots of stuff happened to me. It all seems like bits and pieces of memories or dreams. But yes, I think it all happened even though it doesn't make sense. At one point I was in the gardens, by the statue. The Redeemer. There was a ghost. It was him. Cazlich. We talked. He helped me wake up."

He squeezed the bridge of his nose, eyes closed.

"I saw Sanguir after I woke up," he said. "I think she helped me wake up too. Without her I don't think I would have. I then fought Haem—with this other magic. Gold magic."

Galager turned fully around toward Ada. "Sanguir's dead. I remember that now."

Ada winced. *Not her too.*

"I saw her. Then I went to find you. At the gate."

"The Listener has passed," said Twoheart. "Bosun Rheev told me.

Although I'm not sure when he did. I was barely conscious at the time. I imagine he . . . felt I had the right to know."

Ada and Galager spontaneously embraced. So much had happened to them. So much they didn't understand. Maybe one day they would. But right now, she believed him. Every word. After all, who would believe her story about Vashti and Cabbal?

"When we are finished here, we will return to Lavalor," declared Twoheart, pulling back her shoulders, trying to look strong. "We shall reawaken Cazlich. That's our way forward."

"How will we awaken him?" asked Galager.

"I'll go with you," said Willow in a rare moment of speech. "I possess the required skills and knowledge."

Shaleen whirled around to face her. She started to say something, most likely to object to her offer. But she changed her mind. "I suppose you must," she said, appearing resigned to allowing Willow to leave Firthwood.

"Choose wisely," said Twoheart, directing her advice to Willow. "That would be no small undertaking. You are putting your life at risk if you come with us. Perhaps Ada and Galager can instead awaken the Redeemer?"

Willow scratched a temple. "Lupawa, I do not have the answer to your question. I don't know the extent of their skills."

"What skills are needed?" asked Ada. "Can you describe what it's like to awaken someone?"

Willow glanced at Keil. Her fingers dropped from her temple to her chin as she thought. "It's the opposite of emitting light," she said. The corner of her mouth curled up. "When a person goes into Torpor, healing light is sent into their body, but in such massive amounts that the host must store the light, and in so doing the energy encapsulates and protects every fiber of flesh, and bone, and spirit. When the body stops accepting the energy, it is in Torpor."

She now extended her arms, opened her palms upward, then slowly pulled them back as if gently pulling back empty air. "To awaken someone, we coax the magic from their bodies. We pull it out. It takes but a minute."

Ada scanned her memories. She was sure she had never been taught such a skill, but neither had she ever heard talk of this technique. However, her mind did ping on one comment that Valter Vreman once made once about lodestones. It was something about having the skill to repel or attract someone else's magic. Vreman had said a nimbus could be erected that proactively pushed the offending magic away, rather than simply blocking it. And similarly, there were techniques that could be employed that attracted other magical outpourings.

"When you pull the magic from one's body," said Ada, "might it be described as an attraction? One force attracting another?" She suddenly remembered meeting Sanguir that first night in Fane Tower, the white smoke, the blood, the smoke turning red. *Blood attracts blood.*

Willow's lip curl became more pronounced. She nodded her head slowly. "That sounds reasonable," she said.

"Have you performed such magic?" asked Twoheart.

"Not yet," said Ada.

"Have you awoken anyone form Torpor?" the vangard then asked of Willow.

"I have, yes," the wrullorer said. "There have been occasions when we had need to intercede on grievous injuries, for example, to stem the flow of arterial blood loss. We put such victims into Torpor and then carry their statues to Amaranthine Springs, where I then awaken them so they can immediately immerse themselves in the healing waters, thereby avoiding death."

"Why didn't we do that with Katonkin?" asked Galager, reacting a little too quickly. He shook his head. "Never mind," he said. "I forgot. Amaranthine Springs takes before it gives."

"Willow, are you sure you are willing to help them?" asked Shaleen.

The two healers exchanged a few words. Finally, Keil dropped his gaze into his lap and Ada knew that Willow would be joining the quest.

"It seems I must," said Willow. "Their need is our need."

Twoheart raised a hand to her mouth and coughed into it. She dropped her arm and faced Shaleen. "I think I understand why the Torpor was kept secret from me."

"From all outsiders," corrected Shaleen.

"Yes, outsiders, like me," responded Twoheart.

"I'm sorry. You know what I mean."

Twoheart smiled. Shaleen responded in kind. "You didn't want anyone to find the Bloodstone," said the vangard. "If the entire Commonland knew of the Torpor, then Cazlich's statue would have been revealed for what it truly is. It might have been destroyed long ago by people searching for his talisman."

"That is correct, although we didn't know it was at Castle Lavalor."

Civato suddenly stood up and pointed to the sky. "It's happening," he said. "Look, the clouds are changing."

50

"This way," said Shaleen, leading the troop to the right, along the ten-foot-high wall of gray granite that separated them from their destination. Ada studied the vortex as she kept close to Galager's back. No sign of magic up there, but the clouds indeed looked flatter, as if a mile-wide sheet of clear glass was being pressed up against them from beneath. She hoped the shield would keep those lightning bolts away from them. If they didn't, well, she preferred not to think of what would happen otherwise.

Shaleen stopped in front of a rift in the granite step. It was V-shaped, as if a giant sword had struck the ledge, leaving its mark, as well as leaving a point of ingress to the higher areas above the step. The rift was about eight feet wide at the top, much narrower at the bottom, but just wide enough to allow a person to climb into it. As soon as everyone was standing near to her, the Firthan eludrian clambered into the big groove and started climbing her way through it. Twoheart was next, with Civato behind her, helping her up, step by laborious step.

The groove wasn't very deep, perhaps ten feet in total. It made for a steep angle, but Ada found it as easy to climb as a ladder because of all the stacked-up rubble within the furrow of rock. It only took her a minute or two to emerge on the higher elevation. She noted that during that time that no lightning bolts had assailed either the mountain or the troop.

Keil and Willow separated from everyone else after emerging from the groove behind Galager.

"See you all at the well," said Keil. "We need to search for crystals. Just give us five minutes." The two wrullorers began to walk along the edge of the ridge as Shaleen instead began to cross over the flat expanse revealed before them.

"Follow me," she said. "Almost there."

It was a little windier up here at the summit. And there was nothing left to climb. Amaranthine Mountain had petered out to a plateau that looked to be maybe three or four bowshots in diameter. Ada scanned her surroundings. No other peaks were visible. This mountain was the tallest one in the vicinity. The entire surface was covered in detritus of stone and rock. No boulders were evident, but there were plenty of craters, presumably caused by lightning strikes. The craters were half-filled with shards of rock, pebbles, and dust—lots of black and gray dust! It was a scene from hell—after the fire had gone out. Almost everything looked burnt or charred, except for some recent craters or smaller pock marks that had exposed areas of original gray granite bedrock. No doubt in time they'd also become black by later lightning strikes.

Before too long Shaleen brought them to a roundish hole at the center of the mountain top. It was about twenty feet in diameter at the widest point. Ada stepped to its edge, along with everyone else, and peered over it. She saw water, maybe thirty or forty feet down from the rim of the wide hole.

"This is it?" said Galager. "I expected something . . . different."

"Me too," said Ada. "And where are the flowers?"

"The Amaranthine flowers don't grow up here," said Shaleen. "They occur throughout Firthwood. They are rare. Every day people set out from Thrum to search for them. Some searchers remain out in the forest for several weeks before returning to Thrum, often having failed to find any. Nowhere else on Earth can they be found but in Firthwood."

"These are the legendary healing waters?" Civato asked skeptically, referring to the well and the water contained within it.

"These are their . . . headwaters," said Shaleen. "During rainy season the water level will be higher, closer to the top of the well. But the water level matters not. Amaranthine Springs begins here, with rainfall that is . . . changed by Jhalaveral's Lightning and by other things deep within the mountain. There is a system of water veins and arteries within the mountain, all of which are fed by this single well. The rain enters the well here, but exits the mountain in a different form at a multitude of spots farther down below. The water you see below is not the most potent of the healing waters. The water we seek today is hundreds of feet below us."

"Hundreds of feet?" responded Ada. She didn't understand. Neither did Galager nor Civato, as evidenced by the dumbfounded looks on their faces. "A little difficult to get there from here, wouldn't you say?"

Shaleen laughed. "Not at all. All that is required is a leap of faith," she said.

"Seriously?" said Galager, awareness causing his eyes to bulge with shock and surprise. "You want us to jump into this hole? How would we get out once we did? We'll drown down there."

Twoheart coughed. "You will be safe," she said to Galager. "This will be my second immersion. It is a strange experience, but not uncomfortable or dangerous."

"Tell us more," said Ada. "This is . . . scary. I don't know that I want to do this."

"You'll have to do better than that to convince me to jump into this hole," said Civato.

Twoheart backed away from the hole, gathering the others around her.

"It is true that I am more injured than any of you," she said. "But we are all depleted. Our spirits are bruised. And we have smaller injuries—my lungs, your wrists, your feet, your will—that may seem manageable now, but if infections take root, they will affect your ability to continue fighting. We have obligations now—all of us. The land depends on us. Everything we do, we do for others, not for ourselves. I am Twoheart, wife of Panthertooth. I am of the Claw. And I will ask you to trust me, and to follow me into this mountain. If you do not choose to trust me, then turn and leave. Go back the way you came, but with your tails tucked between your legs."

She paused, letting her words sink in.

"But I do not think you are cowards," she finally said.

She flashed them a brief smile, then dove head first into the well.

Without any further thought, Ada jumped in right behind her.

51

She hit the water like a rock and was driven under its surface by the force of her fall. All sound was driven from her ears. She began to flail her arms and legs, trying to get back to the surface. Ada opened her eyes, searching for daylight, trying to orient herself to swim back to it. She felt starved of oxygen and began to kick even harder. Her lungs were already begging for air. She had to fight to keep from opening her mouth and involuntarily sucking in water. Jumping into this well had been a bad idea. If she survived this, she decided right then and there she would have a word with Twoheart at the earliest opportunity.

She finally broke the surface and gulped in air. She flicked her head, sending an arc of water out to the side. Her sandals touched muddy bottom. *How?* She instinctively stood up and found the water depth to be no more than five or six feet. It came up to her neck, though only moments before she was at least ten-foot under.

How is this possible?

She saw trees a short distance away. And grass. The lush greenery half surrounded a pool of clear, sparkling water, and she was in it. There were panthers lounging in the shade at the edge of the tree line. She saw their Firthan masters there as well, laying in the grass, their backs resting against their sleeping animals. They were the same seven animals—and men—that had carried them up Amaranthine Mountain that morning. She recalled Shaleen saying they'd be waiting for them down here.

She spun around. A mountain rose up on the other side of the pool. A gentle waterfall fell from a tunnel maybe a dozen feet up in the lowest rocks.

Her eyes were drawn back to a figure in the water near to her. Twoheart! She was standing in the shallow pool. She had her hands on her hair, wringing it dry. She was smiling from ear to ear. She looked happy, and strong.

Ada heard her name. She spun around again and saw Galager in the water. He had just surfaced and immediately called to her. Seconds later Civato's head bobbed up over the surface, followed by Shaleen's.

They all came closer together and stood in a circle within the water.

"That was amazing," said Galager. "I feel so . . . good!"

Ada had to admit it, she did too. By all appearances, so did everyone else.

Galager suddenly ripped the bandages off his wrists. He held his arms up for the others to see. "The cuts are gone!" he said. "No pain whatsoever."

Civato reacted by removing his bandages. "Jehlude Jhalaveral!" he uttered in amazement, then laughed heartily. "I am also hale and whole. A miracle. Never felt better."

Galager hastily unbuttoned his tunic. He pulled apart the garments over his chest and thrust a hand inside. "It's healed," he stated with glee, jumping up and down in the water. "My eludria scar! Though I'd never see the day."

Ada checked her own wrists and then her chest scar. She had one of those too. But they were no longer there. *Wow!*

"I remember jumping," said Ada. "Then fighting to the surface. And as soon as I did, I was here!"

"My experience as well," said Civato.

"Same," said Galager. "I almost want to do it again."

Shaleen shook her head. "Just joking," said Galager, forestalling any words she was preparing to utter.

Two more heads suddenly bobbed to the surface. The healers, Keil and Willow.

"How was the hunting?" asked Shaleen. "Find anything useful?"

Willow shook her head. They didn't seem overly excited, but Ada figured they must have made this leap of faith many times over the years.

"Next time," said Shaleen. Willow nodded in agreement.

Ada studied Twoheart. Sure, Amaranthine Springs had healed the group's minor scars, but the big question yet remained: Had they cured Twoheart of serious illness and injury?

Time to find out.

So, she asked her. She knew the Atikan well enough by now that she would remain silent unless someone prodded her for answers.

"I am as before," Twoheart reported after Ada had probed her with a few penetrating questions. "I am completely healed. As are you, and the others. All mistakes have been resolved. All poisons removed."

Odd words.

"The springs can heal mistakes?"

Twoheart speared her with an eye. She slowly nodded. "Natural mistakes." After a moment or two she could see Ada was still confused.

None of the others were listening to their conversation at this point. Galager had taken off his weapons and overgarments and sandals, placed them along the shore in the grass, and was now doing backstrokes over closer to the falls. Civato had done the same, joining him in the deeper water. It's not that they needed to unweight themselves. This water made it easy for them to stay buoyant, clothes and all. The three Firthans were already sitting on the grass, waiting for their visitors to tire of the splendor of the water.

Twoheart came closer. "Nature sometimes makes mistakes," she said, whispering. "Amaranthine Springs can correct them.

She's talking about herself.

"What kind of mistakes?"

Twoheart shrugged. "A dog with three legs," she said. "A snake with two heads. A turtle with no shell. A blind person. A person who feels there is something wrong about their body. Things like that."

"Amaranthine Springs can heal all of that?"

Twoheart smiled. "I personally know that to be true."

"And the poison?"

Twoheart shrugged. "A person who has been poisoned will emerge from the springs clean and healthy. Any poison or unnatural property within one's system will be gone as if it were never there."

The Atikan swam away from her, floating on her back, propelled by her toes, but held up by this miraculous water.

Ada padded her clothing to locate her eludria ruby. It was still there, in the pocket where she always kept it. She started to withdraw it, but decided to first head for the grass. She'd hate to drop it in the water and lose it. Once she was on the grass, water dripping steadily into it, she produced her ruby and tried to invoke an aura. Nothing!

She tried twice more, with the same results, then gave up.

The springs have removed the eludria from my body!

Galager was still in the water doing gentle backstrokes. But he had eyes on her. He could tell something was wrong. An expression of concern came over his face and he stopped swimming and just bobbed there in place.

Ada secured her ruby within her garments, unbuckled her weapon, laid it on the ground, and went back into the water. She swam over to Galager and they floated there, facing one another, hands holding onto arms.

"What's wrong?" he asked, squirting out water from his lips, letting it run over his chin.

She told him.

He didn't react at first.

"Is that a good thing?" he soon asked "Or bad?"

"I don't know."

Galager drew her in a little closer. "Are you worried?"

She pulled him in a little closer. "I don't think so." They bobbed there for a few seconds more.

"We can always infuse ourselves again," he said.

"We can. But I wonder if I can summon Cabbal now? Maybe I've lost the ability to bind him to my will? The malediction. Even if I do infuse myself again."

They were in each other's arms now. Neither of them fought it. Their wet cheeks were rubbing together, so were their chests. Their legs seemed to be trying to work out the best way to intertwine with each other.

"Does this mean we can have babies now?" he asked.

She felt his arousal below the water. And their lips met, not for the first time, but the first time in ways that mattered.

The sound of a horn issued forth from the nearest trees. All heads turned toward it, bodies suddenly still, listening. Shaleen and the two healers seemed mortified by the sound. Ada and Galager separated in the water and moved toward the edge of the pool.

"We must go!" Shaleen shouted. She ran toward the panthers and their riders, all of them already on their feet. The two wrullorers were doing the same, right on her heels.

Already at the edge of the pool, Twoheart leapt onto the long grass, heading in the same direction as the three Firthans. "Come," she yelled to the trio still luxuriating within the water. "Hurry!"

52

Ada smelled the smoke before she saw the flames. The horns had ceased.

The seven panthers and their riders broke out of the forest and into the clearing where the Firthan lodge was located. They had been running for maybe ten minutes since leaving the pool. The lodge was completely on fire. Ada wondered how that could be. *Wasn't it made of Haleburl?* But she remembered seeing glimpses of black floors the previous night and realized that it was only partially built of the fire-proof wood. Embers from a fireplace didn't start this conflagration, something else did.

It was mid-afternoon. The flames reached high, sending a curving arch of black and grey smoke into the bright, blue sky. A ring of people—all around the lodge—stood a safe distance from the fire. She estimated their numbers to be close to a thousand. They were in shock, watching the structure burning, probably wondering what to do, and probably blaming their new visitors for all the destruction they were witnessing. The fire sounded like a beast, a demon from the abyss. It roared and spit embers and sparks into the air. No one was trying to put out the fire, for good reason—it was too late to save the lodge.

Ada heard screams over on the right side of the clearing. Firthans were scattering like rats from that area. *Are they trying to get away from something?* She saw some bodies in the low grass. A pale white figure stood among them, carrying a great sword.

Haem!

A man in a black robe appeared from behind a group of Firthan men who had blocked the advancing group's line of sight up until that moment.

Oh no! Lazlo's here! But how?

Of course, the dome shield is down!

Shaleen turned the sprinting cats, guiding them now toward the demon namril, Lazlo, and the Firthan defenders opposing them.

Twoheart began yelling at her. Firthan words. Shaleen must have heard her, as she immediately signaled all the riders to halt.

They pulled up together about thirty yards from Lazlo and his demon.

Everyone jumped from their cats and ran forward a few yards so the cats were behind them. Ada and Galager instinctively came together, pulled their swords, and stared at the Vilazian and his demon.

My ruby doesn't work!

Civato stood near them, sword drawn, eyes fixed warily on the two dangerous figures.

Twoheart said something to Shaleen and her men, presumably warning them not to approach the interlopers. The Firthans listened, retreating further away from the threat ahead, bringing the cats with them after whispering in their ears and lightly tapping their hands on the shoulders of the mighty beasts.

They coaxed the cats to hunker down into the grass, though they looked ready to pounce nonetheless. Shaleen and her men stood near them, talking to them, trying to get them to pay attention to them and not the threat some thirty yards at their front. The panthers were mighty creatures, but they'd perish quickly if they attacked either Haem or Lazlo. Ada was certain of it, and so, too, apparently, was Shaleen and her men.

Twoheart screamed more words to the men up ahead, the brave ones standing closer to the interlopers—too close. They got the message and began backing away.

"What do we do?" asked Galager, his speech fast and excited. He already had his ruby in his left hand. *But no aura around his fist.* He seemed to be aware of that.

"Put it away," said Ada. "They're useless to us."

He pocketed his ruby. "We have to use that blue and gold stuff," he said.

She flicked her eyes toward Shaleen. "She doesn't have her ruby."

Galager grunted.

"When the time comes," said Ada, "mess him up."

He grunted again.

"Don't doubt yourself. How about we make it two out of two?"

"Two out of two," he said, those amber eyes glinting confidently in the sunlight. "I'll await your move."

They hugged, lingering for just a second, pecked each other on the lips, and turned back toward Lazlo and Haem.

Twoheart lifted a hand to stop them. Civato moved to stand at the Atikan's shoulder.

"Winkite," said Galager. "On our first day in Lavalor, we watched you and Katonkin on Fane Tower do what you do." He smiled at her. "Now watch what we do."

The vangard didn't move.

"It's now or never," said Ada. "If we can't beat these assholes now, after our trip through Amaranthine Springs, after all we've been through, then we've been nothing but a waste of your time."

"Trust us," said Galager.

Twoheart dropped her arm. Both she and Civato stepped aside to let them pass.

Ada walked forward. Galager was on her right, matching her every step. Twoheart stalked forward on Ada's left with Civato anchored on the Atikan's left.

Ada decided to concentrate on Lazlo. He was the bigger threat here. *One problem at a time.* She remembered Weir's words. *Silence. Tranquility. Awareness.*

She stopped walking when the opposing groups were about ten paces apart. There were two Firthan bodies over to her right. She didn't see any obvious injuries; clearly Lazlo had killed them with his magic. She had to fight back anger.

Silence. Tranquility. Awareness.

Lazlo was on the right, as she faced him. Haem on the left.

Civato and Twoheart stood across from Haem.

Ada and Galager stood across from Lazlo.

"There you are," said Lazlo, speaking the common-tongue. His left hand had a red aura around it. "I have to congratulate you on your escape from Vashti. I have to admit, I didn't expect that, although I knew you both had gifts. I underestimated you."

Ada gestured toward the bodies near to her. "You people are murderers. At least for you, that stops today." She was trying to sound confident, but inside she was a mess of fear and anxiety.

Lazlo laughed. "You think you are enough for me and my friend here? You're lucky I haven't already killed you. I'm just amused by your false sense of bravado."

"How did you find us?"

Lazlo waved a hand. "The thrum allowed me to follow your demon. Child's play."

"We know your plans," said Ada, trying to unsettle the man, to get him angry. That's what Weir had once told them to do with their opponents. Angry people make mistakes.

"We know all about The Grand Unraveling," she said. "We know Zaviel has another Bloodstone. We know he struggles with it, and that it hurt him when he first inherited it from his predecessor. It hurt him again when he destroyed part of Cadia Gate six years ago. He's afraid of it. Hell, we know it killed his predecessor and instilled a sickness upon your people in Azinor. That sickness killed Vashti's daughter, Carleea, and many others. And yet you dare believe that you will inevitably defeat us? Do you not see that destiny is not on your side? The Blue and Gold *will* destroy the Vilazian Multitude. Sometimes the mighty pick the wrong fight."

Lazlo's smile disappeared.

Ada laughed at him. "You know, it took me a while to figure it all out. But I did. I pieced together all the different clues. And now the mystery has been solved."

"What mystery?" Lazlo said, all sense of humor gone.

I'm under his skin.

"Galager and I. We were born under a full moon, on the same day."

In her periphery, she saw Galager glance at her.

"It was about the same time you people found another Bloodstone. It was about the same time a historic storm struck the ancient battlefield—the place where your ancestors long ago had their asses handed to them by Cazlich, The Redeemer. Jhalaveral and Ethelliphus have been playing games with us all. But Jhalaveral has the upper hand. And so do we."

She sheathed her mercenary, then raised her open palms toward Lazlo. "Do you see any eludria in our hands? Does it seem as if that concerns us? Vashti was also arrogant and cocky, like you are now, but we ended her reign of terror. And now it's your turn."

Suddenly everything was quiet, except that they could hear the inferno raging behind them. She didn't have to turn around to know that a thousand Firthans were standing behind her and the others.

Galager raised his left fist. A golden aura burst up around it.

Now or never.

Ada called forth her power and raised her own left fist, matching Galager's display. She glanced down and was relieved when she saw a blue aura.

Maybe we have a chance after all.

She expected Lazlo to attack then, but instead Haem suddenly turned into a black crack of dust and began corkscrewing into the sky.

The demon was fleeing from them!

53

Lazlo recoiled when he realized Haem had abandoned him. The vilemaster called forth magic. It flared up around him. Ada wasn't sure what he intended to do with it.

No matter, it was time to end this, one way or another.

A blue bolt of power shot forward from her fist. A golden beam exploded from Galager's fist just behind it. They both struck Lazlo at nearly the same instant. An explosion of green light erupted around the vilemaster, extinguishing his red outpourings. Lazlo screamed in anguish and went silent. He fell to the grass, face first, then rolled to one side. Ada saw his ruby drop to his side.

Ada extinguished her magic. She beckoned Galager to do the same.

Her gaze jerked toward the gyre. It was still gaining altitude and trying to gain distance.

She ran forward to Lazlo's side. Galager and their two protectors, Twoheart and Civato, were there too. Civato bent low and snatched up Lazlo's ruby.

"He may have another one," warned Galager.

Lazlo was alive, but in bad shape. His face was beet red, his hair looked singed, and his black robe was emitting wisps of smoke in places. His terror-filled eyes flicked between the two Commonlanders and his mouth was curled downward in agony and rage, exposing his teeth.

"How?" he gasped.

No one reacted.

"No matter," Lazlo then said. "Zaviel's magic is too strong—even for you."

Galager raised his golden fist, but Ada stopped him. "Not yet, Gal—"

But Twoheart suddenly lunged forward, withdrew a longknife from behind her shoulder, whipped it around in a high arc, and plunged its point deep into one of Lazlo's mortified eyes, killing him instantly.

The vangard's brutal act caught Ada by surprise. Her shoulders snapped backward and a hand shot up to her mouth, trying unsuccessfully to muffle her gasp of horror.

"Look," yelled Galager, his finger pointed toward Haem, almost over the edge of the forest now.

The demon's dusts were suddenly pulsing a red color and were being sucked into the black crack. In the blink of an eye the last particle of red dust vanished, and then the crack seemed to fold in upon itself, and disappeared.

Haem was gone!

"Jehlude Jhalaveral," yelled Civato Jeregoth.

Twoheart bent low over the body of Lazlo Urich. She pulled out her longknife then wiped it clean on his robe. After sheathing it, she began patting down his garments and soon found several more rubies tucked away in the folds of fabric.

Ada and Galager embraced one another tightly.

"I was so afraid," she whispered into his ear.

"Me too," he whispered back. "We're still alive."

The nearest Firthan men and women began to attend to their fallen comrades, at least four of them, tragically burned dead by vilemaster magic.

Shaleen approached Ada and Galager.

"I'm so sorry," muttered Ada, withdrawing from Galager's arms. "This is all our fault."

Shaleen pointed at Lazlo's still form. "It's his fault. Their fault."

"We brought them here."

"He followed you here. There's a difference. The shadow of war reaches far."

They took some moments to watch the Firthans carry away their dead. Willow and Keil were kneeling over one other figure in the grass. He was still alive. A small measure of good fortune.

"We need to leave," said Ada. "Will you allow Willow to come with us? It will be dangerous."

"It's up to her. But she seems determined to help you."

"Do you have leaders we need to talk to about this?"

"We have an elder council. We thought it best not to involve them."

Ada nodded. "For their safety?"

Shaleen grinned and dipped her forehead slightly.

"May I ask you a question?" asked Galager.

"Of course."

"I thought maybe you could clear something up."

"If I am able to," said the Firthan woman.

"It's about Cazlich. You said you knew him?"

She nodded. "What would you like to know?"

"How do you know his Bloodstone is in his statue? Clearly, he wasn't put into Torpor here, in Thrum. Otherwise, his statue would be down in that cavern where Katonkin is now."

Good question.

Shaleen didn't react at first. Maybe she was thinking.

"A trusted friend informed us of that," she finally said.

"Hatano Jonan?" guessed Ada.

"Correct," said Shaleen. "Cazlich came to Thrum to rid Firthwood of the Vilazian remnants after the Battle of Torrent Slew. Then after he and Constance Fane helped us erect the dome shield to guard against the Longclaws, they suddenly and unexpectedly departed."

Galager asked her if Cazlich had his Bloodstone with him while in Firthwood.

Shaleen shrugged. "He never showed it to us. He did say he would soon destroy it."

"Did he use it to build the dome shield?"

"No," she said. "He used eludria."

"Why did he leave so abruptly?"

"We don't know. He wouldn't say. I think the Longclaws disturbed him, changed his mind about the inevitability of the withdrawal of the Vilazian Multitude."

Galager seemed at an impasse.

Ada picked up where he left off.

"I infer that Hatano returned sometime later?"

"Yes. He told us Cazlich's sufferings became too much for him after departing Firthwood. When death was nigh to him he was put into the Torpor, near to the location where Castle Lavalor is now. One of his vangards was a wrullorer."

"What happened to that wrullorer?"

"Lost to history. He disappeared. Likely at the hands of the Vilazians while returning home."

"I'm sorry to hear that," said Ada. "But it was Hatano who told you the Bloodstone went with Cazlich? Into Torpor?"

Shaleen nodded.

"One last question," said Ada. "Yesterday you said Cazlich was ill when he arrived in Thrum. Did he ever make the leap of faith?"

Shaleen thought on that then slowly shook her head.

"He refused," she said. "When we advised him to do so, he told us that poison can be a powerful weapon. The next day he and his one hundred vangards departed Firthwood, and we never saw him again."

It was Shaleen's turn to ask a question. "Why does all of this knowledge matter to you?"

"Because," Ada said, "it seems to me that the Redeemer didn't have his Bloodstone while he was here in Firthwood. You saw him use a ruby though. I think he likely buried his Bloodstone in Torrent Slew, after the battle there, before he arrived here. That's most likely why he needed to depart Firthwood in such a hurry. The Longclaws must have upset him and changed his mind about no longer needing such a powerful talisman, even though it had made him ill. He wanted to return to Torrent Slew to retrieve it."

Ada slid her ring form one hand to the other.

"Just a guess, mind you. But Galager and I found out today that the eternal waters have removed all traces of eludria from our blood system. The magic we wielded today was not eludria-based magic. It was something different, something we knew we had prior to our arrival here. Cazlich must have feared the springs, feared the changes they might instill within him, whether temporary or permanent."

"Does any of this change your plans?" asked Shaleen.

"No," said Ada. "If Hatano said Cazlich had his Bloodstone with him at the time he went into Torpor, who are we to call him a liar? Although now I fear it has been lost. Or it's still buried in Torrent Slew. Cazlich never made it back there, according to what you just told us. Either way, no matter where the Bloodstone is, our next step is to awaken Cazlich and ask him its whereabouts."

Shaleen looked troubled. Ada asked her what was wrong.

"You do realize," Shaleen said, "if you awaken him, it may result in his death?"

"But Willow will be there to help him. She can also give him some of the water."

"We don't know what ails him, or how severe his illness is. He could be seconds from expiring, or days. Our knowledge does not instruct us on the matter. Willow may or may not be able to sustain him long enough to reach Firthwood."

"I see," said Ada.

"We have to wake him," said Galager. "There's too much at stake."

To that, all three agreed.

54

As fate would have it, the quest arrived back at Castle Lavalor around midnight, the day after leaving Firthwood. The return trip had not been the deleterious journey the one to Firthwood had been, likely because Amaranthine Springs had invigorated and revitalized them in the meantime. The quest was now comprised of Twoheart, Civato, Galager, Willow, Ada herself, and of course, Cabbal.

Lord's Keep was ablaze with torch light as they descended toward Lord's Mansion. *Was it in friendly hands?* The remainder of the castle, however, was dark. It was a moonless night so far, but clear. Hundreds of enemy campfires were evident beneath the forest trees south of the impalement field. Ada could just make out the dark shapes of lizards in the second and third wards of the fortress. Hundreds of them!

The plan was simple. First, set down in the gardens of Lord's Keep. Then, inspired by the Firthan dome shield, she and Galager would erect a nimbus dome around the gazebo under which Cazlich's jade statue was located. And finally, protected by the others, Willow would work to awaken the Redeemer, the legend, Cazlich.

Just yards above the gardens, though, Ada already realized fierce fighting was currently underway within Lord's Keep. No lizards were inside the inner walls, as far as she could see, but hundreds of Bipaquans and Commonlanders were meting out punishment to one another atop the nearby walls.

Cabbal set them down near the Gazebo, as Ada ordered. The demon then sailed back into the night, as previously instructed. She figured if Cabbal was on the ground fighting alongside of the quest, the friendlies might get the wrong idea and attack them all.

Shouting and weapon clashes impinged upon her ears from all directions. Men near and far were screaming in pain. She and the other members of her quest whipped around in circles at first, desperately trying to identify any threats. They were standing amongst strangers, Bipaquan redfaces among them.

With little time to absorb every detail, Ada ducked beneath a sword aimed at her face. Civato stepped in and deflected the back-swing aimed at her neck then slaughtered the redface who had been wielding it. But another Bipaquan had followed the other one in. He was behind Civato. Ada tried to warn him, but it was too late. Civato threw his shoulders back as a blade struck him from behind. He shrieked with pain, recovered quickly, spun around, and cut the man down with two chops of his blade. Civato put a hand on his side. It came away covered in blood. His blood.

Things were happening quickly.

Galager came to Ada's side. His fist was already a ball of golden power.

"Ready?" he yelled.

Ada was unsure. *Civato?*

"Let's do it!" Galager screamed, apparently unaware of the Bethurian's injury.

Ada had to act.

Blue and gold magic erupted around them. It turned green once their outpourings combined. She remembered how Valter Vreman had usurped her powers on Cadia Gate to create a nimbus. She now did the same, drawing on Galager's energy, erecting a dome around them, then letting it grow in size. Within seconds it completely surrounded the gazebo and everyone standing within a few yards of it.

Civato may have been hurt, but so far, it wasn't affecting his ability to fight.

Twoheart and the Bethurian got to work killing every Bipaquan within their bubble. Five redfaces went down to their combined fury. There were a few Lavalorans here as well. Four or five. No one she recognized. They were shocked to see the members of the quest and the green magic above their heads. At least they seemed to understand they were all on the same side.

Twoheart yelled something.

Ada's gaze snapped toward her. She was standing under the gazebo with Civato, close to the jade statue.

Willow was lying on the ground between them. A Bipaquan lance had found its mark.

Twoheart shook her head.

Oh no!

It was obvious Willow was dead.

First Civato, and now Willow!

Ada felt the first pangs of grief and panic beginning to constrict her.

Silence. Tranquility. Awareness.

A new plan came to her almost instantly. She had to trust that Civato would continue to be effective, and she ignored the tragedy of Willow's death.

"Drop the nimbus," she said to Galager. "We have to clear the keep of our enemies. I have an idea."

He nodded. "Just say when."

"Twoheart!" she yelled. "Civato!" They both locked gazes on her. She could tell the Bethurian was lagging.

"We're dropping the nimbus! Clear the keep! Watch out for friendlies!"

They both nodded, Civato a little less sharply than Twoheart.

"Now!" screamed Ada.

The nimbus collapsed as quickly as it had been created.

A blue beam shot out from Ada's clenched fist. A Bipaquan just four yards away from her fell.

She aimed at another redface and he collapsed near the first one.

Ada saw a golden beam of light sweeping across two more redfaces, killing them as easily as a sword though the heart.

She became aware of Twoheart, guarding her rear. She wielded an Atikan battle axe now.

Civato was doing the same for Galager.

Ada slowly walked to the north, toward the mansion, slaying every redface that came within her field of vision. She checked behind her. Galager was heading south along the long extent of the gardens, opposite the gazebo, enemies falling before his efficient power.

A stream of Commonlanders ran into the gardens. A dozen swords! No, twenty! They filed out of Lord's Mansion and spread out in all directions. Some of them ran past her to help Galager. Some split left and right, heading up stairways on the keep walls to assist their brethren at those teeming ramparts.

She saw faces she recognized.

Castellan Havless and Bosun Rheev! Running toward her. Havless's sword dripped with Bipaquan blood, as did Bosun's battle axe.

They all hailed each other as they came close.

"Good to see you up and about," Bosun said to Twoheart. "Both of you."

Havless started to speak, but Ada cut him off. *This was no time for pleasantries.*

"Can you hold the keep?" she asked. "Once it's cleared?"

"We can," said Havless.

"You've given us a second wind," said Bosun.

"Have you no eludrian to assist you?" she urgently asked.

"Inside the mansion," said Bosun. "It was a hell of a time getting the Bipaquans out of there. There are some vilemasters there, resisting us. They're still trying to kick us out. But our new fellow, he's good. We'll be alright. Their backs are broken now."

Ada sighed in relief. “I don’t have much time to explain,” she said. “Galager and I need to work over there—under the gazebo. We need you all to keep the redfaces away from us until we’re done. I don’t know how much time we need. I don’t even know if we’ll succeed at our task. But it’s important that we try.”

She took a breath.

“Once we are done here,” she continued, “I am going to summon a demon namril to take us away from here. To someplace safe where we can ascertain the whereabouts, and find the means to end the Grand Unraveling.”

She wasn’t sure they knew what that meant. “It’s their plan to defeat the Five Realms,” she explained, almost out of breath.

“As I was about to say, you and your men must not interfere with the demon once I summon him. It won’t hurt anyone. I won’t let him.”

Bosun and Havless were shocked.

“It looks like Haem, but it’s not. Do you understand?”

“We do,” said Havless. “Good luck,” he added. “To both of you!”

“When will we see you again?” asked Bosun.

“I’m not sure,” she answered truthfully.

“Take me with you,” said Bosun.

Ada wasn’t sure whether she, or Havless, was more surprised at the suggestion.

Bosun wheeled to face Havless. “You’re almost done here. You have plenty of men, and Jasper Fallowthin.” He pointed at Galager. “Panthertooth assigned me to protect him.”

Bosun turned toward Twoheart now. “Can you use my axe? Take me with you.”

“We can use you,” said Ada abruptly. She looked at Twoheart. “Civato is seriously injured. He’ll make it, I think, but we have to leave him here so he can get help when this is all over.”

She looked back at Bosun. “I have to warn you. I’ve a feeling we’ll be walking into a hornet’s nest.”

“Hornets don’t scare me,” declared Bosun.

"Go!" ordered Havless. "Do your job, lad. Protect them. We shall drink to our mutual success when this is all over."

Ada ran beneath the gazebo, Twoheart and Bosun flanking her. She called out for Galager, who was returning to the gazebo. Civato guarded his rear.

Ada knelt down on the dais, near the jade statue, waiting for him. Willow was there, not eight feet away, lying in a pool of blood in a fetal position, that dart sticking through her mid-section. Ada closed her eyes to the horror of the sight. She felt responsible for this tragedy.

Silence, tranquility, awareness.

Someone touched her arm. She opened her eyes. It was Galager. Kneeling in front of her.

"It's not your fault," he said intuitively. "Or mine."

"I know—but."

Galager glanced at the statue. "You think we can get him out of this stone?"

"Yeah," she said. "Pretty sure." *Why am I lying to him?*

"You ready?" he asked.

She glanced at Willow. She spotted a small leather waist satchel peeking out from under a flap of her robe.

Ada jolted upright and went to the still form of the wrullorer. She opened the satchel and removed its contents: a small flask of liquid, two petals of an amaranthine flower, and the green Lightning Crystal Willow had used to help the two vangards. She put the flask and the petals into her own pockets, but left the now useless crystal next to Willow's body. Ada wanted to linger there, somehow pay respects, but sounds of battle rattled her into movement.

She backed away from the unfortunate woman, and returned to Galager.

Side by side, they faced the statue. The trio of Twoheart, Bosun, and Civato moved in close and surrounded them, guarding them with their bodies, their lives, and their weapons.

"This is different from before," she said to Galager. "Instead of pushing magic away from us, like we usually do, we need to pull it toward us."

He nodded.

"I'll talk us through it as we go," she said.

"We can do this," he replied.

They glanced at each other one last time, and went to work.

Almost simultaneously, their fists began to glow, the color of their respective eyes.

"Make your aura bigger," said Ada.

"Good, stretch it toward the statue."

He did.

"Yes, that's good. Now surround the statue with your magic."

Blue and gold began encircling the jade figure. Their powers comingled, but did not explode. But neither did they combine this time. Instead, blue and gold tendrils seemed to twirl around the stone figure like two snakes in a love dance.

Maybe that's what's supposed to happen?

"Now pull," Ada said. "But don't let your magic shrink away from the stone. Imagine the stored energy being attracted into our auras."

Thirty seconds elapsed. Nothing happened, except that the sound of war filled the air all around them and the blue and gold tendrils continued swirling around each other.

Another thirty seconds elapsed.

"It's not working," said Galager.

"Keep pulling," said Ada.

Another fifteen seconds passed—but the statue still wasn't changing.

"I don't know why it's not working," she said. *The crystal?*

Another fifteen seconds passed.

"Hands," said Galager.

"What?"

"They used their hands," he said. "Keil and Willow."

Of course!

Ada reached down with her left hand and tentatively placed it on the head of the statue.

Galager did the same.

All at once, their combined magic turned a bright green.

"That's better," he said.

The statue started to brighten. The green hues rapidly intensified and grew whiter, illuminating the entire garden area of Lord's Keep. Ada remembered the healers backing away from Katonkin at the moment he transformed into jade.

"Get back!" she yelled.

Three sets of hands grabbed at them from behind. The two vangards and the warden. They were literally carrying them away from the statue as a white light exploded from underneath the gazebo, temporarily blinding everyone.

55

When the white light faded, all went dark.

Until a single ball of golden light suddenly appeared like a firefly in the night.

Galager's aura.

Still, everything seemed inexplicably dim, so he called forth more of his power.

It revealed a man in the shadows. He was sitting before them on the ground. Cross-legged. Hunched over his knees. Wearing a black robe and sandals. No weapons. No rubies. And neither did he have a talisman. Not that Ada could see.

She was at Galager's side, his fist still aglow. The two vangards and the warden were there too, standing protectively around them both, axes at the ready, deadly eyes aimed at the sitting figure.

They were no longer under the gazebo.

They weren't even in the gardens at Lord's Keep.

They were in the undercrofts of Castle Lavalor.

"Cazlich," whispered Galager.

The man sat up straight and peered at them.

No one moved for a few heartbeats. Instead, they all examined each other.

"Can you help me?" the man finally said. "I can't seem to move a muscle."

Galager took a step toward him. "I've met you," he said. "In my reverie."

The man had a short beard, black with streaks of noble gray, same as his short, curly hair. Prominent cheekbones, strong jaw. Light skin. A Vilazian, no doubt about it.

He lifted a hand, beckoning for assistance. Galager started forward, but Bosun called him back. In his place went Civato. Ada noted the blood on Civato's side and hip. The Bethurian took the man's hand and pulled him to his feet. He almost stumbled, but Civato caught him despite being injured himself. The man seemed harmless enough, Ada decided. The question was: Was this Cazlich?

"Who are you?" asked Twoheart.

"I think you already know," the man said.

"Speak your name," she demanded, her axe held high in front of her.

He laughed. "If you insist. I am Cazlich, of course. That's why you awakened me from my Torpor. Is it not?" He peered closely at Galager. "How are you, young man? I do remember you."

Galager jerked a thumb toward Ada. "This is Ada Halentine. We both awakened you. I'm Galager Swift."

The man dipped his head in greeting. "I would thank you, but I don't yet know the purpose of our meeting. It could be nefarious in nature."

"You look ill," remarked Ada. "How long do you have until—?"

"Until I die?"

She nodded.

He shrugged. "A few days, at most."

He dusted off his shoulders. "Did you perhaps bring me a cure?"

No one reacted.

"Well, that's too bad." He took a few steps forward, groaning as he did so. "I've been sitting too long."

He looked at them. "That was a joke."

"I'm sorry," said Galager. "But important matters are distracting us." He pointed to the ceiling of the undercroft. "We have friends. They're fighting to retake Castle Lavalor as we speak. Did you bring us down here? I don't see your Bloodstone."

"Ah, my Bloodstone," he whispered. He mumbled something to himself, and nodded. "That's why you have awoken me. I should have guessed. But . . . I know your magic," he then said. "It is . . . familiar to me."

"How so?" asked Ada.

"I buried that magic in a battlefield. I wanted to hide it forever, away from the hands of man. But . . . here it is, despite my best efforts."

"I don't understand," she said.

"Your magic is green, is it not?"

Ada shook her head. But she stopped short.

Yes—it is! When it is combined with Galager's magic.

"What are you saying?" Galager asked.

The man pointed at both of them. "You are the Bloodstone incarnate. I'd recognize your magic anywhere."

"We are what?" stammered Ada.

Galager's jaw hung open. Literally.

"How is that possible?" said Ada. She suddenly waved her hand in the air, erasing her last comment. "Wait, wait," she said. "Never mind. How is it possible you . . . transported us to the undercrofts? You hold neither eludria nor a Bloodstone."

"You awoke me," Cazlich stated. "You laid hands on me. You two are the Bloodstone incarnate. Anyone can invoke magic from the Bloodstone when they are in contact with it. As I awoke, I saw the battle taking place in the gardens and felt it wise we should go somewhere safe. I invoked magic through you. So here we are."

"This is crazy," said Galager. "But I believe him."

Ada had to admit, she did too. On the other hand, time was critical. She decided to get to the heart of the matter.

"Master Cazlich," she began. "We do not have any more time for word games or introductions. Let me make this as simple as I can. You have been asleep for over two hundred years. The Vilazian

Multitude has found a new Bloodstone. The Commonland will soon be invaded. The Vilazian, Zaviel Vogli intends to impart great suffering upon our people with that powerful talisman. And after he's done with us, I think he will take his new power elsewhere and terrorize the world in a way that's never been seen before. Galager and I don't pretend to understand the nature or source of our magic —our blue and gold magic—that has come upon us in recent days. But we need to find your Bloodstone so we can put a stop to Zaviel's plans. We've just returned from Firthwood. A woman there, Shaleen, an eludrian, believed you would help us. She is the reason we awoke you. So, I am asking. No, I am begging you. Can you help us? Will you help us?"

No reaction.

Not at first.

He spoke.

"I would like to ask you about the well-being of Shaleen and her people, but that will have to wait for now. When I departed Firthwood, my plan was to return to the place where I buried my Bloodstone, the place where I defeated my enemy, a people I was born into but grew ashamed of. Their cruel demon birds finally made me understand the Vilazian Empire would never stop its warring ways. I decided to do whatever it took to stop them once and for all.

"I learned of the Torpor while in the city of Thrum. I learned it was possible to pull magic from that which contained magic. When one of my eludrians became injured, I learned that Amaranthine Springs could pull eludria from a person's body. I took those lessons to heart. And so I conceived of a plan to pull all the magic from the Earth, so that magic might be destroyed and the Earth again made safe for good people.

"But I had to return to the battlefield where I buried the Bloodstone. I would need its power one final time to end the scourge of eludria. To end the Age of Blood. That's the only way to stop them— my people. Alas, I was more ill than I realized. I never completed my quest. Now here I stand before you both, the blue and gold, together the green, the Bloodstone incarnate. If you want my help, then bring me to Orial. And there we shall rid the world of eludria. This Zaviel fellow you mention will then have no use for a Bloodstone that has no magic remaining within it."

"But the dome shield," said Twoheart. "If we destroy all eludria, the Firthan shield will no longer exist. Nothing will stop the long-claws from entering their valley. Many will die. And what of my husband, and all others in the torpor? Are we sure we can awaken them, if we do as you propose?"

"Your concerns are now mine," said Cazlich. "It is true that my plan will mean the end of the Firthan dome. But if it is daylight when we do I propose, they will have ample time to protect themselves before nightfall, when the birds attack. Yes, their lives will be different for a time—until we find a way to cleanse the land of all other Vilazian monsters—but they will be safe until then. As to the torpor, it existed before the comet, as did the Firthan wrullore. I see no reason to fear that my plan will endanger anyone within the torpor."

Twoheart dipper her forehead, her concerns suitably assuaged.

"Why did Hatano Jonan lie to the Firthans?" asked Galager.

Cazlich seemed surprised by the question.

"What lie?"

"He told them you had the Bloodstone with you when you went into Torpor."

He considered his answer. "As per my desires, he likely wanted to confuse people as to the true whereabouts of the Bloodstone. Any more questions?"

"You'll do it?" asked Ada. "Truly? You'll come with us?"

He bowed his head. "If I am able. But . . . I am weak."

Ada produced Willow's flask, and the two flower petals. She gave them to Cazlich.

"Amaranthine Springs?" he asked, one eyebrow raised in query. After she nodded, he placed the petals on his tongue, drank from the flask, and then handed a now half-empty flask back to her.

"The last time I refused such gifts as these," he said, "I died." He then emitted a short burst of laughter.

After she pocketed the flask, Ada switched the ring on her finger to her other hand.

Cazlich noticed her gold band and pointed at it. "Is that what I think it is?"

"Yes."

"I gave that to her. To Constance. The love of my life."

Ada felt her heart breaking. "What happened to her?"

"I don't know," he answered. "She was with me when I went into the Torpor. I suppose she had a life to live afterward."

"I'm sorry," she said. "For both of you."

"Let us begin this great quest," Cazlich said abruptly. "We have a long walk ahead of us."

Civato laughed heartily. "I suppose it's time we tell him about Cabbal!"

Ada did just that. A round of questions and answers ensued, but finally the Redeemer was prepared to meet the demon namril.

Everyone exchanged glances. Galager shrugged. "Let's go," he said excitedly. "This may be the only chance we get to set things right."

It took several minutes for Cabbal to reach them once Ada issued the malediction. Longer than she would have expected. She figured he must have come to them through Havless Tower. Her suspicions were confirmed a few minutes later when Cabbal took them back out the way he had come.

The last thing Ada figured they had to do, before leaving Lavalor, was to drop the injured Civato off within Lord's Keep. He objected, of course, but as he was merely dust at this point, he lacked the ability to actually refuse her. After she and the others had sincerely thanked the Bethurian for everything he had done to help them, and after expressing hope to someday cross paths with him again to continue their newfound friendship, it was time to let him go. Cabbal simply touched down briefly and set the Warden on the ground inside the gardens near Havless and his guards. Knowing that the Bethurian would never have agreed to stay behind, even with a serious injury, she figured this act would likely save his life.

56

It took them almost two days to reach the monastery known as Orial, below the Grey Acme, the highest peak within the Greyridge Mountains. It was about noon when they arrived. Legend spoke of Orial as a great place of worship, built sometime after the Sword of Jhalaveral smote the southern extents of the Commonland. The Vilazians later arrived here, drove out the monks and kept the place for themselves, a home away from home. Far below the monastery, deep in the roots of the Grey Acme, were the eludria mines, the dark tunnels from which emerged all the material that would later become eludria rubies. And of course, this was where Cazlich's Bloodstone was found—and more recently, Zaviel's.

If that monster was not currently out in the countryside leading his army to war against Megador, this is where he'd be. As Cabbal dove down to a giant scar in the landscape at the foot of the Grey Acme, Ada suddenly realized this might very well be the last she would ever see of the sunlit world.

Directed by Cazlich's voice, Cabbal descended toward an open mine-pit situated in the crux of a defile that reminded Ada of Little Dog Gorge, only this one was higher. The mining pit itself had the appearance of a vortex because of a dirt roadway that encircled it, winding ever tighter the deeper it got. Hundreds of men labored here, their sunburnt backs glistening in the final hours of daylight.

"Slaves," Cazlich whispered.

Many long ropes with buckets dangling from them were strung up along the slopes of the pit. Eludria wasn't the only precious mineral found here. A multitude of small wooden shacks—mine adits and other structures—festooned the seemingly endless roadway, and many of them were interconnected with a complicated system of walkways, stairways, and ladders.

Cazlich aimed them at one of the adits near the bottom of the vortex. Ada briefly wondered how he knew where to go, then remembered he had been an eludrian in the service of the Empire before he became a servant of peace and justice, the Redeemer. He had been here before, albeit oh so long ago.

"Zaviel is here," said Cazlich as Cabbal plunged them into darkness. "I can feel the vibration of his Bloodstone."

They soared through the empty tunnel, straight into the mountain. The demon's preternatural sight allowed them to see shadowy details although there were also lanterns or lamps partially illuminating the way. They passed intersecting tunnels, all of them dark. They came to an elevator shaft and Cabbal dove down, straight into it. The black walls rushed past them as they descended, and it felt like they were falling. At the bottom of the shaft a wooden elevator car plugged the way but Cabbal's dusts merely sifted their way through the cracks between the boards and exited into an illuminated tunnel. They went past more intersections, and then the tunnel split, one way dark, one way lit with lamps. Cabbal went right, into the light. He took another right, with more lamps, and slowed as they entered a chamber.

Cabbal set his passengers down at this point. Ada felt the weight on her feet again, always a welcome sensation. Cazlich was at her right shoulder. Beyond him was Galager then Bosun. At her left shoulder stood Twoheart.

Because of its shape and size, the cavern reminded Ada of the Firthan cavern where Katonkin was interred. Her heart suddenly yearned for him to be here with them, but those thoughts were suddenly vanquished from her mind when she noted two astonishing things. First, the ground just ahead of them—a spot of dirt about twenty feet in diameter, was glowing red. It was bright enough to illuminate the entire cavern. The second astonishing thing was that a man was standing in the middle of that spot, facing them.

Ada quickly scanned the cavern for other threats. None that she could see, though she noted three exits—tunnels—including the one they had used to enter this space.

"Zaviel Vogli, I presume?" Cazlich sounded calm, self-assured, completely the opposite of what Ada herself was feeling.

"Who are you?" said the man in a Vilazian accent. Ada peered more closely at him. Black robe, same as Lazlo. Gray beard. Craggy face, thin lips, with a forehead that protruded over his eyes like a bulging cliff. His left hand was a clenched fist. No aura.

Bloodstone!

Ada's right foot began to tremble. She had to fight to keep it still.

"Zei kle Cazlich."

She quickly interpreted the simple words. Vilazian words. *I am Cazlich.*

Zaviel took his time responding. "Why are you here? You don't belong here. You're a traitor!" That last phrase was a hiss of anger and disgust.

Cazlich pointed to the glowing ground where Zaviel was standing. "Time to end this," he pronounced. Common-tongue again.

Zaviel glanced down at the ground below his feet. He laughed. He lifted his fist and showed them his Bloodstone. Too far to see details, but Ada knew it was the real thing.

"You no longer have your talisman," Zaviel said, again laughing. "If you do, show it to me."

Cazlich reached down and took Ada's hand. He did the same with Galager. The three of them were like a chain now.

Zaviel scoffed.

Twoheart suddenly stepped in front of Ada and crossed over to where Bosun was standing. Bosun had also reacted, standing his ground, but pivoting to his right. Ada jerked her awareness in that direction and saw a demon namril framed within the dark rectangle of one of the side-exits. It was just standing there watching, over at their far right, a dark silhouette cast in red illumination because of the glowing spot of ground. The two vangards didn't attack, instead, they merely interposed themselves as a human shield between the demon and their three eludrian charges.

Ada suddenly realized Cabbal was no longer with them. In fact, he had never materialized, something she had failed to pay attention to when they first arrived here. She checked her surroundings.

Where is he?

She was about to invoke the malediction when Cazlich shook her arm, dissuading her.

Zaviel uttered some words. His demon lurched from the side-exit, heading straight for the two Lavaloran vangards, a long black sword in its white-clawed grip. Ada instinctively took a step backward, but Cazlich stopped her, though the three of them pivoted slightly to face the demon's onslaught.

The creature's battle-scream echoed in the chamber as Twoheart and Bosun raced forward to meet the threat. Ada stole a glance at Zaviel, but he seemed content watching whatever was about to unfold. Cazlich's eyes, however, were unwavering and fixed squarely on Zaviel.

The three combatants met each other about twenty feet from where Ada stood. She wasn't sure what to expect. Images from the fight with Haem atop Fane Tower flicked through her memory in a single heartbeat.

But already, things were not the same here. Both Twoheart and Bosun had Atikan battle axes, not just swords and longknives, and it immediately became clear their tactics would be very different. Both vangards leapt into the air, whipping their axes around in a vertical off-axis crescent path. Their bodies followed their axes, somersaulting and twisting, applying the forces of leverage to the accelerating weapons that were ripping audibly through the dank air. In a spectacular instant, the demon swung his sword, but seemed confused by the coordinated actions of the two vangards and the giant blade caught only air. Both axes then struck home in the middle of the demon's armored chest, the long spikes sinking all the way to the handles.

The demon fell to the ground on its back, clawed feet raking the air. Twoheart and Bosun landed cleanly on theirs, on each side of the pale creature, their hands still on the wooden handles of their axes. They heaved mightily on long handles, pulling away from the flailing demon. The embedded spikes anchored each other, and immediately tore through the demon's massive chest, effectively ripping it in half until both weapons broke free, bringing with them the upturned ends of broken ribs and bloodied entrails—yellow, bloody entrails.

By the time Twoheart and Bosun had their axes at the ready again, the demon had gone silent and still. Blue and Gold fury had sent it violently to its grave in a matter of seconds!

"To hell with you!" screamed Galager, unable to contain his pride and excitement.

Ada watched as Galager's reddened face turned toward Zaviel. "Now it's your turn, you piece of dirt!" Galager was so animated, his arms jerking in the air, that it was all Cazlich could do to keep their hands joined.

Ada realized the danger if their grips should break.

"Silence! Tranquility! Awareness!" she shouted toward her beloved.

The shouting went against the purpose of those words, but Galager instantly got the message and immediately calmed down. Within a blink of an eye, he looked at her and blew a kiss.

Zaviel, however, was enraged. His fist had begun to glow red.

57

Zaviel summoned his scarlet power and aimed it at the two victorious vangards. But Cazlich had been watching his opponent closely, studying him, predicting his actions. Blue magic seemed to spontaneously flow from Ada's entire body at the same time that gold magic came forth from Galager's. Cazlich had usurped their energies and he threw it all toward Zaviel in an explosion of green magnificence. It widened as it crossed the cavern and sailed over the head of the vilemaster before falling over him like a fishing net. Not a speck of red light escaped Zaviel's outstretched arm before he was completely enclosed by a bright green dome shield.

Zaviel turned to face Cazlich. Ada could see his scowl of outrage behind the green shimmer of magic. An explosion of light blasted the interior of the green dome. Tiny cracks appeared in its surface, revealing traces of a red nimbus that Zaviel was using to counter the green one. The cracks healed themselves, but the green dome stopped tightening around their enemy.

"Run!" said Cazlich to the vangards. "Leave us before it is too late."

Twoheart and Bosun ran back to trio. "We shall stay and help you," Twoheart said.

Cazlich jerked his head vigorously. "Then you shall die, for no reason."

"We stay!" insisted Bosun. "We won't leave you here."

Another explosion of sound buffeted the cavern and the green nimbus again showed red cracks. Zaviel was trying to blast his way to freedom. Cazlich summoned more of Ada's energy, Galager's too, and the green dome healed itself, holding, for now.

"This is our battle now," said Cazlich. His face and neck were tight from the strain of his magical outpourings. "You must leave this place. I can't hold Zaviel off forever. These two embers will join you when we are done here. I promise you. But they will need you later, to protect them afterward. It's a long journey home. I would send them away, but they are the Bloodstone incarnate. I need them to lay ruin to this mountain."

"Run!" yelled Galager. "Get out of here!"

Twoheart decided quickly at that point. She stared deeply into Ada eyes, then into Galager's. "It's been my honor," she said, bowing her forehead to each of them in turn. "Thank you for saving Katonkin."

Bosun nodded at them, lips compressed, eyes wide with emotion. He didn't say anything. Instead, he tapped his chest with his fist, over his heart, and then the two vangards dashed from the cavern, using the same exit that Cabbal had used to bring them here.

Ada hoped with all her heart they'd make it to the surface in time.

With the vangards gone, all eyes turned to Zaviel, who continued to pound the green dome from within its interior. To Ada's horror, Cazlich's dome suddenly collapsed.

The green outpourings didn't die, though. Instead, they rebounded towards the trio. Ada flinched, but needlessly, as the magic quickly enveloped them all in yet another green dome, this one protecting her, Galager, and Cazlich.

But Zaviel was free!

A smirk crossed Zaviel's face. He thought he had scored a tactical victory over Cazlich.

His joy quickly disappeared, however, when Cazlich began

lurching forward, dragging Ada and Galager along by their hands with him. Their green dome moved forward with the Redeemer, inching closer and closer to their enemy. Cazlich's deft magic was a wonder to behold.

Zaviel again called up his own nimbus and surrounded himself with it, intending to fight off Cazlich's advance. The two domes slammed into each other, sounding like swords clanging against one another, only a hundred times louder. Ada's ears were stung by the volume of noise in the cavern. Step by step, Cazlich had his way with Zaviel. His green dome continued advancing, moving Zaviel backward until, finally, the trio was standing dead center in the cavern, atop the red glowing ground.

Cazlich urgently looked at each of them, in turn, while holding his opponent at bay.

"Jhalaveral chose wisely," he said, almost shouting to be heard.

Ada was speechless. She somehow realized they were approaching a major turning point or event. Her eyes met with Galager's. Perhaps for the last time. They pointed at each other then, and like Bosun had done, they tapped their chests over their hearts.

"End game," said Cazlich. "I'll release you," he said to both Ada and Galager. "When I do, bring your magic together and focus your power on the ground below your feet."

A tremendous explosion buffeted their dome, though it held. Zaviel had abandoned his own nimbus and was now trying to breach Cazlich's magic by directly attacking it. He had gone from defense to offense. As he did so, he moved around the dome toward the exit into which the two vangards had disappeared into. He repeatedly threw balls of power at their shield, causing it to wobble each time, though it did not break.

"Reach deeply into the ground," continued Cazlich. "Find the remnant of the comet. It is here, beating like a heart. You must pull its life energy away from it in the same way you pulled the preservative magic from my statue when you awakened me. Never stop pulling—not until this ground we stand upon no longer bleeds red."

Zaviel hit their shield with yet another blast that caused Ada's nose to bleed, though just a trickle.

Then, in the small amount of time remaining before Zaviel's next attack, Cazlich let go of their hands and extinguished his magic. Ada gasped as she watched the green dome start to collapse all around them.

Cazlich suddenly produced an eludria ruby from a pocket. Light erupted around the trio, a red nimbus this time that sprang up from the Redeemer's outstretched arm to replace the green one now expiring and collapsing inward, but still there. When the green dome finally vanished seconds later, a red dome had replaced it, though it was slightly smaller in diameter.

Zaviel threw a curse into the air. He had missed his chance to strike them all down.

"Now!" yelled Cazlich.

Free from their need to give their magic to Cazlich, the two teens let loose with their Blue and Gold power. It turned green where the streams met and then jetted into the dirt. They adjusted their positions, facing each other squarely, a yard apart, and thrust their combined energy deeper and deeper into the ground where they stood. Downward it went, like a sword into the Earth, searching, probing.

"Deeper!" yelled Ada.

"Found it!" screamed Galager a heartbeat later.

Ada felt it. It was as if they had hit a raw nerve. It pulsed with pain, and reflected back up to her the way vilemaster magic had reflected back up to her and Master Vreman atop Cadia Gate.

But this time, she didn't fight it. Instead, she accepted it with all her heart.

"Pull!" she yelled. "Pull, Galager, pull!"

58

Something seemed to snap below them. Ada wasn't sure whether it was the magic or the mountain. Maybe both. She screamed with satisfaction when magic began to flow even more freely up into her as a river of energy, a current, that had been reversed.

She lifted her eyes a degree or two. Galager was working as hard as she was. His eyes were bulging with determination, his mouth a scowl of rage. He saw her looking at him and smiled. A thick column of green magic began to flow up from the ground in between them, where they worked with their feet spread apart in a fighting stance. It shot upward and broke apart, turning into red embers like fireflies before they struck the underside of Cazlich's dome and vanished.

She heard granite breaking apart all around her. Small black shapes plummeted from the cavern ceiling—rocks and boulders—striking Cazlich's dome, sliding off it, and thudding heavily to the ground outside its perimeter.

"Look," cried Galager. "The ground!"

"Yes!" screamed Ada. The dirt they stood on no longer had a red glow.

They heard another explosion. Not magic. The mountain had had enough.

Their celebration cut short, the tunnel behind Zaviel started collapsing and a large section of the ceiling above him turned into a thousand boulders. The vilemaster lunged to his left, their right, and ran for his life, back around Cazlich's dome, as tons of granite fell into the area he had just vacated.

In the middle of all this ongoing devastation, Zaviel then turned for one of the other exits.

"Extinguish your magic!" commanded Cazlich. "Quickly!"

Ada didn't hesitate. Neither did Galager. Blue and gold winked out of existence. But the red dome was failing at the same time. Cazlich was going to let the mountain fall down on all of them rather than let Zaviel escape!

An explosion of red light caused Ada to instinctively close her eyes. She felt herself flying across the cavern at great speed. Her eyes came open a split second later, and she tried to make sense of what she was seeing. She was still standing. But she was no longer in the dome shield. Instead, it was in front of her. Galager was at her side. *What?* She looked at the dome again.

Cazlich and Zaviel were inside of it! Together!

Cazlich switched us!

Before she could say or do anything, Galager grabbed her by the arm and started pulling her to the nearest exit tunnel.

"Watch out!" he screamed, as rocks fell everywhere around them.

She let Galager take her away, into the black tunnel, but she was still looking at the red dome of magic behind her as it weakened around the Redeemer.

We destroyed the Sword of Jhalaveral!

The magic is dying and so is his shield!

The last she saw of Zaviel was as a coward, screaming for his life.

The last she saw of Cazlich was as a contented hero, his quest complete, smiling at her.

Soon after, the mountain claimed both Vilazians in its unrelenting grip.

59

Ada could hear the mountain rumbling behind them as she and Galager wormed their way through the dark tunnels of the Orial mines. They had nothing to illuminate their way. The Grey Acme wasn't finished yet with burying its dead. She could only hope they wouldn't be included in the final tally of names of those who'd disappeared in these age-old excavations.

She tried summoning Cabbal as they carefully picked their way through one tunnel after another, always choosing the path leading up. Yet after an hour or so it was evident he wasn't responding. She didn't know if that meant the demon was dead, or if the death of eludria had permanently broken her command over the beast.

Their blue and gold magic no longer worked either. After all, Bloodstones were based on eludria magic too—even those who were the human incarnation of such.

In a move of desperation, they had produced their old forgotten rubies from their pockets and tried to infuse themselves with them. But, unlike before, neither of them melted into their bloodstreams. They ended up casting them away into the darkness behind them.

Slowly but surely, though, Ada began to get a sense of things. She didn't think it was magic. Or perhaps it was. She wondered if it was a remnant from her time flying around the Commonland within Cabbal's dusts, for the beast surely seemed to possess some preternatural knowledge of places, locations, and pathways. With nothing left to lose, she began to act on those hunches. She took the lead from that point on. And it worked. Maybe twelve hours later she and Galager saw a point of light ahead of them, and they all but tumbled out of an old mine adit that overlooked a different valley than the one in which they had entered the day before.

They found a slow stream and drank prodigiously and slept even more, together, in the shade of a jakroot cluster. Later that day, after it had cooled some, they hunted for berries, finding a few bushes of muscadine and blackberry. There weren't many, but they were enough for now.

At dusk they heard shouts—Twoheart and Bosun. Ada and Galager were standing at the top of a hill when the vangards spotted them. The teens raced down the grassy slope to meet them. They all enjoyed happy embraces and shared laughter and tears. Lots of questions were asked by both sides, and answers given. The vangards had rabbits hanging from their belts.

They decided to make camp, finding a good site not an hour later between some boulders on the leeward side of a small rise, not far from a tiny stream. Bosun started a fire as Twoheart prowled the area for firewood. Ada and Galager skinned and gutted their dinner. Their meal that evening was the best they'd ever had.

The stars were bright that night. Ada was elated there was no sign of a moon.

The teens learned that the mine workers—the slaves—had all revolted when part of the Grey Acme had collapsed and when they then discovered their Vilazian overlords could no longer wield magic. The vangards had watched these events unfolding after narrowly escaping the collapse of the open-pit. They had even helped instigate a few fights between Vilazian soldiers and large groups of rampaging slaves.

Twoheart estimated they'd be fairly safe for the first few days of their journey back to Lavalor. But once they neared the Sunder Line, all bets were off. There were too many unknowns. Zaviel still had an army somewhere out in the Fringe, and there were ogres and skinks, and other creatures they might have to contend with as well. Still, her plan was one of caution and non-confrontation. She wanted them all to sneak their way back to safety, and she was pretty confident she knew the best routes to take to achieve that.

They also talked about their personal plans, after safely arriving at Lavalor, and after doing whatever it took to ensure it was in friendly hands again. Ada was immensely pleased when they, to the person, said they planned to return to Firthwood at the earliest opportunity to find a way to reawaken Katonkin Weir and help Twoheart with her vow to destroy the Longclaws, if they yet lived. Bosun wanted to find Pythia and bring her with him.

When it was time to sleep, Ada and Galager crawled into each other's arms.

"Look!" said Galager, pointing over to the west.

Ada followed his finger, and saw a shooting star.

THE END

AFTERWORD

Thank you for reading my stories!

READER REVIEWS: I would love to hear your thoughts. A short sentence, a single word, or even just a simple rating are very much appreciated. Online reviews are vital to the success of indie-authors like me. Thank you for your support! Convenient review links here:

www.LNHeintz.com/links

BOOKS IN THIS SERIES

The Grand Unraveling (Eludrians I): www.LNHeintz.com/eludrians1

Crossing the Precipice (Eludrians II): www.LNHeintz.com/eludrians2

ACKNOWLEDGMENTS

Thank you Steven Moore, Stephen Brooke, Kathy Cook, Lili Dawidowicz, Steve Dawidowicz, Carolyn Dunn, Cheryl Foehner, Pat Mann, and Ingrid Ellis Schaper.

Made in the USA
Columbia, SC
12 October 2022